TWO

TRUTHS

AND A

LIE

ALSO BY MEG MITCHELL MOORE

The Arrivals

So Far Away

The Admissions

The Captain's Daughter

The Islanders

TWO
TRUTHS
AND A
LIE

A Novel

MEG MITCHELL MOORE

wm
WILLIAM MORROW
An Imprint of HarperCollinsPublishers

P.S.™ is a trademark of HarperCollins Publishers.

HarperCollins books may be purchased for educational, business, or sales promotional use. For information, please email the Special Markets Department at SPsales@harpercollins.com.

A hardcover edition of this book was published in 2020 by William Morrow, an imprint of HarperCollins Publishers.

FIRST WILLIAM MORROW PAPERBACK EDITION PUBLISHED 2021.

Designed by Bonni Leon-Berman

Library of Congress Cataloging-in-Publication Data has been applied for.

ISBN 978-0-06-284010-3

21 22 23 24 25   LSC   10 9 8 7 6 5 4 3 2 1

For Newburyport, my adopted hometown

TWO
TRUTHS
AND A
LIE

Prologue

THAT WAS THE summer we all drank tequila by the gallon. Not really, of course—if that had been true we all would have ended up dead, instead of only one person. Although there was no alcohol involved. It was your garden-variety car accident, the Acura crushed against the pole on that deserted stretch of Hale Street, the driver dead on impact.

Garden-variety. It happened all the time. Except that it wasn't, and it didn't, not in our town.

Prologue

JUNE

I.

THE SQUAD

Later we would remember that we first set eyes on Sherri Griffin on Sawyer's Beach, on the first day of the first session of surf camp. From the beginning, we weren't sure she fit in. In fact, we weren't even sure how she *got* in: surf-camp sign-ups happened in April, and she said she and her daughter had only just moved here. Somebody had to have clued her in before she moved. Or a child had dropped out, leaving a space open, and this newcomer had snapped it up. Perhaps she was savvier than she looked.

We remembered that she asked about the best place to get a haircut for her daughter, whose hair was curly.

"Rebecca would know," Tammy said. "She has a wave in her hair." She indicated the woman standing at the shoreline.

"Rebecca knows everything about the town," Esther added slyly, and purposefully. "And she's a planner."

"Oh yes," Monica added. "She's very organized." It was true. Rebecca decided when we would take our annual trip to Nantucket, where and when we would eat when we got there, and, most important, who would go. It was Rebecca who coordinated the carefully curated shots of us in our white jeans. It was Rebecca who tastefully filtered the photos and posted them on Instagram and Facebook, tagging each of us so that for any outsiders perusing their feeds there would be no doubt about who was there.

And, of course, who wasn't.

Well, that was the old Rebecca.

There were twelve of us, an even dozen. Occasionally we made an exception to allow for more. For example, for Brandy's fortieth, three years ago, we included two of her book club friends on the weekend trip to Chicago, bringing the total number to fourteen.

Fourteen, we all agreed later, was too many. There was the thing with the spiked seltzers, to cite an example. One of the interlopers drank five (!) White Claws without offering to replenish when we Ubered to the liquor store. The other got very drunk during Brandy's birthday dinner out, at Twain, and was later sick at the Airbnb we had rented in Lincoln Park. We all agreed this made everybody uncomfortable and was not to be repeated.

After, some of us remembered the pertinent facts we'd learned about Sherri that first day at the beach. Divorced. Recently moved from Ohio. An eleven-year-old daughter, who would be entering sixth grade at the middle school.

Upon hearing this news, we tried our best to appear inclusive.

"All of us have sixth graders," said Dawn. "So you'll be seeing a lot of us, come fall!"

"It all depends on what team she gets," offered Monica.

"True," said Dawn.

"Teams?" said Sherri. "Like, sports teams?" She was sitting on a striped beach towel; we remembered that she seemed woefully unprepared, having brought only a small mesh beach bag. The rest of us had our Tommy Bahama beach chairs slung low in the sand, Hydroflasks in the cup holders. This woman had no water bottle that anyone could see. No Yeti full of cold brew. Certainly no snacks to share.

Though, of course, in her defense, one of us said later, how could she have known to bring snacks to share?

Gina shook her head indulgently. "No, it's the teams for the middle school. Gold and crimson. She'll be on one or the other, and that will determine everything for the year."

"Everything," confirmed Monica.

We could see that we were making the newcomer nervous (and many of us were okay with that). We were all relieved when one of our favorite surf instructors, Parker, approached the group.

"Who drives a white Acura?" asked Parker, whom we all agreed was very hot, especially when he pulled the top of his wet suit down during the breaks between sessions, showcasing his phenomenal abs.

"I do," said the new woman. Some of us had forgotten her name already. Terri, was it? Mary? No, Sherri. It was Sherri. With an *i*. Some of us remembered that she'd told us that right away, as though anticipating an incorrect spelling.

"Rebecca does," said Monica, a split second later. Rebecca, who was still down at the water's edge, had been distracted all morning. Nicole had seen her on her cell phone, having what she described as a "very animated" conversation.

"Did you park in the metered lot?" Parker wanted to know. We all heard Sherri say that she wasn't in the metered lot, she was in the overflow. She hadn't known to get here early. Rebecca, of course, had known. First spot closest to the bathroom.

"I'm sure Rebecca got a meter," Monica told Parker.

"I think she got backed into," said Parker. "Chloe said she saw someone leaving a note."

"I'll tell her," said Dawn, smiling openly at Parker.

The kids started to come out of the water for their snack break, pulling their surfboards behind them. Rebecca's daughter, Morgan, tripped over her board's leash and landed in the sand, not quite facedown, but close enough. Rebecca wasn't looking—she was on the phone, still or again—and the rest of us pretended not to see. Although, really, wasn't Morgan Coleman's awkward stage lasting quite a long time? Of course we didn't blame her! After what had happened.

When camp was over, many of us stayed at the beach for the afternoon. We'd packed lunch and planned to remain for the day. But not Rebecca, and not the new woman, Sherri, who folded her towel into her mesh bag while her daughter peeled off her wet suit. We supposed we weren't surprised to see Rebecca leave. She hadn't been the same since Peter. Last summer we hardly saw her at all.

We assessed the new girl. Her hair was dark and thick, pretty, even in its wet braid. We could see how it was probably curly when loose. Her skin was promising: clear, with the golden glow that spoke of an easy tan. Bathing suit: Target, last year's model. The shorts she was pulling on over the suit were Old Navy, ill-fitting. And yet we all noticed that she had sort of an ease about her. A way of fitting into her environment.

"Well," said the new woman, "it was so nice to meet all of you."

"Likewise," said Tammy. She cast a meaningful look at Gina. We didn't have to say it out loud. We knew this woman wouldn't try to get into the group. After the Chicago debacle our group had been restored to its natural order, an even dozen, and the borders had snapped themselves closed, like the lobes of a Venus flytrap.

2.

SHERRI

"How'd you like the girls? Were they nice to you?"

"Sure."

Sherri and her daughter, Katie, were on their way home from Katie's first day at surf camp. Katie had never been on or near a surfboard in all of her eleven years, but she'd taken to it surprisingly well, at least as much as Sherri could tell from her vantage point on the beach.

"Was anybody *not* nice to you?"

"I don't know. I don't think so. If they weren't, I didn't notice." Sherri looked in the rearview mirror, perplexed. During the daytime Katie seemed to be fantastically unaffected by everything that had happened before the two of them moved to Newburyport. Was her nonchalance simply a coping mechanism, masking the deep, dark reaction that came only in sleep? Or had Sherri actually done a passable job of protecting her?

The road that led south from the surf beach, Ocean Boulevard, was lined with mansions on the right. On the left were majestic views of the Atlantic Ocean, bordered in places by a rock wall. Along the rock wall ran a sidewalk and on the sidewalk people were running, riding bikes, walking dogs: happy happy summer people in a happy happy summer place. Sherri took a deep breath and released it, just as the counselor had told her to do.

The road had gentle twists and turns like a road in a storybook, and every now and then the ocean would open up wide before them. It was enough to take your breath away. *Here is where the fairy princess lives,* Sherri thought, passing a giant white house that looked like a Southern mansion. One house had peeling paint and a weedy, untended lawn. *Here is where the monster lives,* thought Sherri. She shivered. The counselor had told her to try not to think too much about their other lives. It was not an overstatement to say that their survival depended on it.

"What are you doing, Katie?" Sherri asked. Katie had her head down now, intent on something in her lap. Her phone, which Sherri had bought her against her better judgment, with some of the money they'd been given to start over. She'd been swayed by the ability to track Katie's whereabouts.

"Just texting with some of the girls."

"The girls you just met?"

Sherri glanced again in the rearview mirror and saw Katie nod. Sherri's mother would have said, "I didn't hear your head rattle," and demanded a verbal answer, but truth be told, Sherri's mother and Sherri had had a very different relationship than Sherri and Katie had. Katie tended to treat Sherri less like a parent and more like an overwrought friend whose occasional discombobulation caused Katie some mild bemusement.

When she was packing up to leave the beach, Sherri had heard the women discussing cocktails by so-and-so's pool in two days' time, kids included. Sherri had lingered over her cheap beach bag for a moment, half wondering if they'd invite her, half horrified by the thought that they might. If they did, she would go for Katie's sake. It would be lovely for Katie to make some friends over the summer so that she'd enter school in September with familiar faces to seek out by the lockers or at lunchtime. Sherri felt a pang at the thought of Katie with a cafeteria tray, desperately seeking a place to sit.

"Taylor wants me to come swimming at her house this week!" Katie announced.

"Really?" Sherri felt a flush of nervous excitement. *Calm down,* she told herself. *It's just a swimming invitation.* "That sounds like fun! Which one was Taylor?"

"Blond hair," said Katie.

"Didn't they all have blond hair?" All the kids, all the moms. Sherri glanced in the rearview mirror, hating her own brown hair even more than usual.

Ahead of the Acura a line of cars had stopped, waiting for somebody to turn out of the parking lot of an outdoor ice cream shop. Sherri could see three separate lines of people, at least ten deep, at the shop. THE BEACH PLUM, said the sign. BEST LOBSTER ROLL IN NEW ENGLAND. Sherri had never tasted a lobster roll. Their very existence puzzled her: lobster and bread. It seemed an unnecessary combination.

Across the street was yet another parking lot for yet another beach, with more happy summer people milling about. Sherri had had no idea that the beach scene in their new lives would be so robust. She felt a surge of something wash over her, maybe the memory of a long-ago childhood summer at the Jersey Shore, and she experienced a sudden uplift in mood.

"Let's do it," she told Katie. She followed the car ahead of her into the Beach Plum's parking lot. "Lobster rolls for lunch. What do you say?"

"Okay," said Katie affably. Sometimes Sherri thought that she could suggest dissecting a garden snake and serving it with crackers and Katie would nod and say, "Okay," to that too.

"When in Rome, right?" added Sherri.

"Right," agreed Katie.

Now that they lived in New England, now that they were officially, legally, definitely Sherri and Katie Griffin from Columbus, Ohio, relocated after a nasty divorce, and no thank you they didn't want to talk about it, it was all still quite raw, they should do whatever they could to fit in.

How far, wondered Sherri, as a cloud passed over the sun, momentarily darkening the June day, would she actually go to do that?

3.

ALEXA

Alexa Thornhill cast an appraising eye on her next four sets of customers. Two families, one middle-aged couple, and someone else she couldn't yet see because he or she was being blocked by the second family.

"I can help the next customer!" she said brightly from her position behind the counter, which looked out on the parking lot and the line of sandy, hungry people standing in the sun. It was just past one. Graduation was not far in the rearview mirror and already Alexa was bored out of her mind. After work—she got out at four—she would pop into the clothing store attached to the ice cream shop and see if they had the high-necked O'Neill halter dress in stock in her size (extra small). Her ex-best-friend Destiny had a friend who worked there and promised she'd let Alexa use her discount. Not that Alexa needed it (things had been going very well lately online), but she enjoyed taking advantage of a personal connection when she could. And Destiny owed her something, after what happened in March.

Two parents with identical twin boys, four or five, stepped up to the counter. The parents looked worried, and Alexa could already foresee the disaster that would soon unfold. The parents (Midwestern, maybe, but anyway, not local) would get a look at the prices and try to get the boys to share. The boys would agree on principle but would disagree on a flavor, and one of the parents would ask Alexa if the boys could split the smallest size into two different flavors.

Yes, she could split the smallest size into two different flavors, but no, she didn't enjoy doing it, and, yes, there would be a fight over which boy got the most ice cream because it was impossible to get two half-scoops exactly even. The whole family would leave more distraught than it arrived.

This was exactly what transpired.

People were so predictable.

Alexa's job at the Cottage Creamery, the walk-up ice cream joint on Plum Island, was more of a cover than anything else, part of her endeavor to appear like a normal almost-eighteen-year-old girl. Most of her money she made elsewhere. Also, getting out of the house was critical, and it was nice to be near the beach, during this, her last summer ever living in her hometown. Not that anyone knew that. And not that Plum Island had the best beach scene around. It would be much more fun to work up near Jenness Beach, at Summer Sessions, doling out acai bowls to the surf-camp kids and their moms, watching the hot surf instructors stroll by with their wet suits pulled down halfway. But everyone knew the Summer Sessions jobs went to the surfers and their significant others and Alexa had never bothered to learn to surf. It seemed time-consuming and unproductive. Cold too, especially in New England waters. Maybe when she moved to L.A., maybe then she'd learn.

The middle-aged couple stepped up to the plate, and she could almost see the woman shrink back when she got a load of Alexa's megawatt smile. They each ordered the Ringer, which was a milkshake topped by a doughnut. If she weren't forced to serve it, Alexa wouldn't touch the Ringer with a pole of any length; doughnuts didn't do it for her. Her boyfriend, Tyler, could take down four maple bacons from Angry Donuts in a single sitting. Watching him do this always made Alexa feel a little queasy.

The man put a hand to his retreating hairline and smiled back at Alexa. He was wearing a brick-red Newburyport T-shirt he probably picked up at Richdale, near the postcards and the penny candy. Alexa would bet her toe ring that in high school he was a solid B student with a not-quite-pretty girlfriend everyone referred to as "sweet."

"This place," she said to her coworker, Hannah, once the couple disappeared with their trillion-calorie bombs. What she didn't have time to say, because she was busy scooping, was, *is so freaking homogenous that sometimes I want to throw up.* She couldn't wait to shake the dust of this town from her Granada oiled leather Birkenstocks.

"We're low on napkins, Amazon," said Hannah severely.

Alexa rolled her eyes. *She* had acquired her name seventeen years ago, almost eighteen, could she help it if the world's biggest online retailer had only recently understood its allure? She dispatched the next family and now she could see that the person after that was her mother. Alexa sighed. Attached to her mother, as usual, was her little sister, Morgan.

"Hey," said Morgan.

"Hey, Morgan. Mom. How was surf camp?"

"Good," said Morgan morosely.

"Annoying," said Alexa's mother. "Somebody backed into my car in the lot. So that's a whole thing I'm going to have to deal with."

Alexa's mother would not order the Ringer, and a touch of imaginary lactose intolerance would also steer her away from Alexa's favorite flavor, Moose Tracks, in which Alexa occasionally indulged. Rebecca would go for a raspberry sorbet, small, in a cup, no toppings, or she would have nothing at all. Morgan, who was eleven and built like a collection of paper straws stitched together with dental floss, would get chocolate with rainbow sprinkles, and she wouldn't finish it, but she would insist on taking it home. Alexa's mother would cover the leftover portion with aluminum foil and stick it in the freezer, and eventually Alexa would throw it away. Morgan would never notice or inquire after it. Predictable.

Alexa's mother slipped an extra five into the tip jar, which Alexa found unnecessary, and as predictable as the ice cream order, but sweet nonetheless. She smiled.

It was on their way back to the car that the unpredictable thing happened: Morgan stubbed her toe on the parking dividers made out of driftwood and shrieked. Alexa's mother left her phone on the counter to hurry to Morgan, because God forbid Morgan should be uncomfortable for an eighth of a second. The phone beeped and out of habit Alexa glanced at it: most beeping phones in Alexa's orbit were beeping for her.

But no. On her mother's phone was a text from an unknown local number, which was a surprise, because her mother's in-town social network reached far and wide, like the tentacles of an octopus, and anyone Rebecca deemed worth communicating with she had surely put in as a contact. Before she could stop herself, Alexa was reading the text.

Thanks for the talk today. When can I see you again?

Alexa took several seconds to process this.

Her mother left Morgan sitting at a picnic table and retrieved her cell phone, glancing sharply at Alexa after she looked at the screen, obviously to see if she'd been caught. Alexa made sure her face was a smooth mask. But: was that a tiny smile playing at the edges of her mother's mouth when she read the message? Oh, ugh. Alexa's mother was forty-four years old. Certainly past her prime. Double, triple ugh.

Rebecca slipped the phone into her handbag and indicated with her head that Morgan should move toward the car, stubbed toe or not.

"Bye, Alexa," whispered Morgan.

"Bye, Morgan," said Alexa. She spoke louder than she needed to, making up for Morgan's fragile voice. Morgan had always looked like she was scared of her shadow's shadow, but that had gotten worse since Peter. How in the world was this child supposed to survive middle school in the fall? Alexa should take Morgan on as a project, but she wasn't sure she had the bandwidth. Even so, she made a mental note to talk to Rebecca about Morgan's social media activity. Morgan was at a vulnerable age. Too much of a presence could be damaging, but too little could be damaging as well, and Morgan had a remarkably undeveloped sense of self-preservation.

"Bye, honey!" chirped Rebecca. She was holding her sorbet in one hand and struggling to get the keys to the (dented, Alexa now saw) Acura out of her bag with the other. Alexa tried not to look at the Colby College sticker sitting proudly in the rear window; it made her stomach churn.

"Bye, Mom." Alexa's voice mirrored her mother's in tone but inside she was slowly dying of horror. Her mother possibly had a paramour. Reason number 472 Alexa couldn't wait to get the hell out of this town, and not to the far reaches of Maine, either, where Uggs and Patagonia passed for fashion and keg parties for entertainment. No, Alexa had her sights set west and south from there, all the way from Newburyport to the City of Angels itself.

4.

SHERRI

There were five words that later Sherri believed altered for her the course of the rest of the summer. It happened when she was picking up Katie from a playdate at Taylor Kearney's house. The Kearney family lived down a road off Merrimac Street that led to the river; until Sherri punched the address into Waze she didn't even know there were streets and houses down there. She had a lot to learn about her new town.

The house was an expanded bungalow with a four-car garage off to the side. In back, close to the water, were a gorgeous tiled pool and a sweeping green lawn that rolled gently down to a private dock. At the end of the dock was a motor boat. Sherri didn't know enough about boats to know the size or what kind of hull or motors it had, but her sense of the boat was one of quiet opulence. Emphasis on quiet. She was getting used to the way a lot of the wealth in Massachusetts was hidden down streets like this, behind stone walls or fences, more whisper than scream. In Sherri's old life, when people had money you knew it. When Sherri had money, everyone knew it. Other people saw to that.

The girls were still splashing around in the pool, so Sherri let herself in the wrought-iron gate. Taylor's mother, Brooke, was stretched out on a lounge chair, reading the newest Elin Hilderbrand novel. She sat up when Sherri came in and shielded her eyes from the sun with a hand. Katie waved at Sherri and then resumed the handstand contest she and Taylor were having. *Good luck to Taylor,* thought Sherri. Katie could hold her breath all day long, and into the night.

"Hi, girls!" she said cheerfully, the way she thought a normal mother in a normal situation might.

"Drink?" said Brooke. She unwound herself from the chair. She was wearing, very well, Sherri decided, a small black bikini with a strap over one shoulder. A drink? Sherri glanced at her watch. It was 2:30 in the afternoon. She hesitated, and before she had a chance to decide, Brooke had disappeared into a pool house that Sherri had just noticed and, once returned, was pressing a cold glass of rosé into her hands.

"Thank you," Sherri said.

"Summer Water," Brooke said. "It's my favorite." She pointed toward the sweating bottle, which she had placed on one of the side tables. There was a side table next to each chair, along with a pool towel rolled up the way they did them in resorts. Brooke tipped her wine toward Sherri's and they clinked glasses.

Sherri took a sip. "Delicious," she said. The wine was dry and light and Sherri thought she tasted grapefruit or maybe lemon. In her old life she had gone for the hard stuff, and plenty of it. A glass of rosé felt tantamount to drinking a Capri Sun.

"Sit down," said Brooke, gesturing toward one of the lounge chairs. It was more command than offer. Sherri sat, then leaned back awkwardly into the cushion. She wasn't wearing sunbathing clothes; she was wearing an unfashionable set of khaki capris and a plain white T-shirt. She'd left her old wardrobe behind. She and Katie both had. It was better that way, easier. In fact, it was imperative.

She took in the yard. It looked like it had come straight out of a magazine, all of it, even the two girls in the pool, because they were young, suntanned, and happy. "Is Taylor your only child?" she asked.

"Oh gosh no," said Brooke. Her expression said, *What a question! Who would have only one child?* Her voice said, "She's my baby."

"I see," said Sherri, waiting.

"Alton is going to be a sophomore, and Ceci is going into eighth grade. Ceci went to Salisbury Beach with a friend, and Alton, well, who knows. Once they go into high school, you never see them again." She waved her hand in the air like a magician, whisking her eldest child away.

High school was only three years away for Katie. The thought of never seeing Katie again in a mere three years filled Sherri with a brutal sort of rage and terror. She was not going to let that happen, she had only Katie left in the world. She looked at the pool. There was a diving board and a winding slide. Lined up on the side like soldiers awaiting orders were a series of brightly colored pool floats, not the cheap kind you have to blow up. These were made of thick, expensive foam. They looked like they were floating even when they were on the ground. The pool house had an indoor/outdoor bar with six stools, and Sherri could see an outdoor shower attached to one side of it. This outdoor shower was nicer than the indoor shower in hers and Katie's current accommodations.

What she couldn't see were the heads of two girls. The panic came over her in a flash and she jumped up from the chair and ran to the edge of the pool. The tile was dark gray, so you couldn't make out what was under the surface.

"We're having a contest," said Taylor calmly, and Sherri saw that she had failed to notice Taylor sitting on the edge of the deep end of the pool, holding a phone. "To see who can stay under the longest. I'm timing her. I already lost."

Now Sherri felt foolish. Obviously the girls were okay. And yet. Shouldn't Katie have surfaced by now? Instead of abating, the terrible panic picked up strength and force. "Katie!" Sherri cried. A distant part of her noted the way her voice went up at the end in a kind of ridiculous shriek. Katie's head broke the surface and she gasped for air. "Katie, I'm here!" said Sherri.

Katie was laughing. She was laughing, and Sherri thought she was dead. Sherri had been about to jump in the water after her.

"Two fifty-one," said Taylor admiringly. "That's the pool record."

"Yessss," said Katie, treading water with one hand, fist pumping with the other. "What was the old record?"

"Two twenty-nine," said Taylor.

Sherri put her hand over her heart and wondered if it would ever slow down to its normal rhythm. She turned back to Brooke. Brooke was watching Sherri closely. She looked partly bemused, and partly nakedly curious. She had finished her wine and was pouring herself a second glass. "More?" she asked Sherri.

"No thank you. I'd—we'd better get going." Sherri called to Katie to gather her things and say good-bye and thank you. She was suddenly in a hurry to get out of there. She turned back to Brooke and said, "I'm sorry! My manners. Thank you so much. What a fun afternoon for the girls. What a beautiful home you have." Not that she'd seen the home. She'd have to be more normal next time, see if she could wrangle an invitation inside.

"Thank you!" said Brooke, in a modest/not-modest way.

Sherri fumbled in her bag for her keys, and that's when it happened.

"Hey," said Brooke. She hesitated for a second, and then seemed to give herself permission. "We're all going out to Plum Island Grille tonight. It's Esther's birthday." Sherri waited. And then came those five words. "You should come with us."

"If I went out to dinner tonight," Sherri ventured in the car on the way home, "would you be okay, Katie-kins? There's Miss

Josephine, if you need her." Their neighbor in the half-house, an elderly widow with a Papillon, had grumpily offered to look in on Katie if Sherri ever wanted her to.

"I won't need her," said Katie. "You should go, Mom. You never go out anymore."

Sherri felt a childish excitement, the excitement of being included. *You should come with us.* Funny how five words could change her mood in a flash.

Don't be silly, she told herself. It's just one invitation, probably because she felt bad for you, or because she was tipsy. That's all. You shouldn't even go.

But she should. She would!

When Sherri was getting ready for dinner, Katie slipped into her room and watched her brushing her hair in the mirror over the dresser. The mirror was here when they got here, as was the dresser—the whole place was fully furnished. At the time Sherri had been grateful not to have to buy furniture, but now she felt there was something sad about living with other people's castoffs.

"Can you dress up tonight, Mom? The way you used to?"

Sherri kept brushing and said, "I don't have any of those clothes anymore." Then, softly, an addition: "You know that."

Katie nodded and sat on the bed, tucking her bare legs under her, accepting.

"I was pretty then, I know," said Sherri. She pulled her hair back in a ponytail, then fastened it with an elastic. She looked in the mirror, considering. She turned toward Katie, who was looking at her severely.

"You're still pretty," Katie said. "You're just much less fancy."

"*You're* not fancy," said Sherri, smiling now, indicating Katie's grubby shorts.

"I know," said Katie. "But I was never fancy."

Reasonable enough. Maybe Sherri could try a little harder. Lipstick, at least. She left the bedroom and padded into their shared bathroom, where she dug around in a drawer to see what she could find. Katie followed her and watched her the whole time: sternly, unnervingly, lovingly.

5.

ALEXA

It was your typical summer high school party, except that it was out on the farthest reaches of Plum Island, which was a pain to get to. There was a fire pit on the back deck. Some kids had wandered off to the dunes to make out. Zoe Butler-Gray, valedictorian and resident of the house, was in the kitchen holding forth on Trump's immigration policy, and nobody seemed to be listening. Zoe didn't appear to care. She was headed for Dartmouth; she knew her real audience was waiting for her there.

Alexa, sitting on a couch in the living room, wished she could be elsewhere. How many parties had she attended over the course of her high school career, each one the same as the last and the next? Tyler handed her a plastic cup. She could tell by the shiny look in his eyes that he had been drinking a lot already, or smoking weed, or both, and she wondered how she'd get home. She wondered how *he'd* get home. The cops had been out in full force on the causeway this summer and Tyler couldn't risk getting caught. She should take his keys and get them both a ride.

She took a sip of the drink. Vodka and cranberry. Tyler had been kind enough to put a slice of lime in it for her but even so she could hardly stomach it. The taste of cranberry juice reminded her of a series of urinary tract infections she'd had when she was young, nine or ten, when her mother poured her a glass every morning and wouldn't let her leave the table until she'd finished it. It was a gesture that came from a combination of love and Internet medical knowledge, no harm intended, but still Alexa was positive cranberry juice was a drink she would never enjoy in this lifetime. She had told Tyler this more than once.

"You can't drive," she said combatively. "And I want to go home."

"Let's just crash here. Come on, babe." Tyler snaked his arm around her waist. Alexa disliked the word "babe" almost as much as she disliked cranberry juice, and Tyler knew this too, but sometimes when he was drunk or high he forgot.

She removed his arm and sat back on the couch. "Negative on that," she said.

"Why not?" He returned his arm to her waist, tighter this time. "We can sleep on the beach!"

Nothing sounded less comfortable to Alexa than sleeping on the beach. Her hair was very thick; she would never get the sand out. She removed Tyler's arm again, and this time he resisted more strongly. Say what you will about the #metoo movement and all the rest of it, tell Alexa that times were changing and women could speak up, she knew it was still a very, very fine line that she was walking, that all girls were walking. The line between being attractive and being a tease. The line between needing and not needing. Between independence and desire. If she could give Morgan one piece of advice it would be, Don't grow up.

"I don't want to stay here, Tyler," she said. "Just leave me alone." Besides the fact that she would much rather sleep in her own bed, there was the not-small matter of her virginity, which for some reason, against all odds and contrary to what most people at school and probably in town and probably online thought, she had managed to hold on to for so long that now it seemed awkward and meaningful to let it go. But whatever. It *was* her body; these *were* her choices. She stood.

"I get it," Tyler said. "Take it easy, Lex."

"Don't call me Lex," she snarled, sounding like the bitch that she felt like, that she feared, sometimes, she actually was. The next thing she knew, she was steeling herself and knocking back the cocktail, cranberry juice or no cranberry juice. *Forget it*, she thought. *Forget Tyler. Forget Zoe Butler-Gray. Forget everybody.* On her way out the back door she grabbed a can of beer, a Riverwalk IPA, which had probably been brought out because Zoe Butler-Gray's father worked for the brewery and always had stacks of it in the garage. She opened it and carried it onto the back deck.

High tide and it felt like the waves were going to come all the way up to the furniture. The moon was almost full, but not quite; it looked like somebody squished it between a thumb and a forefinger. Alexa sipped the beer. She hated IPAs—they were so heavy, they sat in her stomach like a stone. She drank it anyway. Her sips got bigger, and they turned into gulps. When she stood, she felt dizzy. Experimentally she lifted her face to the sky and turned around and around. She felt like she was one with the moon. She felt like she was spinning through the night.

When she stopped spinning, she ran smack into a sweatshirt.

"Sorry," she muttered, and the guy inside the sweatshirt caught her elbow and said, "Hey, hey." *Fantastic,* was her first thought. Another guy grabbing at her, just what she needed. She lifted her eyes.

"You okay?" said the guy. The sweatshirt was white, or off-white—she couldn't be sure under the dim outdoor lights—and said "Saint" in purple and "Michael's" in gold. It was wildly unfashionable. She had seen this guy earlier, with Shelby McIntyre, who was a year ahead of Alexa, and some sort of cross-country star at UVM. (Cross country was a sport Alexa had never understood—it seemed hard and cold and messy—although the coach at the high school was said to be legendary.)

"Yes," she said. "Fine. Just going inside." It was then that she remembered the reason Zoe Butler-Gray always brought out the IPA at parties—not the pilsner—was because it had an alcohol content of about a million percent. She remembered that just about the same time she remembered that she had eaten neither lunch nor dinner before the vodka. She felt herself beginning to fall.

6.

THE SQUAD

We took the center table at Plum Island Grille, the only one long enough to accommodate us. Some of us, arriving early, had met beforehand in the bar on the other side of the restaurant, from which you could see the famous Plum Island salt marshes and the turnpike (a grand name for a short stretch of road) we had just driven over to get there. Except for Esther, who lived on the island and had walked down. It was the only time of year it was in any way convenient to be Esther.

In the distance, if we squinted, we could see, or imagined we could see, the Pink House, long empty, much speculated about, which sits in the center of the marsh, paint peeling, roof leaking, cupola choked with birds' nests. The Pink House was built in 1925 as part of a divorce settlement by a disgruntled husband for his ex-wife. *You want your own house?* the husband is rumored to have said. *I'll build you a house!* And, bam, he built a house, in beautiful isolation.

After a time we repaired to our table to meet those who had just arrived. One of us couldn't make it, and we were somewhat surprised to find that Brooke Kearney had taken it upon herself (without consulting the rest of us) to invite the new woman, Katie's mother, to fill the spot. Sherri. With an *i*. Sherri from the beach.

We were surprised, but we weren't going to be rude about it.

We are nothing if not welcoming. Even though the look Esther shot Brooke when she realized what had happened . . . some of us agreed after the fact that that was borderline impolite.

It was a birthday! We started out with tequila shots, twelve of them, with twelve slices of lime and four salt shakers to share. That is how we always do birthdays. It was a good tequila, a Clase Azul, which had just come on the scene for us, and was so smooth you didn't really need the lime. Then appetizers: tempura oysters, shrimp cocktail, crab cakes.

Sherri didn't seem to have any compunction about ordering the surf and turf, we all noted. The rest of us stuck to the grill board with swordfish and pineapple salsa. It was bathing suit season, after all.

With the tequila, and the cocktails that followed, Sherri became a little more animated. Her clothing choices were just this side of okay—when one of us tucked in the label to her dress for her (It was sticking out! We weren't snooping!), we noticed that it said Ann Taylor Loft. That's just an observation, not a judgment. She'd worn lipstick, which was brighter than the rest of ours, and mascara, though studying her some of us thought that eyelash extensions would do wonders. Her mascara was clumping. It was hard to put a finger specifically on the rest of what was wrong. Well, nothing was *wrong*. But something was off. That's the best way to put it. Something desperate in her laugh? Yes, that's just it, that's what it was. Something desperate.

7.

REBECCA

Rebecca took a bite of her scallops and thought, *I don't even know these women*. She thought, *These people are strangers to me. We were thrown together by happenstance, that's all. Happenstance and geography.* These were thoughts she'd been having more and more often lately. It wasn't that she didn't like her friends anymore, that wasn't exactly right—it was that nobody here knew what to do with her sadness after Peter. Immediately after, sure: there was the food and the offers to take over carpools and so forth. But after a time, Rebecca could tell that secretly they thought (and maybe sometimes talked among themselves) that it was about time for Rebecca to get on with it. They wanted the old Rebecca back, the one who planned trips and organized sleepovers. They didn't understand that that Rebecca was gone forever.

Brooke had invited an outsider to Esther's birthday dinner, which was clearly vexing Esther, though she was trying her best not to show it. Rebecca considered the new woman, who was sitting next to her. She had seen her on the beach at surf camp, but Rebecca had been on the phone with Daniel for a lot of the morning. Daniel's brother-in-law was having problems with his daughter, who was thirteen, and Daniel was trying to help him by having her stay with him while his brother-in-law went on a business trip to Cincinnati. Now Daniel himself was having trouble with the girl.

The woman was Sherri "with an *i*" (that was how she intro-duced herself, as though the *i* were of particular value, a bonus). All Rebecca knew about her was that she had a daughter the same age as all of the girls and that she had moved from somewhere (Illinois?) after a divorce.

"Nice to meet you," Rebecca had said automatically, even though it wasn't, not really. She'd been reared on a steady diet of politeness—thank-you notes for every gift, a kind word for any person she ran across—and she'd carried many of these habits into adulthood and tried to instill them in her own children. But manners were thing number 758 that no longer mattered to Re-becca after Peter.

"Oh, hey!" said Esther, who sat on Rebecca's other side. Alco-hol always made Esther's fair skin flush the color of a spring rad-ish. "I've been meaning to say, it's really too bad, what happened with Alexa and her friends. I heard the three of them don't hang out anymore."

Rebecca, startled out of her reverie, was surprised into show-ing her surprise. "Destiny and Caitlin?" she asked. (Rebecca had been wondering for months what had happened between Alexa and those two, but the answer was somewhere in Alexa's vault, locked away, unattainable.) "Nothing *happened*," she added.

Esther assessed Rebecca's ignorance too quickly. "Of course not," she said.

"Why?" Faced with Esther's knowing look Rebecca had no choice but to ask. "What did *you* hear happened?"

"Oh my gosh, *nothing!*" said Esther. "I didn't hear anything." She put a hand nervously to her earlobe as if checking for a lost earring. "I just meant—I mean, I heard it had something to do with Alexa's plans for next year. But you know what? I could be totally off-base. I'm not even sure who I heard that from, now that I think about it. I'm probably thinking of someone else entirely."

Rebecca concentrated for a moment on the buzzing of the other conversations going on around her. She heard Georgia cry out, with a loud laugh, "We'll have to get rid of her!"

"Alexa's plan for next year is to go to Colby." Rebecca didn't say *as you know,* and she didn't say, *obviously,* but both were implied. Rebecca would not get caught up in the wasp's nest of competing agendas. She would finish her scallops, and she would go home, and she would call Daniel to say good night, and she would be asleep by ten thirty.

Then she noticed that the woman on the other side of her, Sherri with an *i,* didn't look quite right. Rebecca laid a hand on her arm and said, "Are you okay?"

"Completely fine," said Sherri. "Really. It's just a little warm in here, that's all. Do you feel warm?"

"I do," said Rebecca (she didn't). She didn't believe that it was the temperature. The woman looked to be in some distress. Her dress was droopy and her eyes were droopy and Rebecca could bet that underneath it all her soul was droopy. A divorce was a loss of a high order: not the death of a person, but the death of a union. Esther had turned away from Rebecca to talk to Dawn, and Rebecca leaned closer to the poor broken creature on her right.

"Tequila does that to me too," she whispered. "I always have seltzer as my second drink. Sometimes I just can't keep up."

Sherri with an *i* said, "Smart," and gave Rebecca a grateful glance, and Rebecca felt a small, empathetic, recently underused part of herself begin to unfurl.

8.

SHERRI

She shouldn't have ordered the second cocktail. After all, she'd already had the wine at Brooke's house in the afternoon. But the first one had gone down so easily, especially after the shot, and everybody else was having another one, and the old Sherri could hold a lot of liquor. (She was thinner now, from the stress of the move, less curvy, more of a lightweight.)

Also, she shouldn't have ordered the surf and turf. She'd been one of the first women to order, and for a moment she forgot where she was, who she was now. She'd never looked at menu prices before; she'd never said no to the best dish in whatever restaurant she was in. By the time she remembered, it was too late.

There were so many different conversations going on—the women had broken off into twos or threes, beautiful heads bent toward one another. She caught little snippets here and there, individual words—*camp* and *horrendous* and *contractor* and *eyelashes*—but couldn't find her entrance into any single discussion. She heard someone at the far end of the table say, "We'll have to get rid of her!" and her blood ran cold.

Only the woman next to her had spoken to her, and it was with such kindness that she felt tears unexpectedly prick her eyes.

She picked up her steak knife and looked at her plate: an eight-inch filet for the turf, and shrimp scampi for the surf. It had been

Bobby who introduced her to good steak; when she met him she was familiar only with the cheap cuts: the chucks, the flanks. Bobby taught her about Kobe and tenderloin and porterhouse. He took her to Mastro's on Sixth Avenue.

"Get whatever you want," he said to her anytime they went out. It had given him great pride to be able to say that. He beamed like a little boy who'd just tied his shoes for the first time. Mastro's was the first restaurant, but not the last, that Sherri had been to without prices on the menu. It struck her like a swift blow that she'd have to look at prices, and very carefully, for the rest of her life. She never should have ordered this dish. She had lost her appetite anyway. She cut into an asparagus spear.

We'll have to get rid of her. No mirth when Bobby said that. Madison Miller was a piece of business that must be attended to, like filling out invoices and managing the fleet of trucks.

Eventually Sherri managed to eat her meal, and the good meat and the good shrimp got to work soaking up the alcohol, and so by the time she was driving the Acura back across the causeway she felt almost normal. (Many of the ladies seemed to have carpooled, so it was a lonely business, climbing into the Acura all on her own, though she did manage a quick good-bye to her savior.) The moon, almost full, was winking above the salt marshes, and she lowered the window to take in the very particular briny smell of the summer evening. She began to feel almost peaceful, and when she parked in front of the half-house on Olive Street she was looking forward to telling Katie all about the restaurant. Maybe they could go there one evening soon and sit on the more casual side, near the bar, and share two of the small plates. (The flatbread had looked very good.)

She called Katie's name as she unlocked the door and entered the house. Every light in the house was on, and the living room, where she thought Katie would be watching television, was empty. Her pulse started to race. She called Katie's name again, then again, and she heard some reply—as quiet as the mewing of a kitten—from upstairs. The hall light was on too, and the lights in her bedroom and Katie's as well.

"Katie-kins?" Instantly Sherri was 100 percent sober, with every hair, every pore and fiber of her body, on high alert. Katie was sitting cross-legged in the very corner of her very bright bedroom, her knees drawn up and into her chest. She had pulled the comforter from her bed to cover herself. Sherri rushed to Katie's side.

"What happened?"

"Nothing happened," said Katie. "I just got scared."

We'll have to get rid of her, came the fragment of memory, floating along on the summer evening, and Sherri felt all of her collective terror gather itself and sluice through her.

"Oh, honey. I'm so sorry. I shouldn't have gone out. I shouldn't have left you alone. I shouldn't—"

"Mommy," said Katie. Sherri opened her arms and Katie uncurled her body and fell into them. Sherri felt her tears leak out into Katie's beautiful hair and they stayed for some time, rocking back and forth in the too-bright room, with Katie's sobs getting louder, until, without any warning, she threw up all over her comforter.

9.

ALEXA

When Alexa woke up the next morning she was lying in an unfamiliar bed, in an unfamiliar room, under an unfamiliar comforter. She was alone. Ohgodohgodohgod. She was alone in a strange bed. On a chair next to the bed she saw her O'Neill dress folded neatly. Oh God. She lifted up the covers and peeked down, afraid she would find that she was naked. No. She was wearing a pair of sweatpants (Sweatpants! Surely this was a first.) and—she felt behind her neck—a hooded sweatshirt. She pulled the sweatshirt away from her body to examine it. It was purple, and it said KNIGHTS on it in gold. Where had she just seen a sweatshirt with gold writing? Fragments from the night before began to filter back into her brain. She was drinking cranberry juice and vodka. She was angry with Tyler. She was looking at the moon. She was spinning.

There was a soft knocking at the door, and when she said, "Yes?" her voice cracked, as if it hadn't been used in a long time. Into the room walked a boy, and the rest of the puzzle pieces clicked into place. She'd drunk two drinks on an empty stomach, and then she'd fallen onto this boy's sweatshirt. She remembered him guiding her gently around the side of the house, and into a car.

"I'm Cameron," he said. "Hartwell. Cam. In case you don't remember. I brought you tea." She noticed that before putting down the tea he laid down a coaster. There was a matching coaster underneath a half-empty (half-full?) water glass, which triggered a memory of two Advils proffered to her.

"Is this your house?"

"Yup. This is the guest room. I slept in my room." That grin again. "It was all very proper. You were shaking in that dress, so I gave you some clothes to put on. Which you did by yourself. In the bathroom."

"Thanks," she said warily. "But where are we?"

"Off Turkey Hill."

Turkey Hill was the neighborhood on the other side of the highway from downtown, where many of the houses were bigger, newer, with yards and driveways and garages. Alexa never had reason to go out to Turkey Hill. Turkey Hill was exactly as far from Plum Island as you could get while still being in Newburyport. What the hell was she doing on Turkey Hill?

"Why were you at Zoe's party?"

"Shelby wanted to go. My, um, girlfriend. You know Shelby?" Alexa nodded. "She and Zoe ran cross country together, they're close." He shrugged.

"What happened to Shelby last night?" Alexa wanted to know, and she also didn't.

"She went home," Cam said. (Was that a grin playing at the corners of his mouth?) "She got a ride with someone else."

Most likely, thought Alexa, *Shelby had to get to bed on time.* She probably had the early shift handing out breakfast to homeless people in Lowell, or she was organizing a charity walk on Boston Common.

"She was mad," added Cam.

"Mad?"

Now the grin was full-on. "She didn't like it that I said I would take you home."

"So why did you?"

"You looked like you could use the help."

"Why did you bring me here?"

"Well, you begged me not to take you home."

"I did?"

He nodded. "You wouldn't even give me your address." This sounded plausible; Alexa sort of remembered shaking her head and making a motion like she was zipping her lips. "I asked you if you wanted to come here for a little while. We watched some Samantha Bee, and you fell asleep. I thought it was best if I just got you to bed instead of trying to get you back in the car and having a whole situation with your parents."

"My mom," she corrected. Then: "Samantha Bee? You're so woke." She was teasing, and also not.

"I try."

"How come I don't know you? Have you always lived here?"

"Since I was three."

"You didn't go to Newburyport High."

"Immaculate Conception through eighth grade." (The Catholic school. Alexa hadn't known many of the IC kids, except for a few girls she played town soccer with in elementary and middle school.) "Then St. John's Prep. I go to school in Vermont now." He pointed to his T-shirt, which was gray. In purple letters were the words SAINT MICHAEL'S COLLEGE and in the middle of the shirt was a drawing of a knighthead.

That explained it. "Wow. I'm so sorry. I have no idea how I got so drunk." Even though she did know: it was simply a terrible mix of liquor and a strong beer and an extremely empty stomach. "What time is it?"

"Just after eight," said Cam. "I'm an early riser. Do you need to call someone? Tell them where you are?"

Just after eight was good. In her house, nobody would expect her to be up before ten o'clock, and since Tyler had picked her up for last night's party, her Jeep was still in the driveway. Even so, precautionary measures were in order.

Alexa picked up her phone, which was on the nightstand, plugged into a charger: a thoughtful bonus. There were five texts and two voice mails from Tyler, which she didn't feel like listening to or reading yet. Her best bet was Morgan. She sent her a text. Soooo tired. Can u tell mom I got up and went back to bed? She knew that she had left the door to her bedroom closed, as she always did, and she knew that Morgan wouldn't question her whereabouts and that her mother had read a long book last year about the power and necessity of sleep for the development of the teenage brain and since then had never judged Alexa for sleeping too much. Alexa could use the 360 app to ascertain when her mom and Morgan left the house, and then she would ask Cam to drive her home.

"Where are your parents?" she asked. *Please don't let there be parents downstairs,* she thought. There was no way she wanted to do a walk of shame, shameless though it may be, past anybody's parents.

"They're not home. They went to the lake."

New England was lousy with lakes, but the way Cam said it, so casually, as if there were only one, spoke to Alexa of legitimate money. She raised an eyebrow and said, like she didn't really care, "Where?" Even though she was pretty sure she knew the answer.

"Winnipesaukee." She waited. "Wolfeboro," he admitted. Bingo! Home of Mitt Romney and the Marriotts.

"I see," she said. She lifted the mug of tea to her lips. It was lightly sweetened, with just a hint of milk. Alexa was not a tea drinker. Her caffeine of choice was a cortado, especially the ones they served downtown at the Coffee Factory, or a double espresso from Starbucks with a small dollop of milk, no sugar. But, in the interest of being polite to this young man who had *not* taken advantage of her, she took a cautionary sip. It tasted like liquid gold, at once cleansing and nourishing. The warmth traveled down her body, all the way to her toes, then back up again, to her head. She had to stop herself from gulping the rest of it. "Thanks again," she said. "For the tea—for everything. You really saved me from getting in a lot of trouble."

"I am your knight in purple armor," he said, grinning. His grin was—well, infectious was too strong a word, wasn't it? Or was it? She found herself grinning back. *Pull it together, Alexa,* she told herself sternly. *You have a boyfriend.*

"You seem like you have a lot of school spirit," she said. It wasn't a compliment, not necessarily, but he took it as one.

"Thanks," he said. "I play golf."

"Golf? College golf?"

He nodded and smiled some more, seeming not at all embarrassed.

She rose from the bed, wondering if he was watching her, not that she cared, but of course he was watching her.

"Bathroom's that way," he said, "in case you don't remember." (She didn't.)

She looked out the window. She could see a pristine pool bordered by iron lawn chairs with bright orange cushions and contrasting turquoise pillows—a color combination of which she approved. She could see a badminton net set up with a crisp yellow border around it, and the requisite corn hole game, painted with the Red Sox logo.

"Be right back," she said, hoping she didn't sound coquettish. The bathroom was en suite. There were two sinks, side by side, the kind where the sinks look like bowls or vessels dug up from a Greek archeological site and refurbished to perfection. She looked in the mirror above one of the sinks. Her hair was a disaster, and her mascara was smeared. She would never, ever let Tyler see her like this, nor would Tyler want to. She washed her face, then opened the cabinet under one of the sinks to see if she could find some passable moisturizer. There was a brand-new tub of Kiehl's ultra facial cream, which would do just fine. She slathered it on, and returned to the bedroom.

Cam was still grinning. He had made the bed and returned the throw pillows to where they must have been before she crashed the night before.

"Breakfast?" he said. "I make a good omelet."

Of course he did. She was really hungry. She acquiesced to the omelet, which, it turned out, was one of the best she had ever tasted; it was positively dripping with cheddar cheese, and also included a costarring role of a gorgeous tomato.

While they ate they played a couple of rounds of the name game. They knew a few people in common; they were only two years apart in school. They went to different preschools, Alexa to Knoll-Edge and Cam to Mrs. Murray's, so their paths had diverged from the beginning. She told him about Colby with a straight face and he said, "I have a buddy there. I'll tell him to look out for you. He'll be a junior, same as me. We went to the Prep together. Ethan Whittaker."

"Great," she said. "Ethan Whittaker. I'll keep my eye out for him."

When she finished her omelet she loaded her plate in the dishwasher and offered to load his as well, not because she considered that woman's work but because he had done the cooking so it seemed only fair. The omelet pan was already clean, set upside down to dry.

"I have to work at nine," said Cam. "We'd better get going. I'll drop you off at home on my way, okay?"

She nodded. "Where do you work?" She figured he'd say something like training guide dogs to help blind war veterans or running summer camps for youth services.

"Market Basket," he said. "Mostly on checkout. And I'm training to be an assistant manager." This revelation didn't add a milligram to the scale on which Alexa had been weighing Cam's cachet, but he looked so proud that she squeezed out this: "My mom loves Market Basket. She almost never goes to Shaw's." And even though she would like nothing more than to repair to the guest room and sink once again into those glorious sheets, under that cloud of a comforter, she said, "I don't want to make you late." She pointed at her St. Michael's spirit wear and said, "Um, I can change back into my dress now and give you this . . ."

"Don't worry about it," Cam said. "I have plenty. You can get it to me another time. I grabbed your dress for you." He handed her a CVS bag with her dress folded neatly inside. Her flip-flops she found in the massive mudroom. Cam swung open the door from the mudroom to the outside. There was a minivan in the driveway. "Your chariot, my lady," he said, bowing and making a sweeping gesture with his hand that should have been completely awkward but was somehow sort of charming.

She could probably have him if she wanted him, this egg-savvy, golfing, guestroom-offering Catholic boy with the nice brown eyes and the promising biceps. She could take him from Shelby McIntyre in a millisecond, in a heartbeat. It wouldn't require more than a toss of her hair, a few strategic texts and one sunset beach picnic. But, there were other considerations. There was Tyler. There were her two jobs. There was the fact that Alexa had attracted the interest of many, many different kinds of boys since the year she turned fourteen but had never dated a golfer.

The air was wet and pulpy with humidity. In the yard across the street a kid of six or so was kicking around a soccer ball, and another kid was zipping down the street on a scooter. It was summer, obviously. But in a funny way it felt like it was Christmas morning and Cameron Hartwell was a present Alexa hadn't yet unwrapped.

Before she got into the minivan she marched up to Cam, placed a hand on each of his cheeks, and kissed him.

10.

SHERRI

It cost nine dollars in quarters to wash a comforter at the Port City Laundromat in the Market Basket plaza. Who had nine dollars in quarters? Not Sherri. What she had was a twenty and three sad one-dollar bills. The change machine rejected each of the dollar bills in turn: one, presumably, for being too wrinkled, one for being torn nearly in half, and one for no discernible reason other than change machine prejudice. Finally she surrendered the twenty, trying not to think about the fact that she'd been saving it to take Katie to breakfast at Mad Martha's on Plum Island, which she'd heard was a local treasure. She watched, half-fascinated, as the quarters poured into the metal cup. It made her think of a trip to Vegas she and Bobby had taken back in the day. They'd stayed at the Venetian and while Bobby hit the craps table, Sherri had played the slots for days. She'd done very well. Not that she'd needed the money, not back then.

How far the mighty have fallen, she thought. She scooped the quarters into her pockets and counted out thirty-six, laying them carefully on top of the washing machine in nine piles of four. When she knocked against one pile with the outer edge of her hand, one quarter rolled off and under the machine. Sherri crouched down and tried to retrieve it, but it had traveled too far under for her to get to it from her crouching position. She'd have to go lower on the floor, Flat-Stanley style. She was not above doing that.

Now the mighty have fallen even farther. That's what she was thinking when she heard the tinkle of the bells, and a semi-familiar voice say, "Sherri? What are you doing?"

Sherri righted herself, then stood. One of the women from the birthday dinner the night before was facing her. Dawn, Sherri thought her name was, but she wasn't certain enough to say it.

"Nothing," she said, trying to maintain the smallest shred of dignity. "I lost a quarter under the machine."

"Ohmygod, do you need a quarter?" Dawn opened her handbag and peered inside. "I was just coming from getting my nails done and I thought I saw someone familiar. I almost never have coins on me but let me see." Dawn was wearing gold platform flip-flops with little jewels on the straps, and her toes were painted a spirited pink. It had been so long since Sherri had had her nails done that it almost hurt to look at Dawn's toes. What Sherri wouldn't give to soak her feet in a warm tub and have somebody rub them with a pumice stone.

"It's fine," said Sherri, smiling through gritted teeth. "I got it."

"You sure?" Dawn crept closer to Sherri and whispered, "Do you not have a washing machine in your place?"

"I have a washing machine," said Sherri untruthfully. "I just need to wash something big, that's all." She smiled a hard, bright smile and turned back to the machine. This was not, she told herself, going to be the quarter that broke the camel's back.

"Hey, you should come to barre class tomorrow," said Dawn. "Nine fifteen. A bunch of us go." She looked again at the washing machine. "Give me your number and I'll text you the details. If you're new to town, I'm pretty sure the first class is free!"

II.

THE SQUAD

"She was crawling around on the floor," Dawn told us later. She said she felt sorry for Sherri Griffin! Scrambling on her hands and knees in the Laundromat for a quarter. Who knew the state of that floor?

(*We* certainly don't—we don't go to the Laundromat.)

"You felt sorry for her, but not sorry enough to walk by and pretend you hadn't seen," said Tammy. The conversation stopped for a moment. But that was Tammy for you, you couldn't always be sure when she was joking and when she was serious.

Dawn and Tammy have never gotten along perfectly; it went back to a beef that Dawn's daughter Avery and Tammy's daughter Izzy had back in second grade, smoothed over but never really forgotten. Dawn gave Tammy a look and said she would have been happy to give Sherri Griffin a quarter but she simply didn't carry cash anymore. And certainly not coins. Everything is credit cards or Venmo these days.

"I told her she should try barre class tomorrow," said Dawn. "Why not, right?" We used to go to a different barre class, but we'd recently switched. And ever since we'd switched, Rebecca had stopped going. We didn't know why.

Tammy said, "Okaaaaay," but didn't look too happy about it.

12.

SHERRI

All through the barre class, Sherri chewed the inside of her cheek to keep herself from screaming. It. Was. So. Hard. And it was the strangest kind of hard. Sometimes you scarcely moved at all, you did strange swingy things with your hips, you picked up teeny tiny weights. But by the time they'd done their damage, you felt like you were holding two four-ton concrete pilings in each hand.

In the first section ("arms"), she thought she was going to throw up. In the second ("quads"), pass out. By the time they got through glutes and abs to the stretching, at the end, she didn't even have the energy to lie down flat on the mat, the way all the other women were doing. "Savasana," apparently. She just slunk out the door and made her way on quivering muscles to her car.

It was difficult to explain the sensation that had come over Sherri during the barre class—it was a feeling of helplessness, of haplessness, such as she hadn't experienced in a very long time, not since she'd been forced to play volleyball in high school gym class. ("Look where you want the ball to go, Sherri!" the gym teacher had cried again and again. "Not where you're afraid it's going!") Sherri had never, ever gotten the hang of volleyball. Nor badminton. Really, anything with a net. And now, apparently, anything with a barre as well. In her old life, of course, she'd been curvier. And if she got too curvy, there was good old-fashioned dieting. A home gym, although Bobby used that more than Sherri.

It was some time later that she fully felt the sting of her failure and her exclusion. She had stopped in to pick up Katie's summer reading book at the lovely little bookstore on State Street. She peeked in the window of the coffee shop next door and saw the whole group, bent over their lattes and cappuccinos, talking earnestly. Her cheeks burned, and she ducked her head, turning away from the window.

She thought she'd navigated the most difficult experiences of her life already, before she and Katie had arrived here. Now, with her legs about to give out on her, looking at these women whose daughters controlled the incoming sixth grade, she wondered if her biggest challenges might still be coming.

There had been talk of a lunch table. Katie *had* to get a seat at that lunch table.

She turned around and almost ran into another woman, the woman who had been kind to her at the restaurant. She combed her mind for the name.

"Rebecca," said the woman. "Morgan's mom? We met briefly at the beach, and then at dinner." Rebecca's eyes flicked toward the coffee shop and back to Sherri. Instantly Sherri understood. Either by her own choice or the choice of others, she hadn't been included either.

"Hey, Morgan and I are planning on going to the beach today. Are you free? You and your daughter should come."

Rebecca offered to pick up Sherri and Katie, explaining that she already had a parking pass to get onto the reservation and it would be silly for Sherri to pay the parking fee. Sherri didn't know what "the reservation" was until they arrived; apparently it was a state-owned beach with a campground and miles of parking for which you could use the special pass. Nothing to do with Indians, as Sherri had initially thought. Oh, she had so much to learn.

Sherri found out a few things about Rebecca right off the bat, after they settled themselves into their beach chairs (Rebecca had brought one for Sherri) and watched the girls run off with boogie boards. Rebecca worked in a nearby town as a second-grade teacher. Her older daughter, Alexa, was almost eighteen, headed to Colby in the fall.

In Sherri's old life her best friends had been the wives of the guys Bobby worked with; they'd been tossed together by circumstance more than temperament or choice. Jennifer with the stables. Lauren with the acrylic nails. Amber with the indoor swimming pool. She'd sometimes wondered what it would have been like to choose her own friends, women she'd met at work (difficult, since Sherri didn't have a job) or in a book club (impossible; Sherri had never been in a book club). She hadn't made a friend from scratch in a very long time—since high school, really, and she'd lost touch with most of those friends when she'd started up with Bobby. None of her friends had liked Bobby.

Rebecca reached into her cooler (it had the word YETI printed across the center, just like all of those coolers lined up at the surf-camp beach) and pulled out two cans of something. "Black cherry or ruby grapefruit?" she asked. Seltzer! Just the thing on a hot day. Sherri had brought only water to drink.

"Either," said Sherri. "Thank you. Unless you're saving one for Morgan."

Rebecca let out a friendly sounding snort and handed Rebecca a can. "Uh, I don't think so," she said. "Morgan's not exactly drinking age."

Sherri took a closer look at the can. White Claw Hard Seltzer. Five percent alcohol. One hundred calories. Sherri thought of Brooke and her rosé by the pool. Did these women drink all day, every day? Well, all right. Sherri could hold her own. She opened her can and took a long sip of the seltzer. She didn't taste rum, or tequila. Maybe it was vodka? She took another sip, then another. The sun was so lovely. She could almost feel the vitamin D seeping into her bones. She was filled with a sensation of peace and tranquility such as she hadn't felt since . . . well, in a very long time.

And then her eyes flew open. From out of nowhere she had that panicky feeling again. Where were the girls? Oh, there they were, not on their boogie boards anymore. They were playing around with their phones, taking beach selfies. No self-consciousness about bathing suits when you were eleven years old, all knees and elbows and vertebrae. Not like now, when there were so many different body parts to worry about, things hanging and wobbling. Maybe Sherri should have gotten the breast implants when Bobby offered all those years ago. Lots of the women did. (Implants, and then some. New lips. Bigger eyes. Bigger cheekbones.) But Sherri had always liked her breasts. They were big enough to be serviceable, even attention-seeking, without getting in the way. Now she kept them covered, like she kept so much else covered.

A klatch of teenage girls caught her eye. They were lying on their stomachs in a semicircle, laughing at something on a phone one of them was holding. The seltzer must have gone to her head, because all of the girls looked like Madison Miller, even though Madison Miller had ginger hair and none of these girls did. But they were about Madison Miller's age, fifteen, sixteen, with bodies that were sleek and brown and hair that sat in tight buns on the tops of their heads. *Be careful!* Sherri wanted to call to them. *Be careful, because you never, ever know.*

"Are you okay?" Rebecca had pushed her sunglasses to the top of her head and was peering at Sherri. "You look like you just saw a ghost."

I did, thought Sherri. *There's a ghost over here, and a ghost over* there. *This beach is full of ghosts.* What she said was, "I think the seltzer might have gone to my head, that's all."

"It's hot," conceded Rebecca. "And that seltzer is strong." She reached back into the Yeti and produced two wraps. She took one herself and handed Sherri the other. "Eat," she commanded.

Sherri did as she was told. Hummus and vegetable. She was ravenous. "Did you make this? This is delicious. This might be the best wrap I've ever eaten." Since she and Katie had become a family of two their meals had been scattershot, made quickly out of boxes and cans. She hadn't felt settled enough to cook properly, the way she had back in their old house, and often she skipped meals altogether.

"No, I got them at the Natural Grocer," said Rebecca. "I didn't know if you or Katie were, you know, vegetarian or vegan or anything so I kept it simple just in case."

Sherri briefly relived the shame of the surf and turf at Plum Island Grille. "No," she said. "We're none of those things. We eat everything. Thank you. This is so—" She felt her voice catch, and she told herself to pull it together. "This is so nice of you." She tucked her T-shirt closer around her bathing suit. Rebecca had disrobed immediately upon arrival at the beach, showing a body that was nicely toned. She'd bet Rebecca could get through the "glutes" at barre class without feeling like somebody was cutting up her muscles with a Swiss Army knife.

Rebecca's eyes were on Morgan and Katie. "Did you ever want to have more than one child? Sometimes I feel like Morgan is an only child, she and my older daughter are at such different stages."

"I definitely wanted more than one," said Sherri. She had wanted four children, but Bobby said only one. Too much noise made him twitchy; chaos threw him off. He liked everything just so in the house, and even Katie's possessions, her shoes tossed here and there, sometimes put him over the edge. For a criminal, he was very fastidious. Or maybe all criminals were fastidious. Sherri had never surveyed the other wives about that in particular. Though some of them volunteered marital secrets without being asked for them, so Sherri knew more than she wanted to know about, for example, Tony Cancio and the toe fetish. She wished she could un-know that one.

Maybe it was the alcoholic seltzer talking, or maybe it was the beauty of the summer day, lulling her into an unwarranted state of complacency. Sherri felt, almost, like Rebecca was someone she could confide in. That was a dangerous feeling, and it had to be stopped at all costs. There was no person anywhere Sherri could confide in. She cast about for a change in subject, and her eyes caught on Rebecca's wedding ring. "What did you say your husband does?" asked Sherri.

"He's gone," said Rebecca. She twisted her wedding ring.

"Like, for good?" Sherri asked. Absconded? A deserter?

"He died," said Rebecca. "Eighteen months ago."

13.

REBECCA

Rebecca had it down to a brief explanation, like a school report with a time limit. "He had a ruptured brain aneurysm at Logan airport, after a flight from Dubai. He managed a contracting company and he was in charge of a long-term project there. He was completely healthy. It came from out of nowhere; it was a huge shock."

"Oh my gosh," said Sherri. "Really? I'm so sorry. I didn't know." The dichotomy between the bright, hot day and this news of a death would probably make Sherri clam up. Rebecca was always doing that, she felt—injecting her tragedy into someone else's sunshine.

She lifted her eyes to meet Sherri's and said, "How would you have known? We just met. It's a perfectly normal question."

"I'm so sorry," Sherri repeated. "I can't even imagine. I thought *my* situation was hard."

"Your divorce," said Rebecca.

"Yes," said Sherri. "My divorce. And the move. But all of that pales in comparison to this—I can't even imagine." She paused. "It must help, to have so many friends around, for you, and Morgan too. People seem really nice. The other day, Katie was invited to Brooke's house to swim with Taylor."

"Oh, *Brooke*," said Rebecca, rolling her eyes.

"What?"

"Nothing," said Rebecca. "Brooke's great. Everybody's great. When it first happened people were so supportive. *So* supportive. Casseroles, carpools, the whole bit." She rummaged in the cooler and cracked a second seltzer, offering one first to Sherri, who shook her head. "I just feel like we've come to the end of our time limit. Like we had six months, maybe a year, to get through it and then everyone expected that we'd all be back to normal. But we're not normal. I don't think we'll ever be 'normal' again." She made little air quotes around the word *normal*. "Mourning isn't a quick process."

"No," said Sherri decisively. "It isn't." She said that like someone who knew, and that felt to Rebecca like an unexpected kindness, like a cool hand laid against a hot cheek.

The first twelve months after Peter's death had been a nest of confusion and anxiety, both of these coupled with a bone-deep, mind-numbing fatigue that nothing seemed to help. Rebecca could get nine hours of sleep, or four, or none at all, and in all cases she dragged herself through her days, especially at school, going through the motions of "getting back to normal" while wondering where she could find a quiet corner in which to lie down, and close her eyes, and forget, and remember.

Her friends were wonderful for the first three months, caring enough for the next three, and after that point she began to sense their fatigue with her fatigue. Oh, they tried to hide it! But she was starting to drain their emotional reserves. They were ready to have the old Rebecca back: they were ready for her to move on.

Rebecca had decided that she would never move on. She wouldn't Tinder or Match or Zoosk or Bumble. She wouldn't swipe left *or* right. She wouldn't accept the invitations of her friends when they asked if she wanted to come to a barbecue

where there might be a recently divorced man from North Ando-
ver who was "definitely looking." (Looking for what, specifically?
Rebecca wanted to ask, but didn't.) Rebecca had had two chances
at love, first with Alexa's father and then with Peter, and look what
had happened. She'd used up all of her turns. Happily ever after
was not in the cards for her.

As the one-year anniversary approached, Rebecca's therapist
suggested she try a grief support group in Haverhill. She gave
Rebecca a printed list of options. Rebecca liked the therapist, and
she retained some of her old schoolgirl eagerness to please. She
took the list, and she promised she'd go.

She walked into the first meeting and saw a half dozen people
sitting in a semicircle. She saw a man at the snack table who looked
vaguely familiar, though she couldn't place him. He was looking
at her in the same I-think-I-know-you way. She nodded, and he
nodded, and together they perused the tray of store-bought cookies. Rebecca wasn't surprised to find cookies: she had learned that
when people didn't know what to do with your grief they settled
on feeding you.

"They should serve alcohol at these things," the man said. "It's
not AA, right? Bring out the Dark and Stormys!" Rebecca laughed
and then immediately thought she might cry; Peter had loved
Dark and Stormys.

"I'm sorry," the man said. "Did I say something to upset you?"

She shook her head, mute, and he said, "I did. I can see that I
did. I'm so sorry."

"No," she said, because she couldn't figure out how to say, "No
need to be sorry," without bursting into tears.

"How can I make it up to you? How about I buy you a drink
after the meeting?"

She looked around and realized she didn't want to be at the
meeting—there was so much *grief* and *sadness* in the room, and

she didn't have space for the grief of so many other people in her withered heart, which could barely contain her own. She hesitated, and he said, "Are you from Newburyport? You look so familiar."

She nodded, still not trusting herself to speak, and he continued, "I teach economics at the high school. I'm Daniel." He held out his hand. *Daniel Economics,* thought Rebecca. Easy enough to remember. "I'm Rebecca Coleman," she said, meeting his own hand with hers. Then some part of her that she thought had died with Peter—the part that danced to Nirvana in high school, the part that used to like sunbathing and sex and staying out until sunrise—said, "How about we skip this whole thing, and you buy me a drink right now?"

They went to a new wine bar in downtown Haverhill, and saying, "Red?" and waiting for her nod, Daniel Economics ordered two glasses of Cabernet. She was grateful for this: there had been so many questions in the past year—coffin or urn? Where's the life insurance paperwork? Do we have the kind of faucets that need to be turned off in the winter?—that she'd have been happy if somebody else answered everything for the rest of her life.

"So . . . ," said Daniel when they were seated. "Let's get the inevitable out of the way."

Rebecca took a sip of the wine and was immediately infused with a great warmth and a sense of peace. Wine!

"Husband," she said. "You may have heard of him, it was news in town at the time. Ruptured aneurysm. Age forty-eight. I have two daughters, seventeen and eleven."

Daniel Economic's brow furrowed immediately. He was sort of adorable when he did that; he looked like an overgrown Sharpei.

"I'm so sorry," he said.

"Thank you," she allowed.

"I know, that's what everyone says. But really, I am so, so, sorry."

"Thank you," she repeated. It *was* what everyone said, but somehow he said it differently—there was something in the directness of his gaze, and in its softness, that made her feel like he really meant it.

He was looking at her very earnestly. "How are your daughters? How are *you*?"

"Okay," she said. "I don't know. Bad. Fine. Terrible, mediocre, fabulous. It depends on the day. It's hard to read Alexa—she's older, and she's in a different situation. But Morgan, she's only in fifth grade. She's taking it hard."

"Ohhh," said Daniel. "Oh. Yes, I remember now. I know about your husband. Peter, you said?" She nodded. "I remember now. You should know . . . you probably know that I had your daughter, for Intro to the Stock Market. I didn't make the connection. Does she have a different last name?"

"She does," said Rebecca. "Thornhill. She kept my ex's name." She squinted at him. She'd had only three sips, but the wine was starting to hit her. Her legs felt pleasantly numb, her lips loose. "Now you go," she said. "Your turn."

"Sister," he said. "Breast cancer, five months ago. She left behind a daughter, who's almost thirteen."

"Oh my God!" she said. "I'm sorry. I'm really so, so, sorry. That shouldn't be allowed to happen."

"I know. It shouldn't. But it did."

"Older sister or younger sister?"

He took a deep breath; it was a breath that seemed to contain all of the sorrow in the world. He let it out slowly, deliberately. "The same age," he said. "I'm older, technically, but only by seven minutes."

"No! Oh, no. *No*. You were twins?"

Daniel Economics nodded. "We were really close. I was married, and divorced. I never had kids. Her family became my family. My niece feels like my own kid. They live in Boxford, so I see them a lot." He shrugged. "It's like a part of me died when she died."

"Of *course* it is," said Rebecca. "You were together from the very beginning."

"That's it. That's exactly it. We were together from the very beginning. I just can't seem to . . . get over it doesn't seem like the right term, because I don't think I'll ever get over it. But I can't seem to get back to regular life. I mean, I'm doing everything I need to do, sort of, but I'm just—"

He trailed off, and Rebecca said, "Going through the motions?"

"Exactly!" He smiled, and an unexpected dimple popped out in his left cheek. "Exactly."

"I get it."

"I know you do."

Daniel's hand was resting on the table, next to his wineglass, and the next thing Rebecca knew she was putting her own hand over his.

"Did you go to the parent-teacher conferences?" Daniel Economics asked. His eyes were very brown, such a deep, chocolate brown that she could scarcely see where the pupil ended and the iris began.

"Peter went," she said softly. "He was so good like that. He traveled a lot for work, and so when he was home he liked to be really involved with the kids."

"That makes sense," said Daniel Economics. "Because I think I would have remembered you, if you had gone." He paused. "Can I ask you a question?"

"Of course."

"Does it get better? I'm still—I'm still in so much pain. Nearly all the time."

Not yet, is what Rebecca was thinking. But she said, "A little bit. No, let me revise that. It gets a lot better, but only a little bit at a time. So you hardly notice it. And then one day you turn around, and it's not as bad as it once was."

"That's really good to hear." He reached across the table and touched her hair. He looked as surprised by this as she felt. "Sorry," he said. "I don't know what made me do that. Other than the fact that you have beautiful hair."

"Thank you," she said. She got quite a lot of compliments on her hair, which was a dark chestnut color with a natural but manageable wave. It was one of the only features that marked her and Alexa as related. But people didn't usually go around touching it. For some reason this seemed as un-strange as her putting her hand over his hand.

"Maybe we can be in pain together, sometime," he said. "Maybe we can just talk, sometimes. Maybe we can be our own therapy group. With better cookies. Or real food, maybe. Maybe a meal!"

"I'd like that," she said. She drained her glass.

He called the next day, and the day after that, and the first time Morgan had a sleepover and Alexa had plans, Rebecca went to Daniel's house and he cooked her dinner—she deemed the restaurant scene in Newburyport too risky to bear witness to whatever it was they were doing. Which was what? Well, she wasn't entirely sure. But after dessert it crystallized. No pun intended (dessert was ginger sorbet with pieces of crystallized ginger scattered throughout). Daniel could cook! Rebecca had cleared the plates and was about to put them in the sink when Daniel came up behind her and put his hands on her shoulders. She turned, and her mouth found his without even looking for it. Then they were kissing, and then they were kissing some more, and then he was leading her into his bedroom, and clothes were coming off, and off.

So that, it turned out, was what they were doing.

After, while Daniel took a quick shower, Rebecca was perusing the shelves in his living room where there stood a few framed photos. There was one of Daniel and what she figured were his parents and the dead twin, standing in front of a boat with crystal-green water behind them. There was one of a young girl who she figured to be the left-behind daughter at an earlier stage of life. And there was one of . . . *Gina? MOM Squad Gina?* No, it couldn't be Gina. But it was, in a photo with a bunch of other people. Here was Gina's husband, Steve, wearing a Red Sox cap. Here was Gina and Steve's daughter, Callie, much smaller and younger, but recognizable by her naturally curly hair and her crooked smile. And here, holding a baby who must be the now-seven-year-old brother of Callie, was Gina!

"What is Gina doing on your bookshelves?" she called to Daniel. He came out with a towel around his waist and damp hair. Rebecca looked modestly away. He had a very nice chest—he confessed to doing one hundred push-ups every day, in sets of twenty-five—but still she felt shy; seeing a man in a towel in front of her, a man who was not Peter, made it seem all the more real, what had just occurred. A blush crept onto her cheeks.

Daniel stood next to her and looked at the photos too. Rebecca pointed at Gina.

"Oh, sure," he said. "Gina. I don't know why I keep this photo up here anymore! It's from another life. So, Gina's husband—"

"Steve," said Rebecca.

"Yes. Steve. Steve is the brother of my ex-wife, Veronica. If you can believe it. So I guess technically Gina is my ex-sister-in-law? She and Veronica were good friends, and they still are." He made a face. "I guess that makes her kids my ex-niece and ex-nephew? But you don't lose a niece and a nephew in a divorce, do you? I hope not. I love those kids. I guess that's why I keep the picture up there, even though Veronica the Cheater is right *there*." He jabbed a finger at a lithe blond woman who was also in the photo. "I still see them. They live over on Jefferson."

"Oh, I know where they live," said Rebecca. "Believe me." Jefferson was only a few streets away from her own house. Her heart sank. Here she thought she had found someone new, unsullied by history or connection, but she should have known better: there was no such thing in a town of this size. If Gina found out about this, she'd shout it from the rooftops, just as she had about the sleeping bag. Every time Rebecca thought about Gina she thought simultaneously about the sleeping bag and felt a rage so potent it threatened to seep out of her pores.

"We can't tell anyone about—this," said Rebecca. She made a motion that indicated his towel and her own fully clothed self. "Especially not Gina." She winced.

"Why not?"

"It'll get out, someone will tell the girls. I'm not ready for a bunch of questions. I'm just—" She let out a little puff of air. "I'm still just trying to figure things out. You know?"

He took her face between his hands and looked into her eyes. He smelled like Irish Spring and also like the ginger from the dessert. He kissed her lightly on the forehead and said, "We don't tell anyone until you are one hundred percent ready. And that's assuming that there's something to tell—that you want to do *this*" (he imitated her hand gesture) "again."

There were so many emotions swirling inside Rebecca that she couldn't have given a name to each of them even if she'd wanted to. But a few were recognizable: relief, fear, sorrow, joy. Hope.

"I think I do," she said. "Want to do this again. Yes, please, actually. I really think I do."

Now, at the beach, with Sherri, Rebecca said, "It's been really hard on Morgan. She and Peter were very close. She's done some funny things since Peter died. She's become really klutzy, tripping over everything. She wet her sleeping bag at a sleepover! She's never wet the bed, ever, not even when she was toilet training. And everybody found out about it." It had been Gina's house where it happened, almost a year ago now. It had been Gina who had whisked the sleeping bag away to be washed. "So naturally she doesn't go to big sleepovers anymore."

"Oh, that's awful," said Sherri.

Morgan and Katie were at the edge of the water taking turns doing handstands, probably videoing for Instagram. Katie's handstands were solid but Morgan kept toppling over.

Two skinny teenage boys, hairless as hippos, were throwing a Frisbee back and forth. Many of the empty spots in the beach had filled in. Colorful umbrellas and their fancier cousins, pop-up beach tents, now occupied nearly every available space. The sand was shimmering with the heat. "Anyway, I'm so happy to see Morgan like this, making a new friend. Playing. She's still a kid, and I want her to act like a kid." She paused. "It's an entirely different story with my older daughter, Alexa. She has a different father." She paused and reached for a bottle of sunblock and squirted some out, rubbing it on her arms. "So in this funny way her grief is more, I don't know, *complicated* than Morgan's. Less clear-cut. I feel like there's a wall between her and Morgan that wasn't there before. Maybe it got too high before I noticed it, I don't know. I don't know how to break it down." She paused again and then realized she'd just spilled at least three-quarters of her life story to a virtual stranger. "I'm sorry! I haven't talked about most of this with anyone. I guess I had a lot saved up. Am I getting too personal, for a first date?"

"No!" said Sherri. "Not at all. I'm happy to lend an ear. Two ears!"

"Thank you," said Rebecca. "It's good to acknowledge some of this stuff out loud."

One of the skinny Frisbee boys missed a catch and the Frisbee sailed perilously close to Sherri, effectively ending the serious part of the conversation.

"Is there any chance Alexa babysits?" Sherri asked, after tossing the Frisbee back toward the boy.

"Are you looking for a sitter for Katie?" asked Rebecca. (Could an eleven-year-old not stay alone? Eleven-year-olds were permitted to take the babysitting class at the Y and babysit for *other* people's children!)

"I know. She's too old to need one," said Sherri. "But it's a new town . . . and our house is old, and sort of creaky, I can see where she gets nervous. It's all new to us, not having my husband around." She cleared her throat. "My ex, I mean. It might not hurt to have a name ready as I start looking for a job."

"Well, let's see. Alexa works at the ice cream place out on Plum Island. The Cottage? She has a boyfriend. She's pretty busy. But if she's not free or interested, she might know somebody who is. I'll send her number to you. Don't tell her I sent you, though. Just tell her it was someone from the Mom Squad. It'll go over better that way."

"Mom Squad," repeated Sherri, as though she were testing out a foreign language. "Mom Squad. That sounds really nice and protective, like a group of superheroes."

Rebecca snorted. "Sort of," she said. She thought again of Gina and the sleeping bag. "But not really. Anyway. Sorry I talked so much about myself! I don't know what got into me. I do that sometimes, you know, since Peter died. I used to talk to him, and now I burden other people. I probably drove him crazy when he was alive, with all of my talking, and he was too polite to say anything. I feel bad about it now." Poor Peter, listening to her for hours on end, pretending to be interested. "Is there anything more depressing than an oversharing widow?"

"I can think of a few things," said Sherri grimly, which gave Rebecca pause. Such a funny phrase, giving pause. What did pause look like, anyway, and how did one receive it once it was handed over?

"What about you?" Rebecca asked. "Was your divorce one of those friendly ones, or an awful one where you only speak to each other when you absolutely have to discuss custody? Are you looking for someone new, or content on your own for a while?"

When Sherri next spoke there was a new edge to her voice. "No, my divorce was not the friendly type of divorce. And I'm not looking for anyone new. There's no custody to discuss." She smiled, but there was something hard in the smile that hadn't been there before. "It's just Katie and me, against the world."

14.

THE SQUAD

Sherri didn't join us for coffee after barre class. She didn't even know enough to wipe down her mat and hang it over the barre for the next person! She was out of there so quickly that it was the instructor who wound up her stretching rope, who placed her hand weights in the appropriate bins.

Obviously Sherri had never been to a barre class in her life. Maybe barre hasn't made it out to Ohio yet? We don't know. Oh, her form in the plank section! Not that we could really see, concentrating as we were on our own planks—it was a particularly difficult series, with one of the most challenging instructors—but as we were turning from front plank to side plank some of us did see Sherri topple. Though we all pretended not to. We tried to remember when we too were new to barre, many moons ago, and if the side plank was difficult for us then. But we couldn't recall. Some of us have naturally strong obliques, and of course that makes side plank easier.

Dawn told Sherri about the barre class and she said, sure, she'd give it a try. The first class is free. Did we mention Sherri ordered the surf and turf at Plum Island Grille? So maybe money wasn't an issue for her. Then again, the Laundromat. So maybe it was.

Come to think of it, we said later, Rebecca hadn't been at the barre class, nor at coffee after. It had been Gina who switched us from the class we used to take, the 8:15, to this one, the 9:15. The switch was due to a change in the schedule of our favorite instructor. Gina, when pressed, told us she had *specifically* mentioned the new class to Rebecca *in person*. We didn't know why she hadn't come—with her teaching schedule summer is the only time she can go to the 8:15 *or* the 9:15. It was yet another example of Rebecca pulling away from us.

And she couldn't hide what she did later that day anyway, because Morgan posted on her Instagram story a video of Katie doing handstands on the beach. When the camera swerved we could see Rebecca. Next to her in a matching chair, the new woman. Sherri. Later, a TikTok appeared. And there we were at Jenness, like a bunch of idiots. We planned it after barre class, at the coffee shop. Some of the kids wanted to bring surfboards, and it's much harder to surf at Salisbury. But we would have been happy to bag the boards! Would it have killed Rebecca to let the rest of us know where she was going that day? The Mom Squad group chat is *right there* for anybody to add to at any time. It's not that hard.

But nobody told us about the trip to Salisbury. I think that's the important thing you have to remember here. Nobody. Told. Us.

Some of us didn't believe it—the new girl? And Morgan? The new mom? And Rebecca? What did they all have to talk about with each other? How did they even know each other well enough to form this little alliance? Those who hadn't seen the video tried to find the proof the following day. But you don't have to be eleven to know that an Instagram story vanishes exactly twenty-four hours after it's been posted. Poof: just like that, it was gone. Like it had never happened.

Also. We don't even know how it got out, the thing about Morgan and the sleeping bag. Gina took it away as soon as she noticed. She had that bag washed and dried before Rebecca picked up Morgan. She never told anyone. Why would she?

Except Tammy, but that was in private. And then Brooke, after Tammy accidentally mentioned it to her, and then one of the girls found out. But we jumped all over Tammy and Brooke and Gina for that. Morgan had lost her dad! Could we please give her a break?

After that things were never quite the same between Rebecca and Gina. There was a certain level of mistrust. Which was too bad: they used to be close.

Looking back at the end of the summer, when everything was over, it was possible to point to that Instagram story from Salisbury Beach and say that that was when the tide started to turn. If you will please excuse our pun.

15.

REBECCA

Rebecca found Alexa in the kitchen, where she was buttering a piece of toast. Bernice was lying directly in front of the sink, as was her wont, so each time Alexa needed to use the sink she had to stand a Bernice-width away and stretch over her. Bernice was a Bernese mountain dog. Peter had named her—he'd been delighted with the play on words.

"Can you follow me to the service station on Bridge Road?" Rebecca asked.

The buttering grew more vigorous and Alexa said, "Now?" Bernice shifted her big fluffy body in the wrong direction, closer to the center of the kitchen.

"Sometime this morning. I've got to get that dent repaired—it's already been over a week." Rebecca felt suddenly nervous, as though she were asking her daughter out on a date. Alexa sighed prettily and glanced at her phone. "Unless you're working," said Rebecca, hurriedly, apologetically. (Why was *she* apologizing? She paid the car insurance on Alexa's Jeep.) "I could always ask a friend." (Could she?)

"No, I'm off today. I have plans later. But, sure, I can drive you."

"Plans with your friends?" Rebecca couldn't keep the inquisitiveness out of her voice. "With Caitlin and Destiny?"

"*Mom*," said Alexa. She stared at the toast. "Stop. Why all the questions?"

"It's not *all the questions.* I'm just—well, something made me realize how long it's been since you hung out with Caitlin and Destiny." *It's really too bad, what happened with Alexa and her friends,* Esther had said, as if she knew something Rebecca didn't. "And I want to make sure everything's okay." If she'd been more on the ball, if she hadn't been wrapped up in Daniel and worried about Morgan, she would have picked up on this a long time ago. It vexed her that it had taken Esther's pressing to force her to bring up the topic.

"Everything's fine. Everything's better than fine. People change in the course of high school. Isn't that what you're always telling me? That it's okay to grow and change? Evolve. We're just not as close anymore."

Rebecca did say that it was okay for people to evolve, and she believed it. But she remembered Esther's face at Plum Island Grille, her smug, knowing smile, and she kept on. "But the three of you used to be so sweet together. You were like Betsy, Tacy, and Tib!"

"Like who?" Alexa was taking very tiny bites of her toast (did she have an eating disorder? Rebecca wondered) and rubbing her earlobe with her other hand (or a touch of OCD?).

"Betsy, Tacy, and Tib. The books? About the three little girls?"

"I don't know what you mean."

"Did I never read those to you?"

"No."

"Are you sure? That's a travesty. Practically a crime."

"If you did, I don't remember." Bernice heaved herself to her feet (paws) and moved to another part of the kitchen, as though this discussion of desiccated friendship was irritating her. Alexa took a bigger bite of her toast and said, "Anyway, I have other friends. I've got plenty going on. So don't worry. I'm not pathetic and alone."

"I'm not *worried,*" said Rebecca. She *was* worried, of course— she was always worried about something. (What *did* Alexa have going on?)

"Do you mind if we go right now?" asked Alexa. "I have some things I need to do later."

At the service station, after she'd arranged with the owner to call her when the work on the Acura was complete, Rebecca saw the young man who was pumping gas looking sidelong at Alexa from under the brim of his hat. Alexa, a foot on the dash, scrolling through Instagram, noticed him while pretending not to notice. *Stop looking at her!* Rebecca wanted to cry. *That is my little girl, and you have no right.*

It had been a long time since Rebecca had sat in the passenger seat with her eldest child. Since Alexa had procured a driver's license and the Jeep she'd become so independent that at times she seemed more lodger than daughter. But here she was, her face washed clean of makeup, her hair in a messy bun, wearing pajama shorts that were for some reason designed to look like men's boxer shorts, driving her mother home, with no shoes on, which Rebecca thought was probably illegal.

How strange it was: you raised these people from their most miniature, floppiest, most dependent suckling form, and then when they were scarcely grown you helped them get a laminated piece of paper and you sent them off in these hulking, crushable monsters of steel and rubber, and you hoped for the best. (Was Alexa hugging the right side of the road a little more than she should?)

They were crossing the bridge now, back into Newburyport, and Rebecca looked at all of the boats in the harbors on both sides of the river, the sun glancing off the water. It was one of prettiest sights in the world to Rebecca, the view from this bridge in the summer, and she'd put it up against the sun setting over the Blue Ridge Mountains or the fjords of Norway, although she hadn't actually seen either of those places in person.

"It just goes so fast," said Rebecca. The car sailed over the last piece of the bridge and stopped behind a line of cars waiting to turn toward town. "Do *you* feel like it's going really fast? Life?"

Alexa made a face and said, "Absolutely not. I feel like every day lasts about a week and a half."

"One day," said Rebecca, "you will be being driven around by your own children, and you will see what I mean. I, at that point, will be toothless and infirm somewhere."

The Jeep idled. "Don't be dramatic," said Alexa. "You'll probably have teeth." She flicked her tongue out, lizard quick, as she waited for the last two cars in front of her to disperse, and that made Rebecca think that she could still see her in there somewhere: the girl who used to stick out her tongue in the very same way when she was tying her sneakers at age seven. Further back in time, the girl who, when Rebecca packed her up in the middle of the night to move her out of a situation that was no longer safe, didn't ask, *Where are we going?* but instead asked, *When will we get there?*—a question that showed such a survivor's determination and such faith in her tattered, shattered mother that Rebecca set her shoulders back and understood at once that she had to make herself worthy of that little girl's trust.

"We need to start shopping for your dorm room soon, don't we?"

"Not *soon*. It's only June."

"Still, it'd be good to get a jump on it. I haven't seen a list yet. Did they send a list? Of what you need?"

Alexa didn't know; Alexa didn't seem to care that much. Rebecca supposed the list, like everything else these days, could be found online.

"What about a dorm assignment? Did we get that yet?" Rebecca couldn't wait to drop Alexa off at Colby and watch her get ready to experience everything she herself had experienced. "I wonder if you'll be put in Hillside," she mused. "Remember, from the tour?"

Alexa didn't answer.

Rebecca's phone, which was in her lap, buzzed. A text from

Gina. Sry we missed u at the beach yesterday! U should have told us where u were going.

Rebecca could feel the passive aggressiveness seeping through the screen. "Oh, *please*," she said.

"Drama?" asked Alexa. She found a spot in the traffic flow and shot across Merrimac Street; they were almost home. "Mom Squad drama?"

"Of a sort."

Alexa's expression simultaneously said, *You are old, so your drama cannot possibly be as interesting as my drama* and, *Despite myself, I'm sort of curious.* After a moment the curiosity must have won out because Alexa asked, "What's going on?"

"Nothing," said Rebecca. The phone buzzed again. This time the text was from Monica. Thought we'd see you at barre yesterday. "I mean, it should be nothing. Morgan and I went to the beach with Sherri and Katie and you'd think I gave the nuclear code to North Korea."

"Who are Sherri and Katie?"

"New people. From Ohio. Jeez, try to make a new friend and it feels like high school all over again. Do you know what I mean?"

"Uh, yeah," said Alexa. "I definitely know what you mean. Remember that time someone called you at one in the morning to find out why her daughter hadn't been invited to a sleepover with Morgan and four other girls?"

"Tammy," said Rebecca. "I remember. I told Morgan she could only have five that time. I can't always host a dozen!"

"Remember when World War Three broke out over a barbecue that someone wanted to have on the same weekend as Brooke's end-of-summer party?"

Rebecca remembered that too. "Gina," she said. "Not even the same day. Just the same weekend. *That* was a kerfuffle. To put it mildly."

"So who would be what, then?" asked Alexa. "If you were all in high school?"

Rebecca thought about it. "Esther would probably be homecoming queen," she said. "And, let's see, Gina would definitely be student body president, and Melanie would be the pretty girl who wanted the lead in all the plays but thought she was too cool to hang out with the theater kids. A theater kid in sheep's clothing, I guess."

Alexa smiled indulgently. "Homecoming queen isn't really a thing anymore, Mom. That's like super old-fashioned."

"Well. Still. You know what I mean." Alexa granted this statement a slightly condescending nod. "In a way," Rebecca continued, "in a way it never ends. We're in high school for the rest of our lives, like it or not."

"Please, no," said Alexa. "I just got *out* of high school. Whatever else you do, please don't tell me that I'm stuck there for the rest of my life." She turned into the driveway and parked neatly, pulling up on the emergency brake just the way Peter had taught her. Rebecca had left the whole of Alexa's driving education to Peter and the professionals at Hoffman Driving School. She didn't have the stomach for it herself. As a result, Alexa could parallel park like nobody's business, and she could drive through rush-hour traffic on Storrow Drive without breaking a sweat.

"Peter would be proud of you," Rebecca said now.

"For what? My parking? It's just a driveway, Mom. Morgan could park here."

"Well, your parking, to start with. But a lot of other things besides."

Alexa winced. There was a moment where Rebecca thought Alexa might hug her, or that she might even cry. But: "Thanks," she said softly, not meeting Rebecca's eyes, hopping out of the Jeep, landing softly on her illegal bare feet.

16.

ALEXA

One day close to the end of June, Alexa locked the door and readied herself for the camera. She surveyed the contents of her closet and consulted her list of what she'd worn in previous videos.

Alexa kept her online outfits in the back of her closet, behind her winter coats, just in case anyone ever came snooping. She selected her Diane Von Furstenberg Julian silk jersey mini wrap dress in Sussex stripe hydrangea; she found that when she wore vertical stripes her viewers took her more seriously. She could tell by the comments. In the bathroom, she employed her hair straightener to tame the curated beachy look she wore at the Cottage and, finally, she used her Tom Ford eye color, which cost eighty-eight dollars at Sephora. Alexa believed this to be a silly amount of money to spend on four shades of eyeshadow, but she also believed in looking the part, and she further believed that when you had money you should spend it on quality items.

She tested the microphone by reciting the first stanza of "The Raven," which she'd had to memorize in eighth grade and had never forgotten. "Once upon a midnight dreary, while I pondered, weak and weary," she began.

A knock at the door. She sighed and turned off the camera. *Suddenly there came a tapping,* she thought. "Yes?"

"Alexa?" Morgan.

"What's up, Morgs? I'm in the middle of something."

"Who's in there?"

"No one's in here."

"I thought you were talking to someone."

Come on, thought Alexa. She just wanted to make her video and get on with her day. "It was just an audiobook," she said. Alexa had never listened to an audiobook in her life, nor did she plan to.

"Can I come in?"

"No." Too sharp, but she couldn't help it.

"Why not?"

"I'm doing something important. Where's Mom?"

"I don't know." Morgan's voice was plaintive. "She's not home. She didn't leave a note."

"Text her."

"I did. She didn't answer yet."

"I'm sure you'll be fine for a little while." Alexa couldn't help the note of exasperation that crept into her voice.

From outside the door came Morgan's irritated little huff. "Why can't you be nicer, Alexa? Like you used to be?"

Alexa winced. "I'm nice!" she told the door. "I'm nice all the time."

"No you're not. Not anymore."

The truth was, Alexa *hadn't* been all that nice to Morgan lately, really not since Peter died. Morgan's grief had seemed so separate from her own—in many ways so much cleaner, so much more deserved and allowed, that Alexa felt herself bumping up against it again and again. Unable to help herself.

"I'll be down in a few," she added, more softly. Picturing Morgan's sad little face, hearing her raspy, innocent voice, brought to the forefront an uncomfortable question.

Alexa's biological father was "no longer in the picture"—a euphemism employed by Alexa's mother and adopted by Alexa herself, even though she knew that the truth behind those words was darker and more ominous. A raging alcoholic. Incapable of or unwilling to seek rehabilitation. A danger to himself and others. *No longer in the picture.* Never to be in the picture again.

So Alexa couldn't help but wonder. If Morgan's essential goodness came half from Rebecca and half from Peter, where did that leave Alexa? Only half good. Half at the most.

"Give me ten minutes, okay?" She kept most of her videos to under four minutes, because she'd found that that was the sweet spot for holding people's attention. She always sat in the same chair. She crossed her legs demurely at the ankle, and she aimed the camera so it focused mostly on her face.

"Welcome to Silk Stockings," she said. "Today we're going to learn about toxic assets: what they are, and what to do if you find yourself in possession of them."

She'd been doing Silk Stockings for just about a year now. The seed first sprouted before that, in that dark time after Peter's death. Those were confusing, unsettling days, when her mother drank a lot of red wine, and Morgan curled up in the living room and reread Harry Potter for the zillionth time. At meals, instead of sitting down and eating something her mother had cooked, as they had in the past, they each foraged in the kitchen and ate standing at the island, or trailed cracker crumbs or shreds of cheese to the television or a corner in which to nurse their melancholy. For her part Alexa found herself watching a lot of YouTube alone in her room.

There were so many videos! And she knew that some of these people were making money from them. She started to pay closer attention. There were videos of people opening boxes and people putting other people to sleep with ASMR whispering; there were people training their dogs and people putting on makeup and taking off makeup and putting makeup on their well-trained dogs and curling hair and straightening hair and baking, sawing, grilling, singing, strumming, arranging, knitting, organizing.

For a while Alexa was intrigued by Hannah Hart, who cooked drunk, but Alexa didn't like to cook. She definitely didn't like to cook drunk. (She didn't even like to eat drunk.) It was around that time that she was taking an Intro to the Stock Market at the high school that she'd chosen as an elective because the teacher, Mr. Bennett, was supposedly an easy grader.

One day she was listening to him talk about bull markets versus bear markets, and idly thinking about how much easier it was to learn from good-looking people, which may be prejudiced or whatever but it was still totally true (Mr. Bennett, for an old person, was not terrible on the eyes), and then it hit her. This could be her entry into YouTube. She could be the pretty girl talking about the stock market.

She made a few videos, explaining terms she'd learned either in class or in *Stock Investing for Dummies*. Price-to-earnings ratio, bears and bulls, diversification. When she was confident enough in the format, and in her hair, she started posting them to her own channel. Viewers and subscribers followed—more quickly than she'd anticipated. It was sort of embarrassing, how fast and furious they came. Soon she had enough subscribers to apply to the YouTube Partner Program, where advertisers paid to appear on certain channels. She got accepted, and she started earning.

What she made was not insane money by YouTube standards. But it was *way* more than she made scooping ice cream at the Cottage. It paid for her clothes, which were not cheap, and it allowed her to tuck away a sizable amount each month. For her future.

Not long before Peter died—halfway through Alexa's junior year—she told him she might want to take a gap year. She thought she might want to live in California for a while. Her class was suffering from collective stress and anxiety; people were having contests about how little sleep they could get by on; it was a particularly long, gray New England winter, where time and time again they opened the door for Bernice to go outside and do her business and they all swore she shook her head and backed away.

Peter didn't say, *You can't do that.* He didn't say, *That's not in the plan.* He said, "Let's do this. Let's do your college visits, and you take your standardized tests, and you do your applications. Just to cover your bases. And when the time comes to decide, we'll have a conversation about it with your mom."

Alexa didn't understand how Peter could be so reasonable and so patient all the time. She had only seen him get truly angry twice, once when somebody keyed his car in the North End in Boston while they were all having dinner at Carmelina's, and in 2018 when the Patriots lost to the Eagles in the Super Bowl.

Then Peter was gone. Poof. She thought that if Peter were here he'd be proud of what she'd built, and somehow his imaginary approval got intertwined with her efforts too. Later, after her fight with Caitlin and Destiny, after months and months of feeling removed from her mother's and Morgan's grief, her desire for a new life, a faraway life, got braided in as well. And now here she was, sixteen thousand subscribers strong.

Neither she nor her mother brought up the college visits: nobody had the time or the energy to make them happen. She visited and applied only to Colby, her mother's alma mater, and to UMass, and got into both. As Silk Stockings gained steam, her interest in college narrowed and narrowed until it was the size of a pinhole. In May she had taken a deep breath, called Colby, and given up her spot. Come September, she would head to Los Angeles, where Silk Stockings would be but the first step in making Alexa Thornhill a brand.

She had a few things to sort out, such as, where would she live in L.A.? How much money did she actually need to get started?

When would she tell her mother that she wasn't going to Colby? She'd confided rather ill-advisedly in Tyler, but she'd sworn him to secrecy. And she'd begun to mention her plans to move to L.A. casually in the occasional video (the one about understanding current market conditions, for example), aware, as any rising You-Tuber was, of the possibility of the eyeballs of a talent scout coming to rest on her channel.

She turned off the camera and checked the comments and likes on her last video, about cryptocurrency, one of her more challenging endeavors. A few hundred comments, including the usual: people who liked her dress, people who didn't like her dress, someone who thought there was too much of a glare coming in through the window, someone who saw fit to bash the person who complained about the glare, and so on and so forth. Not too many people had much to say about the actual content. Never mind: YouTube empires had been founded on less. She scrolled down until her eyes snagged on a comment from *jt76*. This person had been popping up more and more in the comments, and always had something kind to say.

She thought of *jt76* as a he, but of course it could be a love-sick lesbian or a transitioning teenager or a masquerading Mom Squad member. Maybe *jt76* wasn't even kind! Maybe he (or she) was from the SEC and was going to arrest her for some sort of violation she didn't even know she'd committed.

This time it was: *Really succinct explanation, I've never really understood this topic before! Thank you for condensing it so well!*

At least somebody thought she was good at something. Even if nobody thought she was nice.

17.

THE SQUAD

We're not sure where you heard this, but honestly. Somebody told you *Esther* would be the homecoming queen? No. Sorry. You've been misinformed. Esther was more like that girl who manages the boys' teams instead of playing her own sport. You know that girl, right? Always walking around with a clipboard, telling people where they needed to be and what time the bus was leaving. *That* was Esther. Homecoming queen? Please.

18.

SHERRI

Sherri's counselor had done a lot of legwork to help them settle into their new lives, greasing the wheels in important and invisible ways. Apparently the surf camp at the beginning of the summer was nearly impossible to get into without a lot of prior planning! And Katie had secured a spot. Now Katie was enrolled in a series of one-week camps through the Youth Services program in town (this week's was Knitting for Preteens; Sherri had never learned to knit herself and was in awe of the collections of stitches Katie had been bringing home each day) and Sherri, also with the counselor's help, had a job interview. Here she was at Derma-You, a medical spa in Danvers, interviewing with the office manager, a woman named Jan. Sherri was carrying her fake resumé in a new bag she'd bought for $29.99 at Marshalls. She thought it looked like it cost quite a bit more than that, though.

It had been a long time since Sherri had held a job. She'd stopped working after she and Bobby got married. She hadn't exactly been changing the world; she'd been working as a receptionist at a hair salon and frankly had been happy to give it up and concentrate on getting pregnant, which took longer than she thought it would. Now, the prospect of a job interview filled her with equal parts terror and feverish, trembling excitement. She, Sherri Griffin, was going to reenter the work force!

When Sherri walked into Derma-You's waiting room she found it busy, full of women, most of them bent over clipboards and casting furtive glances around at the rest of the patients. She was shown by one of the smooth, ageless front desk employees to a small room in the back to meet Jan.

"We need someone to answer the phones, that sort of thing," said Jan, launching right in. Apparently they weren't going to sit around and engage in small talk. That was all right with Sherri. Small talk made her nervous, because she didn't want to say the wrong thing. Jan could be in her fifties or in her thirties or her forties depending on how many of Derma-You's services she had availed herself of. It was really hard to tell. Sherri tried to listen to her without staring too hard at her puffy lips.

"A lot of the job is answering phones," said Jan. "Being the first face the patient sees, that sort of thing."

"I've got a really good phone voice," said Sherri, trying not to sound too eager.

"Eventually you'll need to be trained in the billing system, which is sort of complicated." Jan rustled the fake resumé, which had Sherri having had a number of clerical jobs in and around Columbus, Ohio. She furrowed her unfurrowable brow. "Have you ever worked in a medical office before?"

"Not specifically," said Sherri. "But I'm a very fast learner." That's what the counselor had told her to say, and in fact it was true.

"Well, we're extremely short-staffed right now," said Jan. "We're opening another branch in Woburn, and half of our front desk staff has had to go over there, so we're scrambling. You can consider yourself hired."

"Really?" It was that easy, to get a job?

"Really," said Jan. She peered at Sherri's face.

"What?" asked Sherri, putting a hand self-consciously to her cheek. The light was extremely bright in this office.

"You should stay out of the sun. You've got sunspots here"—Jan touched Sherri's cheek along the top of her cheekbones—"and here." The edge of her forehead. Sherri reared back; something had activated her "fight or flight" instinct.

"Sorry," said Jan, lowering her hand. "I was just going to say, the lasers can do wonders with that. I didn't mean to spook you."

"You didn't spook me," said Sherri untruthfully.

"There's no shame in wanting to improve yourself," Jan said firmly. "That's the most important thing you need to understand if you are going to work at Derma-You."

"No! No, of course not," said Sherri. "Of course there isn't any shame in wanting to improve yourself." If anybody in the place understood that, it was Sherri. *If only there was a laser for the heart,* thought Sherri. *A filler for the soul.*

They went over some specifics. Jan preferred to train new hires in the evening, when it was a bit quieter in the office. "Not that it's ever really quiet," she said, both proudly and ruefully. The office was open until nine three nights a week. Could Sherri come at six P.M. on the sixth of July, which was next Monday?

Yes, Sherri could come at six P.M. "How long will I stay that night?" she asked.

"A couple of hours," said Jan. "Maybe longer."

Sherri thought of Katie in the corner of the bedroom. Her heart started to beat faster. But she couldn't *not* take the job. They had to eat; they had to pay the rent. "I'll see you on the sixth," she told Jan.

She made her way through the thrum of women seeking self-improvement: the women who felt no shame about their bodies and the women who obviously felt lots of shame. Once she was in her car she allowed herself a little whoop of joy. She had a job! She would get a paycheck and discounts on the lasering of sunspots! She, Sherri Griffin, would be a contributor to the economic wheels that powered the great state of Massachusetts.

Sherri decided she'd bring some sort of treat home for Katie to celebrate. Maybe some of those Angry Donuts from the shop on Winter Street. She hadn't tried Angry Donuts yet—she didn't know what the doughnuts were quite so angry about—but one of the moms had told her they were very good.

She found a parking spot near the shop, and when she got out of the car such a funny, unexpected thing happened. She wasn't far from the river, and some of the scent had wafted her way. A pair of seagulls circled, letting out a mournful, delirious cry. From where she stood she could see the foot traffic and the bike traffic on the rail trail. It was all still so foreign to Sherri, the smells and the sounds and the very particular air of a New England summer. And at the same time, in some inexplicable way, she was starting to feel like she was home.

As it turned out, Angry Donuts sold out early most days and nothing was left for Sherri to buy. So after she picked Katie up at the knitting camp she took her to Mad Martha's. They would celebrate Sherri's new job!

Mad Martha's was nothing more than a little cottage on Plum Island, really almost a shack, with just a few tables, the bigger of which patrons shared with other patrons whether they knew each other or not. Katie and Sherri were seated with a family of five on vacation from Durango, Colorado. The food was delectable, and the community table lent the whole experience a jolly, festive air. The Colorado family was chatty. Durango sounded lovely, with a famous railroad that wound through canyons and a national forest. Sherri put it immediately on her mental wish list of places to visit. The list was long and included India and Africa too.

Realistically she probably wouldn't get to any of those. Her pay at Derma-You was twenty dollars an hour, and she wasn't even working full-time. The waiter was young and nice-looking, with beachy hair, a good tan, an easy smile. Sherri could tell that Katie was smitten, blushing faintly when she placed her order. *Watch out for the good-looking ones,* Sherri imagined telling her when she was a little older, in a few years' time. *I went for a good-looking one, and look what that got us.*

The thing was, Bobby had often been tender and funny. He made a really good pesto sauce. Once they'd played mini golf and he'd crawled through a spiky hedge to retrieve her ball, when she very easily could have gotten a new one from the girl working at the counter. He used to make pancakes for Katie every Saturday morning, which was sort of a cliché of good fathering, but in fact the pancakes were sensational, and he never burned the bottoms. In bed they had an incredible connection—*incredible.* Sometimes, even now, she flushed when she thought about that. And, worse, she missed it.

The waiter at Mad Martha's wasn't even twenty, and it would have been unseemly for a woman of Sherri's age—a mother! A Derma-You employee!—to let herself be attracted to him. But the glimpse of his bicep, the hollow below his cheekbone when he smiled, his firm, tan calves: all of these things made her wonder something that she hadn't allowed herself to wonder since she and Katie had first set foot in that terrible motel that smelled like old cheese and despair. What she wondered was this: Would she ever have a man in her life again? Would she ever have sex again? It didn't seem fair for her to have to give up sex altogether because Bobby had been involved in something so reprehensible. But how, exactly, would it come about, the sex? She lived in a town where everybody seemed already to be coupled off, marching two by two like animals onto the ark. Would she continue to wake day after day alone in the bed in this half-house with only Katie for company?

She took a bite of her breakfast burrito; it was the size of a small country and absolutely delicious. Maybe she and Katie should adopt a dog. Maybe Sherri should join Tinder. Was she too old for Tinder? Probably she was. Were people on Tinder looking for a slightly worn single mother with a secret past? Probably they weren't. She sighed.

"I think we should do some updating," Katie was saying as she worked her way through her pancakes. "To the house? Don't you think it would be fun to do that, Mom? Maybe we could get a rug for the kitchen floor, like Morgan has. Something really bright. And some throw pillows for your bed! Wouldn't you like to have some pretty throw pillows on your bed? They have them at Homegoods, do you think we should go to Homegoods?"

"Maybe," said Sherri, turning her attention back to Katie. "Sure, we can go to Homegoods."

"Today?"

"Why not?" Sherri was feeling flush, with the new job and all. "We'll go today, after breakfast." Bobby would never have wanted Sherri shopping in a Homegoods. He loathed discount shopping—he called it "shopping for other people's castoffs." She'd *liked* that he hadn't wanted her to have other people's castoffs.

"When's your first day at work?" asked Katie.

"July sixth. In the evening."

"The *evening*?" Katie looked stricken. "What will I do? Will I stay alone?"

"Will you be okay if you do?" Sherri asked.

"Yes," said Katie's voice—but her eyes told a different story.

"We'll figure something out," said Sherri. "I promise: we'll figure something out."

While they were waiting for the bill she pulled out her phone and texted Rebecca. I forgot to get Alexa's number from you 😔 (she added the slightly chagrined emoji, to convey that it was probably her own fault). RE: Babysitting.

The first time Sherri found something was an accident. She was in Bobby's office, looking for a stapler, and she dropped the papers she was holding. They slipped right out of her hands, almost like they *wanted* to lead her to something. When she bent to pick them up, she saw that the floor vent register under his desk chair was slightly askew. In her attempt to straighten it—Bobby was fastidious, she knew he wouldn't want anything out of place in the house—she pulled at it, thinking she had to take it all the way off to put it back on straight. After she removed the register, she saw that four of the large floor tiles slid out of place too.

And underneath was not the place where forced hot air came out in the winter. Underneath was a hiding place, sort of a tunnel.

Of course she'd really known before that, hadn't she? Maybe not the specifics, but she knew there was something going on. Something untoward. From the very beginning, there was *so much money*. None of the wives talked about where the money came from, they knew that a simple trucking business couldn't make money like that unless it was trucking something very, very illegal. Drugs or jewels or people.

The wives didn't let themselves think too much about it. They definitely didn't talk about it. They spent it, and they enjoyed it— they practically bathed in it—but they didn't talk about it.

There was *so much of everything*. Clothes, cars. A vacation at a five-star resort in Mexico where Katie played in the pool while Bobby and Sherri drank champagne that cost four hundred and fifty dollars a bottle. Sherri didn't even blink when Bobby ordered it. When she drank it, it tasted like money. They had friends with yachts; they had friends with shares in private planes and vacation homes they'd never set foot in.

The first time Sherri found the hiding place there were two boxes full of hundred-dollar bills in there. *Full.* There must have been tens of thousands of dollars, maybe hundreds of thousands. She didn't count it. She just put it away, and she lined the floor tiles back up, and she put the register back too.

The next time, the money was gone, and there was a box inside a box inside a box—like an ominous set of Russian dolls—and inside the smallest box were twenty large diamonds.

Another time: cocaine, divided in tiny bags, like snacks for a preschool class. Once there were five fake passports, all for different people. Sherri saw all of it. She saw the laptop that looked exactly like the laptop on Bobby's desk but wasn't. (She tried to figure out the password for that laptop many times, but always stopped before it locked up. She tried her birthday and Katie's birthday and their wedding anniversary and Bobby's eight-hundred-meter time from high school. Nothing worked.)

It became her hobby, to keep an eye on the hiding place. It was like knitting or learning Spanish, but different. It was what Sherri did besides looking after Katie and keeping herself looking good for Bobby (nearly a full-time job in itself: the waxing, the nails, the peels, the hair). Even as she was tracking it, she told herself it was okay. Nobody was getting hurt. It was only money changing hands. She told herself that whoever's money it was probably deserved to lose it—they'd probably done something bad in the first place. Brought it upon themselves.

She didn't let herself consider the lives being ruined by the drugs, the kids who might be taking them, the desperate people who were selling them. She didn't think about any of that.

And then came Madison Miller, and all she could do was think.

19.

ALEXA

Alexa parked on Pleasant Street, in front of an old-fashioned Buick that Peter would have liked. He would have known the make and the model and announced it to them all, and they all would have ignored him because that was just Peter being Peter. And now he was gone, and they would have done anything to be able to indulge his interest in old-fashioned cars.

She made her way to the Coffee Factory, which was attached to the Book Rack. Newburyport had settled into its summer self. Sidewalk tables were out in full force. There were dogs on leashes and people who looked familiar to Alexa and also people she'd never seen before, which meant they were likely day-trippers from Boston on their way up 95, with stops planned in Portsmouth and at the Kittery outlets and for lobster rolls and ice cream cones. She saw her tenth-grade geometry teacher heading out of the bank, and Hunter Hayden, who'd been in her psych class senior year, coming out of Richdale.

At the coffee shop she waited in line to place her order. While she was waiting, she checked her e-mail on her phone. The only thing in her in-box was an e-mail from Amazon, which wanted her to rate her recent experience with the Chantecaille mascara she'd purchased. Alexa's mother would freak out if she knew Alexa had spent seventy-two dollars on mascara she'd used once before giving it to Morgan, who was not allowed to wear makeup, but Alexa's mother didn't know just how much her videos had earned her.

Alexa Thornhill, will you rate the seller? begged the e-mail.

Alexa took her cortado to one of the outside tables and sat, considering her short-term future. The next day Tyler would be leaving with his family to spend three and a half weeks at his grandmother's house on the shores of Silver Lake in Michigan, as he did every summer. Last summer, when they had just be-gun dating, Alexa missed Tyler desperately. Now she was sort of looking forward to his absence. Honestly, she would be mostly okay if Tyler met some wonderful Michigan girl this summer and fell in love with her. That would take so much pressure off Alexa. She'd have to pretend to be upset, etc., but she could pull that off.

She was supposed to see him that night. She knew what Tyler was hoping for, as a "good-bye" present, as he had referred to it. She'd been avoiding the topic; she felt like she should be ready to have sex with Tyler, and yet something was stopping her.

Alexa rated the mascara a four. Really it deserved closer to a three from a value to price ratio but she was feeling generous. Maybe Amazon and Chantecaille were onto something. Maybe the world would move along more smoothly if only people asked each other for feedback more often.

Immediately another e-mail came in from Amazon. Alexa Thornhill, how likely would you be to purchase this product again? With one being unlikely and five being extremely likely.

Seriously? She filled in the first star only, to make a point. It was truly desperate to ask for extra praise after you'd already gotten praise. It was something Destiny would do.

Then her phone pinged with a text. It was Caitlin, who wanted to know if Alexa could meet her for lunch in Portsmouth. She was still really pissed at both Caitlin and Destiny for what had happened in March, but it might be fun to take a drive up to Portsmouth, maybe see if there was anything new at Lizology.

March, a biting wind going at the walls of Destiny's house.

Destiny lived out on Plum Island, far out, close to the lighthouse at the very northern tip. Destiny's parents had gone to Boston for the night for a cousin's wedding, so Alexa had driven Caitlin and herself out to Destiny's in her Jeep. Destiny was supposed to stay home with her thirteen-year-old brother, Ethan. There was talk of a party at Jason Harrington's house, but that was all the way out by Maudslay, miles and miles and miles away.

"We could go for a while," suggested Caitlin. "Just to see who's there."

"I can't go to a party," said Destiny. "I promised I'd stay here with Ethan and his buddy."

"They won't even notice if we leave," said Caitlin. "I just walked by Ethan's bedroom and they're absolutely one hundred percent glued to Minecraft."

"Well, I'm not leaving," said Destiny. "You guys go if you want." The wind gave an extra-loud howl, as if it wanted to remind them that winter wasn't over yet, and that it could send the water crashing over the Plum Island dunes anytime it wanted to.

Alexa glanced at her phone. She had three texts from Tyler practically begging her to go to the party. Can't, she texted in reply. Hanging with the girls.

Caitlin looked uncertain and then she said, "Never mind. We'll have our own party here. We can stay over, right? We're staying over?" She looked to Destiny for confirmation and Destiny nodded. Caitlin opened the liquor cabinet and poked through it.

"Jeez, Dest, did your parents start marking the bottles?" She was examining a fifth of Tito's. "I think they did it wrong though. This line doesn't even match up."

Destiny yawned. "Yeah," she said. "They did. But I heard Savannah's mom telling my mom the trick about turning them upside down to mark them so we can't just fill them up with water like we used to."

Caitlin frowned at the bottle. "It's kind of a good trick," she said. "I can't figure out how we'd fill it to the right place." She turned the bottle upside down, then righted it, then, shrugging, returned it to the cabinet. "Leave it to Savannah's mom," she said.

Alexa knew she should be joining the conversation but she didn't really feel invested in it, or even interested. She wondered if she should just go home, where her mom and Morgan were finding their way around their reordered family. Her mom and Morgan were probably cuddled up together on the couch, watching one of those interminable Disney Channel shows that Morgan loved, or else a movie featuring strong female central characters: *Brave*, or maybe *The Hunger Games*, although the latter was likely too violent for Morgan, who disliked blood and spears.

Caitlin rummaged in the very back of the cabinet and found a bottle of triple sec that was so old and irrelevant that nobody had bothered to mark it. "Here we go," she said. "Party time!" She took out three juice glasses and lined them up, sloshing the triple sec more or less equally into them. More than a shot, less than a juice serving. She pushed one toward Alexa and one toward Destiny. Alexa took a sip of hers and coughed a little. It tasted like a clementine and a bottle of cold medicine had decided to have a child together and had put that child into Alexa's juice glass. "I don't think I can drink this," she said.

"Of course you can," said Caitlin. "Pretend it's Tito's."

"We need a game," said Destiny. "A drinking game! Quarters?

Thumper? Buzz?" Destiny had gone on a college visit to UMass the month before.

"You need more people for all of those," said Caitlin authoritatively. She sipped pensively at her triple sec. "I've got it!" she said suddenly. "How about Two Truths and a Lie?"

"I don't think that's a drinking game," said Alexa.

"It can be," said Caitlin. "Anything can be a drinking game if you drink while you're playing it."

They repaired to the living room, taking their glasses and the bottle of triple sec with them.

"I'll go first," said Destiny. She looked to the ceiling for a moment, thinking. "Okay," she said. "Ready. One. I have never been to China. Two. I made out with Shane Miller in ninth grade. Three. I cheated on my Spanish exam first semester junior year."

"Okay, wait," said Caitlin. She had knocked back her entire serving of triple sec and was already looking bleary as she poured herself another. (Caitlin was such a lightweight.) "I know for sure that you have never been to China."

"I could have gone to China," said Destiny. "I didn't meet you guys until we were ten. Maybe I went to China when I was seven." Destiny had moved to Newburyport from Nashville in the fourth grade.

"I'm pretty sure you would have mentioned it," said Caitlin. "So that's a lie or a truth? *I have never been . . .* A truth. Okay, let's see. And you would have absolutely told us about Shane Miller when it happened, right?" Destiny's face gave away nothing. "Alexa? Would she have? What do you think?" Without waiting for Alexa's answer Caitlin said, "So that's a lie. Right? That's a lie. Which means that you *did* cheat on your Spanish exam?"

Destiny's head made a tiny nod and she said, "Amber's older sister sold me a copy of hers from the year before. I *aced* that thing."

"Aha!" cried Caitlin. "Drink!" Then, "Wait. Who drinks? Me, because I figured it out? Or Destiny? Because I figured it out."

"I guess all of us," said Destiny. She tipped all of the triple sec into her mouth and made a face. Alexa pretended to take a sip of hers and wondered if she could excuse herself to go to the bathroom and pour it down the sink.

"Your turn," said Destiny, pointing her glass at Alexa. The wind huffed and puffed some more, and Alexa wondered if it might actually blow the house down. Had her mom made her special Dutch oven popcorn with plenty of salt and pepper?

"Go," said Caitlin bossily. "Alexa. *Go*." Alexa searched her mind and came up empty. "If you don't go," said Caitlin. "I will." She refilled Alexa's glass, which didn't need refilling. And for some reason that very causal gesture set something loose in Alexa. It was something about the presumption of the triple sec, about the alcohol-softened, expectant, *predictable* faces of her friends, maybe about the fact that they still had their fathers and Alexa no longer had Peter, or maybe, beyond that, the fact that they didn't know grief. They had never known real grief—they were untouched by its cold, dark fingers, and that wasn't their fault, obviously, but it somehow made her unable to stomach being in the same room with them, especially when her mom and Morgan were cozy at home together. Without Alexa. She half-hoped the wind *would* blow the roof off. She wished, illogically, fervently, for something to happen that would take her attention from the sorrow and the rage she felt bubbling up inside her, that she could tell was about to spill over onto Caitlin and Destiny, whether she liked it or not. It was preordained. (It was Destiny.)

Caitlin was on her third serving of triple sec. Destiny's eyes were turning glassy. They were both looking at her. Looking, and waiting, and expecting. Alexa could hardly stand it.

"One. I failed my driver's test the first time I took it and never told you guys. Two. I'm not going to college. Three. I've cried every day since Peter died."

"Whoa," said Destiny. "This just took a turn."

"You failed your *driver's test*?" said Caitlin.

"I don't know," said Alexa savagely. "Did I?"

"I think the game is supposed to be a little more lighthearted?" said Caitlin. She was clearly buzzed, because she had started ending every one of her sentences with a question mark. "Something along the lines of how Destiny did it? Here, I can go. Want me to go, Alexa? One. I have never been swimming on a beach where there's been a shark sighting. Two—"

She stopped and stared, because now Alexa was standing, almost quivering.

"Well I'm sorry if I don't feel like playing this game. I'm sorry I'm not lighthearted enough. I'm sorry that my *dad died* and I didn't get over it immediately. I'm sorry if it's been a little—complicated on my end."

Destiny glanced nervously at Caitlin. Alexa watched their eyes meet, watched a look pass between them that was definitely not meant for Alexa to share. It was the look an exasperated set of parents would pass back and forth over the head of a toddler in a tantrum, a look that said, *Here we go again. Let's just wait it out.*

"But it's been a long time now, Alexa. And it's not like—" Caitlin clapped a hand over her mouth as though she could keep the evil words inside.

"It's not like what? Say it, Caitlin." The rage was rising, rising.

"Nothing."

"Say what you were about to say."

"*Nothing,*" said Caitlin, around her hand.

"You were about to say, it's not like he was my real father, right?" Alexa could tell by Caitlin's face that this was 100 percent correct.

"No, I—"

Alexa's voice was steel. "Then what were you going to say?"

Miserably, mutely, Caitlin caved. "That?" she whispered. "But I'm so sorry. I didn't mean—"

"Forget it," said Alexa. "This game is stupid. I'm going home." She started toward the kitchen, where her phone and car keys were.

They both said things like, *What?* And *Why?* And *We didn't mean anything!* And (this was the most infuriating one, the one that set her teeth on edge): *Stop being so sensitive!*

"Are you mad at us?" Caitlin was pleading now. Good. Let her. "Alexa, please don't be mad at us? We didn't do anything?" She looked at Destiny for confirmation.

"Big surprise," said Destiny. "Alexa's leaving."

Alexa turned around slowly. "Big surprise?" she repeated. "What's that supposed to mean?"

"You leave everything, if you even show up in the first place. You're, like, totally disengaged. And it's not just around us. Tyler told me the same thing."

"I'm sorry," said Alexa. "*Tyler* told you the same thing?" Problem number one with this story was that Tyler was unlikely to use a word like *disengaged*. Problem number two: why was *Tyler* talking to *Destiny* about *Alexa*?

"Yeah." Caitlin looked like she used to in middle school, when she had an overbite and zits along her hairline, before she had a big glow-up and learned how to dress to flatter her skinny legs. "He talks to me sometimes too, you know. He's allowed to have other friends."

"I know he's allowed to have other friends!" Alexa snapped. "Caitlin, obviously I know that." She wasn't *that* kind of girlfriend. Tyler could have all the friends he wanted. But she didn't think he should talk to *her* friends *about her* behind her back. That felt sneaky and mean.

"He worries about you, Alexa. That's all. Because he cares. But he said you can be prickly sometimes." That was Destiny.

Alexa let out a short, derisive laugh. She faced Destiny and spat, "Now you're both turning on me? Now I'm *prickly?*"

She and Destiny and Caitlin had existed as a threesome since Destiny moved to town in fourth grade, with a trace of Southern accent lingering from her early Tennessee years. Three had never been a crowd with them. But now Alexa felt like the loneliest person in the entire universe: lonelier than a hermit living in Siberia. She was a third wheel here, and if she went home she'd be a third wheel there too.

"I'm going home," she said anyway.

"Don't be mad?" said Caitlin. "I'm sorry for what I said?"

Alexa's head was aching and her heart was aching. "I'm not mad," she said. "I'm tired. And I forgot I have to get up early tomorrow."

Two truths, one lie.

Now Alexa heard someone saying her name, and she looked up. It was Cam Hartwell, smiling that giant, goofy smile. She felt herself flush. She remembered the cup of tea he'd put by her bed. Something about this memory made her feel happier than she had in a while.

Next to Cam was a reddish golden retriever attached to a navy blue leash. "This is Sammy," he said. "You didn't meet him the other day because he was at the lake with my parents." Sammy looked like a dog in an L.L.Bean advertisement. He was sporting a navy blue bandanna to match the leash and a collar with anchors on it. Very nautical. Sammy licked Alexa's hand and then did a thing where he pulled back his gums and really looked like he was smiling. It was hard not to smile back.

"What are you up to?" asked Cam.

"Headed up to Portsmouth a little while later," Alexa said.

Cam nodded. "Good day for Portsmouth." Sammy let out a little whine and started to pull at the leash and Cam said, "Sorry, boy, we're going now. We really are." To Alexa he said, "Duty calls! But I'll be in touch soon."

Who was he, Alexa wondered, to be so confident that she *wanted* him to be in touch? She remembered the kiss in his driveway. He had definitely kissed her back.

Alexa Thornhill, will you rate your experience with Cam Hartwell?

She'd give him a four and three-quarters out of five. *Could be a little less earnest,* she'd put in the comments. Then she pictured Cam reading that and becoming sad. He'd say something like, *I'm not that earnest, am I?* He would say that very earnestly, of course.

Alexa Thornhill, how likely would you be to see Cam Hartwell again? On a scale of one to ten, one being not at all likely and ten being very likely.

She brought her cup back inside and placed it carefully in the dish bin, noticing as she saw her reflection in the glass that she was grinning. Yeah, okay, sure, she'd go see Caitlin up in Portsmouth. She could feel herself getting nicer by the minute. Must be the Cam Effect.

20.

THE SQUAD

We were not obsessed with Alexa Thornhill, if that's what you're thinking. We were grown women, with husbands and children and jobs, some full-time, some part-time, and many, many appointments. It would have been unseemly to take an interest in a seventeen-year-old.

But when we found out that Alexa posted videos on YouTube of course we took a quick look. We're not sure what we were expecting. Something salacious, maybe. Alexa Thornhill is a very pretty girl. We've always wondered about her biological father because Alexa and Rebecca do not look that much alike. The hair, maybe. Not that Rebecca isn't pretty enough. But Alexa is drop-dead: another league.

We were hoping for information that would give us a little something to talk about on the beach, or on our early morning walks, which some of us took three days a week, rain or shine.

We were not expecting to watch a video on cryptocurrency.

Serious walking is one of the best ways to lose weight, you know. We try to walk five miles at a stretch. The New England summer humidity sweats everything right off you. Some of us were eating Keto that summer too. Keto is very effective.

It was on one of these early morning walks a couple of weeks after Esther's birthday dinner at Plum Island Grille that Michelle posited that there was something "off" about Sherri Griffin.

"What do you mean, 'off'?" we said. Most of us knew that Michelle was at work writing some sort of psychological domestic thriller set in our town. She called it "Girl on the Train-esque" but honestly we didn't think it would amount to much. She wasn't even a writer. But that was Michelle for you, always taking up something new, throwing pasta at the wall to see if it would stick. There was the scented candle business, a few years ago. The shares she bought in an ice hotel up in Montreal, then sold again after the warm winter. The alternative preschool that she thought up to compete with the Montessori school on Inn Street. Nothing came from any of those endeavors.

"She seems like someone who's got some grit in her oyster," said Michelle. She told us this was a phrase she'd picked up from one of the writing blogs she was always reading. She explained that it meant that somebody had something dark in their past. Something they were trying to escape, or something they were trying to figure out. Obviously we already knew what the phrase meant, but we let Michelle have her moment. "Definite grit," she repeated.

Our route took us from Cashman Park down the boardwalk along the river, past the new harbormaster's hut, and onto the new section of the rail trail, which is really something. We had to break into smaller groups when we hit the rail trail, so that we weren't taking up the whole thing. In the past we have been accused by some of the town's old-timers of "traveling in a horde."

Michelle was still on the oyster and the grit. Those of us who were walking with her suspected that she preferred talking about the elements of a psychological thriller to actually writing a psychological thriller. "Mark my words," she said ominously.

Some of us went back to talking about Alexa Thornhill's

YouTube videos, and whether or not Rebecca knew that Alexa had decided not to go to college to focus on her "career." We can't tell you where we heard that—it was told to us in confidence. But we can say that the information came from more than one source, and that the sources were reliable.

Rebecca didn't join us on the walks anymore. We didn't blame her! She was still adjusting to the new normal. But without the walking and without the barre class, we weren't sure how she was staying so thin.

Of course we were there for her, when it happened. It was a shock to the community too. Peter had been so healthy, so vibrant. He ran in the Yankee Homecoming ten-mile race every summer. He was on the school committee and the board of Our Neighbors' Table. He was not yet fifty! There one day, and then gone. We set up a Meal Train for an entire month after the funeral. We took Morgan whenever we could, to give Rebecca a break. Believe us, we were there.

"I don't think we mention it to Rebecca," Dawn said finally. "It's not our business."

"Agreed," said Gina. "Let's keep our noses out of Rebecca's business. She's still mad at me about that thing with the sleeping bag, and I didn't even tell a soul."

We refrained from mentioning that if we all knew what Gina was talking about, it was *literally impossible* that she hadn't told a soul. We just kept walking.

"Sherri came here from out of nowhere, right? Isn't that sort of strange? I mean, why Newburyport? Does she even have any ties here? It seems random, that's all. Kind of funny," said Michelle.

We were certain Michelle was creating a mountain out of a molehill. But sometimes we can all be prone to that tendency. In a town like ours, not a lot happens, and sometimes we look for the excitement where we can get it.

21.

ALEXA

Caitlin, who had a summer job peddling jewelry at Bobbles and Lace in Portsmouth, had suggested they meet at Popovers on Congress Street. Alexa, cautiously optimistic, arrived first and saved them a table. When Caitlin slid in across from her she said, "Hey," breathlessly, followed by, "I've only got twenty minutes. It's crazy at the store today. I'm super stressed." She was wearing a simple pink sundress and a beaded knot necklace—a bobble, no doubt bought with her employee discount.

Alexa wanted to tell Caitlin she was selling earrings and sandals, not performing open-heart surgery on premature babies, but she bit her tongue. It was the first time she'd hung out with Caitlin since March, and Alexa wanted to see where this might go.

They took turns holding the table and going up to the counter to order their salads. (Alexa had the Wedge and Caitlin the Caesar; each came with a popover, hence the name of the restaurant.)

"Hey, so listen. I've been feeling so bad about what happened. That night at Destiny's, that stupid game, the whole thing. We really didn't mean to upset you. We feel terrible about it. We talk about it all the time. We never thought we'd go this long without hanging out with you."

Alexa felt herself softening. "I know I overreacted," she acknowledged. She'd been just as angry at—felt just as excluded from—her mother and Morgan as she did from Destiny and Caitlin that night, to be fair. "There were a bunch of things bugging me that night, I don't know, I didn't mean to take it all out on you guys."

You can be a little prickly sometimes, Alexa.

One thing she remembered learning about porcupines for a school project in seventh grade was that their quills lay flat until they were threatened. And then, *bing*, they came out, and victim beware.

Caitlin was looking at her beseechingly. "We wanted to hang out with you so many times, Dest and I. Around graduation and everything? It wasn't the same without you? But we still felt like you were mad at us. And you were always—busy. With Tyler, I guess? Or whatever. You just weren't around."

"Yeah," said Alexa. "Thanks. I appreciate that. I've been pretty busy with a whole bunch of stuff."

Caitlin glanced at her phone, probably checking the time; she wanted to get back to her hugely taxing job at Bobbles and Lace.

"There's one more thing," she said. "To be honest, though? I'm only telling you this to be a good friend? You know that's the only reason I would ever tell you something like this."

"What?" Alexa felt her quills rise.

"I'm not mentioning any names but someone I know says they saw Zoe Butler-Gray getting out of Tyler's car in the parking lot of Blue Inn on Plum Island. Recently."

Ah. Now Alexa saw why Caitlin asked her to cross state lines and brave the parking on Market Street on a perfect summer day to have lunch with her. It wasn't to try to mend their friendship, or at least not entirely. It was for this.

Blue Inn was a boutique luxury hotel whose most expensive room went for more than one thousand dollars a night in the summer. There was no way Tyler had either the cash or the desire to take Zoe Butler-Gray to Blue Inn for any sort of rendezvous.

(But did he?)

No! Tyler's idea of romance, in Alexa's experience, was limited to the three-for-twelve flower specials at Shaw's and, on a special occasion, pre-boxed chocolates from one of the downtown stores. He had never bothered even to put together a custom box at Simply Sweet.

She dignified this story with a raised eyebrow, no more, no less. Caitlin shifted in her seat and picked a crouton out of her salad, watching Alexa the whole time.

Alexa's phone rang with an unfamiliar, local number. Normally she'd decline a call from an unknown number, but she had the urge to show Caitlin that she was busy and important. She answered.

"Alexa?" said the caller. "Hi, sorry, hi, my name is Sherri, my daughter Katie is friends with your sister. Morgan?"

"Okay," said Alexa. Her mother had mentioned something about a new mother and daughter.

The woman, sounding flustered, went on to explain that she was looking for a babysitter for her daughter and someone on the Mom Squad group chat suggested that she try Alexa. Alexa thought, *They let a newcomer on the Mom Squad group chat?* As far as Alexa knew, the borders between the Mom Squad and the rest of the world were like those of Castro's Cuba: closed until further notice.

Alexa turned away from Caitlin and said, "I don't really babysit." She wondered which of her mother's misinformed friends had put forth her name.

"Oh, I see." The woman sounded disappointed. "Okay, I'm sorry. It's hard when you're new to town, you know? To find all the stuff you had where you lived before. Especially as a single mom. Do you have any friends who might be interested?"

She could offer the babysitting job to Caitlin. Caitlin would probably take it, and she'd somehow make it look like she was doing Alexa a favor even as she got paid. Alexa thought about that and got mad. She thought about Tyler disembarking from his car in the parking lot of Blue Inn and got madder. She was even mad at the popover that came with her salad for being so good that without noticing she'd eaten the whole thing.

So she did two things in a row. First, she asked for details. Second, she told Sherri she would be more than happy to babysit her daughter the Monday evening after the holiday weekend. And then she did something else, brought on by—oh, who knew. Brought on by Caitlin's vainglorious posture, by the fake apology, or maybe by the very simple fact of being in a different city, over the state line, with the rest of the day spread out in front of her, as unfilled as a blank notebook. She kept her body turned away from Caitlin and she texted Cam Hartwell to see what he was up to that night.

Immediately after she sent the text, three dots appeared, then the text itself.

Got plans. Against her will—she didn't care, truly she didn't, why should she care about someone she hardly knew, and anyway that kiss in his driveway was just a kiss, *nothing more*—she deflated.

Another text plopped onto the screen.

The plans are with you, it said. I'll call you later with the details.

"What are you smiling about?" asked Caitlin.

"Nothing," said Alexa bitchily. Now she wasn't even mad about what had happened in March; she was much more irritated about the ruse Caitlin used to draw her closer before inserting the knife. She put her phone down and said, "You're missing an earring."

Caitlin's panicked hand rose, found a hoop in each ear.

"Not that one. Third hole up. The little diamonds? The ones you got for your birthday? One of those is gone."

Alexa rose from the table, deposited her dishes into the correct bin, and escorted herself out of the restaurant before Caitlin had a chance to find out if Alexa was lying.

22.

SHERRI

Sherri climbed the stairs to Katie's room carrying a basket of laundry that she'd just dried at, yes, the Laundromat.

The door to Katie's room was closed, and Sherri put down the basket of laundry to open it. They weren't a doors-closed sort of household, especially now that it was just the two of them. Sherri had always prided herself on her openness with Katie, on using the anatomically correct terms when referring to body parts, both male and female, and if Katie should ask her any questions about sex, Sherri was going to tell her everything she knew. Which, admittedly, was far less than you could find out online these days. But Sherri would do her best.

"What are you doing up here, sweetheart?" she asked, as she was opening the door.

"Mom!" cried Katie, and almost immediately after that, "Nothing!" She was lying on the bed, holding something, and whatever it was she was holding she shuttled swiftly under her bottom. She lay there stiffly, staring at the ceiling, like a corpse awaiting the attentions of an undertaker.

Out of nowhere Sherri was angry. The rage came upon her so quickly that it carried with it its own personal heat, like a sudden sunburn. She was angry at Bobby, and she was angry at the adjustment counselor, with her pantsuits and her work pumps and her gentle smile and her freaking advice. She was angry at the cheap cotton comforter on Katie's twin bed, and she was angry at this town, where she and Katie, who had been somebodys where they came from, now had to prove themselves worthy, like college girls pledging a sorority. She was angry at her stupid ugly shirt and her sensible shoes and her hair color and her short, ugly nails. She pulled at the thing that was sticking out from under Katie, and Katie said, "Mom! Don't!" Katie grabbed part of the comforter in each hand and pressed her back down, trying not to surrender her treasure. But Sherri was motivated, and she was stronger, and she pulled and pulled until she had it in her hands.

It was a notebook, one of those black-and-white composition books sometimes required for school.

Sherri hadn't bought this notebook for her daughter.

She started to open it and Katie reared up, grabbing the notebook out of Sherri's hands. "*Don't*," she hissed. (Katie never hissed. They were not hissing people, just as they were not closed-door people.) "It's mine," Katie said. "It's *private*." She held the book close to her chest, wrapping her arms around it.

"What is it?" Sherri demanded.

"It's just a notebook."

"Where did you get it?"

"Morgan gave it to me."

"Morgan? Why was Morgan giving you a notebook?"

"No reason," said Katie. "She has like ten of them. It was never even used." Morgan had told Katie that her mom kept buying her the notebooks for her to write about her feelings after her dad died.

Katie stuck out her bottom lip in a way that reminded Sherri of what she'd been like as a little girl—breezy and self-possessed, until you crossed her—and Sherri's rage left her as quickly as it had come. None of it was Katie's fault, not Bobby or Madison or any of the rest of it, not the cheap bedding or Sherri's ugly nails. She sat on the edge of the bed, nearly panting with the exertion of having been so angry and of trying to hide it. "I'm sorry, Katie-kins," she said. "I overreacted."

"That's okay," said Katie. She stared at the ceiling, back to her self-contained, unflappable self. She was waiting for Sherri to leave so she could continue writing in Morgan Coleman's cast-off notebook; eventually Sherri did leave. So what if it was a diary? Shouldn't all young girls be allowed to keep a diary? In fact, wasn't a diary actually a refreshing change from all of their iScreens, and shouldn't this behavior be encouraged? What could be the harm in it, really? Katie didn't know a lot of the specifics—Sherri had been very careful to shield her from the worst of it, and the counselor had declared her remarkably well-adjusted, considering.

And yet. What if Sherri was mistaken about that? What if Katie knew more than she was letting on? What if Katie put secrets in that notebook? Not little-girl secrets like who had a crush on whom but big, bad, grown-up secrets, the kind that nobody could ever, ever, ever read.

What then?

Did Bobby remember the night they met the way Sherri did? She'd never know, now. They were at a bar in Jersey City. She was with two of her girlfriends, the same friends she'd had in high school. The three of them were twenty-one, fresh-faced and innocent. Sherri was alone in the world. Alone! Her mother had died when she was seventeen, and her father started drinking and never stopped. She had no place she belonged. No siblings, not even a cousin nearby.

At the bar that night Bobby smiled at her. He bought her a mudslide. That's how young she was, she thought mudslides were sophisticated! He tipped the bartender with a twenty and she was agog.

Sherri fell for Bobby Giordano from that first minute. She fell and she fell and she fell.

Typically Bobby conducted his business outside the house, but every now and then the guys came over and they all met in his office. Who, Sherri always wondered, was sitting closest to the register that held all of the secrets? Did the guys know about it? Did each of them have a similar hiding place in their homes, and did the wives know about those hiding places?

The guys coming over was a signal to Katie and Sherri that they should disappear. Sometimes they watched a movie from the comfort of Sherri's king-size bed. Sherri brought up snacks: big bowls of popcorn, apple juice for Katie, a glass of wine for herself. No more mudslides; she'd learned about good wine. She never minded those nights. If she was being honest with herself she looked forward to them, with Katie and her curled up together like puppies. Katie often fell asleep partway through the movie and Sherri would listen to her rhythmic breathing and feel a tremendous sense of peace. She didn't think about what was going on downstairs. It wasn't her business. When Bobby came to bed he never woke them. He climbed in on the other side of Katie and that's how they slept. Like a tableau of the perfect family.

But one night the guys were over and Katie had a sleepover to go to. A birthday party. It was a Friday. Without Katie there Sherri was at loose ends. She wandered around the kitchen, wiping counters that were already spotless. Then she had the idea to put together a snack for Bobby and the guys. She never did that; he had made it clear that he didn't want to be bothered. But surely they were all getting hungry in there. They had their rolling bar cart, their glasses and ice, but no food. Sherri put together a plate of cheese and crackers, a little of that nice prosciutto, sliced as thin as a cell slide, that came from the local deli, some dark chocolate caramels dotted with sea salt. She made it look so nice.

She stood outside the office, trying to decide if she should somehow knock with her shoulder or call out for Bobby to open the door, when something stopped her. Maybe it was the word *girl* that snagged her attention; maybe it was the tone of the conversation, which was low and urgent. Something made her put the tray down on the little table in the alcove outside the office and lean closer to the door until her ear was pressed up against it.

The girl, they kept saying. The girl wasn't going to keep quiet, the situation with the girl would have to be addressed. It was a shame, she had seen something she shouldn't have seen, but there was nothing they could do about it, except what had to be done.

"Wrong place at the wrong time." That was Bobby's voice.

"We'll have to get rid of her," said one of the other guys.

The words were like ice water poured down Sherri's spine. She froze for a moment. Then she carried the tray back to the kitchen, put the cheese and prosciutto in the refrigerator, the crackers in the pantry. She poured herself a shot of vodka to calm her shaking nerves. Then another, then another. She should do something. She couldn't do anything. She should warn the girl. But she didn't know who the girl was. She didn't know what the girl had seen. She should, she couldn't, she wouldn't, she didn't. Maybe she'd heard wrong. She'd been on the other side of a heavy door. It would have been easy to imagine hearing things that nobody had said.

After a time, she put it out of her mind. What other choice did she have, with no proof of anything? Even if she'd wanted to talk to anybody about what she thought she heard, she had nobody. Bobby and Katie were her family. They were her entire world.

And didn't she love that world? Didn't she love the glitz and the glamour of living with money? She didn't want to do anything to jeopardize that, and she had nowhere to go if she'd wanted to leave: no job, no resources. She had grown up without any money at all. They never had extra for school supplies or nice shampoo or even a gift to go to a birthday party, should she be invited, which she never was. Unless the whole class was invited, and that was always obvious and somehow even worse than not being included at all.

When Sherri was in fourth grade a girl in her class accused her of smelling like garbage because her mother worked in the kitchen of a restaurant and somebody had spotted her one afternoon taking the food scraps to the Dumpster in a big white bucket. The worst part was that the girl was right. Sherri's mother did sometimes smell like garbage.

Once she married Bobby Sherri bought the most expensive shampoo money could buy, the kind you could only buy at a salon. She bought nail polish in every color, and gorgeous blouses made of silk, and designer bags, and shoes, and shoes, and shoes. When they bought the house with the pool, they also got the guy who came twice a week to balance it. She never had to touch any of the pool chemicals or the skimmer baskets. When they threw a party, which they did all the time, she never had to take a step into that top-of-the-line kitchen, because two hours before the party started an army of caterers showed up with their beautiful food and their beautiful cocktails for all of the beautiful guests to enjoy. All Sherri had to do was choose from her beautiful dresses and match the dress with a fabulous pair of heels and attach herself to Bobby's arm.

Eye candy, she believed that was called.

Nobody would call her eye candy now. They'd call her practical looking, a mom with a reliable part-time job, struggling, like a lot of other people in the world, to pay the rent.

She knew the money wasn't clean. But honestly she never imagined people getting really hurt over it. She never imagined anyone dying.

23.

ALEXA

"Hampton Beach?" said Alexa when Cam called her later to solidify the plans. She thought she might have heard wrong. Hampton Beach was not a place she typically hung out. North of Salisbury, south of Rye, there was a certain . . . well, for lack of a better word, a certain element there. The beaches themselves were beautiful, and there was supposed to be phenomenal surfing by the Wall, but. It was a little biker-y, a little weed-and-Miller-Lite-ish, and when the sun went down the freaks came out. When Alexa thought of Hampton Beach, she thought of tattoos. And not tasteful little hip tattoos (Alexa herself sported one of a starfish that she got when she turned sixteen) but dark, heavy, sleeve tattoos.

Alexa could practically hear Cam grinning over the phone. "Yup," he said. "I scored two tickets to see a Dave Matthews cover band at the casino. And tonight is your lucky night, because one of those tickets has your name on it."

"Dave Matthews?" said Alexa. "The Hampton Beach Casino?" The casino, though storied, was where the has-beens played, and where the old people went to get drunk and reminisce. What she was supposed to be doing tonight was saying good-bye to Tyler before he left for Silver Lake, but she had conveniently left his texts unanswered. When she thought of what Caitlin told her, she didn't feel an ounce of guilt about this.

"The one and only," said Cam. "Well, not the one and only be-cause that would be the real Dave Matthews. But close enough!" Dave Matthews was one of Alexa's mother's favorite artists. When she had more than one glass of Cabernet, she'd been known to play "Crash Into Me" on repeat at an excessively loud volume. Since Peter's death she did that a little more often than she used to. Rebecca and Peter had seen Dave Matthews together live three times. Even Morgan liked Dave Matthews! Somehow the gene for that had skipped Alexa. Maybe the Dave Matthews gene was re-cessive and her biological father hadn't passed it on to her: another reason to feel left out. Maybe it was the same as the nice gene.

"Um," she said. "I don't know . . ." She scoured her mind for an excuse but came up empty. The truth was, Caitlin's tidbit about Tyler had put her in a tailspin. Her mother was going out "with the ladies," which probably meant early cocktails and fish tacos at the Deck. Even Morgan had plans—she was sleeping over at Katie's house.

"I will brook no refusal," Cam said. "And I'll have you home before you turn into a pumpkin. I'm the lector at the seven AM mass tomorrow at the IC. I need to get my beauty sleep."

Was. This. Guy. For. Real. A church lector at Immaculate Con-ception? "Okay," she said. "I guess if you're not brooking refusal I can't refuse."

"It's a date!" he said. "Where should I pick you up? Home, or work?"

"Home," she said. "I'm off today." She would wear her new Ramy Brook tank top in bright blue, which brought out the color of her eyes. She'd bought it for two hundred and eighty-five dol-lars at Neiman Marcus online. When her mother complimented her on it, she claimed that she got it at Marshalls, marked down 75 percent, even though anybody who knew anything knew that you would never find Ramy Brook at Marshalls.

She would have only one drink. Maybe two drinks. She would behave herself even though her mind was full of chaotic, unsettling thoughts.

When they were in the minivan, driving up 1A (Cam had chosen the coastal route, which Alexa appreciated even though the highway would have been faster), Alexa broached the subject of Shelby McIntyre. As it turned out, Shelby had left two days earlier on a service trip to Kenya with Newburyport Youth Services. "This will be the fourth year in a row she's done it," said Cam. He shook his head and smiled, as if he could not believe the marvel that was Shelby.

"Oh," said Alexa. "Wow. That's really amazing. Good for Shelby. Those service trips are supposed to be incredible." Alexa had zero interest in a service trip, where you went like six days without showering and had to eat things like goat meat and gruel. Clearly Shelby McIntyre was on the fast track to Heaven. "Will she mind?" she asked. "That you're doing this, with me?"

Was it Alexa's imagination, or did Cam's hold on the steering wheel tighten?

"We're not exclusive anymore," he said. "That's over."

"I see," said Alexa. "I'm sorry?"

"Nothing to be sorry about," said Cam. He pressed his lips together and kept his eyes on the road. Alexa looked off to the right, where the sun was just beginning to lower over the Atlantic. The strips of beach that whizzed by them were nearly empty.

Alexa couldn't resist her next question. "Whose idea was it? Not to be exclusive?"

"Both," said Cam. He stopped at a crosswalk and they watched a sandy family—two parents, a stroller, and a kid on a scooter— make their way across. *It's never both,* thought Alexa, *it's never both,* but she let it slide. Then Cam said, "We agreed it was better for her to go back to UVM unencumbered." Alexa took that to mean that Shelby decided it was better for *Shelby* to go back to UVM unencumbered.

"What about you?" Cam asked.

Tyler was on a 7:35 A.M. flight the next day, which meant he would leave for the airport at 4:30. If Alexa wasn't seeing him right now, she wasn't going to see him until he returned from Silver Lake in three weeks. She thought again about Tyler and Zoe Butler-Gray getting out of Tyler's car at Blue Inn, and her blood boiled.

Alexa said, "Unencumbered."

24.

REBECCA

Morgan had been invited to stay the night at Katie's house, and Alexa was out with Tyler, who was leaving the next day for Silver Lake. Rebecca was happy that Morgan wanted to spend the night somewhere—since the sleeping bag incident she'd turned down all sleepover invitations.

Rebecca checked the 360 app and saw that Alexa was at the Hampton Casino. *The Hampton Casino?* She opened her laptop, checked the casino's Web site for the schedule, and saw that tonight there was a Dave Matthews cover band. That didn't seem very Tyler-like, or very Alexa-like. Come to think of it, Rebecca didn't really know Tyler's musical taste. She knew he liked Cap'n Crunch cereal, and that he was a good lacrosse player and a solid C student in non-honors classes, and that Alexa had to get a ride home with someone else from junior prom because Tyler had had too much to drink at one of the after parties. She knew that Alexa could do better than Tyler. She knew that a mom, even a loving one, even a grieving one, couldn't interfere too much in her teenage daughter's romantic life as the daughter was learning to make her own decisions. She knew that Alexa had sprouted some protective edges since Peter's death that, like the quills of a porcupine, hurt more coming out than they did going in. She knew enough to be careful.

She was supposed to go to the Deck with the ladies, but she was dragging her feet. She'd go in a few minutes. Or never. She checked her e-mail. There was a message with the title *Holiday House Tour Initial Meeting* from Patricia Stone, who was the head of the committee. Rebecca had volunteered to help with the house tour five years in a row, but last year, after Peter, she dropped out. Gina had temporarily taken her place on the committee. Now Patricia probably wanted to know if Rebecca wanted her spot back. The idea of it all made her feel tired. She closed her computer. As she was contemplating how much she didn't feel like getting dressed to go out, a rogue wave of nostalgia hit her, probably brought on by the thought of Dave Matthews. Peter had loved Dave Matthews. They had loved Dave Matthews together through various live shows in various venues.

Rebecca poured a glass of Cabernet and indulged in an energetic round of crying while she listened to "The Space Between." Bernice came and sat on her feet, and she got through "Satellite" and "Crash Into Me" before the tears subsided.

Peter had loved lots of things, not just Dave Matthews. Hazelnut ice cream. Lobster tacos. The soft skin on the inside of Rebecca's arm. Travel! He'd been so excited to go to Dubai for the first time, and then he'd gone and died before he made it all the way home. From Dubai he had texted them the most stunning pictures. The city skyline at dusk, with an orb of pink lowered over it, as if by the hand of God. The flamingoes at Ras al Khor. The observation wheel at Bluewaters. A farmers' market with signs in Arabic in front of a rainbow of peppers and tomatoes. *I have all the time in the world*, he probably thought, as he touched the camera button on his phone again and again. *This is just one of the amazing things I will see in the rest of my life, and there are many, many more to come.* It tore Rebecca's heart in tiny pieces when she thought about what his face must have looked like, the way his eyebrows shot up when he got excited, the way he looked around for someone with whom to share the wonders. He was probably eagerly nodding at perfect strangers the whole time he was taking those pictures. That was Peter.

Morgan had Katie. Alexa had Tyler. All the ladies at the Deck had husbands they'd left behind with the children so they could have cocktails and fish tacos. Rebecca was a puzzle piece discarded under the corner of the carpet at the end of the vacation, forgotten.

Her phone rang. Daniel. She didn't have him put in as a contact—she didn't want the girls to pick up her phone and see his name—but by now she recognized his number, even knew it enough to dial it by memory. She wiped her tears and cleared her throat.

"Any chance you can grab a bite?" he asked. "Or are you saddled with children and responsibilities for the evening?"

She turned the music down. "As it happens," she said, "I'm available. And hungry. Suddenly I'm really, really hungry. For a steak, or a burger. Something like that. Do you want to pick me up?"

"Sure! Where would you like to procure this burger or steak? I'm open to anything."

"Anywhere but the Deck."

"Give me ten minutes," said Daniel.

Rebecca turned off her phone and waited outside, on the porch, watching the cars go by, the occasional bike and dog walker. As it turned out, the summer evening really was sort of lovely.

25.

ALEXA

Before Alexa had too much time to think they had parked in one of the lots behind the casino, given over their tickets, been ID'd and braceleted. Alexa's bracelet marked her as under twenty-one. Cam had a really good fake ID and his demeanor and haircut both suggested maturity; it went unquestioned. Alexa was surprised Cam even had a fake ID. Did he go to Confession after procuring it?

Cam got them both beers and warned Alexa to be mindful of the security guys. The band took the stage. The music started. Cam and Alexa sipped and swayed to the music with the old people and the drunk people and the people who acquired their hairstyles, like, more than two decades ago and never changed them, and Alexa started to feel a subtle shift in her attitude toward Hampton Beach. It was refreshing to be close to home and yet feel so far away. Nobody knew Alexa here, and she knew nobody. The band's rendition of "The Space Between" was not half bad, and the not-Dave-Matthews Dave Matthews was wicked cute. All things considered, Alexa was beginning to have a good time.

You cannot quit me so quickly, Cam, she thought. She swayed a little closer to Cam, allowing her Ramy Brook silk to rub up against his scratchy plaid shirt. He smelled good, clean and masculine. She gave her hair a toss and wondered what he would do if she leaned over and kissed him. Just as that thought was forming she noticed a man staring at her from across the room.

The guy was older, like Peter's age, and at first she wondered if he could be the dad of one of her friends or the husband of one of her mother's Mom Squad members. But then she realized that he wasn't looking at her that way, like a dad or an uncle, but in a different, creepier way. *No*, she thought. *No no no.*

"The wicked lies we tell," sang not-Dave Matthews. *The wicked lies we tell*, thought Alexa.

"Going to the bathroom," she told Cam. "Be right back." She hightailed it toward the restrooms but she knew—she was positive—that the guy was following her. She could feel his presence behind her, and of course she was right. It was quieter by the bathrooms, the music was muted, so she heard him loud and clear when he said, "Hey!"

She ignored him. She was almost at the bathroom door. She was about to open the door.

"Hey," said the guy again. "Aren't you that Silk Stockings girl?" And he had his hand on her shoulder, just like that.

She turned. "You must be mistaken," she said quickly. "I think you have me mixed up with somebody else."

He slid his hand down her arm and kept it there. She wanted to shake off the hand, she wanted to call for help, but a), she didn't want Cam to know any of this was happening, and b), she was still holding the beer and she didn't want to attract attention and get arrested for underage drinking, which would also get Cam in trouble for buying it for her.

"You're lying," said the guy. Up close she could see that he was maybe in his late thirties or early forties, younger than Peter, with a stubbly beard and small brown eyes that were set far apart, like the eyes of a snake. "You know what my friends and I call you?

Little Miss BTP." She didn't want to know what that stood for, but she had a feeling he was going to tell her. "Better than porn." He licked his lips. "Because you wear those fancy clothes, but all we can think about is what you look like without them."

Alexa flicked his hand off her arm so hard she was surprised it didn't hit him in the face, and pushed the bathroom door open. Her heart was racing and her pulse was racing and she felt like she was going to throw up. She'd never been recognized like that before, and it felt more disconcerting and invasive than she'd ever expected that it would. She knew her videos got a lot of eyeballs; if they didn't, she wouldn't make any money. But she'd never thought about all of those eyeballs belonging to specific people, to potential perverts or stalkers.

There was so much pot smoke inside the bathroom that Alexa thought she might have gotten high just from walking in there. Alexa dumped her nearly empty beer cup in the trash and joined a woman with frosted hair and frosted lips and frosted nails at the mirror considering her frosted reflection with a sour expression.

"I look like a friggin' corpse," the woman said, glancing up at Alexa and then back at the mirror, frowning. "This friggin' light, why do they have to make it so bright? It's like, you're out there dancing, feeling good, then you come in here, and bam. Reality."

Alexa said, "Amen, sister," though she herself avoided the mirror, not wanting to see how scared she might look.

"You okay?" said the woman. "Because you look like something just spooked you." She had a real North Shore accent and a cigarette-addled voice.

"Yeah," said Alexa. "Fine. Thanks."

26.

THE SQUAD

Text from Georgia to Rebecca, 6:42 p.m.: We R here holding the table

Text from Tammy to Rebecca, 6:57 p.m.: Where are U? R U coming? Should we order U a Drink?

Text from Gina to Rebecca, 7:12 p.m: Hello????

27.

ALEXA

"You were gone awhile," said Cam when she made her way back to him. "Everything okay?" The band was taking a break.

"Yes," she said. "Good."

Her hands were shaking so much that she dropped her phone and it went skittering across the floor. Cam retrieved it, and she saw him glance down at the screen before handing it back to her. Three more texts from Tyler had come in in the last ten minutes. She watched Cam see the texts. The last one said Where R U I thought we had plans. Then her phone rang and Tyler's name flashed across the screen.

Cam set his mouth in a tight line and said, "Should I answer?"

"No!" said Alexa, horrified.

"You don't seem so unencumbered," Cam said. "Is that why you were gone so long in the bathroom?"

"Oh, calm down," she told Cam. She meant for it to strike a light note, but it came out wrong, she was too shaken up by the guy near the bathroom to joke properly. She wrenched a smile from her jittery lips, but she could tell by Cam's face that he didn't think it was funny. On the contrary, he was looking at her regretfully, the way her mother looked at Morgan when she knocked over a glass at a nice restaurant. She could feel his regard for her slipping away.

"Listen," said Cam. "I have to ask you a question." He gave the impression of straightening a tie, even though, obviously, he wasn't wearing one. "Is Tyler still your boyfriend?"

"No," said Alexa. "I mean, yes. No. Sort of."

Cam looked stern and disappointed. "If you have a boyfriend, then why'd you kiss me?"

"Why'd you kiss me back?" she countered.

He stared at her.

"Screw this," she said under her breath, but not so much under her breath that he couldn't hear her.

The band began to play "Crash Into Me." Appropriate.

Cam shook his head. She recognized that shake. She'd seen it before. It was a sign that people were disappointed in her. She'd seen it on Caitlin and Destiny when she'd stormed out in March. She'd seen it on Morgan when she'd closed her bedroom door and told Morgan she wanted to be alone. Cam glanced at his watch and said, "You about ready? After this song?"

Alexa thought of Morgan saying, "Why can't you be nicer?"

(Why *couldn't* she be nicer?)

"Sure," she said to Cam, keeping her voice even. "Ready when you are."

Because nice doesn't get you anywhere, Morgan, she thought. *Nice just gets you to the back of the line.*

On the way out, Cam didn't touch Alexa. He didn't put his hand on her lower back to guide her through the middle-aged crowd. When they were on the sidewalk, moving toward the minivan, he kept a safe distance. On the way home, he talked to her some, but his words were clipped, and she could tell that he was trying his best not to engage fully.

She glanced at him as he drove, looking at his strong profile, the small dent underneath his cheekbone. Alexa was experiencing an unfamiliar feeling. If she had to put a name to it she might call it . . . yearning. She wanted to kiss that stupid dent. Alexa Thornhill was not accustomed to being the yearner; she was always, always the yearned for.

These fickle fuddled words confuse me, Cam, she thought.

When he pulled up in front of her house she said, "Thanks. That was fun." She waited a half second before opening the car door.

Cam said, "No problem. See you around." He didn't look directly at her.

She slammed her door extra, extra hard. How dare he make her feel this way. *He* was the one who invited *her* to the concert. All she did was make one comment, under her breath, even, and he gave up on her.

Bernice was sleeping in her dog bed; she woke up long enough to thump her tail twice and then she went back to sleep. For a few minutes Alexa stroked Bernice's ear, which was as soft as a silk blanket.

She sat with Bernice for a long time, watching the rise and fall of her ribs, what looked like a smile on her giant black lips. Bernice was the least judgmental creature in Alexa's world.

Alexa Thornhill, how would you rate your evening at the Hampton Beach Casino, with one being not very irritating and ten being very, very irritating?

Eleven, she thought. *No, twelve. Definitely twelve. And a half.*

JULY

28.

THE SQUAD

Text from Rebecca to Mom Squad Group Chat, July 2nd, 3:06 p.m.:
I invited Sherri to come along on Gina and Steve's pontoon ride
on 4th, Hope ok?? ☺

Text from Gina to Mom Squad Group Chat, July 2nd, 3:07 p.m.:
Maybe ask privately before you invite someone else? ☹

Text from Dawn to Gina, July 2nd, 3:08 p.m.: Hey you know you
sent that to the whole group chat? ☺

Text from Gina to Dawn, July 2nd, 3:08 p.m.: Nooooooooo!! Crap.
What do I do?

Text from Dawn to Gina, July 2nd, 3:09 p.m.: Play it off? ☺

Text from Gina to Mom Squad Group Chat, July 2nd, 3:12 p.m.:
Of course! The more the merrier! ☺

Gina had sent Rebecca, like, five texts about the Holiday House
Tour, and whether she was going to reclaim her spot on the com-
mittee. The first meeting was in August, so it was natural that
Gina wanted to know. It was fine if Rebecca wanted the spot back;
Gina just needed to plan her fall.

Rebecca left those texts unread. But she had time to text about
Sherri coming on the boat. So we'll let you decide where her pri-
orities were.

And *obviously* nobody minded having an extra person on the pontoon. We were going to have to squeeze, but that wasn't a big deal. *The more the merrier* is definitely a phrase we live by.

It was what Sherri *did* on the boat that was a little strange. We mean, you're out on the water, you have to watch yourself! It was just a pontoon, we were only on the river, but still. You can't be too careful. You can't just go crazy like that.

29.

SHERRI

When did she become aware that a teenage girl from two towns over was missing? Days after that night with the snack tray? Weeks? She became aware in the way that people do in this age of social media—a flash across her Instagram feed, a snippet heard on the little TV in the corner of the kitchen one morning over breakfast, a Facebook post. White, upper-middle-class private school girls simply did not go missing all that often, and when they did, it was news.

Her name was Madison Miller. She was sixteen years old, a sophomore in high school. She'd gone shopping by herself at a nearby Target for supplies for a school project and had never returned. There was security footage of her entering the store and leaving the store, and nothing after that. Her car had been abandoned in the parking lot.

She'd had her driver's license for thirteen days. She'd made only three solo driving trips before: her parents were the overprotective type. The careful type. But as it turned out, not careful enough.

"How awful!" Sherri said to the television. She was making Katie's lunch, trimming the crusts from her peanut butter and jelly sandwich. The FBI was involved: it was a suspected kidnapping. There was Madison Miller's picture. Madison Miller was just exactly in between plain and pretty, with ginger hair, a little space between her front teeth. A center part, a teal shirt, double piercings in both ears. "Terrible," Sherri said, shaking her head. She kept making Katie's lunch. She sliced carrots, washed an apple.

Now here were Madison Miller's parents, holding a press conference, begging for information that might lead to their daughter's safe return. The dad had thinning gray hair and a strong jaw; the mom looked exactly like Madison, except with a drawn and worried face and deep purple pockets underneath her eyes.

Bobby came in then. He glanced at the TV and there was the very slightest change in his face, almost a twitch. A flash, really, and then it was gone. Was the seed in Sherri's mind planted then?

We'll have to get rid of her.

Madison Miller was all over the news for a week. From this Sherri learned exactly what she was wearing at the time of her disappearance: Hollister jeans, ripped at the knee, size four, a gray hoodie, pink high-top Vans, size eight. A silver ring on the middle finger of her right hand made of interlocking leaves. A charm necklace with three charms: her birthstone (ruby), the number 16, the letters MRM, for Madison Rose Miller.

There was speculation, of course. She didn't seem like the type to run away, by all accounts, but teenagers are notorious for keeping their real selves hidden from those who love them best. That's what the psychologist on the television said. Was she an addict? Did she have a boyfriend nobody knew about, maybe an older man? Did she have secrets?

"What do you think?" Sherri asked Bobby once. "About this missing girl?"

He shook his head regretfully. "Hell of a shame," he said. He squinted at the photo in the paper she held out to him. "Cute girl," he said. Then he looked at her quizzically. "Why are you spending so much time on this girl, babe? People go missing all the time. Shit happens."

Was the seed planted then?

Once, entering a supermarket to buy a carton of orange juice and a tub of the cream cheese Katie liked on her bagels, Sherri found herself face-to-face with a poster that showed a different photo of Madison Miller than what she'd seen in the past, which was a casual family photo in front of an ocean. But now here came a school photo, fall foliage in unnatural shades of red and orange: a background. On the bottom of the poster at the supermarket was a number to call with any information: an FBI tip line. Sherri copied the number on a receipt and shoved the receipt back into her wallet.

She brought the groceries home and toasted a bagel for Katie.

What could she say if she called the FBI? Could she say, "I have a bad feeling about this"? What did she know, for sure? She knew nothing to connect Bobby and the guys with Madison Miller. She knew he had a secret computer, and she knew he engaged in business that was not quite legal. But did that make him a kidnapper? Was a bad feeling a tip? If she called the FBI, their lives would crumble around them.

"They still haven't found the girl," she told Bobby later that evening.

He said, "What girl?" But before he said that he paused, and she watched him arrange his face carefully. She watched him reach for the right words.

Was the seed planted then?

After that, she spent hours at her computer, getting lost in what she found. Rabbit hole after rabbit hole. Madison Miller didn't come back, and she fell out of the news cycle. But there are dark places on the Internet where stories never die, and where they morph into conspiracy theories. Madison Miller was kidnapped to be part of a sex trade operation run by a ring of South Americans. Madison Miller was a drug dealer, a porn star, a Russian operative, a garden-variety runaway.

Sherri couldn't stop, and she couldn't stop, and she couldn't stop, because she knew that Madison Miller was none of those things. She was somebody's sister and somebody's daughter and Bobby had said himself, Sherri had heard him: she'd been in the wrong place at the wrong time.

She couldn't shake the thoughts. They swirled around her like tumbleweed. They were with her always, her quiet, evil companions.

And then, seventeen days after Madison Miller disappeared, a dog walker found her body.

Rebecca told Sherri that if she wanted she could bring an appetizer to share. Sherri worked all morning on individual Brie bites made in a mini muffin tin with phyllo dough. Each bite had a little dot of pepper jelly inside, like a friendly surprise. She'd found the recipe on an app Katie had kindly downloaded onto her phone. Once they got their lives in order, Sherri vowed to use the app more often.

Rebecca had explained to Sherri that the town of Newburyport did not have fireworks on the Fourth of July; instead the town celebrated something called "Yankee Homecoming" at the beginning of August and did its fireworks then. However, there was a group going out on Gina and Steve's pontoon on the Fourth, as it fell on a Saturday. Sherri should come.

Sherri's first thought was *Hell no*. She wasn't going to leave Katie at night. But then Rebecca said, no worries, Katie could stay with Morgan until Alexa got home from work at seven thirty, then Alexa would keep an eye on them. It would give Alexa and Katie a chance to get acquainted before Sherri's first full work shift.

"Doesn't Alexa have plans? On the Fourth of July?"

No, said Rebecca, she didn't seem to. She acknowledged that that was unusual, and looked troubled for a moment. Alexa's boyfriend was out of town, Rebecca said.

Sherri debated for a long time about what to wear. She didn't want to dress too much like her old self, but she didn't really want to be her new self either. In the end she chose white jeans and a flowy navy blue tank top that she hoped whispered *upscale nautical* but worried screamed *Marshalls*.

Once on the boat, which was docked near Michael's Harborside restaurant, Sherri counted six couples, plus herself and Rebecca. So not the whole squad then. Some people must be on vacation, or busy with extended families. At least half the women were wearing white jeans, and this felt like a small victory to Sherri. She had never met the husbands before, and Rebecca introduced them quickly—SteveJoeDavidHenryMattOtherJoe. They all looked more or less the same, like overgrown frat boys gone a little thick, and she felt a sharp pang of nostalgia for how she and Bobby used to make heads turn when they walked into a party together. Bobby had never let himself get soft.

But never mind all that now. She accepted a drink in a red cup that somebody handed her, and she took a sip. "Delicious," she said. She attempted a friendly laugh but it came out more like an awkward squeal.

"Tito's and blueberries with just a touch of tequila," said Gina. She took the Brie bites from Sherri.

"I didn't get a chance to make anything," Rebecca told Gina. "I'm so sorry! The day got completely away from me."

Gina and Rebecca exchanged a glance that could possibly have been described as frosty.

"Well, *these* look phenomenal, anyway," said Gina, peering at the Brie bites.

With that endorsement, Sherri began to relax. The seats were like giant cozy couches, and there was a dark green canopy covering the captain's chair. Steve was at the helm. The pontoon began to glide in a stately manner down the river.

Rebecca sat on one side of Sherri. On Sherri's other side was a husband. (One of the Joes? David?)

Rebecca leaned over and said, "Joe, Sherri's new to town. She came from landlocked Ohio, and yes we all feel bad for her, but now she's found her way to the right part of the country. She's never eaten a whole lobster, you know! We're going to rectify that soon. Can you give her a little bit of a geography lesson?"

"Ohio!" said Joe. "I lived in Ohio until I was ten."

"I didn't know that!" said Rebecca.

Sherri flushed and ducked her head. This was okay: she was fine. She had prepared for a moment like this. *Redbrick,* she thought. *Livingston Park. Carpenter Street.*

"Cleveland," Joe said to Sherri. "Well, just outside."

Relief washed over Sherri. She tried to make her voice sound regretful as she said, "Oh! Too bad. We lived outside of Columbus. I don't know Cleveland very well at all."

Joe pointed out to Sherri that they were moving toward Amesbury, away from the mouth of the river that led to the open ocean, and that the pontoon was for inland use; Gina and Steve had another boat for the open ocean. "There's Brooke and David's dock," he said, pointing. "And straight ahead is the Rocks Village Bridge, which connects West Newbury to Merrimac and Haverhill."

"Got it," Sherri said. She looked around and was able to appreciate the beauty of the summer evening. The threads of color still tangled in the sky. The riverfront houses with docks and boats tied up at the docks. A lone kayaker. The smell of silt and salt and summer. The Brie bites were going like hotcakes—the plate was almost empty. "I feel like I'm in a floating living room," she said. Joe chuckled appreciatively: another small victory.

The pontoon glided; somebody refilled Sherri's red cup; people were laughing and talking and it was all very festive. A motor boat passed them going the other way and passengers on both boats waved at one another. Sherri waved too: why not? It was the Fourth of July. The lavender evening was gorgeous. Joe had laughed at her joke. She was doing fine.

Then, almost as suddenly as a curtain dropping over a stage, darkness descended. The little bit of light left in the sky was gone.

And, *bang*, came a sound, *bang bang bang*. Each time, Sherri's heart jumped a little bit more.

She turned away from Rebecca. "I thought you said there weren't fireworks?" she said. If there were no fireworks, it must be gunshots. She fumbled in her bag for her cell phone. She had to check on Katie. *She had to check on Katie.* But there were no bars on her phone: no signal.

"Not in Newburyport," said Rebecca. "Those are the Amesbury ones that we can hear. Are you okay, Sherri?"

"I need to get off the boat," Sherri said, softly at first, and then, because she couldn't help it, more urgently. There were no walls surrounding her, but somehow it felt as though they were closing in on her anyway. Her stomach lurched; her brain and heart lurched. She didn't care who heard her, or what they thought of her. She cared only about Katie. "I don't have a phone signal. I need to get off the boat," she said, to Rebecca, but also to anyone who was listening. "I need to make sure Katie's okay, I need to get off the boat. *I need to get off the boat!*"

30.

THE SQUAD

Nobody had a good cell signal out there. Nobody. It's a river! Cell service is unreliable. Eventually, Rebecca calmed Sherri down, and we finished the pontoon ride and went back to the dock. But seriously. Talk about a mood killer.

Somebody, we can't remember who now, said they thought they'd seen Sherri flirting with Joe. And that maybe he was flirting back. After the year that Esther had, and that thing with the office assistant, believe us, that was the last thing that Esther needed to worry about. They were still in therapy!

On another note, that was the night all of the girls were at Brooke's house. They were going to swim and watch a movie. Brooke's sister was there to watch over them. And where was Morgan? At her own house, with Katie and Alexa. Who had, what, nothing better to do on the Fourth?

It was almost like they were *trying* to exclude themselves.

31.

ALEXA

Alexa hadn't heard from Cam since the not-Dave Matthews concert. *Fine,* she thought, when she allowed herself to think about him at all. He was probably busy finding homes for orphaned puppies. Which was fine. She had a lot of work to do on Silk Stockings, and also to get ready for her move: she could afford no distractions.

On her way to Olive Street to babysit for Katie Griffin for the first time, she checked her phone anyway. Nothing from Cam. (She didn't care.) Nothing from Tyler either. Not that she was surprised by that; she did blow him off the night before he left for Silver Lake. She had checked his Instagram a couple of times to see if he'd posted anything from Michigan, but he hadn't. Caitlin hadn't tried to make any more overtures since lunch at Popovers, and Alexa hadn't reached out to Destiny.

Congratulations, Alexa, she told herself. You have successfully alienated just about everyone.

Sherri and Katie lived in one half of a two-family on Olive Street, not far from the high school, where the houses were crowded together and the sidewalks a little crumbly. Could Alexa have walked to Olive Street from her home on High Street? Yes. But did she? Nope. Alexa had never been one to walk when she could drive.

Alexa expected that Sherri would be like most of her mom's friends, with good hair and well-groomed eyebrows and a decent sense of fashion, at least for an older person. But Sherri was wearing khaki pants and a polo shirt with a logo on it, and her drab hair was in a low ponytail.

Sherri told Alexa that when they first moved to Newburyport she left Katie alone when she went out to dinner, but that Katie got a little freaked out because of all of the creaks and groans the old house made.

"I told her it's just the house settling," Sherri said. "But you know kids." She lowered her voice to a whisper and added, "She thinks the house is haunted. Which obviously it's not. But we've had a lot of changes lately. It's been"—she raised her eyes to the ceiling, as though selecting the perfect word, but produced only—"hard."

"I get it," said Alexa. Alexa knew Katie's parents were recently divorced. She reminded herself to be extra kind. Alexa refrained from saying that the house probably *was* haunted, because it was her belief that most of the older homes in Newburyport were. She knew that her own house was, but she thought that the spirits that haunted it were most likely friendly, especially in her bedroom. More than once she had woken in the night to sense a warm, comforting presence surrounding her, almost like somebody had laid a light blanket over her sleeping body. When she turned on the light she saw nothing, and the feeling disappeared. She tried to tell Tyler about this once. He said, "I'll show you a warm comforting presence in your bed, bae," and after that she didn't talk to him about it, or to anyone.

Sherri departed, and Alexa turned her attention to her charge. She was hoping Katie went to bed on the earlier side; Alexa had some research on L.A. apartments to do. There were so many different neighborhoods! Four hundred and seventy-two, she'd learned online. She knew the Valley would be too hot, and downtown L.A. too crowded, but that was as far as she'd gotten in terms of ruling out areas. There was Echo Park and Pacific Palisades and Koreatown; there was San Pedro and Fairfax and Santa Monica and Topanga Canyon. Each of these names tasted exotic on her tongue when she said them aloud in the privacy of her own bedroom. Playa Vista. Sunset Junction. Los Feliz.

Katie was as efficient and self-contained as a Roomba, a nice change from Morgan's overparented other friends. When Alexa asked her what she'd like for dinner Katie told her she'd made herself some pasta with a little bit of butter and cheese before her mom left, and that she sliced some red peppers to make sure she got her vitamins. Alexa was not sure that Morgan was familiar with how to boil water, never mind slice a pepper. She was impressed.

Katie settled down to watch *Cupcake Wars* in the living room and invited Alexa to join her. The living room was so small that Alexa had the impression that if she sat down her knees would knock up against the television set—and she had topped off in ninth grade at five feet, five inches.

"I'll join you a little bit later," she told Katie. "I just have a couple of things I need to take care of."

She left Katie immersed in the wars to go on a little snoop. Back when she used to babysit, the snooping was the best part of the job. In the past she'd found vibrators and porn magazines (old school!) and stashes of cash and photos of old girlfriends and boyfriends. In one case, she found the photo of an old boyfriend of a dad who was happily married to a mom. She'd found antianxiety meds and baggies of weed and hidden credit cards. Most people, it turned out, were hiding something from the people they love. She'd never done anything with any of her discoveries; she'd held them in a secret place in her mind, coiled like a coral snake, ready to strike.

Alexa headed up the narrow set of stairs that led to the second floor. The painted banister was peeling. It could totally be lead paint, in a house this old, so just in case Alexa didn't touch it. Her own house had been professionally de-leaded.

Sherri's room revealed nothing. There was a double bed made up neatly, with a patchwork quilt folded in thirds at the foot of it. There was a dresser and a nightstand, and the nightstand drawer was empty. Who had empty nightstand drawers? The absence of secrets felt like a secret unto itself. The closet was small, the way closets were in these houses, with non-fancy wire shelving, the kind you bought at Home Depot and that left marks in some of your shirts if you weren't careful. Four pairs of shoes were neatly lined up on one of the shelves. Who, Alexa wondered, had only four pairs of shoes? It looked like the closet of a nun.

One bedroom was empty—like, literally empty, nothing in it, and Alexa thought about how her mother would have turned it into some kind of funky home office with maybe a standing desk and a few succulents from Sage. Well, Sherri was a single mother, a working mother, so no surprise that she hadn't quite gotten around to interior decorating just yet.

Alexa progressed to the third room, which was clearly Katie's. It was messy in the way that Morgan's room was messy, with scattered bottles of nail polish on the floor, probably not closed all the way, and a paperback open on the bed. The dresser drawers were closed only partially, with pieces of T-shirts and pajama bottoms sticking out of them. On the pillow—the *pillow!* This was so something Morgan would do—was an uncapped marker, and Alexa reached for it. She saw the cap on the nightstand, which was on the far side of the bed, and as she was reaching for it she put her hand on top of the pillow to steady herself. There was something hard under the pillow (Morgan would do that too, leave something weird under the pillow—a contraband snack, maybe, or a copy of *The Fault in Our Stars*, which she'd been told she was too young to read until at least seventh grade) and before she could even think about what she was doing Alexa slid the object out.

It wasn't a snack. It wasn't a copy of *The Fault in Our Stars*. It was a composition notebook with a black-and-white marbled cover, very similar to the "grief journals" her mom had bought for Morgan. *Don't open it,* Alexa told herself as she was opening it. *Don't you dare open it, you know that bad things happen when you stick your nose places it doesn't belong.* In eighth grade, for example, she sneaked on to Google Docs and read Mia Rosenberg's narrative nonfiction draft and found out it was all about how angry she was at Alexa for stealing her boyfriend, Elijah Connor. In fairness, Elijah Connor had never cared that much about Mia, and everybody knew it, and anyway Alexa only dated him for two weeks because he turned out to be really, really boring.

And it was not like it was a diary, for Heaven's sake! It was probably full of math equations. Diaries of eleven-year-old girls were typically pink and hardbound and closed with those tiny padlocks with keys that went missing all the time. This was just a notebook. Alexa would prove it, by taking a small peek inside.

The first line on the first page said, "I'm not supposed to write any of this down. I'm not even supposed to talk about it."

"Alexa!" Katie called from downstairs. "Where'd you go? Alexa! They're going to announce the winner!"

Alexa slammed the notebook shut. Was there actually something *interesting* going on in this drab little half-house? She called, "I'll be right down!" and tucked the notebook back under the pillow. She wasn't sure if Katie heard her so she yelled, "Coming!" even louder, and instantly there came a banging from the other side of the wall. Ghost, or neighbor? She wasn't sure. She banged back, three times, and after that there was only silence. Probably a ghost.

She hightailed it down the stairs and into the living room to see who won the cupcake war. It was not yet dark, not even really twilight, and there was no need to turn on either of the mismatched table lamps that sat on the elderly tables in the living room. Even so, Alexa found that she was suddenly considering Katie Griffin in a whole new light.

While they were watching, there came a knocking at the front door. Katie and Alexa looked at each other, startled.

Outside the door stood a shriveled specimen of a woman. She was holding a small dog with giant ears. The woman made Alexa think of what would happen if somebody took a walnut and glued it on top of an old rag doll. She was looking at Alexa sternly.

"Can I help you?" asked Alexa. She had no problem being stern right back.

"Noise!" the woman said, her face crumpling into even more wrinkles, if that was possible.

"Excuse me?" Alexa couldn't stand looking at really old women up close. It was depressing. Supposedly their tiny little eyes contained the wisdom of the ages or whatever, but all Alexa saw was a complete lack of collagen and the absence of an actual neck.

"Too much noise!" said the woman, pointing an angry finger toward the house. "Somebody was just banging on the wall at me."

"You banged first!" protested Alexa.

The woman ignored this. "The crying all the time, the screaming. It's too loud!"

Alexa smiled her sweetest smile and said, "It's under control. I'm so sorry we bothered you. Thanks for stopping by."

"Who was that?" asked Katie when she returned to the cupcake wars.

"An angry old lady," said Alexa.

"Miss Josephine," said Katie, nodding sagely. "From next door."

Alexa was about to ask Katie about the "crying all the time, the screaming," but she decided to hold her tongue. There was something going on in this house. And she was going to find out what it was.

Cupcake Wars had become a real nail-biter, and she asked Katie if she could get her anything from the kitchen while they waited for the winner. She was going to start right now being the world's best babysitter so that she got asked back again.

32.

SHERRI

You are strong, said Sherri in her head at Derma-You once her training was complete. *Katie is safe, and you are strong.* This was her mantra for the evening. Her counselor in the program had taught her about mantras. Sometimes she recycled, because it was difficult to think of a new one every day. They were all variations on a calming and empowering theme: *Your body is capable, your spirit is capable.* Or, *The rest of your life is the best of your life.* (She'd been pretty proud of that one, with the rhyme.)

She reached for the file of a woman named Penelope Butler, who would be in at seven thirty for her fourth laser treatment to remove her underarm hair. Unwanted hair was just one of the things you could make disappear at Derma-You. You could also say good-bye to lax skin, liver spots, spider veins. Moles, cellulite. Skin discoloration. Scars. It was shocking, really, how many things could be removed from the human body.

The doctors were three smooth, ageless women—at once the advertisers for their goods as well as the dispensers—who flew in and out so quickly in their white coats that Sherri could hardly keep them straight.

The door opened and a woman walked in. Miranda Ramirez, who had a seven o'clock consultation for fillers. She smiled uncertainly, the way Sherri had learned all new patients smiled on their first visit. They wanted to change something about themselves, but they were ashamed to admit to that want. They looked around to see if anyone they knew was in the waiting room.

Sherri smiled back. She had noticed that some of the other women who worked at the front desk—there were usually three at a time, one checking patients in and one checking them out, while a third manned (womaned) the phones—were often hurried and graceless when they talked to the patients. They could have been dealing with oil changes or tax appointments, not the precious, vulnerable parts of these women's bodies, the over-hairy or over-scarred or flabby bits that required special attention.

Sherri tried to make up for this deficit. She smiled her extra-wide, welcoming smile. She tried to let them know that she got it. She understood what it was like to take on a disguise.

The phone rang. She jumped. Alexa! Then she chided herself. Of course it wouldn't be Alexa. Alexa didn't even have this number; she had Sherri's cell phone number.

"Thank you for calling Derma-You!" she said in her friendliest, most accepting voice. "How can I help you look your best?"

After work two of the girls asked Sherri if she wanted to go for a drink with them. Sherri texted Alexa to see if she minded staying later; she didn't. The women were younger than Sherri; she was flattered to be asked. She would go and have a friendly drink. She would be a person without history.

They went to a giant, anonymous, air-condition-blasted Mexican restaurant around the corner from the office, where they sat at a tall round bar table and ordered three margaritas and a bowl of chips. One of the women was married without kids—this was Clara—and one was married with a three-year-old boy. This was Sandy. As they waited for their drinks to arrive, Sandy complained about her mother, who called her four times a day and said nothing. Sandy ended each of her sentences on an up-swing. "She just keeps calling?" she said. "And I'm like, Mom, nothing's changed since lunchtime?"

"That's better than my mother," said Clara. "She's dating a man ten years younger than she is and she keeps texting me photos of her outfits to see if they're 'on fleek.' I keep telling her nobody says 'on fleek' for real, but she's not getting it." They all had a good laugh about that, and the waitress delivered their drinks.

Clara and Sandy turned to Sherri expectantly and said, "What about your mother?"

"My mother died when I was seventeen," said Sherri.

"I'm sorry!" the women said in unison. A pall fell across the table, and Sherri reproached herself for bringing the festive mood down.

"Don't be," said Sherri. "It was a long time ago." She almost said, "It had no bearing on the rest of my life," but of course it had all the bearing on the rest of her life, because when she met Bobby she was so fragile and motherless that she succumbed fairly read-ily to his charms. She took a giant swig of her margarita to show that it was all right.

"Oh, you know what?" said Sandy. "I'm taking this mindful-ness class? And this one thing they suggested? Writing the story of your life in fairy tale form!"

"Why would you want to do that?" asked Clara. She dipped a chip in the salsa.

"Apparently it results in big waves of self-acceptance wash-ing over you?" said Sandy. "I haven't tried it yet. Mine's due next class?"

"I think it sounds like a lot of fun," said Sherri. "I might give it a try myself."

She could see Sandy and Clara looking at her sympathetically, as though they all knew that Sherri's fairy tale would be pathetically boring but were too polite to say so.

Once upon a time, thought Sherri. There was a woman who lived in a house with a pool and had a maid who came three times a week and a husband named Bobby and a kitchen straight out of a magazine. And then one day, this woman learned something terrible.

It was always a dog walker, wasn't it?

Madison Miller's body had been buried in a semideserted stretch of woods one town over from where she went missing. Heavy rains had recently hit the area, washing away some of the soil. The dog happened to be a hound; the owner happened to let him off the leash at just the right place. Right place, right time, you could say.

Now her picture was in the paper again. Now there were more articles. No known motive, said the articles. Authorities were seeking information. Madison Miller had died from asphyxiation. There were marks around her neck that suggested a thin piece of wire.

Sherri left the paper open to the article. When Bobby came down for breakfast she said, "Look at this. They found that girl."

"What girl?" Bobby asked. If he had anything to give away, he didn't give it to her.

"The one who's been missing. Remember?" She held the paper in front of him. "The one who was all over the news a couple of weeks ago. Madison Miller."

"Poor kid," he said. He met her eyes directly.

"What do you think happened?" Sherri asked. She felt like she was poking a bear but she couldn't help herself.

He was fresh out of the shower; he smelled like aftershave and shampoo. He whistled when he opened the refrigerator. He *whistled*. "Must have been in the wrong place at the wrong time," he said. "Terrible." He shook his head and sounded regretful, like a teacher delivering a disappointing grade to a student.

Sherri remembered those words from the night she'd stood outside the office with the cheese tray, and she knew that the thing she'd feared was true. Her own husband, the man she'd slept with and vacationed alongside and cooked eggs for so many mornings—*the man she'd made a child with*—could say words that were so nonchalant, so unconcerned, while Madison Miller lay in a coffin.

Bobby kissed Sherri on the mouth, hard, and for the first time his lips felt like icicles. Then he picked up his car keys and left.

The next day there was an obituary. Sherri read it through six times. Madison Miller was a member of the National Honor Society and the Environmental Sustainability Club. She was a straight-A student; she wanted to be a doctor. She had three brothers, and a dog she loved, a King Charles cavalier spaniel named Betty. In lieu of flowers mourners were asked to give in Madison's honor to the Make-A-Wish foundation, Madison's favorite charity.

Sherri went to the bathroom and threw up her breakfast. Then she anonymously donated five thousand dollars to the Make-A-Wish foundation in Madison's name. She dared Bobby to notice.

He didn't.

She went to Madison Miller's funeral. She sat in the very back of the church. It was a Wednesday, midmorning, a dreary day. It was a Catholic mass. Sherri had never been to a Catholic funeral. She was unprepared for the fact that the coffin would be front and center the whole time, covered with a cloth, an open Bible, a crucifix. She was unprepared to be looking at the coffin during the service, imagining the lifeless body inside it.

The church was packed, of course. Madison's mother, unable

even to hold herself up, was supported on one side by Madison's father, and on the other by a man who looked enough like the mother—the same ginger hair and pale eyebrows—that he was probably Madison's uncle. At one point in the service, as the priest was shaking the incense over the coffin, Madison's mother let out the loudest, most unearthly wail that Sherri had ever heard.

Was Bobby aware of what happened after that? It got so Sherri couldn't stand to be in the same room with him. He was out a lot. That helped. But when he was home, if they passed each other, in the kitchen, in the hallway, she found herself turning at a slight angle so that their arms wouldn't brush up against each other. Did he notice her doing that? Did he notice how she threw all of her focus into Katie, into making sure she didn't know anything was wrong? They baked a lot. Sherri encouraged Katie to invite friends to sleep over and in the mornings she made pancakes for all of the girls. But the specter of Madison was there, all the time.

Sherri joined a Facebook page devoted to Madison's memory. She read every single post and every single comment. She drank up details about Madison like a cactus taking in water in the desert. Madison ran the thousand meters in indoor track and the mile outdoors. She was a counselor in training at a summer camp in New Hampshire, where she specialized in teaching swimming lessons to special needs children.

Sherri found out where Madison's family lived. She took to driving by the house at all hours, hoping for a glimpse of someone in the Miller family, a small morsel to feed her hunger. The parents, the brothers, Betty the dog. Once she saw a minivan in the driveway. Two boys got out, both in baseball uniforms, with mitts. The younger one was punching his fist again and again into the mitt, to soften it, or out of anger.

What must it be like to be these boys, the brothers of a dead girl? Sherri wondered. To grow up alongside a ghost?

The mother got out several minutes later. She walked slowly to the front door of the house, and Sherri thought about all of the tasks she must have ahead of her: dinner to prepare, the third brother to be collected from wherever he was, Betty the dog to feed and walk, all with the unanswered question of her daughter's death hanging over her.

How could anyone bear this? How could life go on? But it had to.

For Sherri, life went on, and on, and on. Meals. Katie's schedule, her dance classes and dentist appointments. Sex. Bobby couldn't have known how much she dreaded the sex by that point. He probably didn't know that after every time she scrubbed herself extra hard, until her skin turned pink and raw.

Breakfasts, and dinners, the packing of Katie's lunch box and the dropping off and picking up of the dry cleaning. On all of these tasks Madison Miller accompanied Sherri, like a pet parrot attached firmly to her shoulder.

To the dark Web she went, again and again, every time she was alone in the house. She found photos of Madison that weren't on the news. Pictures of her body as it had been found. Her face was swollen, unrecognizable. Sherri only looked at that picture once, and she never let herself do it again, but she also never forgot it.

The charm necklace came up in some of the posts, because Madison had been wearing it when she disappeared, and she wasn't wearing it when she was found. Sherri saw photos of the necklace online: the ruby, the sixteen, the MRM. Her parents had given it to her for her sixteenth birthday, four months before she disappeared.

When Sherri thought of Madison's parents choosing that necklace and watching as Madison opened the box it came in, her heart broke in a thousand little pieces.

All this time, Sherri stayed aware of what was in Bobby's hiding place under the register. The contents changed again and again.

Once when it was money Sherri took some and left it in Madison Miller's mailbox, in a plain white envelope. Would Bobby notice? Would Madison's parents trace it to Sherri somehow? She hadn't thought to wear gloves. But she'd never been fingerprinted, so a record of her prints wouldn't exist. Sherri imagined the Millers using the money to treat the three brothers to something special: a meal out, maybe, or a day at the ballpark.

Did Bobby know that every time he left the house she pulled off the grate with trembling hands, moved the floor tiles, looked to see what was different?

Sometimes there were zip drives. Often there was money in different denominations and currencies. Passports for people she didn't recognize. And then one day there was a new box, and in that box was a charm necklace with a ruby, a number sixteen, the initials MRM.

Some women complain about their husbands being messy, the socks they leave around, the toothpaste with the cap off, the toilet seat up. Sherri had nothing like that to say about Bobby. He was always fastidious, about his clothes, his things, his business. He never left things lying around. He was so careful. When the housekeeper came, sometimes she'd joke about how there was nothing for her to do. Every now and then Sherri would leave a few dishes in the sink, a wineglass in the living room, so they would look like a normal, careless family, a family with clutter, a family with nothing to hide because it was all laid out in little piles on the kitchen island, on the end tables.

In the end, though, he wasn't careful enough.

33.

REBECCA

Rebecca was in the kitchen, looking through her favorite food blog, Dinner by Dad, to find something to make that night. It would be fun if Daniel could come over for dinner, she'd enjoy cooking for him, watching him interact with her daughters. Daughter. Alexa was never home for dinner. They were in the kitchen, Morgan sitting at the island and Rebecca leaning against it, eyes on her laptop.

"What should I make, Morgs?" she asked, glancing up from the screen. "Are you feeling tacos?"

"No," said Morgan.

"Hmm. Salad? With grilled vegetables and a tahini dressing?"

"Definitely not. I hate grilled vegetables." Morgan did actually hate grilled vegetables. Why were Dinner by Dad's children, two young boys, so willing to eat everything put before them?

Maybe they weren't. Maybe it was all a front, a ruse. Maybe Dinner by Dad didn't even have children. Real little boys didn't eat eggplant without complaint. She closed the laptop and looked more carefully at Morgan.

"What's wrong, Morgs?" she asked. "You look positively downtrodden."

"I don't know what that means," said Morgan combatively. She kicked her feet against the island in exactly the way she knew she wasn't supposed to because it left marks.

"It means you look really sad. What's going on?"

"Nothing."

"Come on, sweetie, you can tell me." She wondered if she should take Morgan back to the grief counselor, get her on a regular schedule again. Her own therapist had told her that mourning was full of peaks and valleys, and that the up and down motion could last a long time. Perhaps Morgan had slipped into a valley and needed help getting out of it.

"It's just—" Morgan kicked at the island again, and Rebecca tried really hard not to tell her to stop. "It's just, why is Alexa always babysitting for Katie now? And never home with us."

"Oh, I wouldn't say she's *always* babysitting for Katie. This is only her second time!"

"But when I want to do something with her, she's always busy. When Sherri needs her, she's not busy."

Rebecca chewed her lip. This was a fair point. "Do you want me to talk to her about it?"

"*No*," said Morgan. "I don't want her to feel sorry for me. I just want her to be like she was."

34.

ALEXA

In her room, before she left to babysit Katie for the second time, Alexa checked Tyler's Instagram feed. No new posts. Then she logged out and logged back in as Tyler—his password for literally everything was *laxattackertyler*—and checked to see if he'd been tagged in any recent posts or had any DMs. And here was Tyler with his two brothers—one two years older, one a year younger—and some random Silver Lake hottie, a girl in short shorts and a completely unimaginative tank top from, like, Target or something, and she was completely ratchet. Cleavage all over the place, an arm around Tyler and another around his younger brother, Conor. *Hanging with the boyz from back east,* said the caption.

Oh please, thought Alexa. She looked more closely, and she saw that Tyler's arm was around this girl's waist. She looked for Conor's hand. It was by his side, just as it should have been. She checked the time on the post. Twenty-three hours ago. So this was what Tyler had been doing when he wasn't calling or texting Alexa. She considered making a snarky comment on the post in the guise of Tyler, but forget it. This girl (@silvergurl) wasn't worthy of a comment. Alexa checked @silvergurl's feed. Lots of selfies, lots of thirst traps. Typical.

Fine, she thought. *Let him.*

Then she checked her Silk Stockings Instagram account, which was different from her personal account, the one her mom had on her own feed. Alexa hardly ever posted on her personal account—an occasional sunset, a cute photo of Bernice, just to stay in the game. She posted on the Silk Stockings account any time she put up a new video, pointing her 21,000 Instagram followers to it. Nothing fancy, just a tasteful selfie (*tasteful*, @silvergurl!) where she displayed her outfit of the day and summarized the topic of the video. She thought she'd probably gotten a lot of new viewers that way, although there was no way to tell exactly where they'd come from.

Cam's Instagram was mostly golf-related. Alexa didn't spend much time there.

Her direct messages were as open as the day was long. To be a public figure you had to make yourself available. That was part of the game.

Direct message from @jt76 to @silkstockings via Instagram: Heading to L.A. soon, huh? You'll love it out here!

She clicked on jt76's profile. No photo. Followers: zero. Following: one. Silk Stockings.

Okay, possibly jt76 was creepy. Or he/she was a talent scout, setting up shell accounts to contact potential clients. She'd heard of that happening.

She typed back, Thanks! I'm sure I will!

At the Griffins' house, after Sherri departed for work, Alexa made some small talk with Katie. She couldn't go right for the notebook. She asked Katie if she was hungry or if she wanted to walk over to Kent Street playground, which was not far away. But Katie gave her a baffled look and declined.

"I don't really do playgrounds anymore?" she said.

"Of course not," said Alexa. Katie and Morgan were at that in-between age: too old to use playgrounds seriously, too young to use them ironically, the way the high school kids sometimes did, swinging in the dark of night with their vape pens or their edibles.

Alexa tried again. Did Katie want to walk down to the water-front or go for ice cream at Haley's? They could get to Haley's via the rail trail.

"I'm good," said Katie, her face placid. Alexa's mother hated when people said *I'm good*—she considered it a non-answer kind of answer—so both Morgan and Alexa had been conditioned not to say it. But Alexa believed in free speech within the walls of one's own home so she just nodded. "I'm reading," Katie added. She held up *Sisterhood of the Traveling Pants*. Alexa recognized the book as her own copy, the one she'd handed down to Morgan, because of the jagged tear in the cover. Katie was reading the first of the series, the one where Tibby meets the girl who has cancer. Alexa loved those books when she was in middle school; she had hoped that her own female friendships would turn out to be as sustain-ing, as reliable and life-affirming and, well, *fun*, as those of Tibby, Bridget, Lena, and Carmen, but, alas, Destiny and Caitlin simply didn't seem to have what it took.

"Okay," said Alexa. "If you need me, just holler. I'll be around." Katie went back to her book and Alexa clattered around in the kitchen for a few minutes, for show, in case Katie was listening. She inspected the contents of the refrigerator (disappointing) and the cupboards (barren). She looked for the liquor cabinet (non-existent).

There was a copy of the *Newburyport Daily News* on the counter, and on the front page was one of those advertising stickers with an ad for Canobie Lake Park, the amusement park not far away in Salem, New Hampshire. As a kid Alexa loved Canobie—it was small enough that she used to be allowed to go off with friends (back when she had friends), and big enough that some of the rides were legitimately scary. In the past few years they'd put in a new roller coaster, Untamed, and Alexa hadn't tried it yet.

Maybe it was the knowledge that she'd be gone soon, or maybe it was the realization that she didn't have any friends, and if Tyler kept it up with @silvergurl she soon wouldn't have a boyfriend either (not that she cared), but Alexa found herself overcome by a fit of generosity, as powerful and unexpected as a punch. "Hey, Katie," she said. "Do you like roller coasters?"

Katie looked up from her book. Her eyes were bright and shiny. "I love roller coasters."

"Morgan does too," said Alexa. This was true—surprisingly true, given Morgan's fear of so much else in the world. "Have you ever heard of Canobie Lake, the amusement park?"

Katie shook her head.

Alexa held up the sticker she'd peeled from the paper and pointed it toward Katie. "I'll take you two," she said. "You and Morgan. On my next day off. It's really fun."

"Really?"

"Sure," said Alexa. "Why not?" Katie was very pretty when she smiled; she had potential, Alexa decided. Obviously she wasn't going to inherit any fashion sense from her mother. But if Alexa took her under her wing, maybe then there would be some hope. Plus it would make her mother happy to see her doing something with Morgan. In fact, it would make Alexa happy too. She'd been a crappy big sister lately.

She waited until Katie had turned back to her book and made her way craftily up the stairs. She was so quiet that she figured if the Silk Stockings money dried up she could probably get work as a ninja. Silk Stalkings.

She found the notebook in the same place she'd found it before, under the pillow. Katie would probably *not* make a good ninja, judging from her uninspired hiding choice. Alexa sat on the edge of the bed, careful not to mess up the comforter.

And then she started to read.

I'm not supposed to write down any of this. I'm not even supposed to think about it, because it is all a secret.

I am supposed to be Katie Griffin and not that other Katie I used to be.

I have a new friend named Morgan who is just as nice as my friends were at home, and in some ways she is much nicer. I had to say good-bye to all of those friends anyway. Except I didn't say good-bye because I wasn't allowed to do that. I wasn't allowed to say good-bye to anyone. We left in the middle of the night, when everyone I knew was sleeping. So I said good-bye in my head.

We live in a nice place now, in a pretty town by the ocean, where there are beaches and ice cream shops and restaurants that sell fried fish and lobster rolls. We have eaten the lobster rolls but we haven't tried a whole lobster. I don't know if we will because they are a little bit weird and you have to crack the shells on your own and dig inside to get the meat out. Morgan likes them and she promises that I will too.

(Morgan liked lobster? This was news to Alexa.)

Morgan is friends with a big group of girls and I have met most of them. I am trying to remember all of their names but it's hard. I went over to swim in Taylor's pool. It was a nice pool and really fun and we had a contest to see who could hold their breath the longest underwater. I won. I always win contests like that because I don't ever give up. And I never, ever tell secrets, even the big secret that I have.

In the fall I will go to the Nock Middle School which is a brick building that is not that pretty from the outside but I went inside when Mom registered me and it is much nicer on the inside. The library has couches in it and lots of books and there is a small courtyard that Morgan says sometimes has ducks in it that you can watch from the windows. I like the idea of being able to watch the ducks during school.

(Alexa remembered the ducks from when she was in middle school. Most likely they were different ducks now.)

In school I will be on either the Crimson or the Gold team but I hope I am on the same team as Morgan. She said that we can eat lunch together even if we are on different teams. I will get a binder from PB Teen with my name stenciled on it, which is what Morgan said all the girls get for middle school. I have already picked mine out online. It is ombré and starts off dark purple but becomes teal by the end. My first name will go sideways on the Velcro pocket. Or my initials. But I think I will use my first name because that is the part that has always belonged to me. Actually, my initials are the same even if my last name is different now.

Inside the binder are places to put all of your pens and pencils and erasers and a ruler punched with three holes, which Morgan says is definitely going to be on the school supply list. She said that when we get the list we can go shopping together. I asked Mom when we can order the binder and she said, Soon, which I hope she means because Morgan says the binders sell out very quickly, and sometimes Mom says, Soon, about something and then it never happens. She is distracted a lot since we moved here.

I've never had a diary before. I always thought they were kind of dumb. Morgan gave me this notebook when I went over to her house. She has a lot of notebooks. She also has a bed with a canopy and a trampoline in her backyard and a big beautiful kitchen that reminds me of the kitchen we used to have before we moved. Morgan's house makes me miss our old house, which I am not supposed to think about anymore.

She also has an older sister who is really beautiful and fancy.

(Alexa smiled at this.)

And also a little bit scary.

(Alexa frowned.)

When I brought the notebook home I thought I would draw in it. The lady with the brown eyes told me it would be good for me to draw whenever I was feeling sad or confused.

(The lady with the brown eyes was probably some sort of child psychologist Katie saw because of the divorce.)

So, hello, diary. It's nice to meet you. Thank you for keeping all of my secrets.
Here is secret #1:
Even though I don't miss Daddy that much I miss him sometimes. Also sometimes I have bad dreams. I don't like to talk about what the dreams are about, even to Mom. When I scream in the night Miss Josephine bangs on the wall and then I try to quiet down.
Here is secret #2:
I was allowed to keep my hair because I'm a kid. I just wear it in a braid all the time now instead of down and curly the way I liked it. Mom had to change hers. She used to have beautiful blond hair and now she has boring ugly brown hair. She changed it for the first

time in the motel room and when she came out of the bathroom I cried and cried because I wanted my old mother back, the glamorous one who used to wear dresses and super-high heels and always had nail polish on her fingers and her toes and wore a gold bikini on vacation. But I can't have her back because of the crime.

Here is secret #3:

My job now is very simple. My job is to fit in. My job is to not think about Daddy in jail. I am to be Katie Griffin. Katie Griffin is nice and friendly and popular and doesn't feel scared if she wakes up in the middle of the night. Everybody likes Katie Griffin and wants to get to know her. It's okay that she doesn't know how to surf because she moved from Ohio, which is in the middle of the country and has no ocean around it. It's okay that she asks if there are sharks in the water. It's okay that she doesn't have a dad because Morgan doesn't have a dad either. This is all normal.

I asked Mom if she can call me by my other name, the name from New Jersey, sometimes, just when we're alone. She got a scary look in her eyes and she said, no, never, don't you ever ask that again, Katie. Don't you ever even say that name out loud again. You have to promise me. Right now, Katie, you have to promise me.

So I can't say it, because I promised her. I can't tell anyone, because I have to keep us safe. I can't ever tell who my father is or what he did. I can't talk about the Witness Protection Program. But I can write my name here. Katie Giordano. Katie Giordano. Katie Giordano.

Alexa slammed the notebook shut and shoved it back where she found it. Her hands were trembling. Something was going on here, and she didn't know what.

"Katie!" she called.

There was no answer.

"Katie!" Still nothing. Alexa flew down the stairs and rounded the corner to the living room. Katie's chair was empty. "Katie!"

"Sup?" said Katie. She was coming out of the kitchen, elbow deep in a box of Cheez-Its. "I'm right here." She held the box out to Alexa. "You want some?"

Alexa Thornhill, did this evening's babysitting gig meet your expectations? On a scale of one to ten, how would you rate your experience?

35.

THE SQUAD

It was early July when we began to notice that Alexa's interest in the Griffins had become, well, for lack of a better word, surprising. One of us saw her leaving their house on Olive Street on a Monday evening. Another one of us, getting cones with her daughter and a friend at the Cottage during Alexa's afternoon shift, heard her tell her coworker, a standout on the Pingree girls' lacrosse team named Hannah, that she was babysitting the following evening as a favor to her mother's friend. Gina reported it to a few of us via text, but not on the main text. A subtext, if you will. Tension between Gina and Rebecca had been high since the sleeping bag incident of 2019. Like we've told you, we have *no idea* how that story got out. And even if *a couple* of the moms knew, we never told our children. We thought maybe Rebecca was holding the whole thing needlessly against Gina. Not that we blamed her! She was grieving!

(Some of us still wondered. What was Rebecca doing with her summer? Except for that ill-fated pontoon ride, we'd hardly seen her.)

To the text about the babysitting we sent back various bewildered emojis. We thought, *babysitting*? Our children had finally reached the age where babysitters were unnecessary, unless we had younger siblings to consider, which the Griffins did not. Or unless we were going into Boston or Portland, or unless we were going to be out very, very late—for the famous/infamous Dalton Club Christmas party, for example. But surely Katie Griffin was old enough to stay by herself during the day or into the early evening. Surely she didn't need a babysitter.

It was Esther who first posited that maybe something else was going on.

After that, we couldn't help but wonder, every one of us.

We mean, Alexa Thornhill was a big deal. Her Silk Stockings account was verified on Instagram.

If Alexa Thornhill had some reason to hang around with Sherri and Katie Griffin, were we missing something? And if so, what was it?

We swear Nicole wasn't thinking about any of this when she sent out the evite to Riley's Boda Borg birthday party. If you don't know, Boda Borg is a real-world gaming environment where you divide into teams and go through these "quests" with challenges both mental and physical. You've never done it? You should. You totally should. It's really a good time. It's in Malden, sort of a haul from us, but worth it. They don't say this on the Web site, but a shot of tequila really makes the experience sing.

A few of us did it on a couple's night out a while back. It was a lot of fun: we rented a van and a driver. All of our teams had color names. The Green Team won, not that we're bragging. We invited Rebecca, but she didn't come. (We didn't blame her! She was still grieving!) Even so, it would have been nice if she'd specifically declined instead of just not showing up. It was that night that Brandy said she saw Rebecca getting a blowout on a random Thursday evening in February, when nobody had any plans to go out. And she was dressed up too. Not in her teacher clothes. She was wearing a pair of to-the-knee leather boots Brandy had never seen before.

It was probably nothing.

Boda Borg is not cheap. Nicole was on a budget that summer, not that she wanted everybody to know about Mason losing his job, but Riley begged and begged and begged for her Boda Borg party. She'd been counting on this all year. So Nicole had to put a limit on it, that's all. That's why she ended up not including Morgan or Katie.

It was nobody's fault. Looking back, at the end of the summer, we suppose it's possible that that's where some of the drama started.

Call Boda Borg yourself, if you don't believe us about the price.

36.

ALEXA

Once Katie was asleep Alexa sat cross-legged on the couch, deep into Google.

She tried "Giordano" and "crime." "Giordano" and "jail." "Giordano" and "New Jersey" and "crime" and "jail."

Bingo.

Google returned approximately one million articles on the arrest of a man named Bobby Giordano and three other men for the murder of a teenage girl named Madison Miller in New Jersey. The first article Alexa clicked on said that the men were rumored to be a little-known part of the New Jersey Cambellini crime family—an offshoot, as they were described. A smaller branch. They made it sound almost friendly, like the smaller, suburban banks that went with a larger city bank.

Madison Miller's body had been found in a shallow grave in a wooded area on the outskirts of a city park by a dog walker seventeen days after she had gone missing from a local Target. She had been strangled. The four men who were tried for her murder admitted in court that Madison Miller had seen something in one of their trucks that she shouldn't have seen.

Alexa felt like she was going to throw up, especially when she saw the photo of Madison Miller, in which she looked perky and nice, like somebody Alexa might like to be friends with, or anyway, like someone who might want to be friends with Alexa.

She kept reading. She continued googling. The trial was all over the Jersey news. Google, google, google. Her fingers flew over the phone screen.

One article talked about a "protected government witness." The courtroom was closed during the trial; no media allowed, the identity of the witness was not disclosed. Alexa tried "Bobby Giordano" and "New Jersey" and "wife." Bingo. Up came a grainy photograph from a local paper. Bobby Giordano was wearing a tuxedo and standing at what looked like a fancy party with a woman clinging to his arm. *Bobby Giordano and his wife, Sharon, arrive at the third annual New Year's Eve gala to benefit the Hope Society of Jersey City,* said the caption. The photo was dated eight years ago. Alexa tried to enlarge the photo, but when she did it became even grainier, so she returned it to its original size and leaned in very close to the screen. The woman's hair was very blond, and it was piled on top of her head. She looked a little bit like early photos of Ivana Trump, before she shed Trump. The dress was not something Alexa would ever wear but then again it was eight years ago and fashion had totally changed since then. The woman had her head turned slightly to the side . . . and, yes, there was something familiar in the tilt of the head, the angle of the nose. Yes, this could be the Sherri Alexa knew: blonder, more full figured, younger, with a surprisingly rocking body.

She googled "Witness Protection Program" and picked up several salient facts, although overall the machinations of the program seemed to be largely undocumented. She learned that witnesses were usually given a lump sum with which to start their new lives and that after that they were on their own, and that it wasn't very much—around sixty thousand dollars. Sheesh.

She learned that Sherri and Katie had to take their new identities to their grave. Even if Sherri met someone and fell in love and decided to get married, she had to do it under her new name. She learned that some witnesses requested an improvement in grades for their children along with doctored school records (usually denied). She learned that it was common for witnesses to be allowed to keep or alter only slightly their first names and the first letter of their last names so that they had time to catch themselves when signing paperwork or a check. She learned that there had been over 18,000 witnesses protected in the program, and that 95 percent of them were criminals themselves, making Sherri and Katie a tiny subset of an already small group.

She tiptoed up the stairs again to check on Katie. Still sleeping. She stood in the doorway of Katie's room and took a deep, deep breath, feeling the weight of this new secret, which she had wanted to possess so badly and now wanted only to jettison.

She returned to the notebook and flipped past the page where Katie's writing ended. There was a blank page, and another blank page. Alexa continued flipping. There was a little more writing on the next page. It was smaller and more scrunched up than the other writing, as though the person who was writing it wanted to both hide it and put it out there.

> *There's one more thing I haven't told anyone.*
> *Whatever you do, diary, you can't tell.*

The writing ended there. Alexa flipped again.

> *Here it is. Secret #4. This is what I want to say when Mom asks me why I wake up screaming. I don't want her to get that sad and worried look on her face so I don't say what I'm thinking.*

Which is that I'm scared that the bad men are still out there. I'm scared the bad men are coming for me.

Alexa slipped the notebook back under Katie's pillow.

Sherri came home around ten. They did the how'd-everything-go-oh-totally-fine routine, and then Sherri reached into her shoulder bag (front rack at Marshalls, Alexa guessed) and pulled out her wallet. Alexa thought of the large Silk Stockings sum she'd recently deposited into her secret account, and she shook her head.

"This one's on me," she said.

"Oh, don't be silly," said Sherri. "I'm not expecting you to work for free!"

"No, really," said Alexa. Granted, she had only a nebulous idea of how much it cost to be a real person, but she was pretty sure sixty thousand dollars didn't go very far in Newburyport, and Sherri was working just part-time, which couldn't pay very much. How could Alexa possibly take money from this woman, *this government witness,* and sleep comfortably at night? "It was fun for me," she told Sherri. "I promise. Honestly, we watched TV and hung out. It doesn't feel like work at all. I insist."

"Really?" Sherri stopped rummaging in the bag and looked at Alexa, relieved. "Are you sure?"

"Positive." Alexa squinted at Sherri and tried to see the woman from the newspaper articles. Sure, hair color could do a lot. So could makeup. And clothes. Alexa squinted harder. It was difficult to see, but the other woman, the former Sharon Giordano, was in there somewhere.

"Is everything okay?" asked Sherri. "Anything wrong with your eye? I swear the people who lived here before kept cats even though the landlord swore up and down that nobody has had pets in here. Are you allergic?"

Alexa recovered, blinking. Yes, she could definitely see the woman from the newspaper. "Everything's great," she said. *I'm scared the bad men are coming for me,* Katie had written. Her heart thumped. "Couldn't be better."

She was gathering her keys and her phone when Sherri said, "Alexa? Can I ask you something?"

Alexa immediately started to sweat in panic. *She knows,* she thought. *Somehow she knows I know.*

"Sure." She couldn't believe how normal her voice sounded.

"What's a Boda Borg party?"

"A what?" Alexa was momentarily disoriented, wondering if *Boda Borg* was some kind of mob term. Then she remembered that it was a real-world gaming environment that had been all the rage for a while in middle school. Not for Alexa—she wasn't a gamer, real world or fake. But some people got into it.

"A Boda Borg party. Katie mentioned that someone named Riley is having one? She was distraught over not being invited. And naturally when you're new to town you can't expect to get invited to everything right away, I told her that. I told her it was nothing to get so upset about. But try explaining that to an eleven-year-old." Sherri sighed. "It's hard starting over, no matter what age you are."

It won't be for me, thought Alexa. *Not in L.A.* But she felt hurt and angry on Sherri and Katie's behalf.

"Boda Borg parties are the worst," she said. "They're chaotic and stressful and the traffic getting there is always terrible and nine out of ten times a kid throws up on the car ride home. Believe me, Katie is *lucky* to miss it."

37.

REBECCA

"You sure you want to take on Canobie Lake?" Rebecca asked Alexa two days after Alexa had brought home the coupon and the idea.

Alexa shrugged. "Why not? I'm free all day."

"Sister bonding time!" Rebecca couldn't hide her delight. She went to hug Alexa but Alexa grimaced and ducked and said, "Calm down, Mom, it's just Canobie Lake." When she was clear of the hug she said, "Hey, is Morgan going to some Boda Borg party?"

"No," said Rebecca. "Not that I've heard about. Why?"

"No reason."

Rebecca called Sherri to make sure it was okay for Alexa to take them to Canobie. She told Sherri that Alexa's driving record was clean, which mostly it was. She didn't mention the speeding ticket Alexa had gotten the year before on Hale Street. Everybody went too fast on Hale Street—it was impossible not to.

One of the benefits of dating a childless teacher was that on a summer day he was likely to be free. While the girls were getting ready to go, she snuck upstairs and called Daniel, suggesting an impromptu date.

"I'm in!" he said. "Where do you want to go? The beach? Plum Island? Salisbury? Jenness?"

"I was thinking a faraway beach, like Wingaersheek or

Crane's—" Most people from Newburyport who went to those beaches did so by boat and stuck to the boaters' only sections; they wouldn't see anyone if they went by car.

"If we don't want to go that far, we could do a hike!" he said. "Old Town Hill? We could bring Bernice."

Rebecca hesitated. Old Town Hill was close, just over the line in Newbury. Lots of people walked their dogs there. Once, a couple of years ago, she and Gina had run into each other on Old Town Hill, Rebecca with Bernice and Gina with her rescue dog, Sadie. Sadie and Bernice had dipped into the river together (Bernice reluctantly, not being much of a swimmer) and Gina and Rebecca had a long walk together. This was B.P. (before Peter) and B.S.B. (before sleeping bag), but there was nothing to say Gina and Sadie wouldn't be there again today.

"I'm not sure . . . ," she said. "Maybe somewhere farther away! For fun. Mount Major?" The chances they'd know anyone hiking Mount Major on a random weekday were slim.

Now it was Daniel's turn to hesitate. "That's a drive, though," he said. "And since we're getting a later start, the parking might be full. If we stay closer to home, we can get a bite to eat after. We can go to Michael's and sit on the deck and have a cocktail. Or we can go to the Deck. And sit on the deck."

"I'm sure they have cocktails in Alton," said Rebecca.

Something changed in Daniel's voice at that point—a sort of peevishness set in. "If I didn't know any better, I'd think you were ashamed of me, Rebecca." He was attempting a jocular tone but the words stung.

"Of course I'm not ashamed of you," she said. "Perish the thought."

How to explain what was really going on? How to tell Daniel that her heart was a road map, crisscrossed with complications, strung through with fault lines? Alexa's fraught relationship with

Morgan. Rebecca's anger toward Gina, Gina's connection to Daniel, Rebecca's ongoing struggles with grief. How to say, *I need you to be a refuge, nothing more, nothing less?*

She closed her eyes and waited and Daniel said, as she knew he would, "Let's go to Alton. Mount Major sounds great. We can park on the road."

Rebecca was on her way upstairs to change her clothes when her eyes snagged on a photo on a shelf in the living room: the four of them, Peter, Rebecca, Morgan, and Alexa, on the Spanish Steps in Rome a little over two years ago—the April vacation before Peter died. Rebecca paused and picked up the photo. She probably passed by it a hundred times a day, but it now seemed important to study it. Peter had his arm around Rebecca and Alexa was positioned between them and a little bit to the front, with Morgan just to Alexa's left. Morgan and Alexa looked so young! They all looked young. Rebecca studied Peter's head. Was the aneurysm already in there, waiting to rupture? She tried to read his expression. He couldn't have known what was coming. Could he? What if he had? What if he'd known, and he hadn't told her?

"I'm sorry, baby," she said. Sorry that what? Sorry that he was dead and she was alive? Sorry that she was thinking of ways to while away a summer day with another man? Sorry that some days she couldn't stop crying but other days she forgot to cry at all?

She looked more closely at Peter's face. No, he couldn't have known what was coming. He just looked healthy and happy and full of gelato.

38.

ALEXA

The morning of the Canobie Lake trip Alexa shot her Silk Stockings video early so they could get to the park when it opened, before the summer crowds swarmed. Once she had looked over and posted the video—hard assets, it wasn't her best, but it would do, considering the time crunch—she changed into cutoff shorts, a strappy tank top, and a pair of Vans and knocked on Morgan's bedroom door. No answer. Was she still sleeping?

The knowledge of Sherri and Katie's secret past was acting like a caffeine hit to Alexa—she was buzzing with the knowledge of it.

"Morgan!" she called through the door, irritated. "Come *on*, we're going to be late!"

Why can't you be nicer, Alexa? Like you used to be.

But. "Down here!" came Morgan's voice. Alexa found Morgan in the kitchen, already having eaten breakfast and applied sunscreen to her face, ears, and arms, even rubbing most of it in. Morgan was practically quivering with anticipation, and Alexa's heart softened.

"Sorry," said Alexa. "I thought you wouldn't be ready." Alexa ate her own breakfast—a Chobani yogurt sprinkled liberally with cinnamon—and repaired to her room to brush her teeth.

It was only then that Alexa realized something, and that something caused her to stop short and stand still in the middle of her bedroom. She realized that a current of fear was running alongside the caffeinelike buzz of excitement. What if Katie was right? What if there were bad men out there? What if they'd been following Katie and Sherri, and by association they were now following Alexa? Weren't there, like, people who could spy on your Web searches if they knew your IP address or something? Did phones have IP addresses? What even was an IP address? What if she'd left a digital trail, and someone had found it? *What if somebody knew that she knew what she knew?*

What if those people followed her all the way to Canobie Lake, where she would be responsible for two young girls amid throngs of people? She needed backup.

She held her phone for a moment, studying her contact list. There was literally nobody to call. Caitlin and Destiny were out of the question. Tyler was still in Silver Lake, probably with @ silvergurl.

There was one person, actually. But he probably didn't want to hear from her: she'd burned that bridge before construction had even begun.

The bad men, the bad men, the bad men.

He answered on the first ring.

"Hey," she said, all cautious. "Sorry about how I acted at the casino. I—I had some things on my mind. I wasn't myself." She didn't wait for a reply. "Anyway. I'm taking my sister and her friend to Canobie Lake and I was thinking it might be more fun to have somebody who's not, like, eleven, there to keep me company, so is there any chance you're free today and want to come?"

She said all of that without taking a breath; she exhaled and waited in an agony of regret, chastising herself. She shouldn't have called. He'd never want to go.

"No apologies necessary, Alexa," said Cam. "I would love to accompany you to Canobie Lake." She could practically *hear* him smiling. "The Boston Tea Party? The Yankee Cannonball? I love that place."

She and Morgan collected Katie on Olive Street, then headed back out to Turkey Hill for Cam, then hit the highway.

Morgan, for all of her general timidity toward the outside world, was positively fearless when it came to amusement park rides—when she was younger she used to stand on tiptoe to meet the requisite height minimum for the roller coasters—and she and Katie spent most of the drive to the park on their phones, looking through Canobie's Web site so Morgan could tell Katie what was what. Wipeout was overrated. The pirate ship was only worthwhile if you were at either end. The Corkscrew Coaster was more jarring than scary, but Starblaster was pretty good. Yankee Cannonball was old-fashioned but fun, and the newest roller coaster, Untamed, was the best.

Here Cam turned from the front seat to deliver a history lesson on how the Yankee Cannonball was the oldest continuously running wooden roller coaster in the country and how it was moved in 1936 from Waterbury, Connecticut, and how they had to shorten each section by six inches to get it into the space where it now resided. Alexa glanced in the rearview mirror, expecting to see the girls' eyes glazing over with boredom, but instead they both seemed riveted. They were staring at Cam like he was solving for them the riddle of the Sphinx, and Alexa remembered that these girls were young and neither one had an older brother or a father. The attention of a fairly charming and, it should be noted, pretty good-looking example of the male species was probably exotic enough to be entrancing.

Once inside the park, a wave of nostalgia washed over Alexa. She still had a photo of herself with Destiny and Caitlin standing in front of the Boston Tea Party at about the age Morgan and Katie were now, when life was easier to navigate. Their T-shirts were soaked—you got positively *doused* on the Boston Tea Party—and they were smiling hard, with the July sunlight glinting off their braces.

Of course the girls wanted to go off on their own. Alexa hesitated, thinking about the bad men. She glanced around. The park was getting crowded.

"They'll be okay," Cam said. "I mean, if you're worried, we can stay with them. But I think they'll be fine." He was wearing a St. Michael's baseball cap, but other than that he was surprisingly, refreshingly free of spirit wear.

Morgan said, "Pleeeeeasssse," and practically went down on her knees on the asphalt to beg, and Katie gave Alexa puppy dog eyes.

"Okay," said Alexa finally. "But if anybody bothers you, you scream as loud as you can, got it?" Morgan opened her mouth as if to demonstrate and Alexa said, "Not now! Only if somebody bothers you."

She took a photo of the girls together just inside the entrance, so she'd know what they were wearing in case anything untoward happened, and she gave them each ten dollars for when they needed snacks. She made them promise to check in with her by phone every twenty minutes. When she and Cam spotted them by the giant swings, they trailed them for a few minutes to make sure no creep-os were bothering them. Then they got in line for the Caterpillar.

If she was being honest, Alexa didn't mind it when, just as the canopy cover to the Caterpillar was going up, obscuring them from each other's view, the centrifugal force threw Cam practically on top of her. But in general she was keeping it platonic, and

Cam was too. He was good company, and the girls were reliable about checking in, and the time flew by, and every now and then Alexa even managed to forget about the bad men.

They met up for a late lunch with the girls in the early afternoon. When Morgan's vanilla twist toppled from the cone and onto the ground, Cam was back in the line, buying her a replacement, before a single tear had time to form. Morgan looked at Cam not only like he hung the moon but like he was also responsible for both the Big and Little Dippers, and, when they'd finished their ice cream, they parted ways again.

As Katie and Morgan headed back to the Yankee Cannonball, Alexa pointed to the teacups. "Want to try these?" she asked Cam.

Cam grimaced. "I'm not great with the rides that go around and around," he said.

"Aw, come on," she begged. "You did the Caterpillar."

"That's different," he countered. "There's something about the things that go individually around that get to me."

Alexa remembered going on the teacup ride with Peter when she was really young, maybe eight or nine, and Morgan was small enough to be pushed around in a rent-a-stroller. "Please? They don't go very fast at all. And we can control them individually. Look! There are, like, four-year-olds on there." It was true.

"Okay," Cam said, relenting. "For you, Alexa Thornhill. Only for you."

In point of fact the teacups spun faster than Alexa remembered, and, contrary to what she thought, the riders did *not* control the spin. The ride seemed to go on for a semester and a half. Alexa loved the feeling—she even found herself emitting an out-of-character whoop—but when she caught sight of Cam's expression she thought she might have gone too far. Queasy was an understatement.

Finally the teacups stopped. Cam was still holding on to the center wheel. His head was bowed.

"Sorry," she said. "Too spinny?" They were the last ones left in a teacup, and the ride operator was looking at them sternly.

"A little too spinny." He looked up; his face had taken on a greenish tint. "A little too spinny after eating. I'm just going to—" He pointed toward a trash can, unable to finish his sentence, and hightailed it out of the cup. Alexa got herself out, located Cam's back near the trash can and turned away, to give him privacy. But then a good amount of time passed. Not just seconds, definitely minutes. She wondered if he was okay. She turned back to the trash can and didn't see him. She checked out the game booths. She looked in the line for the lemonade stand. Then she spotted him, over by the line for the junior sports cars. Cam was more than okay. He was smiling and laughing. He was in an animated conversation with . . . Shelby McIntyre.

Alexa walked closer. Shelby was back from Africa, apparently; she was overseeing a day camp field trip. Her hair was in a ponytail and she was wearing a T-shirt that said COUNSELOR on it in block letters.

"Hey," she said. "I couldn't find you, Cam. Hi, Shelby."

"You two know each other, right?" Cam looked uneasy, but it was possible his stomach was still roiling from the teacup rides.

"Absolutely," said Shelby. Her mouth opened and closed and she looked from Alexa to Cam and back again.

"Great to see you," said Alexa to Shelby amicably.

Shelby did not take the opportunity to say that it was also nice to see Alexa. Shelby turned to Cam and said, "I have to get back to the kids now. But I'll definitely call you about that thing, okay?" She touched his arm when she said that.

"What thing?" asked Alexa. Nobody answered her.

Once Shelby was gone, Alexa could feel that Cam's attention had wandered off, perhaps following Shelby to the Jungle Bounce. She couldn't have that.

"There's something I want to tell you," she said. "Nobody else knows this, but I want to tell you. Just you, Cam. Only you." She spoke quickly, before she had time to lose her nerve. "You know Katie? Well. You won't believe what I found out about her."

Cam's attention was right where she wanted it. "Something bad?"

Alexa hesitated. "I'm not sure. I mean, yes. I mean, it's not good."

He looked worried. "About her? That little girl? Isn't she like ten?"

"Eleven," said Alexa. "Same as Morgan. And it was actually about her and her mother, what I found out. About both of them together. I'm not sure, but I think it's a pretty big deal. I just—I just feel like I have to tell someone, Cam. Like I can't keep it a secret any longer. I'm scared." With each word she could feel the power of Shelby McIntyre receding.

"Scared?" he said. "What are you scared of?"

"Never mind," she said. "I shouldn't have said anything. I'm sorry." She lowered her eyes, and then she looked up at him out of the corner. She was nailing this.

Maybe Cam Hartwell was not so perfect after all. Maybe, like everyone else on the planet, he was human, and he was curious. He met her eyes. His eyebrows lifted. And then she was pointing at a bench and they were sitting down next to each other and she was telling him everything.

39

THE SQUAD

Sometime during July Alexa Thornhill posted on her Instagram a photo of Katie and Morgan at Canobie Lake.

(We all followed Alexa's Instagram account. She knew a lot about fashion! And makeup! When she Rented the Runway for her prom dress she posted the three dresses she was deciding among. Most of us voted for the KaufmanFranco red high low gown, which she did, in the end, choose. Though two of us stood firm for the Giambattista Valli sweetheart dress.)

Anyway, when we saw that photo we were all like, *Whaaaat?* Canobie Lake is typically a group activity. Three of the moms take all of the girls. It's always been that way, since they were too small to go on the Yankee Cannonball, since before they built Untamed. Maybe not everybody can go every year, maybe somebody is at summer camp or on a family vacation or what have you, and the moms rotate in and out, depending on who is available, but at least everybody is included! Everybody is invited! Everybody is given the chance to opt in!

This year, apparently, it was a couples' activity, the couple being Morgan and Katie.

After that, Maya and Riley went to Canobie together. Then Callie and Izzy. Taylor and Audrey ran into Anna and Abby, and it was said that they didn't even make eye contact in the line for the log flume.

It was almost funny, but not that funny, how Katie Griffin changed everything. Forever, the girls had all been one big happy group, and suddenly there were these . . . well, for lack of a better word, these factions forming. Everybody starting to break off in twos. We'd been working hard since these girls were in Pull-Ups to keep this group together, and it was not nothing to do that. The organization required. The group texts that had to be tended several times a day. The plans that had to be considered and reconsidered before being offered to the whole group. We had done all of this upfront work for a reason. We were going to go to middle school as one, a united front, a whole lunch table.

And then one new person came in, and look what happened. Things started splintering like pieces of a felled tree. Breaking off like icicles from the edge of a roof.

Maybe we are mixing our metaphors here. But surely you get the picture.

40.

SHERRI

"Do you want to cover this bit of gray here?"

Sherri put an alarmed hand to her temple, where the stylist, Brittany, was pointing. Sherri had come to the salon that Rebecca had recommended, Shanti, for a simple cut, although she wished she were getting full foils, like she would have in the old days. She missed her glimmering, shimmering hair. It wasn't in the budget, even if she could have allowed herself.

"Yes!" she said. "Absolutely." Sherri had been blond for so long; she'd only gone back to her natural color in that tiny bathroom in the awful motel room. She hated her natural color—a beigy brown that made her think of sand after it had been doused by a wave. She hadn't noticed the gray in her temples. How long had it been there? She supposed the blond highlights had covered the gray all that time.

"It's just a tiny bit," said Brittany merrily. "No worries."

Well, that was easy for Brittany to say. She was probably twenty-four years old. It worried Sherri plenty.

"Lean back," said Brittany later, when she'd retrieved Sherri from the cozy chair where she'd been dozing while the color set. Brittany's skin was smooth and plump and her eyes were gigantic. She wore several bracelets on each arm that clinked musically as she went about her business, and after she washed the color out of

Sherri's hair and put the conditioner into it she gave Sherri a scalp massage that was so good it was practically orgasmic. It had been a really long time since another person had touched Sherri with any sort of tenderness.

Suddenly Sherri thought about Katie at the amusement park. What if she got separated from Morgan and Alexa? What if somebody from their past had followed them there and was going to snatch her from one of the lines? An amusement park would be a very easy place to snatch a child. Sherri never should have allowed Katie to go.

She strained very briefly against Brittany's hand as though she planned to lift her head out of the sink, wrap it into a towel, and drive to Canobie Lake herself. Brittany kept her gentle grip, and Sherri forced herself to settle. The girls were with Alexa, not by themselves. Everybody had a phone. Katie knew to shout for help—no, to *scream* for help—if she ever found herself in trouble; and the girls knew to stay together the whole time, even in the bathroom. Especially in the bathroom.

Soon enough, because of the warm water, the ambient white noise of the salon and the comforting sensation of Brittany's fingers, she allowed her mind to drift.

Three days after she found the necklace, Bobby told her he'd be out of town for two nights. Business, he said. She didn't ask where: she never asked.

The morning he left she called the FBI. She'd expected that when she spoke her voice would be shaky, but it was sure and strong. She said, "I have information on the kidnapping and murder of Madison Miller."

They asked her to come to the local office. They greeted her politely, like she was a dinner guest. They got her coffee. They brought her to a room and sat her down with three FBI agents, two male and one female. Sherri kept her gaze on the female agent. She felt more comfortable talking to her. The female agent had hair in a blunt bob and a no-nonsense way about her but at the same time she had really kind eyes. She was part badass, part therapist. She wore a wedding ring, and Sherri could picture her at home in her kitchen, mixing oatmeal for breakfast, checking a child's math homework. This image made Sherri want to do a good job for her; she wanted to do a good job turning in her criminal husband.

She started with Madison Miller's necklace, and then she worked her way backward. She had so much to tell them. Years' worth. She had details about meetings, and she had dates and times, and she had a good mental record of all the different items she'd seen at different times in the hiding place. She told them that she'd never been able to figure out the password to the laptop.

The female agent smiled at her. "Our guys can get around that," she said. "Why don't you just tell us where the laptop is, Mrs. Giordano, and we'll take care of everything else."

Sherri talked and she talked and she talked, until it came time to pick up Katie from school. The agents asked her if she felt safe returning home. She said she did. They said they would get to work right away securing a search warrant.

That night Sherri didn't sleep. She imagined Bobby might come back home unexpectedly. She imagined Bobby would kill her the way he'd killed Madison Miller.

The next day she kept Katie home from school. She told her she had a mother/daughter day planned. She told her they'd go to breakfast and for a manicure. The whole time they were at breakfast, Sherri was shaking. She spilled her coffee. The manicurist had to hold her hand steady so she could paint her nails.

When they got home Sherri told Katie to go up to Sherri's room and put on a movie. She called the agent with the kind eyes and she said seven words. She said, "I was wrong. We aren't safe here."

If the agent batted an eye, Sherri didn't hear it over the phone. She said, "Sit tight, Mrs. Giordano. Someone is coming for you and your daughter. It won't be long."

The rest of it happened so fast, and also in complete slow motion. The FBI took Katie and Sherri into protective custody. Under the protection of the search warrant, they took apart Bobby's office, bit by bit by bit. It was easy for them to find the hiding place because Sherri had told them about it, but no doubt they would have found it anyway. By the time Bobby got home, there were FBI agents there to arrest him. The same thing happened at Joey's house, and at Sonny's, and at Carmen's: all four within the span of a few hours. Gone.

Sherri didn't let herself think about Bobby's face when the agents approached. She didn't let herself think about him looking around their house, their big beautiful home, feeling confused—feeling scared. Instead she thought about Madison's parents walking by her empty bedroom. She thought about Madison's dog lying near her bed, waiting for Madison to come home. She thought about the last minutes of Madison's life, the wire tightening around her neck. She thought about the little brothers.

Once Bobby was remanded into custody, awaiting trial, Sherri and Katie were allowed to go back home. Sherri told Katie Bobby was gone because he'd been accused of some very bad things. Katie said, "Did he do the bad things?" Sherri looked at her for a long time, and then finally she said, "I don't know, Katie-kins. I don't know. But I think he might have. We'll know more, after the trial."

It was a small grace that Katie's school was in another town, but it wasn't on another planet. People talked and talked and talked. Sherri didn't get out of the car at drop-off or pickup, the way she used to. She didn't chat with anyone. While Katie was at school, she hardly left the house. If she did, she shopped in other towns. She wore a hat. Glasses. Whatever it took. She stopped sleeping. She stopped eating. She pulled herself together in the mornings and the afternoons for Katie, and in between she fell apart. Every. Single. Day.

Weeks went by. A month, two, while they prepared the case. Six months, then nearly nine. At some point someone from the U.S. Attorney's office came to see her. Sherri poured him a glass of lemonade and he said, "We need you to tell a jury everything you've already told the FBI, Mrs. Giordano. We need you to testify at the trial. Do you think you can do that?"

Sherri's answer was immediate. "No," she said. "Absolutely not."

He persisted. She was the only reliable witness. She was the only one who knew everything. She was the one who'd heard them talking in the office; she was the one who had talked about Madison with Bobby, who had gauged his reactions, who knew the time line. If she didn't testify, there was a chance all the men could go free.

In Sherri's dreams that night, *Katie* was wearing the ripped jeans, the pink Vans, the charm necklace. *Katie* was leaving the Target, approaching her car. Sherri woke up just as somebody reached for Katie.

The man from the U.S. Attorney's office returned the next day at the same time. She poured more lemonade. He sipped and looked at her over the rim of his glass.

"I'm sorry," she said. "I wish I could help more. But I've done all that I can do. If I testify, somebody is going to kill me or my daughter."

That's when he leaned forward, and he set the glass down, and he looked at her without blinking. He had gray eyes—an unusual color, the color of storm clouds. He said, "I'd like to talk to you about a program that protects witnesses in certain cases."

Sherri said, "Yes?"

The man said, "It's unusual for a noncriminal to seek this protection, but it's not unheard of, and in the case of you and your daughter we think it might be warranted." Bobby and the others were being tried specifically for Madison Miller's death, but the other evidence—the trafficking, the money laundering—could eventually implicate others. Bobby's operation had tentacles, and nobody knew how far they reached. "Have you ever heard," said the man with the unusual gray eyes, "of the Witness Protection Program?"

"I think so," she said. "Like in the movies?"

"It's not an automatic that you and your daughter would be accepted, but in a case like this, where your testimony is crucial, and where others who might be later convicted of criminal activity remain free, we can certainly talk to the right people about it, and see where we are. I think that's something we should do. Do you agree with that, Mrs. Giordano?" He looked at Sherri intently and also indulgently, like she was a child, and he was offering her an ice cream. Somehow he managed not to blink as he waited for her to answer. He waited a very long time.

Finally: "Yes," she said, her voice no more than a whisper. "Yes, please. I'd like to hear more."

There were no cameras allowed in the courtroom; all media was banned. But they couldn't ban the defendants from the courtroom—they couldn't ban Bobby from seeing his wife, from hearing everything she had to say. They couldn't ban Sherri's heart from breaking anew at the start of each of the eleven days. Four defendants, one trial. Four convictions, four sentences. One protected government witness.

And then Sharon and Katie Giordano disappeared forever and ever.

What Sherri remembered most about the time they spent preparing for their new lives was the bathroom in the room that she and Katie shared, in a dingy motel in an "undisclosed location." She couldn't disclose it now even if she wanted to because she didn't know where it was.

All these motels look the same: a rutted parking lot, a row of doors with two plastic chairs set outside each, a front office that smelled like old French fries, a chain-link fence surrounding an underutilized pool. The toilet ran unless you jiggled the handle, and there was a rust stain in the tub. Bobby would never, ever, ever have taken Sherri to a motel like this. Or any motel.

Sometimes, when Katie was sleeping, Sherri went into the terrible bathroom and sat on the toilet seat and looked at the rust stain in the tub and cried and cried for everything they'd lost.

They lost so much. The money, of course. Their social security numbers. They got new ones, but they were hard to memorize and Sherri still had to look hers up anytime she needed them. Their last name, although Katie got to keep her first name and they both retained the G from their last names. They altered Katie's school records to reflect attendance at a different school, essentially rewriting her past.

In the motel room they made Katie write her new name again and again and again. *Katie Griffin Katie Griffin Katie Griffin*. Sherri practiced hers too. Slipups could be deadly. They role-played meeting new people and introducing themselves. They practiced what was called "cocktail party conversation."

What Sherri was supposed to say at a cocktail party was that she and Katie moved from Ohio after a nasty divorce. Then she was supposed to gracefully change the subject, but if anybody pressed her she had the details ready to go. (Columbus; Bobby took up with a woman at his office; they lived in a neighborhood called Livingston Park on a street called Carpenter Street; their house was made of redbrick.)

During those hours and days and weeks in the motel they wrapped their minds around the fact that they were taking nothing from their old lives with them, not the photo album from Bobby and Sherri's wedding, not the phenomenal drawing of a dinosaur that Katie did in second grade that Sherri had framed and hung in the kitchen near her calendar. Not the calendar either. They simply walked away from everything.

And when all was said and done they landed in Newburyport, Massachusetts, this pretty little town on the sea, with pretty little girls with their colorful surfboards and pretty mothers who had sharp serpent tongues.

41. Alexa

Direct Message from @jt76 to @silkstockings via Instagram: If you're
looking for a place to stay when you come to L.A. I know a great
Realtor. This will all make sense once you know the whole story!
I promise!

@silkstockings to @jt76: (no reply)

Cam texted Alexa two days after Canobie Lake.

Can you go out with me tonight? I'll buy dinner.

She was at work, off at four. Definitely, she texted back. Where?
(She needed the context to figure out the right outfit.)

She wondered if Cam might take her to Brine. Their menu was
supposed to be fantastic this summer, and over the past two years
Alexa had acquired a taste for oysters, something she'd never liked
as a kid. She figured if she was going to live in L.A. in the not-
too-distant future, if she was going to have the kind of life where
people have, like, caviar and champagne for a midmorning snack,
she'd better start getting used to the finer things. Next on her list
were fois gras and dishes involving truffle oil. If they were going
to Brine she was definitely going to have the bacon-and-egg fried
oysters. And wear her new Halston dress.

Sylvan Street, came the reply.

Sylvan Street? Alexa deflated. For real? Sylvan Street was the chain
restaurant out by the movie theater in Salisbury. It was the restaurant Morgan used to pick to go to on her birthday because she liked

the Potachoes, which were potato skins that had been recklessly bred with nachos, but even Morgan had tired of the Potachoes and had started choosing Oregano Pizzeria downtown instead.

Ok, she texted back. *Whatever,* she thought. She waited for him to tell her he would pick her up, but the next text caused her to deflate even more.

6:30. See you there.

When she arrived at Sylvan Street, the parking lot was already full to bursting and the lobby was crowded with large families and cranky kids waiting for their tables. Cam had put his name in but he informed Alexa that it was going to be a forty-five-minute wait, which she could have predicted. There was always a wait at Sylvan in the evenings, especially if there was a big movie playing next door. But the seats at the bar were first come first served, so they took a quick walk around, where a lot of people were glued to the Sox-Yankees game. It was the third of the series, and it would mean a sweep for the Sox if they won this one. There was a collective sense of anticipation among those watching the TVs.

Then, in a stroke of luck, a couple vacated two seats on the far end, and Alexa beelined toward them, just edging out two guys in their late twenties. She didn't make eye contact, because she knew that when you are taking something from somebody you just have to go for it. No hesitation.

Alexa wondered if they might try to get served, and she perused the cocktail menu just in case. There was a summer lemonade with vodka that looked good. But Cam ordered a Coke so she ordered a seltzer, figuring that he was probably being smart. In general, the bigger the chain the more stringent the ID policies. The seltzer arrived in a cup big enough to do the backstroke in, and as she removed the paper hat from the straw she said a silent apology to Morgan, who had joined the Straw No More campaign this summer.

The Sylvan menu was bigger than the book of Job. Alexa skipped straight to the salads and chose the chicken spinach, dressing on the side. Cam was really taking his time, frowning at the menu, reading through the wraps and combos and pasta and seafood dishes like his first language wasn't English. Finally he said, "I think I'm going to have the scallop pie. And maybe Mama Louanne's Brickle Pie for dessert."

"Big pie night," said Alexa. Scallop pie sounded like something her grandmother would order, but she didn't get the sense that Cam was in a joking mood so she refrained from adding that. She said only, "I've never understood brickle. I mean, what is it?"

"I guess we'll have to wait and see," said Cam. He looked at the TV closest to them. It was the top of the seventh, and the Yankees had pulled ahead by one. The guys that Alexa beat out for seats found some after all and they seemed to be taking the score personally.

"I did some reading," Cam said once they'd ordered. His expression was grave. "Online." He leaned closer to Alexa so she leaned into him a little bit too. "About the Witness Protection Program."

"Oh!" said Alexa. "Oh. *Now* I understand why we're eating here instead of somewhere in town—this is an undercover operation."

Cam ignored that. "How much do you know about it?" he asked.

"Enough," said Alexa.

"This is serious stuff, Alexa. Serious, serious stuff. Like, we could be talking Tony Soprano sort of stuff." He took her hand and an electric charge shot through her. But there was something unromantic about the way he was holding it more like he was protecting her, or maybe even looking for protection himself. "Whatever this girl and her mother saw, whatever they knew, and the people they knew it about . . . it had to have been a really big deal. For them to be put into this program, moved here like this. There must be people out there looking for them, or the government wouldn't have bothered to hide them." *The bad men*, thought Alexa. "If you tell anybody else, Alexa, it could be a really big problem. Or if you've already told anybody else."

"I haven't told anyone," said Alexa. "I am positive nobody else knows."

"I just don't like the way it feels," said Cam. "I don't want to put a little girl and her mother in danger by knowing something I'm not supposed to know. I wish I could un-know it." He looked positively downtrodden, so downtrodden that he barely brightened when the scallop pie arrived.

"I'm sorry," said Alexa. "I'm sorry, but you can't un-know something that you know. I can't un-know it either."

"Yes, but you—" Cam let his voice trail off, but Alexa knew what he was going to say before he said it. "You could have kept it to yourself. You didn't have to tell me."

He was absolutely right. She didn't have to tell Cam, but she had anyway. She did it for no other reason than that she wanted his attention, and somebody else's secret was the most valuable thing she could find to trade for that. She should apologize. She should acknowledge accountability. But Alexa had never been good at admitting when she was wrong. So instead, she said the only thing she could think of to say, which was, "That scallop pie is gigantic. Do you think you're still going to want the brickle?"

"Listen," said Cam. "I'm going to do my very best to forget that I know this thing. I can't un-know it, you're right, but I can do my best to wipe it out of my mind. I have no other choice, and I don't think you have another choice either, Alexa. I mean that with the utmost seriousness." He frowned at his pie.

All at once a collective sense of anticipation rose around the bar. Alexa glanced at the television. The Sox were up, bases loaded. Mookie Betts stepped up to the plate and a chant of *Moo-kie, Moo-kie* broke out.

"Alexa? You're with me? There could be people out there, you know. Looking for people who know things. There could be really dangerous people out there."

Before Alexa could answer Cam, Mookie did his thing, hammering the hell out of the ball, and it went high and deep, over the Green Monster. That ball was a goner. The bartenders started high-fiving the patrons, and the patrons high-fived each other. One of the twentysomethings Alexa had beaten to the seat was off his stool and heading over. He hugged her. She hugged him back: there were no hard feelings, because of Mookie. The guy high-fived Cam.

But underneath the thrum of happiness, Alexa could feel her heart skipping along like a frightened animal.

It turned out that the brickle pie involved ice cream covered by Heath bar and marshmallow, all of which sat on top of a cookie crust and were covered by some sort of "brickle sauce." It was sort of horrifying and sort of delicious, but after one bite Alexa couldn't eat any more. Cam's words felt like they were taking up all the room in her body.

There could be people out there. Looking for people who know things.

"I want this to be the only time we talk about this," said Cam when they parted at her Jeep. He looked extra cute when he was serious but his eyes weren't on her at all; he was staring straight ahead, at the traffic on Route 110.

"But—" said Alexa.

"No," said Cam. "No but. That's it, this was the only time. I'm sorry, but it has to be that way."

"Okay," Alexa said. She believed that Cam meant this, but she also believed that he had not yet been introduced to the full powers of Alexa Thornhill; if she needed to talk about it, if she had something to say, surely he would change his policy and listen.

"Good night, Alexa," he said formally, even dipping his head a little bit.

She thought about saying nothing at all (because who did he think he was? making her feel *bad* about wanting help? making her feel terrible for sharing information?) but her good manners prevailed and she said, "Thank you for the lovely dinner," and she climbed into her Jeep and closed the door, hard.

Alexa Thornhill, will you please rate for us the evening you had with Cameron Hartwell? Did dinner at the Sylvan Street Grill meet or exceed your expectations? On a scale of one to ten, how likely are you to seek this kind of experience again?

Fuck off, she thought.

42.

REBECCA

Rebecca stood in the doorway to the living room, looking at Katie and Morgan, who were fast asleep on the couch, the television playing in the background. Neither had had the foresight or perhaps the desire to lie all the way down so they were slumped toward each other, heads lolling forward, looking more like victims of a double homicide than like co-viewers of a Netflix movie. In fact just now they looked almost like sisters, even though in daylight they bore very little resemblance to each other: Morgan small and straight-haired, elfin, except lacking perhaps in the grace that descriptor implied, and Katie sturdier, curlier, with more heft. When Alexa had come home she'd gone straight upstairs. The old Alexa might have come in and sat down and watched a little bit of whatever Morgan was watching.

Rebecca switched off the TV, and now she could hear a soft knocking at the front door. She looked at her watch—it was nine thirty; this would be Sherri, coming to pick up Katie on her way home from work.

"They're both asleep," she said, opening the door. "Come in." She opened the door wider, and Sherri stepped into the foyer. Ponytail, khakis, blue polo shirt with the DERMA-YOU insignia over the pocket.

"Sorry," Sherri whispered. "I actually thought I might get out a little early tonight, but they kept me all the way through." She reached up and tightened her ponytail by pulling the two halves of it in opposite directions. It was a funny gesture—more that of a high school track athlete than of a suburban mother.

"Why don't we let them sleep a little while?" Rebecca said. She led Sherri to the living room and pointed at the couch. "You wouldn't know it by how they're sitting, but I think they're actually comfortable. I'd hate to disturb them. You could stay for a drink? I've got some really nice tequila just begging to be mixed with seltzer and a little bit of lime juice. We'll sit outside, by the pool." Sherri hesitated and Rebecca said, "Come *on*! Please? You'd be doing me a favor; I'll drink far too much if I open this tequila when I'm on my own."

"Okay," said Sherri finally. She set her lips together and nodded her head sharply, as though giving herself permission. "Okay, I will. That sounds really nice. Thank you."

Glasses, ice, limes, seltzer, bottle: together they carried everything out to the pool and set it up on the small table that sat between two lounge chairs, and Rebecca mixed the drinks. A brief evening shower had driven out the day's humidity, leaving the air crisp and almost cool. The moon was a pale, distant wafer, and there were a few stars scattered about. From the far edge of the lawn Rebecca could hear the gurgling of the small stone fountain Peter had installed for her for Mother's Day three years before. He'd been so proud of that fountain—she'd always said she wanted a water feature for the yard. He had wanted to get a little gnome to stand beside the fountain "for good luck," but she'd thought the gnome was creepy and had put her foot down. Now she wished she hadn't been such a grump about it. If someone had only told her, "He'll be dead in less than two years!" of course she would have let him get the gnome.

"This tequila is really good," said Sherri.

"Have more," said Rebecca. She'd almost finished her drink already. The danger with good tequila was that it went down clean and easy.

"I have to drive Katie home," said Sherri. "I really shouldn't." She tugged again at her ponytail.

"Just take it out," suggested Rebecca. "Don't you get a headache, wearing a ponytail all day?"

Sherri shrugged. "No. Sort of. Yeah, I guess." She reached up and pulled the elastic out. Her hair fell around her shoulders. It was wavy, like Katie's, and thick, with no sign of a telltale ponytail bump.

"Your hair is so pretty," said Rebecca. "How come you always wear it pulled back?"

Sherri grimaced. "Oh, I don't know. I guess it's just easier, nothing to mess with." Because of the way the outdoor lights fell, her face was half in shadow and Rebecca couldn't read her expression. "My husband really liked my hair, and after—after everything that happened, I just sort of wanted to forget. I wanted to be a different person. I almost cut if off! But I settled for a different look. Does that make sense?"

Interesting, Rebecca thought. "That definitely makes sense," she said. "That *definitely* makes sense." Emboldened by the tequila, she felt like reaching over and wrapping Sherri in a bear hug and telling her that everything was going to be okay. She settled for mixing her another drink. "Did he cheat on you?"

There was a pause, during which Rebecca wondered if she'd gone too far.

"Something like that," Sherri said finally. "It's complicated."

"It's always complicated," said Rebecca. "Marriage. Right? What's that thing Dostoyevsky said, about happy families? *'Happy families are all alike. Every unhappy family is unhappy in its own way.'* The same thing goes for marriages, don't you think?"

"I think so," said Sherri. "I guess." Rebecca pushed Sherri's drink closer to her, in case she hadn't seen the refill. "I really shouldn't have another," said Sherri. "I have to drive Katie home."

"Let her sleep here," said Rebecca. "And honestly you can too. We've got a guest room that nobody ever uses—it's all made up." She belched softly and added, "Whoops." Then: "The guest room has *really* nice linens. It's perennially made up with nice linens." She hesitated. "Wait, does that mean it's always made up? Or it's made up once a year?"

Sherri appeared to consider this question seriously. She took a sip of her drink. "I think once a year would be annually made up," she said finally. "But I don't know for sure." After a moment she said, "In our old house we had a really nice guest room. We hardly ever had guests, but I loved that room."

Rebecca listened for a moment to the gurgling of the fountain, and something about the moment made her think of earlier friendships, high school and college friendships, when you exchanged confidences with ease, and intimacy was measured by depth rather than longevity.

"If you tell me the bad stuff about your marriage, I'll tell you the bad stuff about mine," she said. It must be past ten now, and High Street was quiet. This was an early town, even in summer; by ten o'clock the traffic was sparse, and most of the restaurants in town were finishing up for the night.

"But your marriage wasn't unhappy," said Sherri. "From everything you've said."

"Not my marriage to St. Peter," said Rebecca. "*That* marriage was happy."

Sherri's laugh was a genuine, unexpected sound, like the trill of a bird in the dark. She seemed like someone else entirely when she laughed. "Are you serious, did you really call him St. Peter?"

"Not out loud," conceded Rebecca. "But in my head—

sometimes, yes. He really was the definition of a good person. Kind and funny and thoughtful and sweet. Never in a bad mood. Everybody loved him. I mean it: *everybody*. Dogs and little kids at the grocery store and old people and people who worked for him and people he worked for."

"Oh come on now," said Sherri. "*Never* in a bad mood?"

"Never."

"Everybody is in a bad mood sometimes. It's human nature."

"Not Peter."

"I don't believe you."

Rebecca sighed. "Okay, maybe very occasionally, if he got overwhelmed at work, or if he didn't get enough sleep. If he was jetlagged." She smiled. "He really liked his sleep. Once he had the flu, and he was in a bad mood for about two weeks. But that was unusual, and in his defense it was a really bad year for the flu. But honestly, that was rare. The minor irritations in life, the crap that gets me cranky? It didn't even faze him."

"I'm jealous," said Sherri. "There are days when I feel like everything gets me cranky."

"Me too," said Rebecca. "*Me too.*" She swiped savagely at her eyes. "I didn't deserve Peter. He was too good for me." Her emotions were taking a sharp left turn, and she tried to rein them in. Deep breath, then another: in, out, in, out.

She didn't deserve Daniel either. Eventually he would figure that out. Her long-term relationship odds were already crummy: fifty-fifty if you were looking at good choices versus bad, zero for two if you were scoring on longevity. If she and Daniel didn't work out she'd be down to zero for three.

"Of course you deserved him," said Sherri. "Of *course* you did." She reached across the table and squeezed Rebecca's hand, and the gesture was so unexpected and so kind that Rebecca had to wipe once more at her eyes with her free hand.

"Alexa's dad was an alcoholic," she said. She hadn't talked about Alexa's father in a very long time—even thinking about him dredged up old feelings, feelings that were as messy and muddled as decomposing leaves in the middle of a forest.

Sherri made a noise that was halfway between a *tsk* and a sigh. "Oh, no," she said. "I'm so sorry."

Rebecca's second drink was three-quarters gone. "It was one of those leave-in-the-middle-of-the-night situations. Like, I had to get Alexa and myself out of there or I thought something really bad might happen. He wasn't a jolly drunk who just fell asleep and was sweet and regretfully hung over the next morning. He got *really* angry when he drank. He turned into another person—an awful person. And he wouldn't get the help he needed to get better. He tried, a couple of times. But it never stuck."

Sherri was sitting very still, listening. For a moment, when Rebecca stopped talking, the only sound was the fountain and a very distant siren, probably coming from near the hospital. "So what happened?" Sherri asked. "To make you leave?"

"He drove drunk with Alexa in the car, and that's when I said, *That's it*. I had threatened to leave before, and I knew if I didn't do it right then, I'd lose my nerve. So that very night, we packed up, and we left. Alexa wasn't even three."

Sherri sipped her drink and then said, "Just like that? You left?"

"Just like that. I mean, there was all kinds of legal crap we had to deal with later, lawyers and mediations and the whole bit, but the night we left was the last night we were all three under the same roof. I got full custody of Alexa, and that was it."

"That was it completely? You don't even talk to him anymore?"

Rebecca held her hand out in front of her. In the moonlight it looked pale and ephemeral, the hand of a ghost. "Well. Yes and no. He got in touch last year. He wrote me a letter, wanting to see Alexa. Claims to be sober now."

"What'd you do? What'd you *say*?"

"I didn't say anything. I didn't answer him. I pretended I never got it. I never told Alexa! That's terrible, right? But he has such a history of disappointing Alexa, when we were together he used to let her down constantly, even though she was so small he didn't think she noticed or remembered. But I think she did notice. And this was just a couple of months after Peter died. We were all so fragile." She squinted at Sherri. "You're the first person I've told about that. Do you think I'm awful?"

Sherri snorted in a friendly way, if a snort can be said to be friendly. "My bar for awful is set pretty high," she said. "So: no. I don't think that's awful. I think you did what you had to do."

"By law he's allowed to contact her directly once she turns eighteen, which will be in September. I don't know if he will or not. But at some point I need to have a conversation with her about him." She turned her head to face Sherri more fully. "See? I'm sure you have nothing quite that bad."

Sherri held out her glass and said, "Can I have just a smidge more tequila?"

"Of course." Rebecca wondered if she'd gone too far. "I'm sorry I spilled all that. But it felt good to say it. I never talk about that part of my life. Everybody here seems so perfect, and obviously they're not, not on the inside, nobody is, but I never feel comfortable sharing this part of my past. It seems sort of shameful and sordid in the context of everybody else. You know what I mean?"

Sherri's answer could have been mistaken for a breath, it was so soft: "I know."

Rebecca shifted and turned to face Sherri more fully. "But how about you? What about your ex? Katie's father? How much is he still in your lives?"

"He's—" Sherri paused, seeming to be choosing her words carefully. "He's hard to get in touch with right now. So for now, it's just me and Katie." She stretched her arms above her head. She swung her legs to one side of the chaise and stood, wobbling. "I think I'll wake Katie and we'll walk home," she said. "And pick the car up tomorrow, if that's really all right."

"Are you sure? You don't need to leave. Or if you need to get home, you can leave Katie here and I'll return her in the morning."

"Thank you. I'm tired. It was a long day. But I'm sure Katie would be delighted to wake up here tomorrow, if you're positive about that?"

"I'm positive."

"Do you want me to help get them into bed?"

Rebecca waved her hand. "I might just tip them over and put blankets over them. They'll be fine. Do you want me to walk with you?"

"No," said Sherri. "Thank you. You stay with the girls. And, Rebecca—thank you. It was so good to talk."

After Sherri had gone Rebecca went around the patio straightening the cushions and picking up the glasses and retrieving a stray cocktail napkin from where it had wafted into the shallow end of the pool. (She was definitely drunk; she realized this when she almost slipped into the water reaching with the skimmer to get the napkin.) The pool pump was running quietly and efficiently in its energy-saving night mode. All was peaceful.

It wasn't until she'd covered up the girls and said good night to Alexa and was lying in her bed, waiting for sleep, that she realized that she'd spilled everything about her history while Sherri had said almost nothing. Again.

43.

ALEXA

The next day Alexa was so jittery that she did a terrible job on her video about accrual bonds. It was so slipshod that she didn't even post it: she decided she'd try again later in the day.

She was working at noon at the Cottage. Her mother asked her if she could drop Morgan and Katie at Theater in the Open camp at nine thirty—Rebecca had a meeting at the school.

When Alexa was young, before she understood that theater was mainly for the misfits, she too loved this camp, which took place completely outside, in the middle of Maudslay State Park. As she waited in the line of parents to pass through the turnaround line, where the counselors did awkward, theater-y things as the kids jumped out of the cars, she noticed that Morgan and Katie were two of the tallest, oldest campers here. They looked like full-grown trees among the small sprouts of younger kids. Alexa felt a stab of sadness for their departing childhoods. She almost started crying, thinking about how far she'd let herself get from Morgan lately.

After the girls got out of the Jeep, Alexa thought she saw a man she'd never seen in the rearview mirror, driving a black SUV. He wore dark sunglasses. Her heartbeat picked up, and her hands instantly began to sweat and slide across the steering wheel.

There didn't appear to be anyone else in the car. Didn't *gangsters* drive black SUVs? *Was this car following her to theater camp drop-off?*

Then three kids with backpacks and lunch boxes slid out of the back seat, and she realized it was just a carpool dad.

Inhale, exhale. Calm down. The bad men are coming. Inhale, exhale. Calm down. No they aren't. Yes they are.

Alexa glanced at her phone. It was only 9:40. Alexa had lots of time to kill before work. From Maudslay it was an easy drive up Hoyts Lane and into Turkey Hill, Cam's neighborhood, and then down his street. Not that she'd see him. What were the odds that he'd be out front at the very minute she was driving by? He was probably at Market Basket, or raising baby chicks in an incubator, or working on a community garden.

As luck would or wouldn't have it, Cam was in his front yard, practicing his golf swing. Peter used to play some golf and he'd once taught Alexa the three parts of a swing: backswing, impact position, follow-through. She was never interested in going to the driving range with Peter. Now she wished she had.

Alexa slowed the Jeep to a crawl and watched Cam. She didn't know enough about golf to know if he had a good swing or not, but she admired the way his shoulder and back muscles moved under his shirt.

Then he saw her. He lifted his hand in a wave. His face remained sober. She pulled into the driveway and jumped out of the Jeep.

He was wearing a St. Michael's visor. He smiled, but she calculated it at only half a smile.

"You look like you're still mad," she said.

"I am still mad."

"About the Griffins?"

Cam said, "Shhhh!" and looked around the neighborhood. Nobody was out except two little kids riding their bikes around the cul-de-sac in furious circles. They looked like they were going to crash into each other, but somehow they never did.

Alexa said, "Cam. Those kids can't hear you. And if they could, they wouldn't know what you were talking about."

Cam laid his golf club down on the grass, gently, like he was putting a baby to bed, and walked toward Alexa. He was frowning. "I know those kids can't hear me, Alexa, but what if somebody else does?"

They both surveyed the street. From far away came the sound of a car starting, along with the usual summer noises of chirping birds, faraway lawn mowers. A truck for a lawn care business rolled down the street. The guy driving waved, and Alexa shivered. What if it wasn't a lawn care company? What if it was a front for something? Wasn't that how the Mob operated, making fronts out of everyday businesses? The woman across the street was weeding her garden, wearing a big floppy hat. But what if she wasn't really the woman from across the street? What if the floppy hat was hiding someone more sinister? Alexa turned back to Cam and saw her own fear reflected in his eyes.

"Listen, Alexa. I know we talked about this the other night. And honestly, like I told you then, I don't really want to talk about it again. But since you're here, and since you're asking, yeah, I'm still mad. This is somebody else's secret, Alexa. This is serious, serious stuff. I don't think you thought it through before you spread it around."

"I didn't spread it around," Alexa said defensively. "I told *you*, Cam, only *you*." Her voice cracked on the last word.

He didn't seem to have heard her. "You know what makes me the most mad about this? Nobody gave you this secret. You read it in a little girl's diary. You took the secret. And when it got too heavy for you, you handed it to me!"

Her face burned. She was tan enough that she didn't think it showed, but she could feel it. She thought back to the day she first opened the notebook. In fairness, she didn't know what it contained. But part of her, glittering evilly in the darkness of her psyche, knew that she would have done it anyway, had she known. In fact, she might have done it faster. In a very small voice she said, "I didn't think—"

"That's right," Cam said. "You didn't think. And that's the problem with this whole situation." There was something so teacherly about the way he said this, so fatherly and judgmental, that the flame of anger in Alexa burned higher, licking at her, activating the very meanest parts of her.

"Forget this," she said. "I don't care anymore. I'm getting out of here as soon as I can anyway. And not to college either. I gave up my spot at Colby. I'm going farther away than that." She was trying to shock him into something, some sort of reaction, but when she searched his face she didn't see any shock. All she saw was a deep, deep well of sadness, so deep she couldn't find the bottom.

"Come on, Alexa," he said. "You don't mean that."

"I do mean it." Her voice rose. "I did give up my spot. It's *gone*. There's nothing here for me!" She thought of Destiny and Caitlin exchanging glances with each other, walling her out. *There goes Alexa again.* "I'm not like you, Cam. You have your . . . your spirit wear and your golden retriever and your lake house and your pitch-perfect family." She hadn't met Cam's family, but she assumed they were as innocuous, as sunshiny, as Cam. She thought of Caitlin clapping a hand over her mouth. *It's not like he was your real dad anyway.* She thought of Morgan: *Why can't you just be nice, Alexa?* "I don't have any of that!" She was screaming so loudly that her throat started to hurt, so loudly that the woman weeding her garden looked over.

Cam's voice got soft and he said, "Lots of people care about you. If you'd show everyone your nicest, best self, you'd know that."

"This is my best self!" she snarled. She was shaking when she got in her Jeep and peeled out of the driveway. When she was halted at the stop sign at the end of Turkey Hill, waiting for a break in traffic on 113, she realized that she'd never said what she'd come to say to Cam. What she'd come to say was that she didn't tell Cam about the Griffins to be an asshole, or to burden him just for the hell of it, or to brag about her snooping capabilities. She told him because she was scared. Because she was scared of the bad men, and she wanted his help.

She turned down Cherry Hill, passing the soccer fields where she'd played as a kid on the town teams. She hated town soccer, all those stupid cheers they made up, the endless standing around, waiting to be subbed in or out.

What was *wrong* with her? Who hated soccer?

Suddenly she was crying, for all sorts of reasons. She was crying for Peter, whose loss she had never felt entitled enough to truly cry about, and for Madison Miller, who left her house one day and never came back, and for her mother, who might have a new boyfriend, who was moving on, leaving Alexa behind. She was crying about Morgan, who needed her big sister but didn't know where to find her.

The tears kept on coming, streaming down her face, blocking her vision. It didn't seem safe to drive when she was crying so hard, so she hooked a left on Curzon Mill and pulled into the giant parking lot that belonged to Maudslay State Park and she found a spot in the very back, near the smelly bathrooms, where she cried and she cried and she cried. The parking lot was full of summer hikers and people getting ready to exercise their dogs and people examining their post-walk legs for ticks. There was a moment when one of the park rangers in his khaki outfit walked over to her, probably to see if she had an annual parking pass or if she cared to pay the daily fee instead, but when he saw her crying he backed away.

She appreciated the ranger's understanding. It felt like the kindest thing anyone had done for her in a long time.

When she was all done crying, she looked in the rearview mirror and was met by the terrifying sight of her red, swollen eyes. Clearly she wouldn't be able to re-do the video about accrual bonds until at least tomorrow. No amount of concealer was going to fix this.

44.

REBECCA

"It's so big," said Rebecca. "Way bigger than I ever imagined."

"Why, thank you," said Daniel.

She hit him on the arm and said, "Get your mind out of the gutter." They had gotten gelato and were sitting on a bench among the hordes of people, looking at the replica of the *Nao Santa Maria*, one of the tall ships that was visiting Newburyport Harbor and had docked at the waterfront.

Rebecca studied the steep, narrow gangway, the multiple decks, the tall wooden masts. "To think," she said. "The ship this one is based on was responsible for the *discovery of America*. I can't help but be cowed by it."

"Well, yes," said Daniel. "Although of course the country had already been discovered by the Native Americans."

"Yes of course," said Rebecca, abashed. "But it's still a beautiful ship."

"It's still a beautiful ship," agreed Daniel.

Once they finished their gelato, Daniel stacked their cups neatly and walked to a nearby garbage can. When he regained his seat beside her, he put his hand on the back of her neck and turned her face gently toward his. They kissed. She was going to pull away—*what if somebody saw them?*—but just for a second, hidden by the crowds, she didn't care about keeping Daniel a secret.

When they pulled away—it was a brief kiss, but enough to get Rebecca's heart racing—Daniel had a faraway look in his eyes.

"What?" Rebecca said. "You look like you just found the pot of gold at the end of the rainbow."

"I was thinking about the houseboat," he said, pointing. Sure enough, there was a little floating house out there that Rebecca had never noticed. On the upper deck she could see two people sitting in Adirondack chairs.

"It's adorable," she said. "Is that someone's actual house?"

He had his phone out. "It could be ours," he said. "I mean, for a night." He tapped on the screen. "It's a rental. Newburyport Houseboats. A buddy of mine manages them. Look, they have availability for the day after tomorrow. Should I book it? Here, look at this." He held the phone out to her. "See how great it is? There's a little kitchen with a two-burner stove, and a bathroom. There's a hair dryer! And a bed, of course." He winked. "There's a really nice bed. Let's book it!"

"Daniel!" She tried to keep the note of exasperation out of her voice. "I can't do that. I can't just—stay on a houseboat with you. I have children. And they don't know about you. What would I tell the girls?"

"I don't know," he said. "That you're seeing somebody? That you're a tiny bit happy?"

"No," she said. "Nope. I can't do it. They're not ready. I'm not ready."

He put the phone in his pocket and sighed. She fixed her gaze on a family looking up at the tall ship. Their heads were all pointed at the exact same angle. She didn't want to fight with Daniel. She really, really didn't want to, but she could sense the fight coming the way an animal could sense a thunderstorm from a change in the air. "Rebecca, we've been together for almost six months now. You know I'm going to be as respectful of your grief as anyone else, but I don't think I can live in the shadows forever. You don't even have me as a contact on your phone!"

"I know your number by heart."

"That's not the point."

"You don't know what it's like for me, Daniel. You don't have kids. That part of it is really complicated."

Daniel's face had taken on an expression Rebecca had never seen on him before: a cross between a teacher who'd stayed up too late grading exams and a Boston-bound commuter who'd just encountered construction on the Tobin Bridge. When he spoke, it was with someone else's voice, a sharper, harsher voice. "With all due respect, Rebecca, you don't know what it's like for me. I feel I'm grieving *your* loss and *my* loss, while you're only grieving yours. I've got to be honest with you. It feels unbalanced."

The family moved on. A curly-haired dog put its front paws on the adjoining bench, looking at its owner's ice cream cone.

"I can't do something before I'm ready, Daniel. I know that might not make sense to you, but it makes sense to me. This is the only way for me to handle things right now, by keeping parts of my life in different boxes." Daniel in one box, Morgan and Alexa in another box, Gina in a third (smaller) box.

"If it is," he said sadly, "I don't think I can be a part of it right now. I'm sorry, Rebecca. I think I'm falling in love with you. I really do. But I don't want to be in a box. I don't think I can keep being your secret."

She didn't know what to say to that. Their first fight! It was a quiet, civilized fight; they hadn't even raised their voices, but something had cooled, the atmosphere had reordered itself around them, and everything felt different. A first fight was always momentous.

Daniel rose from the bench.

"Are we still walking tomorrow?" Rebecca asked, a little bit desperately. "In Maudslay?" Three days a week they met early, at six, before anyone was out, and walked Bernice.

Daniel fixed her with a sorrowful, troubled gaze, and her heart plummeted. "I don't think I can do it tomorrow," he said. He took her hand and squeezed it once, then let it drop. "I'll talk to you soon, Rebecca."

The next day, instead of going to Maudslay on her own, she waited until midmorning and walked Bernice down to Cashman Park. She'd show Daniel. How dare he! Insisting that they do things the way he wanted. Claiming to be *falling in love with her.* How dare he.

She sat on one of the benches that faced the water. How dare he.

Bernice settled herself under the bench and Rebecca poured a little bit of the water she always brought with her into Bernice's collapsible bowl and put the bowl where Bernice could reach it. She contemplated the river and the scrubby grass that grew between the water and her bench. There was a line of inflatable Zodiacs waiting to take boat owners out to their boats. Far to the right she could see the Route 1 bridge, which sometimes shifted into drawbridge mode to allow tall-masted sailboats through.

She leaned back and looked at the clear blue summer sky. She felt something against her back and twisted around to get a better look. It was a plate indicating that the bench had been dedicated in memory of Gilbert Lane, "The Chief." The chief of what? she wondered. Should she dedicate a bench to Peter? That seemed like it might be a nice concrete way to solidify his memory. Maybe when she got home she'd talk to the girls and see what they thought. They could come sit on the bench when they were particularly missing him.

Daniel. Peter. Her ex-husband. How was it possible that she'd lost all three of these relationships?

I think I'm falling in love with you, Daniel had said. And also: I don't think I can keep being your secret.

The longer she sat on the bench and watched the river slide by the more she realized the crux of the problem. The problem was that what Daniel wanted and needed from her wasn't the same thing as what she was able to give him. That was it. Did that mean doom?

She was dancing with these thoughts, doing a little tango, maybe some samba, when she saw the familiar figure of Patricia Stone come along the trail, heading toward her. Patricia was walking with purpose, moving her arms with every step. Power walking. Patricia was head of the committee for the Holiday House Tours. Rebecca thought about getting up and quickly walking in the other direction, avoiding Patricia, basically abdicating her committee spot for all time. As far as Rebecca was concerned, Gina could have it permanently.

"Rebecca!" Patricia said. "Long time, no see. Mind if I sit down?"

"Of course not. Just don't be frightened of the attack dog under the bench." Bernice panted agreeably and then laid her head between her paws and promptly fell asleep.

"I'm thinking about walking the entire rail trail today!" said Patricia. Down the way, the trail hooked up across Water Street and meandered through the South End neighborhoods before emerging triumphantly by March's Hill on High Street, and if you were bold enough, you could cross Route 1 and pick up the other section by the train station, circling back to where they now reposed. "But I'm just going to gather myself first." She sat. "We'd love to have you back on the holiday tour committee this year, you know, Rebecca. We missed you last year."

"I'm not ready yet, I don't think, Patricia," said Rebecca. They watched a boat trailer back up toward the water and deposit a Boston Whaler into the river.

Patricia looked at Rebecca shrewdly and said, "I understand." She seemed like she had more to say, but that maybe she wasn't going to say it.

"Thank you," said Rebecca. "Well, it was nice to see you,

Patricia. I hope you make it all the way around the rail trail in one piece!" She stood up and started unwinding Bernice's leash from where she'd somehow gotten it caught around the bench.

Patricia said, "Did you know, Rebecca, that when I was forty-nine years old my husband died?"

"Nooo!" said Rebecca. She sat back down. "I didn't know that!"

"Yes. He was in a horrific car accident on 95 in Topsfield. It was a bright-white winter's day. No snow on the ground. The other driver was at fault—he was a teenager, still on his provisional license. This was before texting, of course, but he was distracted by something in the car, I don't know if he was fiddling with the radio or what, they never knew for certain, and anyway in the end it didn't matter. He was going too fast to begin with, and he took his eyes off the road, and he forced my Jerry right into the guardrail, at sixty-five miles an hour. Jerry never had a chance to react."

"That's *terrible*," said Rebecca. "I'm so sorry, I didn't know. I thought you'd been married to Bob forever. Your kids—"

"Jerry is the father of my children. Bob and I just celebrated fifteen years," said Patricia. She lifted her sunglasses and winked at Rebecca. "We're practically newlyweds." She paused and reached down to pat Bernice's head. "Anyway. I remember like it was yesterday, being in the stage that you're in now. You're grieving, but you're living, and some days you're doing more grieving than living and some days you're doing more living than grieving. And you never know which kind of day it's going to be until you open your eyes in the morning."

"That's exactly right," breathed Rebecca. "*Exactly* right."

"And I remember how it was after I met Bob too. He would do something, I don't know, something silly that would rub me the wrong way, and I'd think, 'Jerry would never do that.' But that wasn't fair to Bob, you see. Maybe Jerry *would* have done the thing that rubbed me the wrong way! But I was holding Bob up to some impossible standard. The standard of a dead man. So. I don't pretend to be an expert on the topic, but I have been through what you're going through now. And it's terrible, and it's painful, and it's exhausting. But if I could go back in time to my forty-nine-year-old self, I'd tell her not to discount the value of getting back into the world." Patricia rapped on the bench three times, as if to signal that she'd dispensed all of the advice she'd come to give, and rose. "It was lovely to run into you, Rebecca. Your spot is always available, should you decide to return to the committee. Even if someone else has ostensibly claimed it. We'll always have room for you."

"Thank you," said Rebecca.

Rebecca watched Patricia resume her purposeful stride toward the rail trail, and she thought long and hard about what the older woman had told her.

Of course it hadn't all been perfect with Peter, no matter what Rebecca had told Sherri that night by the pool. Sometimes he left his socks on the floor, and when his seasonal allergies kicked in, he snored so badly she had to sleep with headphones, and sometimes he was too strict about keeping the garage tidy. And by the way *she* was no picnic to live with when it was almost time for winter break and all of the kids at school were sick and she couldn't keep their germs at bay; she was always snappish in the winter. At least twice a week they quarreled about whose turn it was to unload the dishwasher. Rebecca *absolutely hated* dragging out the recycling in the winter when Peter traveled and she complained about that more than she should have because, come on, it was just a couple of bins. She watched Patricia walk on, and she thought about the sorrows, small and large, that people carried around with them. Patricia walked past the spot where they often sat to watch the Yankee Homecoming fireworks, and past the playground where the girls used to play when they were little. Patricia got smaller and smaller until finally she disappeared altogether from Rebecca's line of vision.

45.

THE SQUAD

If you turn down a spot on the committee for the Holiday House Tours two years in a row, you're not going to get asked back. You're just not. We know people who have been trying to get on that committee for four or five years—longer, in some cases. If Rebecca wanted to give her spot to Gina, obviously that was her choice. But she could have at least answered Gina's texts about it, so Gina would know what she was thinking.

(By now it was almost August, and we had seen almost nothing of Rebecca.)

One of us thought maybe she was seeing somebody, but why would she keep that a secret?

We wouldn't blame her if she was! Peter had been gone for a year and a half by this point!

46.

ALEXA

For the next several days the conversation with Cam roiled around Alexa's stomach like a batch of bad oysters. She vacillated between self-righteousness (how dare he refuse to help her with this very scary situation!) and self-doubt (was there a chance he was right?). At the Cottage, she worked one five-hour shift, during which she made six Ringers, three milk shakes, and who-knows-how-many ice cream cones with rainbow sprinkles. She was scattered and klutzy. She dropped a doughnut, and then she stepped on it. She gave the wrong change to two different customers. She forgot to tell her boss that they were on their last container of chocolate ice cream, so they ran out—a huge problem, obviously.

"Whoa," said her coworker, Hannah. "Amazon. What's going on with you? You get in a fight with Tyler or something?"

"No," said Alexa tightly. "No, I did not get in a fight with Tyler. Tyler isn't even here. He's still in Michigan."

She sat on the beach for forty minutes after her shift, long enough to add a light golden topcoat to her tan without going too far.

Alexa simmered and simmered. She made and posted one video, about market orders and stop-loss orders, which she had planned on doing separately but then realized she could easily combine into two. She reorganized her closet and her bathroom drawers. In a fit of do-goodness, she took Bernice down to the boardwalk, to see the tall ship (Bernice loved boats).

Finally, when she could stand the terrible feeling no longer, Alexa got in her Jeep and made the short trip to Market Basket.

Alexa generally tried to stay away from Market Basket because you couldn't get down an aisle without seeing someone you knew. Sure enough, near the yogurt she ran into her eighth-grade English teacher, Mrs. Sanchez, who never failed to remember and mention Alexa's "cogent" essay on *To Kill a Mockingbird*. (Topic: Discuss the concept of fear in the novel.)

"It's so nice to see you, Alexa!" Mrs. Sanchez gushed. And then, right on cue, "You know, I still use your *Mockingbird* essay as an example. Every year, I pull that thing out, and I read the *whole thing* out loud, and I try to explain to my students that it's a close reading of the text that really makes for a stellar piece of work." She beamed for an uncomfortably long time and then said, "Please don't tell me you graduated. Is time going by that fast?"

"I did," said Alexa. "It is."

"Where are you headed next year?"

"Um," said Alexa. "I'm not sure." She was scanning the aisles for Cam. She was pretty sure he worked checkout, but then again she could imagine him cheerfully restocking the salsa and answering customers' questions about where to find the Bob's Red Mill flour. "Probably Colby."

"How wonderful! And I hope you're going to put those fabulous writing skills to use," said Mrs. Sanchez. Alexa was pretty sure that when she moved to Los Angeles and got natural highlights in her hair from the sun and dated surfers and actors, she would not be using the skills that allowed her to delve into Jean Louise Finch's young psyche, but she didn't want to crush Mrs. Sanchez completely. Mrs. Sanchez, after all, seemed to be in the very tiny camp of Alexa fans.

"I might go more in a—financy direction," said Alexa. "I've become pretty interested in the stock market." Before she could register Mrs. Sanchez's disappointment, both in her future and in her use of the made-up word "financy," Alexa said her good-byes.

By the hard cheeses, she saw her neighbors from two doors down, the Walkers. She kept her head pointed toward the floor and avoided eye contact. In the nonorganic fruit aisle she saw the mother of the first family she ever babysat for, Mrs. Reyes, but she was *sans* children and thus easily circumvented. In the organic fruit aisle she came upon Caitlin, of all people, who was taking a selfie with a container of raspberries. Alexa didn't know why and wasn't about to ask. She skirted out of the fruit aisle, undetected.

She gathered enough random food in her cart (broccoli, seltzer, those crostini Tuscan crackers Morgan liked, as an olive branch of sorts—a cracker branch) so that her trip looked legit but not over the top, and she headed toward the checkouts. Cam wasn't working any of the registers. She chose a line with a young checkout person who might be friendly with him. Everyone else working was at least forty-five.

"You could have gone in the express line," the girl chirped, surveying Alexa's items. "You wouldn't have had to wait!"

Alexa shot her a withering glance that said, *I know, but I didn't want to.* Then she tossed her hair and said, "Hey, do you know if Cam's working today?"

"Did you bring your reusable bags or do you want paper?"

Was this an answer? "Paper," growled Alexa, and she repeated her question about Cam.

"I don't know," said the girl. She called, way too loudly, over to the manager's station. "Bill! When is Cam working next?"

"He's off for a few days," said Bill. He moved over to the end of the checkout lane and began bagging Alexa's groceries. "No reusables?"

"She didn't bring any," said the checkout girl. She shrugged at Bill as if to indicate that *she* couldn't help it if people didn't care about the planet.

Bill said, "I think he's at the lake."

"Thanks," said Alexa. She took her paper bag and hightailed it back to her Jeep before she could run into anyone else she knew.

The first thing she did after putting away the groceries, and—out of some inexplicable spite toward the checkout girl—throwing the paper bag in the garbage can instead of recycling it, was to climb the stairs to her bedroom and call Hannah to see if she would switch shifts with Alexa. Alexa would work for her the following day if Hannah would work for her this afternoon at four.

"I don't know, Amazon," said Hannah. "I'm at the beach."

Alexa gritted her teeth at the nickname and set her wheels turning. "Which beach?"

"Jenness."

"Oh boy," said Alexa.

"What?"

"Aren't they getting those crazy thunderstorms up there today?"

Hannah hesitated. "I don't think so? It looks like really clear now?"

"Hang on," said Alexa. "Let me put you on speaker phone so I can check." She paused as if she were checking her weather app and said, "Yeah, right around three. Trust me, that beach is going to clear out."

There was a faint murmuring, which Alexa took to indicate that Hannah was passing this information on to her fellow beach-goers.

"Crazy," said Hannah. "I didn't see anything about that on my app."

"Are you using the app that came with your phone?"

"Yes."

"Don't do *that*, Hannah. That app is terrible. You've got to download Dark Sky. It's so much better."

"Really? Dark Sky?"

"Trust me. It keeps up much faster. These summer storms can come from out of nowhere, you know."

"I do have something I was hoping to do tomorrow," Hannah considered. "So if you took my shift—"

"Perfect!" said Alexa. "I owe you."

Hannah was fair-skinned and freckled so probably should limit her sun exposure. If you looked at it correctly, Alexa was doing her a favor.

Back downstairs, she could tell that somebody had come home because the paper bag from Market Basket had been dug out of the garbage and lovingly folded into the recycling bin. She sensed the hand of Morgan the Environmentalist in this, but she didn't stop to look around because she wanted to get on the road.

She turned off the locator app on her iPhone. Her mother didn't know how often Alexa did this; she just thought the app was given to "malfunctioning" and wondered when "they" were going to come up with a tracking app that actually tracked reliably.

A quick Google search led her to Cam's Winnipesaukee address, which she plugged straight into Waze.

The drive to Wolfeboro took her to Alton and then northeast along Winnipesaukee, but she wasn't paying attention when it was time to make the turn from Route 11 to Route 28, and before she knew it she was heading the wrong way around the lake, adding at least thirty miles (maybe more) to her drive. But that was okay. It was a kick-ass summer day, sunny and cloudless. Along the arm of Alton Bay, the pontoons and the other pleasure craft were out in full force. The lines for ice cream at the myriad outdoor stands were long, and traffic was slow. She didn't mind. She was enjoying being somewhere different, away from the fishbowl of Newburyport.

She passed the parking for the Sandy Point Beach Resort, which looked like something out of a 1950s movie, and the parking area for Mount Major. She wound through Meredith and Center Harbor and Moultonborough. Finally, just as she was approaching Wolfeboro, she followed her GPS across a skinny, skinny road with water on both sides, made two turns, and arrived at Cam's house. In case Alexa had any lingering doubts about the address being correct, they were immediately assuaged by the sight of not one, not two, but three vehicles in the driveway (one being the minivan) bearing St. Michael's College stickers.

She sat for a moment in the Jeep, wondering if she should just turn around and go back home. What, exactly, was she doing here?

There was a movement behind one of the windows. She'd been spotted. Nothing to do now but get out of the car and knock on the door.

"Alexa!" Cam said. He didn't say, *How'd you know where I live, you psycho stalker?* He didn't say, *Don't you remember that I don't like you very much?* He simply smiled and nodded—that broad, welcoming smile—as though he'd been expecting her all along, and he said, "I'm really happy to see you."

"You are?" Tears sprang inconveniently to Alexa's eyes. She blinked them back and didn't let her hand reach up to wipe them away.

"Yeah. I've been feeling bad about the fight. Really bad."

"Me too," she whispered.

"I think I was agitated, that's what it was. About—the thing you told me, at Canobie Lake. And I let my agitation get the better of me. I'm really sorry, Alexa. I didn't mean to take it out on you."

"But it's my fault," she said. "That's why I drove up here, because I did a really bad job talking about it the other day—and I got, I don't know, I just got upset over nothing, and it all spun out of control. I came here to apologize. I'm really, really sorry."

Wow. Apologizing felt really good. Unexpectedly good. How come nobody had ever told Alexa that it would feel so good?

"Alexa Thornhill, I accept your apology." Cam spoke ceremoniously. He stood up straight, the way she imagined he might if he were about to accept a golf trophy. "And I'd like to offer you one of my own. I'm truly, honestly sorry for what I said." There was something in his gaze that made her stomach flip, and then flop, and then flip again. "Will you do me the honor of accepting *my* apology?"

Alexa rolled her eyes at the formal language and smiled at the same time she was rolling her eyes; she couldn't help it. "I will," she said. "I definitely will."

"Shake?" He offered his hand and she took it. The skin on Cam's hand was soft, with a slight bump in the palm that might have been a callus from a golf club. He held on to her hand longer than a typical handshake would require and her stomach went through another round of gymnastics. Then Cam said, "Well, what are we waiting for? Welcome to my humble abode." He swung the door wide, and in she went.

In the kitchen stood a woman with short, stylish hair, white shorts, and a peach-colored tank top; she was slicing lemons. She was barefoot and suntanned—older than Alexa's mom, but not so much older.

"Mom, this is Alexa. The one I told you about. Alexa, my mom, Linda. Beware of her, please, she's on vacation from the law firm for two weeks so she's dangerously relaxed."

Linda looked up and smiled, and Alexa said, "Hi, nice to meet you." She tried to study Linda without being obvious about it. She could see where Cam got his dimples.

"Nice to meet you, Alexa!" Linda said. "I'd shake your hand, but, well—" She gestured to the lemons.

"I get it," said Alexa. "We'll just wave." She waved.

The counters sparkled. The refrigerator was industrial-size, with one half devoted to a glassed-in beverage fridge. An upside-down canoe attached to the kitchen ceiling held rows of wineglasses and cocktail glasses. It was all so sunny and good, Alexa felt like there must be a catch. Was a murderer about to jump out of the butler's pantry? A rabid dog loose somewhere on the grounds? A girlfriend hiding upstairs, in the guest quarters? (Surely there were guest quarters.)

"Want to see the house?" said Cam. He was as eager as a little boy. "Did you eat? Are you hungry?"

"No," she said, and he looked crestfallen. "I mean, no, I'm not hungry, yes, I want to see the house." Cam smiled, and she followed him out of the kitchen.

The upstairs hallway formed a loft that overlooked the massively cozy living room. In the living room, there were deer heads mounted on the wall (real?) and a friendly pot-bellied bear made of some sort of metal or stone (definitely not real) standing proudly on one side of the fireplace, one paw extended, like he was giving a tour. A pair of old-fashioned skis was crisscrossed above the stone fireplace, and just below it hung a single snowshoe that was woven like a basket.

There was a bunk room where the bunks were made out of roughly hewn logs and covered with quilts that looked like they were sewn by a thousand perfect grandmothers. In the corner of another bedroom sat a tiny, inoffensive pile of clothing. ("Mine," said Cam. "I'm the only slob in the family.") She should have known: some of the clothing was purple. The only other sign of inhabitance was a book opened facedown on the bed. *Dreams from My Father*. ("Early Obama," said Cam.) She rolled her eyes and tried to hide her smile. This guy was too much.

"I saved the best for last," said Cam. "We're going outside," he called to his mom, who was still in the kitchen, and she called back, "Okay, honey!"

What could be better than everything they'd already seen? Well, the lake, of course. Alexa followed Cam out the back door and down a flagstone path to a semicircular rock wall enclosing the world's most adorable private beach. There were four lounge chairs and a boat garage that was a miniature version of the house, also made of wood and also with a green roof. To the right of the semicircle beach was yet another deck, or really more like a little dock, with two Adirondack chairs and a small table. It was here that Cam led Alexa.

Alexa settled into the chair he indicated. "Cam! This is insane. You know this is insane, right?"

"Yeah," he said. "Sort of." He ducked his head modestly. "This was Mom's present to us when she made partner. I mean, to herself too, sure, but she was trying to make it up to us for being gone so much, working when we were growing up. She worked really hard to get where she is." He began to look wistful—maybe even a little sad, and Alexa found herself putting her hand over his.

"Winnipesaukee," she said. The word came out of her involuntarily, like a hiccup or a spasm.

"This is technically Winter Harbor," Cam said, recovering from his memories of his less-than-perfect childhood, which actually seemed about as close to perfect as a childhood could get. "It feeds into Winnipesaukee just down there." He pointed. "Dad's out on the boat right now, or else I'd take you around. When I do, I can point out Mitt Romney's house, which makes this place look like a two-star-on-Trip-Advisor shack. Hey, want to go grab something to eat in town? Or do you have to get back?"

Alexa thought about Hannah, scooping ice cream for the customers who should be Alexa's. "Nope, there's nothing I need to get back for," she said. When she thought about the rooms full of cozy beds she wanted nothing more than to lay her head down on one of the pillows and curl up under one of the grandmother quilts.

"In that case," said Cam, "I'm going to take you to Wolfe's Tavern, at the inn. It's a famous landmark around here. You'll love it, I promise."

"You don't have to ask me twice," said Alexa. "Some of my favorite places are landmark taverns."

He laughed, and his laugh was a genuine sound, no malice in it, no ill-will or awkwardness. People didn't often laugh at things Alexa said that way, and her face and heart both warmed.

Alexa offered to drive the Jeep but Cam demurred and said they'd take the minivan. "I'm more used to driving in the crush of people and cars that is the heart of Wolfeboro in the summer," he said. "Pedestrians leap out into the roads without warning or provocation."

Alexa figured she must be imagining it when she looked in the minivan's rearview mirror and saw a black SUV. Well, she wasn't imagining the SUV: it was really there, and really black. But she must be imagining that it had come for her: she wasn't even in her own car. Still, the chorus started again in her head, like the far-off beating of a drum. *The bad men, the bad men, the bad men.* She shivered so visibly that Cam reached for the AC button on the console and raised the temperature.

Discuss the concept of fear in your trip to Winnipesaukee, Alexa.

At the tavern, Cam showed Alexa where his father's silver mug was hanging from the ceiling, along with the mugs of all the other people who had completed the one hundred beer challenge; he showed her the moose that people kissed after completing the fifty martini challenge. They shared an order of asparagus fries, the Nashville hot wings, and pork pot stickers.

By the time they returned to the house, someone had put lights on in a few of the rooms; the house looked so welcoming and unblemished that Alexa's throat caught. The house was beautiful, yes, but more than its beauty was the fact that its coziness, its familial feeling stood in contrast to Alexa's own lonelier home, bowing still to grief. As if specifically placed to complete the tableau, from somewhere out on the water came the soulful, haunting cry of a loon.

"That's a yodel," said Cam knowledgeably. "Which is different from a wail. Only the males yodel. Listen—"

Cam stepped closer to her and they leaned together against the minivan, listening. Cam intertwined his fingers with Alexa's and, despite her worry that some of the Nashville hot sauce lingered on them, she was scared to move, almost scared to breathe, lest she destroy the moment. A loon called again.

"That was a wail," he said. "Did you hear the difference? They're talking to each other with the wail, regaining contact. It's pretty amazing how they do that, make sure that they're never lost from each other."

"I love that," said Alexa softly. "I really, really love that."

She didn't want to let go of Cam's hand, but she said she should think about getting home. It was a long drive, and her mother would start to worry. She moved toward her Jeep, still holding on to Cam's hand. *Kiss me*, she was thinking. *Please, Cameron Hartwell, please kiss me before I leave.*

And then he did kiss her; he *was* kissing her. It wasn't like the time she kissed him in his driveway at home, when she took him by surprise, and it was a one-sided thing, a show of power or *chutzpah*. This kissing was mutual, reciprocated and reciprocal, urgent.

"You should go," Cam whispered, when they came up for air, and his voice was gruff and sexy. With his thumb he traced her cheekbone. "Before I do something I might regret."

"Go ahead and do it," she said. "I dare you." She pressed against him—she couldn't help it; her body led her mind. Cam rubbed his hands up and down her upper arms, gently but firmly, like he was warming her after some chill, although even without the glow of the sun the air was perfectly temperate.

"Don't tempt me," he said. "We have the rest of the summer." He opened her driver's-side door and said, "I'll see you soon." He kissed her twice more, once on the forehead and once on the nose, and those types of kisses could have seemed avuncular but actually they were sexy too. She climbed behind the wheel, and he stood in the driveway as she executed a three-point turn and departed, leaving behind something as glimmering and hopeful as a promise.

47.

SHERRI

On this particular day Sherri was not on the schedule at Derma-You so she was able to drop Katie at theater camp herself. After Katie hopped out of the car without so much as a by-your-leave, Sherri saw Rebecca's white Acura—a mirror of her own—three cars behind her in line. As she was pulling out of the turnaround, a text came into her phone. Pull over when you leave. Sherri did as she was told, and Rebecca drove up alongside her and lowered her window. Sherri pressed the button to lower the window on the passenger side, and Rebecca said, "Let's have lunch later."

Sherri hesitated. She'd been spending so much money lately. Katie's summer camps, rent, groceries. Gobs and gobs of ice cream. She hadn't sat down and made herself a real budget. She still had to find a pediatrician for Katie, and a dentist. Possibly dance classes, if she could afford them.

"My treat," said Rebecca.

"Oh no," said Sherri, embarrassed that her thoughts might be transparent. "That's really not necessary. I was just trying to figure out if I had time."

"I insist. You're new to town and you haven't seen all the good places yet. Consider me an ambassador of Newburyport. And anyway, it would be a favor to me. I could use someone to talk to. We'll go to Michael's Harborside. Have you been to Michael's yet?" No,

Sherri had not been to Michael's. "I'll pick you up at noon. No, eleven-thirty. We'll have a better chance of snagging a table on the deck that way."

They got the last open seat on the deck, which overlooked the Merrimack River; across the river, they could see the town of Salisbury, and the deck of another restaurant (which was actually called the Deck). There were boats everywhere: boats docked just below them, boats docked across the river, boats docked to the left and to the right, boats moving and boats tied up. Sherri had never seen so many boats in her life. She thought of the pontoon ride and cringed.

When the waitress—an adorable college-aged girl with a messy bun and a really good tan—came to take their drinks order, Sherri asked for an iced tea.

"Two," said Rebecca. Then: "Actually. You know what? Plot twist. I'll have a sangrita." Sherri looked at the menu; the sangrita was sangria mixed with tequila. "She'll have one too," added Rebecca, pointing at Sherri. "Forget the iced teas."

By the time their food arrived—a lobster roll for Sherri, fish and chips for Rebecca—their drinks were half gone. Sherri's lobster roll was delectable; it was served on a grilled hot dog bun, in what Sherri understood was the New England way, without too much mayo. Rebecca popped a fry into her mouth and when she was done chewing she said, "So here's the thing. I've been seeing someone."

"You *have?*" said Sherri. "That's—exciting?"

"Confusing," said Rebecca. "But also exciting." She took another slug of her sangrita. Already she was faintly flushed. "I'm telling you because—well, because I want to tell someone. And so far I haven't told anyone, not a single soul. I've had to keep it very much under wraps. *Very* much."

"None of your friends?" said Sherri, feeling flattered. "Not Melanie or Brooke or Gina or anyone?"

"No. *Especially* not Gina." Rebecca leaned over her fish and chips platter. She looked furtively around her. "Daniel and I just had a fight about this. Our first real fight! He's tired of sneaking around, acting like we're doing something wrong. But obviously, I can't tell Gina."

This wasn't obvious to Sherri. "Why not?"

"Because," said Rebecca. "Because it turns out that Gina's husband Steve's sister, Veronica, used to be married to Daniel! A long time ago. She cheated on him, and then she left him. She was *not* good to him. Veronica the Cheater." She sat back, took a bite of her fish and looked at Sherri expectantly.

"It seems convoluted," said Sherri. The sangrita had diluted some of her politeness. "Why does that mean you can't tell anyone?"

"It's not that convoluted. Gina is still close to Veronica the Cheater. I used to be really close with Gina. Then came the sleeping bag incident that I told you about at the beach."

"Oh, right. I remember."

"I'm still mad about it!"

"I don't blame you."

"Morgan is still figuring things out, you know, and I don't want to pull the Mom Squad into everything." Rebecca leaned forward again, her voice settling into something approaching a stage whisper. "And now I'm sleeping with basically a Mom Squad relative! Daniel could easily say something to Steve. He's still close to Steve, even though Gina took Veronica the Cheater's side."

"And . . . ?"

"*And*," said Rebecca. "And, Gina has the biggest mouth north of Boston. She would immediately tell, oh I don't know, probably Georgia, who'd tell Esther, and then all of Plum Island would know, and then it would take about forty-five seconds before one of the kids overheard and it got back to Morgan!"

"And?"

"Well, and! And, then Morgan would know. That I'm seeing someone. And. It would crush her, after losing Peter. She's not ready for that. Alexa, *maybe*, almost. But not Morgan! I mean, I know our situations are different, but you must see what I mean? Wouldn't Katie have a hard time if you started dating right away?"

Sherri thought about that. There were so many times when she wasn't sure what was going on behind Katie's whitewashed, cheery exterior. She knew she'd been upset about the Boda Borg party. What if she was upset about other things?

"If I started dating *right away*, yes. But this isn't really right away, is it?"

Around her she heard snippets of conversation: *Patriots preseason* and *couldn't get a plumber in* and *boarding school* and *up to Ogunquit*.

Rebecca looked troubled. "I think I thought you were going to be on my side. Tell me I was right."

"I am on your side," said Sherri. "I am, I promise. But I think Daniel might be right about this one. I don't think you need to hide him."

She watched a wide range of emotions travel their way across Rebecca's face: confusion, defensiveness, maybe even a little fear. A small helping of hope.

"Just consider it," said Sherri. It felt really good to step outside of her own problems and into somebody else's for a moment, or an afternoon; it felt more than good to consider the possibility that she might be helpful. "Think about it," she continued. "And if you need to talk more about it, you know I'm here." She picked up her sangrita and went to town on it.

"Two more," she told the pretty, tan waitress. "One for me, and one for my friend here."

48.

THE SQUAD

What we heard about the Tyler/Alexa breakup was this. We heard that immediately when Tyler got back from Silver Lake toward the end of July he stopped by the Cottage during one of Alexa's shifts. She refused to talk to him while she was working.

One of us had gone to get a Ringer one evening after dinner and witnessed the whole thing. We won't say who it was, and also we would *never* say that the person in question should not have been consuming a Ringer, claiming as she did to be lacto-intolerant and eating low-carb. That is not our place.

The person in the Cottage bought her Ringer, walked up to the beach and back again, and upon returning to her car saw Alexa and Tyler arguing near Alexa's Jeep.

Tyler accused Alexa of ghosting him the whole time he was in Silver Lake, and Alexa shot back that one look at @silvergurl's Instagram told her that it didn't look like Tyler was thinking too much about Alexa.

Alexa then asked Tyler what was the point of continuing their relationship anyway, since he'd be headed to UMass in the fall and she'd be long gone herself. (Alexa was going to Colby, according to Rebecca, but some of us who had watched her video on understanding current market conditions swore that she'd mentioned something about moving to L.A.)

"So you're just, like, giving up on us?" Tyler asked, perplexed. "That's it?"

"That's it," said Alexa. Cucumber cool, according to our source.

We heard that Tyler was insanely angry and that he shouted, "You're going to regret this, Alexa Thornhill! For as long as you live you're going to regret this!"

The person in question waited in the shadows at that point, in case Alexa needed help. Because Tyler was known to have a temper.

Alexa said, "I doubt it," and drove away in her Jeep. Tyler *ran after* the Jeep, but he didn't get very far, because lacrosse season had ended some time ago, and he wasn't in shape.

Okay, it was Gina, all right? If you must know. It was Gina who heard and reported on the whole thing. But please don't tell anybody that we told you that. We promised we'd keep it to ourselves.

Next we heard that Tyler immediately started dating Zoe Butler-Gray, whom he'd taken to Blue Inn earlier in the summer.

We also heard that he'd never taken Zoe Butler-Gray to Blue Inn.

We heard that Zoe Butler-Gray *worked* at Blue Inn and Tyler had given her a ride one day—they were old family friends.

We heard that Blue Inn was closing.

And also that it was expanding.

And that Alexa, with her Silk Stockings money, was one day going to buy Blue Inn outright.

After that, when Alexa wasn't with Cam Hartwell she was often spotted around town with her little sister, Morgan, and Katie Griffin.

Speaking of Cam Hartwell. We did seek out Cam's checkout line when he was working at Market Basket that summer. He was incredibly efficient with the scanner, and managed to make a little conversation at the same time, which wasn't easy. It was a real shame, what he got caught up in later in the summer.

AUGUST

49

REBECCA

"There are way too many people using plastic straws around here," said Morgan severely. "Don't they know that the Pacific garbage patch is now the size of Russia?"

Rebecca, who had been planning on indulging in a cold brew at Commune, respectfully reconsidered. After shopping they were planning to go for poke bowls at Lolo Poke. Rebecca understood the folly of this endeavor—Morgan would get a build-your-own bowl but would build it with only rice and cucumber—but she herself wanted the signature Kai bowl. She'd noticed that since she'd begun dating Daniel her appetite had begun to return, tiptoeing in quietly like a teenager home past curfew.

They were on Pleasant Street, coming out of Pretty Poppy, where Morgan wanted to look at earrings and scrunchies. She was clutching her wallet but in the end had decided against parting with any of her allowance—she was actually rather tightfisted. They had parked Bernice outside, her leash looped around a pole.

"Can we get Bernice one of those dog cones from Harbor Creamery?" asked Morgan. "Just as a little treat?"

"Honey, no," said Rebecca. "You know we have to be careful with her caloric intake. It's not good for her heart or her joints to be overweight."

"Also it's bathing suit season," agreed Morgan. To Bernice she said, "I'm sorry," and rubbed the top of her head. "I know, the struggle is real."

Rebecca was only half listening, because she had caught sight of a calendar item on her phone: first tuition payment for Colby due on the fifteenth of August. She hadn't gotten a bill, though. It must have been sent through the student portal—she'd heard another parent complaining recently about how colleges communicated with students more than parents even though parents were obviously the ones paying. It was ironic, since the complaint about this generation of parents was that they did too much for their children.

When she looked up she saw a figure with a familiar stride moving toward them on the other side of the street. *Daniel.* She tried to catch his eye and shake her head warningly, but he was smiling broadly and had his hand lifted in a wave. *No,* she thought. *No, no, no.* Then she realized he wasn't looking at her at all. "Hello, Ms. Thornhill!" she heard him say in his teacher voice, and he moved on down the street without so much as a glance their way. (Even as she was relieved, Rebecca was also just the teeniest bit insulted.)

"It's Alexa," said Morgan. "Look, Alexa's over there. Let's go over."

"Let's stay here." Rebecca didn't want to risk Bernice recognizing Daniel; Bernice could be capricious and occasionally standoffish, but she and Daniel walked together in Maudslay often enough that she thought Bernice might greet Daniel with a telltale tail thump. A tell*tail* thump.

"She's with a boy," reported Morgan. "She's holding hands with a boy *who isn't Tyler.* She's holding hands with the boy we went to Canobie Lake with."

"She broke up with Tyler," said Rebecca. Alexa had told Rebecca the story—@silvergurl, the argument in the parking lot of the Cottage—but apparently she hadn't told Morgan. She turned. It was all true. Alexa was holding hands with a boy who wasn't Tyler.

"Over here!" Morgan called. "Alexa, come over here!"

Alexa crossed the street, dropping hands with the boy, who followed one step behind. The boy had blond hair. He wore khaki shorts and a golf shirt. In Rebecca's day he would have been called preppy, but she didn't know if that was a term anyone used any longer. Probably not. Most of the terms and phrases she had once used had sailed away on a stiff breeze. Cheesy. Dweeb. Nobody puts baby in a corner.

"Hey, Mom," said Alexa. "Hi, Morgs." She knelt down and greeted Bernice. "This is Cam," she said, gesturing to the boy. She shot Rebecca a look that said, *Not now, no questions,* so Rebecca just smiled and shook the hand Cam held out. Cam looked directly at Rebecca when he greeted her, which she appreciated. Tyler had always looked down.

"Morgan and I are acquainted," Cam says. "Nice to see you again, Morgan."

"We're going to get poke bowls," said Morgan. "If you want to come."

"We just had smoothies," said Cam. "But I love the Kai bowl."

"Did you get straws with your smoothies?" asked Morgan.

"Compostable," said Alexa, and Morgan looked relieved.

"I'm trying to get this one to go to the driving range with me," Cam said, pointing to Alexa. "But so far she's resisting."

Rebecca expected Alexa to roll her eyes at that but when she looked at her daughter, she saw that her face was—well, for lack of a better word, *alight.* Glittering with something familiar. It was only after Cam and Alexa had continued down the road that

Rebecca realized that Alexa's face was a mirror image of how her own often felt since she'd started seeing Daniel: it was the rudimentary, timorous, budding image of genuine happiness.

Morgan, Rebecca, and Bernice crossed the street and paused in front of the dress shop.

"That would look pretty on Alexa," said Morgan, pointing at a dress.

"You think so? It's not really her style, though. Don't you think it's sort of conservative?" The dress had capped sleeves and diagonal stripes in alternating colors, purple, dark green, and black. It was pretty, but it looked a little lawyerly. Alexa generally favored ripped denim shorts and spaghetti-strap tank tops, or, when she dressed up, dresses and tops that only a teenager could pull off. And not just any teenager.

Morgan pursed her lips and studied the dress. "Not for every day," she said finally. "But it would be perfect for Silk Stockings."

"For what?"

"For Silk Stockings. Alexa's YouTube channel."

"I'm sorry," said Rebecca. "For what?"

Morgan looked like a teacher who had to explain a very basic concept to a particularly slow student. "Her YouTube channel," she said. "Where she explains about the stock market and stuff. We all watch it. Me and my friends. Don't you watch it too?"

This was how Rebecca knew she was thrown entirely off guard: she didn't make Morgan repeat her sentence with *my friends and I*.

50.

SHERRI

On a Wednesday in the beginning of August Sherri went to meet her transition counselor, Louise, at the mall. It was really nice, that they gave you a follow-up visit with your counselor to see how you were getting along in your new life. She was trying to find the silver lining in every situation. *My witness protection program comes with free follow-up at no additional cost! I would definitely recommend this program to a friend!*

They met at the food court, at one of the dingy center tables that had been recently vacated by a mother and two little kids and so was strewn with crumbs and streaks of who-knows-what. Louise got to work efficiently with a thin food-court napkin.

Sherri hadn't seen Louise since the grim motel where they'd spent their "transition time," and seeing her now, with the noise of the shopping mall swirling around them, she felt like hugging her. But she knew she couldn't.

"You're looking wonderful!" said Louise, beaming at Sherri. Sherri knew this was a lie. Every time she looked in the mirror she felt like she was living and reliving a bad, bad dream: her hair so plain, her clothing so loose and unflattering. Bags under her eyes big enough to fit shopping into. As soon as she'd saved enough credit, she might avail herself of some of Derma-You's services. "You look like you got a little bit of sun?" Louise said.

"Well, yes," said Sherri. "I—we, we've been to the beach a couple of times." She put a hand to her cheek and thought about Jan's eagle eye on her sunspots.

"Ah!" said Louise. "Yes. The beaches up this way are supposed to be marvelous." She beamed some more. "How are you finding everything . . . socially? And with the house? And the job? I'm so happy to hear about the job. I was really glad we were able to make that happen for you."

Did Louise really want to hear about the intricacies of the social world, about Katie having been left out of the Boda Borg birthday party, about Sherri's gaffes? Did she want to hear about the leaky faucet in the bathroom, and the way Miss Josephine banged on the wall when Katie had one of her nightmares? Was Louise somebody Sherri would be able to call upon, like an old friend, when she had a down moment and needed somebody to lend an ear?

No. Louise was a paid employee of the U.S. Marshals Service, a woman doing her job, a woman who possibly had to miss a son's baseball game or a good friend's birthday so she could travel up here and sit with Sherri in the food court of a mall and make sure she wasn't going to blow her cover.

"All good," said Sherri. "All very, very good. We're really just so grateful for everything, for the fresh start."

"And do you feel as if your new identity has been compromised in any way, Sherri? As though you or Katie have let anything slip?"

"No. Not in any way." Sherri sat up a little straighter when she said this, as if she were back in school, looking for the teacher's praise. What a good little government witness you are, Sherri! (She had not actually been a wonderful student. She'd been solidly average; she had never cared that much about school, truth be told. It turned out she was much better at witnessing.)

Louise stood. Sherri stood also. Louise said, "I'd shake your hand, Sherri, but you know how it is. We're just supposed to be two old friends, meeting up on our lunch hour."

"Of course," said Sherri. "And in fact I do need to get back to work!" They were fairly strict about the lunch hours at Derma-You. What she wanted to say instead to Louise was, "Don't go! Please please don't go!" It felt to Sherri like when Louise left she'd be taking the very last vestige of Sherri's old life with her, leaving only this shell, this brown-haired stranger.

Louise must have seen something in Sherri's face because she did reach across the table and touch her fingers briefly to the top of Sherri's hand.

"It will get easier, in time," Louise said. "Believe me. It will get easier."

51.

THE SQUAD

July had just melted into August when Melanie went to the North Shore mall. She had to return a bathing suit for Molly.

She was heading out of the exit near the food court when she noticed Sherri. Melanie did a double take, not quite sure if it was Sherri or not. It was. Sherri was sitting at one of the food-court tables, across from a woman Melanie had never seen before. The other woman was small, with brown hair, wearing a blue dress with a collar. Neither woman had any food in front of her, according to Melanie. Not that you'd voluntarily eat at the mall food court, right? Not with the Cheesecake Factory right there, not with Burton's Grill! But still. It was odd, to be sitting at that table, without any food.

Melanie told us she got a funny feeling in her stomach. Not like anything bad was going on, exactly. We're not implying anything untoward, or even anything toward. We're just telling a story. We're simply saying that it was an interesting place to see Sherri Griffin. She certainly wasn't hitting Nordstrom, if you know what we mean. The circumstances of her meeting seemed to be somewhat mysterious.

That's all we're saying.

Mysterious.

There might be more to her than meets the eye, texted Melanie to all of us later.

(It could be noted here that Rebecca was left off of this group text, Melanie having wisely understood that Rebecca and Sherri had formed a friendship outside the group. Please see previous entries about the trip to Salisbury Beach, and the girls going off to Canobie Lake, la-di-da, as if nobody else would want to be in on an *annual tradition*. But we digress.)

Melanie followed her "meets the eye" text with a series of emojis: a few different smileys, the little guy with his teeth showing, the LOL and the single tear emoji.

But then, that was Melanie. She never understood how to choose just one emoji to make her point.

52.

ALEXA

Alexa dreamed that she was inside the Pink House. She had passed this house on the way to Plum Island a million times, as a passenger, as a driver, on a bike, once on foot, but she had given very little thought to it. All she knew was that it was widely rumored to be a spite house, built in the 1920s by a man for his ex-wife who demanded a replica of their home as part of their divorce settlement. He put it in the middle of a salt marsh—that was the spite part.

Wasn't it just like a guy, to do something like that for no freaking reason other than that he could?

As far as Alexa was aware, nobody she knew had ever been inside the Pink House, though people had speculated far and wide about what the interior looked like.

The dream was shot like a movie, so that first she saw the outside of the Pink House, with the narrow stone path leading up to it. The camera zoomed in on a close-up of the chipped pink paint, the sign that said GOVERNMENT PROPERTY—NO TRESPASSING! Birds nested in the cupola.

Then the dream Google-earthed her into the center of the house, and up a rickety staircase to a bedroom. The bedroom was decorated with an ornate armoire, a dusty oval full-length mirror and a four-poster bed. There was a woman lying in bed, or a girl. She was dressed in a cobwebby wedding dress. Miss Havisham?

The camera cut again, and now *Alexa* was looking down at the wedding dress. *She* was Miss Havisham. Left at the altar? She fingered the heavy silk. She looked at her arms, which were covered by lace. This couldn't really be happening. Alexa would never, ever choose a long-sleeved wedding dress.

Also, who would leave Alexa Thornhill at the altar? *Please.*

There came a gentle rapping on the door to the bedroom, and before Alexa could say, "Come in," the door opened and a face poked around the doorway. It was Cam. He surveyed the room, grinning. He said, "I need to get you out of here, Alexa. This place is lousy with asbestos, you know."

"How do you know that?" asked Alexa.

"It's what I wrote my college essay about," said Cam. "It's what got me into St. Mike's."

"This house?"

"Yes. This house is iconic. This house has inspired the imaginations of so many people."

In the dream, this all seemed completely plausible. In the dream, this was an acceptable topic for a college essay.

Cam was still talking. "Did you know, for example, that because this house is owned by the Parker River Wildlife Refuge, which is part of the U.S. Fish and Wildlife Service, it can't be sold for money, only traded for other property? Did you know that snowy owls and hawks nest in the cupola? No? You didn't? Did you know that it was fully occupied until the early two thousands even though it's never had running water?" Alexa shook her head. She didn't know any of this.

"Well, Alexa," said Cam. "Let's get you out of here." He held out his hand to Alexa, and she took it. She swung one foot over the edge of the bed, and then the other. She was barefoot, and her toes were painted a pearly pink. (Despite the long-sleeved wedding dress, her wedding shoes must have been open-toed.) There was a mirror above the heavy dark dresser opposite the bed, and she let go of Cam's hand and approached it with trepidation. She cleaned the dust off the mirror with the sleeve of her wedding dress. (The sleeves had come in handy after all.) She expected to see that she had aged years or maybe decades. She took a deep breath before looking.

There were cobwebs in her hair, but otherwise she looked exactly the same. This was an enormous relief. She turned to Cam and asked, "Why'd you leave me at the altar?"

"Leave you?"

"Yes." She gestured to her wedding dress.

"I didn't leave you."

"You didn't? Who did?"

"*You* left *me*."

"I did?"

He nodded.

"I'm sorry," she whispered. "That's so rude. I didn't mean to."

"Oh, I think you did," said Cam. "I'm really pretty sure that you did."

"Are you mad?"

"Of course not. It's not a big deal. Just a silly wedding!" He took her hand again and led her out of the bedroom and toward the landing.

They were about to walk down the stairs when suddenly the staircase crumbled beneath them, turning to pieces of dust and rubble.

"Darn it," said Cam pleasantly. "Sorry about that, Alexa. I was trying to get you out before that happened. Oh well! I guess you can't win them all."

From the stair landing they could see down to the front door. Out of nowhere came a sharp series of raps on the door.

"Who could that be?" Alexa asked Cam.

"Oh, it's probably the bad men."

"The who?"

"The bad men," he said. He turned toward her and smiled, but there were no teeth in his mouth. "The bad men are coming for you," he said. "I told them you'd probably be here."

She woke sweating, clutching *Stock Investing for Dummies*.

53.

REBECCA

Rebecca peeled her eyes from the screen. Her daughter was a . . . YouTube personality? She perused the comments following the three videos she had watched. On each video there were many, many comments—dozens! Hundreds! One of the first comments on each video came from someone called jt76. *Love how succinct this is!* Also: *Great explanation of balancing risk and reward. You're so talented!*

There were a lot of other comments too, most encouraging, some obnoxious. But the thing that stood out the most to Rebecca was the number of views: Alexa's videos averaged in the *tens of thousands!* The highest viewed video Rebecca saw had been viewed *thirty-seven thousand times!*

A *lot* of people were watching Alexa Thornhill do her thing online.

Then there was this. Not a single one of the dresses Alexa was wearing in the videos looked familiar to Rebecca. Morgan was exactly right: they were more conservative than Alexa's usual garb. They were very pretty! But where had they come from? Where did they live?

Granted, Alexa was almost preternaturally self-sufficient. She'd been doing her own laundry since the age of nine, and now that she could drive, Rebecca supposed it was possible that she had her own account at Anton's dry cleaning. How much money was she *making* from this YouTube thing? And how far apart had she and Alexa grown, that Alexa could have this whole identity, this whole life, this whole *wardrobe,* that Rebecca knew nothing about? In the past this was something she would have taken immediately to Peter, of course, and failing that, to one of the Mom Squad members. Probably Gina! Before the sleeping bag incident, Gina would have been happy to lend an ear, and Rebecca would have trusted her. But now—now the earth had shifted beneath her feet in all kinds of unsettling ways, and now she had nobody. Well, not nobody.

She pulled up Daniel's number on her phone and typed out a text.

Can you meet me tomorrow at Maudslay? I want to tell you something.

She held her breath, but the reply came almost immediately. I would love to.

After that, the three dots, then another text came in.

I miss you.

She didn't even hesitate before texting back, I miss you too.

The next day they did their usual thing, which was to park on opposite ends of the parking lot and meet up once they'd gotten on their way. They usually walked down the road a bit before entering the park; Rebecca liked to go in by the Gates of Hell rather than via the more common entrance, by the rangers' cottage at the beginning of the property.

"First things first," said Rebecca. "Daniel, I'm sorry. I'm really sorry about that whole thing at the tall ships." She took a deep breath and turned to face Daniel. "I'm sorry I told you that you need to live in a box."

Bernice gave them a baleful look, as if to say, Are we walking, or are we spending all day apologizing?

"No, *I'm* sorry," said Daniel. "I need to let you do things in your own time. I didn't mean to pressure you, or rush you. I understand that our situations are different, I do. I can wait until you're ready, Rebecca. It turns out that being in a box with you is way better than being outside the box without you."

"It is? Are you sure?"

"*Way* better," said Daniel. "Way, way better."

Just like that, an enormous weight lifted itself from Rebecca's shoulders and disappeared into the summer morning air. *Just like that.* Maybe everything didn't have to be so hard after all.

The Gates of Hell were wrought-iron gates that used to lead to one of the mansions on the property, back when the mansions still stood. There was a rumor that the Gates were haunted, and that late at night you could see the heads of decapitated family members on the spikes, even though no murders had ever taken place on the estate to anyone's knowledge. Nevertheless, Rebecca shivered and tried not to look at the gates.

"Are you worried about the decapitated heads again?" Daniel asked.

"Maybe a little," she admitted.

Daniel glanced up. "If we saw the ghosts of murdered people, I would do everything in my power to protect you." He stepped behind Rebecca and wrapped his arms around her waist and rested his chin on the top of her head. This was one of the things about dating someone new after years and years with the same person: you got to see how your body would fit with someone else's, and sometimes there were unexpected surprises in that. Peter had been very tall, and would have had to stoop to rest his chin on Rebecca's head. It was never worth the effort.

Immediately Rebecca felt disloyal for thinking that about Peter. He would have stooped for her all day long if she'd wanted him to.

They passed through the gates and began to walk along the dirt path.

Daniel tapped the side of his thigh for Bernice to catch up— she tended to lag, especially early in the morning. She was not a morning person. Obviously she wasn't a person at all.

"Oh!" Rebecca said. "Here's what I wanted to tell you. You're not going to believe this. I just found out that Alexa has this entire YouTube channel called Silk Stockings. She dresses up in pretty, tasteful clothes, and she sits in this chair in her bedroom, and she explains things. Terms. Economic terms, things about the stock market."

"Oh yeah?" said Daniel. He stopped and turned toward Rebecca. "Like what sorts of things?"

Rebecca named the topics she remembered: stop-loss orders, crypto currency investments. "Blockchain, maybe?" she said. "Is that a thing?"

"It's a thing," Daniel said. He was smiling to beat the band.

"What?" she said. "What are you so cheerful about over there?"

"Nothing. Just that *I* taught her a lot of those things."

"You did?"

"Sure thing. Intro to the Stock Market. Remember I told you I had her in class?" He looked proud, spine straight, eyes eager and alert, like Bernice when she'd done something special and was waiting for a reward.

"Wow," said Rebecca. "Well, I think you did a really good job. She seems like an actual expert. But—" She paused. "But don't you think it's terrible, that I didn't know about it? It makes me feel like such a bad mother. I found out from *Morgan,* of all people. I used to be the one who told Morgan things that she didn't know, and now Morgan is schooling me. My own daughter." They continued along the path to where it curved toward the formal Italian and rose gardens, which were part of the original estate and were still kept up by the park service. In these gardens roses and other flowers grew willfully, abundantly.

"I don't think it's terrible at all," said Daniel. "I think it's the opposite of terrible. I think it's fantastic. Really. Teenagers do all sorts of things without their parents' knowledge. You know that."

"I know," said Rebecca morosely. "I was a teenager once too."

"Much of it way, way worse than secretly learning about the stock market. Believe me. I've been teaching high school since the dawn of the Internet. And at the risk of sounding self-referential, I couldn't be happier. I can't wait to see some of these videos myself!"

Daniel's unbridled enthusiasm put Rebecca at ease, and she reached down and unclipped Bernice's leash from her collar, allowing her to indulge in some illegal off-leash walking. "I guess you're right," she said. "No, I don't guess you're right. You *are* right. You are. There's no harm done, right? And it's just for now. She probably won't keep up with any of this once she leaves for college."

"Exactly," said Daniel. "I think that's exactly right."

"But what do I *do*? Do I confront her about it? Do I put some limits on her?"

She could tell Daniel was thinking long and hard about this because furrows appeared on his forehead. "You know what? I wouldn't. I'd give it some time, a week or two, maybe more. Does she seem happy?"

Rebecca thought about seeing Alexa and Cam walking pleasantly down Pleasant Street; she thought about how Alexa was helping Sherri out whenever she needed it—sometimes, Sherri had told her, free of charge! "Happier than I've seen her in a long time," she admitted.

"Then let it be, for now. Give yourself some time to figure out how *you* feel about it. When the time feels right, have a talk with Alexa. That's what I would do. Wait here for a sec," he said.

Daniel climbed the few small steps to the rose gardens, and Rebecca stayed behind with Bernice, who was sniffing around the small pet cemetery, where the estate owners had purportedly buried favorite horses and dogs. Rebecca at first imagined that Bernice was paying homage but then she saw that actually she was relieving herself.

Every time Rebecca was in Maudslay she thought about all of the lives spent on the grounds, where once people had lived grandly and where now there remained only a few scattered outlines of structures: parts of the stone foundation of one of the homes, a thicket-choked understructure of a swimming pool, a root cellar. These surroundings at once gave Rebecca a sense of peace and well-being and shot her through with a reminder of the smallness of her life in the vast historical landscape, where one day they would all be rubble and dust.

Wow, that was morbid. She looked up to see Daniel coming toward her with a rose plucked from one of the bushes.

"A rose for my rose," he said.

"That's illegal!" said Rebecca, delighted and horrified. She looked around to see if a ranger might be lurking. First her dog had desecrated the pet cemetery, and now this. "This is a state park! You're going to get us arrested."

He tucked the rose behind her ear and kissed her, in front of God and Bernice and everyone else. "I don't care," he said. "It's worth it. I've missed you, Rebecca Coleman. I'm glad you've come back to me." Then he said, "Are you free today? Maybe we can find a summer adventure."

54

ALEXA

Alexa's mother rapped on her door at nine in the morning, which was about ninety minutes earlier than Alexa generally considered acceptable, and then opened the door without being invited to do so. Alexa, who had been sleeping deeply, raised her head and said, "What?"

"I'm sorry to wake you," said her mother. "But I have to be gone for a lot of the day and Morgan will be at loose ends. Do you think you could keep an eye on her?"

Alexa had the day off from the Cottage. She flopped back on her pillow and pulled the comforter over her face. "Okay," she said, her voice muffled by the comforter. "I can do that. But where are you going?"

"Oh, here and there," said her mother. Alexa felt her mother pause in the doorway but she didn't move her head from the comforter. "Alexa? Are you sure you're okay? About Tyler and . . . Cam? Is there anything you want to talk about? Or maybe something not related to Tyler and Cam? Just . . . anything at all? You can talk to me about anything, you know."

"Nope," said Alexa. "I'm good."

Since her trip to Cam's lake house, Alexa and Cam were hanging out a lot. They did an old-person walking tour through Maudslay State Park, where the rangers told them all about the home that used to sit on the grounds. They kayaked down the Merrimack all the way to Amesbury and back. Seen through Cam's eyes, even this tired town had begun to send out fresh green shoots of appeal or attraction. Her mother's request to spend the day with Morgan failed to provoke the irritation it might have earlier in the summer. Was there a chance that spending time with Cam had made her *nicer? Was niceness contagious?*

Her mother was still standing there. "Maybe *do* something with Morgan, okay? Don't just let her sit around on her phone."

"Got it," said Alexa. She peeked out from under the comforter. "No sitting around on her phone." In fact she thought it might be fun to do something special with Morgan, which was not a thought she would have had in June. It was therefore confirmed. Niceness *was* contagious.

"I can leave you some money to go to lunch if you want. A burger and a shake at Lexie's, maybe?"

"Not necessary," mumbled Alexa. Her bank account was, to put it mildly, robust. Besides that, Lexie's was great, but a burger and a shake seemed sort of ordinary. If she wanted to show Morgan a good time, she was going to take her someplace nicer. She was going to get her an experience, not just a burger.

Her mother was *still* standing there, as if she had something more to say.

"*What?*" said Alexa irritably.

"Nothing," said her mother. She looked at Alexa for another long moment and then she departed, closing the door behind her.

Alexa decided on the Deck, because it was a beautiful day, and they could sit outside and look at the water. She let Morgan ride in the front seat of the Jeep, even though technically she was supposed to keep her in the back because she was still too small to withstand the crush of the airbags should they deploy. But they didn't have to drive far, and they didn't have to drive on the highway, so Alexa felt okay about it. "Don't tell Mom," she told Morgan.

"Of course not," said Morgan, sounding like a little adult. She took a deep breath as she buckled the seat belt across her spindly chest and looked around like she was rounding the Cape of Good Hope for the first time.

They crossed Merrimac Street and Alexa immediately saw the line of cars stopped ahead of her. "Go figure," she muttered. The drawbridge was on its way up, which meant they would sit here for at least five minutes, maybe ten. She could see the Deck from here; she could practically taste the street corn with cojita cheese. She tapped her fingers on the steering wheel, thrumming with impatience. If they'd left two minutes earlier or eleven minutes later, they could have avoided this.

But Morgan said, "Yess! I love it when the bridge goes up," and her enthusiasm reminded Alexa of Cam, who in this situation would say something corny and soothing, like, *That's okay, we've got nowhere to be.* Alexa had to admit, it was a fairly majestic sight, the view from this bridge, with the sun waltzing off the water. To their right, dozens and dozens of boats were docked in the slips at the harbor, with more out on moorings, and the river extended beyond the boats, all the way to the open ocean.

They watched as the mast of a grand sailboat cleared the bridge, and Morgan let out a cheer. The bridge eased down—it looked like it was exhaling—and the line of cars moved ahead.

A girl a year behind Alexa was at the hostess stand at the Deck, and two girls from her class were waiting tables. One of them came up to their table: a hard-core soccer and lacrosse player named Maya. Alexa gave her a *hey*.

"Let's put our phones away," Alexa said to Morgan. "Shall we?" Her mother would be proud of that. Alexa held out her hand and

Morgan relinquished the phone—reluctantly, because she was playing some online game against one of her little friends. "Your generation is totally addicted," said Alexa. "I worry about you guys." She was kidding, but only a little bit.

Alexa ordered the fish tacos with the street corn. Morgan first claimed to want a grilled cheese from the kids' menu but Alexa nixed that right away. They were in coastal Massachusetts! In summertime! Grilled cheese was not a native dish. Morgan sighed and ordered the fried fish plate. Better. The fish was cod, and local. Morgan requested no straws for either of them.

When Morgan lifted her arm to shield her face from the sun, Alexa could see that underneath her Ivivva tank top she was wearing a sports bra. *A training bra,* their mother called those, embarrassingly, and Alexa felt a surge of tenderness for her little sister, because she seemed to be training for a race for which she hadn't yet registered. How long had it been since she and Morgan had done something alone together? Too long.

"Did you break up with Tyler?" Morgan asked. "Or did he break up with you?"

"Getting right to it, huh?" Alexa sipped her straw-less water.

"Well, did you?"

"Technically, yes," said Alexa. Their food arrived, and for a few minutes they were busy and silent, eating. Alexa offered the street corn to Morgan, who shook her head violently.

"I don't like Tyler that much," said Morgan.

"No? Why not?"

Morgan dipped a fry into ketchup and considered this question. "I just don't think he seems very nice all the time."

Alexa was almost seven when Morgan was born. The year Morgan turned six and entered elementary school Alexa was already ensconced at the middle school, wearing a bra and getting noticed for her well-put-together outfits. That was the year the crop top came back, and Alexa got dress-coded more than once. She'd come home from school, tugging off the T-shirt they'd given her at the nurses' office, and there Morgan would be, wearing her certified Disney Anna dress and wig and singing "Do You Want to Build a Snowman?" at the top of her phlegmatic lungs.

In one year Morgan will be the age Alexa was when she first had a boyfriend (an ill-fated romance, please don't remind her); in two, the age when she sneak-watched *Fifty Shades of Gray* with Destiny. (Their mothers had dropped them at Cinemagic for what the mothers thought was the evening showing of the second Sponge-Bob movie: *Sponge Out of Water.*) She supposed she hadn't given her little sister enough credit for maturing all of these years—for having her own, sometimes possibly anguished, interior life.

"No," agreed Alexa. "He's not very nice all the time."

"Is that why you broke up with him?"

After *Fifty Shades*, emerging from the lobby into the parking lot, Alexa and Destiny were shell-shocked, unable to meet each other's eyes. Neither would ever admit it, but both wished they had stuck with SpongeBob. Sometimes, after all, innocence was a blessing.

"Yes," she said. "And you should do the same, if you ever have a girlfriend or a boyfriend or anyone in your life who doesn't treat you well. Okay?"

"Okay," said Morgan.

"I mean it for real, Morgs. Seriously. That's really important, okay? You have to take care of yourself. Promise me."

"I promise," said Morgan.

Alexa had so many other things she wanted to say to Morgan: don't grow up too fast, stay true to yourself, think for yourself and talk for yourself and don't turn down dessert, and show your body if you want to but not if you don't. "You know what I do if I find myself in a tricky situation?" she asked.

"What?" Morgan was all ears—well, and elbows and collarbone and ketchup-smeared face, but mostly ears.

"I ask myself what Peter would say to do. I find I really don't go wrong if I do that."

Morgan stared at the water for a moment, taking this in, and tears filled her eyes. One dropped onto the napkin in front of her, and then she nodded. "I like that," she said. "I'm going to do that too." After a beat she said, "You know who I do like?"

"Who?"

"That one who came to Canobie Lake with us. The one you were holding hands with on the street the other day."

"Cam?"

"Yes. Cam."

They ate and looked at the water. The sun shifted and Morgan started to squint.

"I like him too," Alexa said at last.

"Maybe he should be your boyfriend."

Morgan's features had been changing steadily over the course of the summer and probably before that. There were new mature hollows in her cheekbones that offered a preview of what her face would look like when she was a teenager and then an adult. Her eyebrows, once they were professionally shaped, would be stunning (those came, frustratingly, from Peter; Alexa would have loved to have them too), and after Dr. Pavlo, the orthodontist who was responsible for Alexa's smile, worked his magic on the space between her front teeth, Morgan's smile too would be irresistible.

"Maybe. Or maybe nobody should."

The rest of the meal they ate in companionable silence, and when Soccer Maya dropped the check, Alexa tipped extravagantly, just because she could.

55.

REBECCA

Brooke always sent actual paper invitations for her end-of-summer party, which Rebecca had to admit was classy. Most people believed that paper invitations deserved to go the way of the milk truck and earbuds with wires. Even so, when she opened the envelope her stomach clenched and she let out an involuntary *Ugh*.

Last year she had skipped the party altogether, and had been excused because she was still technically in mourning. This year, mourning would be a harder sell. But she didn't want to go alone. She was tired of going places alone. She wanted to bring Daniel. At the same time, she didn't want to bring Daniel.

Rebecca could write the script for the whole evening right now. There would be a signature cocktail that people would drink too fast. Eventually, some drunk husband would jump in the pool. There would be at least one scene of marital discord—or possibly two. An unhashed-through argument between friends might make its way to the surface.

Brooke's children would watch all of the madness from their bedrooms windows, and the sight would cement in their minds the image of adults behaving badly, which they would then lay out as part of their defense when they were caught drinking or vaping weed in high school or (God forbid) middle school.

On a more positive note, the food would be superb, and there would be dancing.

Was that a positive note, though? Did anybody *really* need to see people over forty shaking it on the dance floor? Well, it was a note anyway.

I'll be there! She hesitated, then scrawled on the card, *Plus one.*

56.

THE SQUAD

Naturally Brooke told us that Rebecca had included a Plus One on her RSVP to the end-of-summer party.

Who was it? we wondered.

Esther said Rebecca would bring her Mystery Man. But Tammy and Melanie got all over her for that. If Rebecca had a man, why would he be a mystery? We'd never judge her for having a new man! We wouldn't judge her for anything! We're her *friends!*

57.

ALEXA

"Ready?" said Cam.

"Ready for what?" Alexa was wary. The last time Cam showed up at her door and asked if she was ready, he was on his way to pick her up for a brisk hike straight up Mount Major.

"For the water stop. Remember? Yankee Homecoming Ten-Miler? Mile five? I volunteered us. I'm positive you said yes."

Alexa groaned. "I'm pretty sure I didn't."

"You did," Cam confirmed. "You definitely said yes."

Yankee Homecoming was the big summer event in Newbury-port. It lasted a week, with different events every day, and would culminate with fireworks on Saturday followed by a parade on Sunday. The Yankee Homecoming race was on the Tuesday evening before the fireworks and comprised a 5K and a ten-miler; it was almost always unbearably humid during the race.

"Can't we at least do mile nine?" asked Alexa. Mile nine would be almost at the finish. It would be so much more interesting to watch people who were really close to achieving their goal than those who were seriously considering dropping out halfway through, just before the hills.

"Nope," said Cam. "Mile five. It's the best mile. It's where people really need encouragement because they're starting to falter. Here, put this on." He handed her a shirt that said RACE VOLUNTEER on the back. Alexa couldn't remember the last time she volunteered for anything, or wore an ill-fitting cotton T-shirt, but she put the shirt on. It hung down to her knees. "Sorry," said Cam. "They were out of smalls by the time I picked them up. I had to get large for both of us. If it helps, you look hot in that."

"It doesn't help," muttered Alexa, even though actually it did, a little.

Once they were set up with their supplies, Alexa peered down Merrimac Street, which was an asphalt wasteland. The sun was so bright and so high she couldn't imagine running to the corner and back. She wished she'd thought to wear a hat. Most of the volunteers were wearing hats, and Alexa knew a brim suited her. Cam's hat was from the Newburyport Brewing Company and had a picture of a greenhead on it, for the Greenhead IPA. The green of the hat did something wondrous to his brown eyes. She knew that if she asked, Cam would give her the hat right off his head. But if the old Alexa would have asked for the hat, the new Alexa would let Cam retain it. Moral growth!

After some time there rose a stir of excitement as the lead runner came toward them. There was a slight bend in the road before the five-mile point, and with the sun and the undulating heat he looked almost like a mirage. The people lining the street cheered. One volunteer held out a cup of water, but Cam leaned over to Alexa and said conspiratorially, "The first ten guys never take water. They're too focused. They can't break pace."

He was right, but after the fastest people went by and the pace became somewhat normal, people were happy to have the water. Some of them even paused to say thank you, or at least to grunt pleasantly. Cam had prepared a string of helpful platitudes, and he said them over and over. "You can do it!" he said. "You're stronger than you think you are! You've made it halfway! The worst is over!"

Alexa wasn't sure that the worst was over at all (wasn't a big hill coming right after this very water stop?) but still she appreciated Cam's optimism and she could tell that the runners did too. She found herself getting a little caught up in the excitement. When one man went for the cup and missed, spilling it all over Alexa, she jogged a few steps after him with a fresh cup. He was so grateful that she couldn't help herself: she panted, "The worst is over!" She ran out of breath before she had a chance to add, "You can do it," but she figured he got the point.

The number of runners decreased from hordes to large groups and eventually to a slow trickle. After some time the pace slowed even more and the stragglers started to pass by. Many of them stopped outright to take the water, and some walked a little before recommencing their slow jog. And then Cam said, "Isn't that Tyler?"

"Where?" said Alexa. And, "I doubt it." Tyler was not a distance runner. However, as the figure Cam was pointing to grew closer she did recognize something in his gait (Tyler was the tiniest bit bowlegged) and in the musculature of the shoulders.

"Ugh," she said. "It *is* Tyler." Instinctively she held out a cup of water. She wasn't going to shirk her duties because of a personal issue.

When Tyler got to her, he stopped. It was almost as if he knew Alexa would be here, as if he'd run five miles just to get to her.

"Hey," she said uncertainly. "Good job?" She smiled.

Tyler did not smile back, nor did he take the water Alexa held out. Alexa was getting a bad vibe. An angry vibe, the vibe Tyler gave off when the lacrosse team lost a big game; the vibe that appeared when it took him three tries to pass the test for his learner's permit. (He twice got stuck on the question about how far ahead high beams and low beams let you see.)

"I didn't know you were running," Alexa said.

"I just jumped in with some of the guys at mile three. I didn't want to pay the entry fee. How would you know if I was running or not? And who's that?" He nodded his head toward Cam. Cam was busy refilling water cups from gallon jugs at the far end of the table.

"Nobody," said Alexa. "Don't you want to keep running? To finish the race?"

"I know who he is," said Tyler. "Don't worry, I know exactly who he is." And then he turned his head away, and then back toward her, and if she hadn't actually been there she never would have believed it, because Tyler spit on her. Like, *actually spit.* On Alexa's arm. There was a *gob of spit* on Alexa's arm.

"What the hell?" cried Alexa.

"Oh, sorry," said Tyler. "My bad." And then he smiled a smile so awful that Alexa's blood ran cold despite the hot evening. She could not believe she ever ever ever was attracted to Tyler. She couldn't believe she'd bought him the Bluetooth headphones he was too cheap to buy for himself the previous Christmas, and that she very seriously considered sleeping with him after junior prom, and probably would have had he not passed out in the back of Lucas Spaulding's father's BMW.

Tyler broke back into a slow jog and continued along the course, rounding the corner that led to the hill. Alexa wiped her arm with the bottom of her volunteer shirt (she was grateful now for all of the extra material) and walked back toward the water table. She wanted to cry—she felt shocked and violated and frankly she couldn't believe what had just happened—but with everything in her she forced the tears to remain in her eyes.

"Did he just *spit on you?*" asked Cam.

"No," said Alexa, because she was too embarrassed to say yes.

"Really? Because it looked like he spit on you." Cam's mouth was set in a severe line.

"I think he was just, like, spitting out water or something,"

explained Alexa. "You know how runners are." (She had no idea
how runners were, and they both knew it.)

"You want me to go after him?" asked Cam.

"No," she said. "Of course not. Don't be crazy." For one thing,
Tyler had rounded the bend on Spofford and was now suffering
his way up the hill. Or he had dropped out. Either way, he was
gone. For another, Alexa thought that Tyler could turn Cam into
pulp with a flip of his massive paw if he wanted to. She filled more
water cups from one of the gallon jugs even though they probably
had plenty. Her hand was shaking, and she couldn't get the water
into the cups without spilling it.

When the last runner had gone by, the volunteers fanned out
into the road and picked up the empty cups. There was something
very team-oriented about the whole process that Alexa liked, even
if they were literally clearing garbage from the street.

"That guy's a jerk," Cam said sternly as he held a giant garbage
bag open for Alexa to dump the cups into. "I can't believe you
dated him."

"I can't believe it either," said Alexa.

"Well, we all make mistakes," said Cam. "I'm just glad you've
come to your senses." He grinned at her, and then he leaned down
and kissed her. Just like that.

"What's that for?" she asked, smiling.

"I just wanted to say thank you," he said. "For being such a
good volunteer."

She rolled her eyes. "You kiss all the volunteers like that?"

He nodded. "It's what keeps them coming back year after year.
It's why we have such a robust presence at mile five." The way he
smiled at her made Alexa's stomach do that flippy-floppy thing,
and she tried to concentrate on that, instead of the place on her
arm where Tyler's spit had landed.

58.

SHERRI

Sherri took a sponge to the stovetop in the kitchen on Olive Street. In her old life she'd hardly ever touched a sponge—the cleaning ladies did all of the dirty work. But she'd grown up as a regular kid with regular chores: she knew how to clean. This stove, though, was almost too much: the marks around the burners had probably been made by years and years of renters, of spilled pasta water and stove-top popcorn.

Sherri took a break and leaned against the counter for a moment, and that's when she heard Katie's quick feet down the stairs, rounding the corner into the kitchen. She was holding her phone, and her eyes were shiny with excitement.

"There's fireworks," she said. "Tonight, for Yankee Homecoming, at the waterfront. Can I go, Mom? With Morgan and the other girls? Can I please go?"

Sherri remembered the awful night on the pontoon, the *pop pop pop* of the fireworks she couldn't see, the panic rising in her chest. "Oh, Katie. By yourselves? Or with a grown-up?"

"By ourselves. All the girls are going, it's totally safe, please, Mom, please please please. *Please.*"

"No," said Sherri. "Absolutely not." The risks were too great. The dark, the crowds, little girls alone. Anybody could grab Katie. Anybody. "I'm sorry, honey. You know I can't let you do that. You know we have some rules that the other kids don't have. I don't want you wandering around downtown in the dark. It's not safe."

There was a split second of silence, and then Katie's face took on a new, hard, mean expression, and she said, "Daddy would let me go. And it's your fault that he's not here to let me."

This was the first time in all this time Katie had said that. It was almost like she'd been saving it up, the single arrow in her quiver, and now she'd released it. Sherri took a deep breath and let the pain from the shot settle. She wanted to say, *Daddy is the reason you can't go.* She wanted to say, *Daddy is the reason we live* here, *and my hair looks like* this, *and I'm working as a receptionist.* But she couldn't say any of that, because that wasn't her job. And however great her own pain was, Madison Miller's family's pain was greater, like a screw pushed through a fingernail, again and again, for the rest of their lives.

"Maybe," she said. "Maybe he would. But he's not in charge. I'm in charge."

"Well, I wish he was in charge," said Katie angrily. "I miss him." Then, more quietly, "Do you miss him?"

There were a lot of complicated answers to that question. Louise the counselor had said, "Let Katie talk about Bobby on her terms, not yours. She's going to need that." Sherri crawled out of the tangled web of her own feelings and said, "Sometimes. What do you miss about him?"

Katie's face changed again, became softer. "There was the Father-Daughter dance at the club a long time ago, remember?"

Sherri had let herself forget about that, a snippet slipping through her fingers and then gone. "I do," she said, letting the memory resurface. She'd bought Katie a new dress, bright blue, with a dropped waist and small embroidered flowers in a row over each shoulder. Bobby had worn his best suit. Sherri had done Katie's hair in a fancy updo with curly tendrils hanging down, and when Bobby had seen her he'd said, "Nobody told me I was lucky enough to take the princess to the ball!" Katie had been six then, with one front tooth missing and the other just starting to grow in, a little stub. Somewhere in the houseful of things they'd left behind was a picture of the two of them before the dance, standing on the porch, Katie's smile as wide as the day was long.

Katie was now fully absorbed in the recollection. "That dance was so much fun. Daddy was a good dancer. He showed me how to do the tango. Nobody else was doing the tango, but we did. We took up the whole dance floor, and everybody was looking at us. I remember he wore his fancy cologne, and he was the handsomest dad there, and all of the other girls were jealous. Even though they didn't say it, I could tell. And they served Shirley Temples and these little square cakes that were so small but each one was frosted like a wedding cake." She sighed. "Are you mad at me for remembering that, now that Daddy is bad?"

"Oh, Katie-kins," said Sherri. "Of course not. That's the hard part, that's the important part. People who do bad things aren't one hundred percent bad. Hardly *anybody* is one hundred percent bad. But what Daddy did was so bad, he had to go to jail for it. It's okay for you to miss him, and to love him anyway." It took everything Sherri had to say that.

Katie took this in. "Okay," she said finally. "Okay then." She sighed again, and this time the sigh carried the weight of the world. "But I still want to go to the fireworks. Please, Mom. *Please.* I didn't get invited to Casey's sleepover and not the Boda Borg party either and I did get invited to this, I don't want to miss it." Her lower lip began to tremble.

"What do you mean? What sleepover?"

"Last week."

"How'd you know about it, then?"

"I saw a picture." Then in a whisper, "They tagged me."

"But you weren't there. Why'd they tag you?"

Katie shrugged, and then Sherri got it.

"Oh, honey," she said. She opened her arms and Katie went into them. "That was a crappy thing for them to do. I'm sorry." Sherri breathed in the scent of Katie's just-washed hair.

"I know we have to be careful, Mom. I get it. But does that mean we can never be normal again? Can we never just, like, go places without worrying?" Her voice broke. "Can I never go to the fireworks?"

Sherri sighed. It sort of *did* mean Katie should never go to the fireworks. "What about if I go with you? I won't go *with* you with you, I'll just stay nearby. You won't even know I'm there. I promise."

"*No*," said Katie. "No. Definitely not. The whole point is to go with the girls." She pushed herself away from Sherri, out of the kitchen, and then Sherri heard her feet go up the stairs.

As soon as Katie was out of earshot, Sherri called Rebecca. Rebecca said all the right things. She said that she was of two minds about it herself; she said that it did get crowded down there, and that the fireworks drew people from all over. And then she said the best thing of all. "I'll talk to Alexa. And if she's free, I'll have her meet up with them and keep an eye on them. Would that help?"

59.

ALEXA

Alexa was perusing the Yankee Homecoming sidewalk sales when she got a text from her mother about keeping an eye on Morgan and a bunch of her friends during the fireworks that night. Old Alexa would have politely declined this offer, but this Alexa, the Alexa who was trying on her Nice Big Sister shoes to see if they still fit after a long time in the closet, texted back No problem.

Then came another text: Katie's Mom is worried.

The bad men, thought Alexa. Her heart thumped.

I'm on it, she replied.

It was easy enough to locate Morgan and Company, because there were about a zillion of them clumped up by the playground, doing that awkward in-between thing tweens do. Oh, eleven.

Then again, what the hell age wasn't in-between? Twenty-five, Alexa decided. When you were twenty-five you must feel as though you were exactly the age you were meant to be. Alexa couldn't wait to be twenty-five. She'd live in a funky bungalow in L.A., and she'd decorate it with succulents and tasteful throw pillows, and she'd press her own juice, which she would drink standing on her deck that would overlook some sort of canyon.

Aside from Morgan and Katie, she couldn't pick any of the other girls out by name. They all had similar sandy blond hair and short shorts and skinny prepubescent colt legs. The big lights around the baseball field next to the park were all on, so it was practically as bright as daylight in this area even though the sun was almost down.

Then Katie saw her and waved and Alexa couldn't help it, that warmed the cockles of her heart, which Alexa had learned in anatomy and physiology junior year were actually just the heart's ventricles, and which could not actually be warmed by emotion.

Then she saw Tyler coming toward her down Merrimac Street, weaving in and out of the crowds and the vendors. He saw her; she could tell by the way he picked up his pace. Ugh. No. She didn't want to see Tyler.

Her feelings about what had happened at the water stop on Tuesday were complicated and difficult to unwind. She was ashamed that it happened, and she was ashamed that Cam had seen it happen. To make things even more confusing she was ashamed that she was ashamed, because she knew that that was exactly the sort of reaction that kept girls from speaking up when they were sexually assaulted. But the spitting was not assault exactly (was it? *was* it?). It was just so strange and so hard to categorize, she wasn't quite sure what to do with it, so she'd packed the whole thing up in a box and stuffed it into the closet of her mind.

She addressed the knot of girls. "Hey," she said to them in general, but more to Morgan than anyone else. She sensed their attention shift. The more fashionable among them took in her outfit approvingly. She was wearing white cut-offs and her Free People Beacon tank, though she brought along a sweatshirt because she knew the mosquitoes would be wicked in about ten minutes. "When the lights go out and the fireworks start, I want you to stay right here," she said. "So that I can find you when it's over, and walk you back home, okay?" She was talking to Morgan but looking mostly at Katie. Katie and Morgan nodded and then went back to what they were doing, which was pretending to be engrossed in their phones while stealing furtive glances around at their friends.

Then Tyler was upon her. He leaned toward her, and she backed away from the girls. "Hey," he said beerily. "I'm sorry about the other night."

The box in the closet of Alexa's mind began to creak open. "When you spit on me?" she said.

"That's not what happened!" He furrowed his brow. He was either perplexed or pretending to be perplexed. A confusing thought crawled out of the box. What if Tyler was right and Alexa was wrong? What if she'd misunderstood? Maybe he didn't spit on her. Maybe he . . . sweated on her. And she got confused. But if he didn't spit on her, what was he apologizing for?

He had her by the arm and he was pulling her behind a tree where she couldn't see the eleven-year-olds.

"Tyler!" she hissed. "I'm supposed to be watching Morgan and her friends. What are you doing?" She turned her head to peer around the tree. *The bad men,* she thought. There was a thrum of noise and energy running through the park. She needed to make sure Morgan and Company were all together before the fireworks started. She especially needed to keep an eye on Katie.

Tyler put one hand on either side of her head and turned it so she was facing him again. "I just can't stand the thought of you with anyone else, Alexa. It just makes me. So. Mad." With every syllable he squeezed her face a little harder.

His face was very close to hers; she wasn't sure if he was going to kiss her or bite her. "Tyler," she said. "Stop it. Let go. You're hurting me." Was nobody seeing this? She was surrounded by hundreds, thousands, of people, yet she felt completely alone. *The bad men*, she thought. *The bad men, the bad men, the bad men.*

Then the floodlights near the baseball field went out. The world plunged into darkness. There was a *pop pop pop* coming from the river. A *bang bang bang*. The crowd let out an appreciative ooooooooh. Tyler dropped his hands from Alexa's face, and as suddenly as he'd appeared, he was gone.

60.

THE SQUAD

The first two weeks of August always go by in the blink of an eye. That's just the way summer is. You start July thinking the season will last forever, wondering how you'll fill the days, and then the next time you turn around the nights are longer, the days are shorter, and there are back-to-school advertisements everywhere.

61.

REBECCA

Alexa was lying on one of the loungers on the back patio in her black strapless bikini. There wasn't much sun left—evening was coming—and the air was cumbrous with humidity.

"Put some clothes on," said Rebecca. "And shoes. We're going out for dinner. I'm buying. Bob Lobster." She poked Alexa's leg with her toe. "Come on." She had exactly one item on her agenda. She'd been holding on to her knowledge of Alexa's YouTube channel for two weeks now, waiting, as Daniel had advised, for the right time to bring it up. And now was the right time.

Alexa groaned and said, "Why do you want to go all the way out there?" Bob Lobster was on the turnpike leading to Plum Island.

"I just do," said Rebecca. "I like their clam rolls, and I haven't had one all summer." She moved toward Alexa like she was going to tickle her, and that got her going. No seventeen-year-old wanted to be tickled by her mother. "Come on. Morgan is at Katie's. It's just the two of us."

Alexa groaned again and pulled on ripped jeans shorts and a tiny, tiny T-shirt. "Tourists love Bob Lobster because it's 'quaint' and 'no-frills,'" she said. "But when I go on vacation? When I'm a grown-up? I'm going in the opposite direction. I'm going to go to the Royal Villa of Grand Resort Lagonissi in Athens, which costs fifty thousand dollars a night. I'm looking to embrace the thrills, not avoid them."

Is that because you are a YouTube personality? wondered Rebecca. But what she said was, "That will be nice for you, one day. For now we're going no frills. I'll drive."

The sky over the Merrimack was a delicate pink bordered here and there by orange. There was the sense of summer coming to a close, of days and nights diffusing and re-forming as nostalgia. They rolled down the windows of the Acura and took in the briny, summery smell along the turnpike. They passed the weathered wood-shingled Joppa Flats Education Center, where Alexa had once attended a summer day camp, learning all about the native birds and marine life, and then they passed the Plum Island Airport, where Rebecca had once bought Peter a piloted ride on a WWII fighter plane for his birthday. He'd emerged looking green about the gills, but he claimed to have loved it.

They ordered their food—the clam roll for Rebecca, chicken Caesar wrap for Alexa—and, once they had it, repaired to one of the outside tables, where they tried to ignore the buzzing flies and concentrate instead on the loveliness of the sky. Alexa was facing away from the road and Rebecca toward it; she could see the light playing on the Pink House. She kept her eyes trained across the street so she wouldn't have to meet Alexa's when she said, "I watched your YouTube channel."

Alexa put down her wrap. Her voice shook a little. "You what?"

"You heard me." Rebecca selected an onion ring from her basket and met Alexa's eyes. "Silk Stockings. I watched it."

"How'd you know about it?"

"From Morgan. Apparently all her friends watch it. *And* at least half the Mom Squad."

"They *do?* Are you serious?" Alexa looked the way Peter had after the WWII plane ride.

"I am very serious. You're a big local hit, apparently. Morgan told me about it that day we saw you and Cam on Pleasant Street, but I wasn't sure then how to bring it up. So I've just been watching. Catching up. Waiting, I guess."

There was a long pause during which Rebecca watched a lot of emotions cross Alexa's face: surprise, anger, stubbornness, a little bit of pride.

"Did you like it?"

Rebecca was touched by how eager Alexa sounded; she was for an instant the eight-year-old bringing home her self-portrait from art class and presenting it to Peter and Rebecca.

Rebecca poked through the onion rings to find another winner, and she spoke carefully: she'd been preparing for this.

"You have a great presence in front of the camera, and a way of condensing the topics into a digestible, educational format."

"Thank you," said Alexa.

"But that isn't the point. My liking it isn't the point."

Alexa kept her eyes on Rebecca. "What's the point?"

"Honey, you're seventeen years old, and you have a very public online personality. Sixteen thousand subscribers?"

"Almost seventeen thousand," corrected Alexa. "I've picked up a bunch of new ones recently."

"But people don't have to subscribe to watch, right?"

"Right."

"So *anybody* can find you. Anybody can watch those videos, and do—whatever they want with them. To them."

"Ew. *Mom.*"

"Not just people who want to learn about the stock market, but any old pervert or freak."

Alexa sighed, exasperated. *"I know,* Mom."

Rebecca felt her voice take a turn toward sharp. "You might *not* know, Alexa. I know you think you're all the way grown up, honey. But you're not grown up. You're not even eighteen yet."

"Almost."

Rebecca had done what Daniel had advised. She'd sat on the knowledge of Silk Stockings while she watched a lot of the videos and read through many of the comments. But now she had to speak up. Alexa was about to step into Rebecca's shoes at Colby— she was about to go off on her own! When Rebecca had matriculated at Colby she'd hadn't been just wet behind the ears; she'd been positively sopping. She cringed when she thought of some of the mistakes she'd made. And that was pre-social media, when kids had the luxury of anonymity while they were bungling their young lives.

"Listen, when you go to college I want you to take a break from this. I'm not saying stop it forever, but promise me for at least the first semester you'll concentrate on school, and making friends, and all of the things you're supposed to be doing in college."

Alexa said nothing.

"Alexa? I need you to promise."

In a very tiny voice, so tiny it could have been coming from a far corner of the eating area, or even from the outer reaches of the marshes, Alexa said, "I'm not going to college."

"I'm sorry," said Rebecca. "What?"

"You don't owe that first tuition payment. Don't pay it. We don't owe it. I'm not going."

"What do you mean? You mean you're not going as in you want to take a gap year?" Rebecca was against gap years but she tried really hard to be open-minded, the way Peter might have been.

"I turned down my spot."

"You *what?*" The background noise receded; it was as if both

Rebecca and Alexa had gone into portrait mode, with everything around them slightly blurry and unimportant.

"I turned down my spot. I have a plan. I want to move to L.A."

"By yourself?"

"Yes."

"Absolutely not."

"You can't tell me *absolutely not*. I'm almost an adult."

"Yes I can. You're not moving to L.A. No way, Alexa. No way. You shouldn't have given up Colby without talking to me about it. We should have discussed this." She couldn't believe it! Alexa had taken her future, crumpled it into a ball, and tossed it in the garbage. How had Rebecca not known she'd given up her place at Colby? She'd been too distracted by her own life, that was how. She'd failed.

Rebecca watched the old Alexa rear up, the defensive, contemptuous Alexa, the one that these past weeks with Cam had mellowed and calmed, and this version of Alexa spit back, "Oh yeah? Well, you should have told me that you're seeing someone!"

Rebecca felt herself flush. "What do you mean?"

"You are, right? If you're not, feel free to deny it."

Rebecca stayed silent.

"I knew it! I saw a text on your phone, in June. And ever since then it's been clear that you're sneaking around."

Rebecca remained silent, marveling at Alexa's abilities to turn the tables.

"Why didn't you tell me, Mom?"

Rebecca sighed and wiped her fingers neatly with a paper napkin, one by one. "Lots of reasons," she said. "For one thing, I didn't know if it was something lasting. For another, you know him."

"I do? Who is it?"

Here we go, thought Rebecca. *From here on in there's no going back.* "Mr. Bennett. He teaches at the high school."

Alexa looked horrified. "Mr. Bennett, my *Intro to the Stock Market teacher* Mr. Bennett?"

"Former Intro to the Stock Market teacher."

"Ew, Mom. *Really?*"

Rebecca held up her hand. "Maybe this is why I didn't tell you. This reaction, right here."

"I'm sorry!" said Alexa. "Sorry, I am. It's just—I mean. First of all. Do *you* call him Mr. Bennett?"

"No. Of course not. Daniel. I call him Daniel, which is his name. I just called him Mr. Bennett because that's how you know him. And I haven't told anyone. I wasn't sure if people would think it wasn't long enough after Peter, or too long, or the wrong person, or what. I just didn't feel like dealing with people's questions, or comments. And Morgan—I didn't think she was ready. Also, if you can believe it, Daniel's ex-wife is Gina's husband's sister. It all just felt too close to home."

Alexa winced. "Wet sleeping bag Gina?"

"Wet sleeping bag Gina. And I guess the final reason is that even in the middle of all of this, meeting someone new, *laughing* with someone new, I still miss Peter."

Alexa took a sip of her drink and then met Rebecca's eyes. "I know," she said. "I know you do. I do too." She paused. "You know, I talked to Peter about not going right to college. Just before he died. I was thinking of it even back then, even before I started Silk Stockings."

Rebecca was torn between feeling intrigued about that conversation and envious that it hadn't been with her. "What did he say?"

"He was really supportive. I mean, he wasn't like, yeah, gap year! Definitely! But he was willing to keep the conversation going. He was definitely willing to think about it. And then all of a sudden he was gone." She gave a little shuddering breath that again called to Rebecca's mind the eight-year-old with the self-portrait. "I miss him a lot too, Mom."

"What do you miss about him?"

Alexa looked like she was thinking about this. "He was so patient when he taught me to parallel park—remember? In that parking lot across from the Towle building? I ran over those cones the first thirty times I tried it and we got chased out of there by the cops because officially the parking lot is private. He was always so—so nice." She swiped at a tear. "That sounds lame, but it's the right word for what I'm trying to say. He was so kind. I wish he was my real father."

"Alexa! He was your real father."

"Well. But he wasn't. Morgan was his actual daughter, the one he had from the beginning of her life. I was just this . . . this interloper who was always hanging around. This barnacle attached to you. He couldn't pry me off, but he wanted you, so he took us both."

"Stop it. Alexa! That's ridiculous." Rebecca considered her daughter. For such a long time after Peter's death she'd been consumed by her own grief—its inability to be contained, its bewildering peaks and valleys. Her sadness was so unwieldy, sometimes unpredictable, irascible. And Morgan was so young and needed so much. Sometimes Rebecca forgot to acknowledge that Alexa had her own grief that was complicated in its own way. She saw now that this had been a failure of hers. "You know, when your dad and I first split up, I figured there was no hope for me. A single mom with a three-year-old! Even though you were the cutest three-year-old around, I just wasn't sure."

"Yeah," said Alexa, smiling weakly. "I can see how I might have cramped your dating style."

"I was prepared to be alone," Rebecca said. "Forever. I thought it would be just you and me, and we'd have this tidy little life, and then you'd grow up and leave me eventually, and I'd just, I don't know, shrivel up and die or something. Or get a cat."

"Not a cat," said Alexa. "Never a cat."

"The first time I went out with Peter, years later, I waited to mention you until the very end of the evening. Not because I was ashamed of you. No, don't look at me that way! But just because I wanted to know what kind of person he was before I trusted him with the idea of you. Does that make sense?"

Alexa nodded.

"And then when I told him, do you know what he said?"

"'*No can do*'?" said Alexa.

"Stop. No, of course not. His eyes lit up—I mean, they lit up, that's an overused expression but honestly they did—and he said, 'When do I get to meet her?'"

Alexa's eyes were wet. "He did? He said that?"

"He did. The second time we went out, we took you to the Big Apple Circus. You might not remember that."

"I don't."

"You were terrified of the elephant, and we had to leave early."

"Oh no!" said Alexa. "I'm sorry! Were you and Peter bummed out?"

Rebecca laughed. "Not at all. I think you did us a favor. Barnum and Bailey it was not."

"I'm so jealous of Morgan sometimes," Alexa said. "Because she got him from the beginning of her life. She got a good one. And my father—well, he's just gone."

Rebecca hesitated. Now would be—could be—the time to tell Alexa that her father had initiated contact. But then she thought about all the times he'd promised to change and hadn't been able to. She knew he had a disease from which a lot of people never recover. She knew he might not be better.

"I know we haven't talked about this in a while—" she said. "But when you turn eighteen, the official custody agreement allows you to get in touch with your father if you wish. And if that's important to you, I'll help you find him. But there's no hurry. You have your whole life to do that. Please believe me when I say that Peter *was* your real father for all of those years you had him. He was as real as it gets."

Rebecca put her greasy, clam-roll hand over her daughter's chickeny hand and they sat like that for several seconds while the sounds of the evening settled around them: the cars going by on their way to and from the island, the kid at the next table having a temper tantrum, raucous laughter from a group of teenagers. In this moment Rebecca felt a shift, as quick as the heartbeat of a bird. It was, maybe, a shift toward possibility. Toward a new kind of happiness.

Although there was still the Colby thing. Which wasn't happy at all. "We'll talk about the Colby thing later," she told Alexa. "We are *not* finished with this discussion."

Eventually Alexa took her hand back (clearly, enough was enough) and she said, "Are you done with this?" And she gathered up the paper containers and the balled-up napkins and she shuttled them into the garbage.

62.

ALEXA

Alexa studied her face in the mirror behind the sun visor in Cam's minivan. She looked the same, but she had felt different, since things between her and Cam had really heated up. Since the race. They'd hung out nearly every day. They'd gone mini golfing and go-carting and swimming. She spent a night at the Winnepesaukee house, safely installed in one of the guest bedrooms, hoping the whole time Cam would sneak in in the middle of the night—he did, but only until unexpected hallway noises put an end to their tryst. Cam took her around the lake in the speedboat, and they stopped to fool around on the far side of Rattlesnake Island. He'd put in a lot of shifts at Market Basket, and Alexa had done the same at the Cottage. She had continued to record her Silk Stockings videos, even, with Cam's help, choosing a few topics she hadn't thought about on her own.

Cam got really into the research. Sometimes too into it, maybe, but it was helpful having someone off whom to bounce ideas, and his assistance freed her up to do more planning for her L.A. move. She found a couple of long-term Airbnbs where she could potentially stay while looking for an apartment.

Every time she put up a new video, Cam posted a salient, adorable comment; it was as if he was competing with jt76 for the award given to the nicest channel subscriber.

The minivan sailed over the bridge from Newburyport to Salisbury, and Alexa cracked the window to let the ocean smell move in. They had crested the hill of summer and were heading down, down, down.

They'd also spent a lot of time talking, Cam and Alexa, in a way that she hadn't talked with another person in a long time—maybe ever. They talked about Alexa's former friends, and they talked about Tyler, and Shelby McIntrye, and they talked about Cam's favorite philosopher (some guy named Blaise Pascal), and they talked about Peter and Morgan. They talked about how Alexa tried to pay her mother back the five-hundred-dollar deposit to Colby that she'd put down in April, but her mother refused, because, even though Alexa had the money, *it wasn't about the money*. They talked about what it was about: her mother's disappointment that Alexa didn't want what she'd wanted, and her fear that Alexa would move far away and never come back.

Now they took the turn off Route 1 and toward the beach, passing the dingy motels with their cracked pools, the newer condos, the defunct ice cream stand where Alexa used to love to go as a kid. Foote's. Funny name for an eating establishment, but there you were.

Every now and then, but not very often, in hushed voices, they talked about Sherri and Katie, and Alexa learned that it was possible to be scared and happy at the exact same time.

They had kissed, a lot, and more than that too—though not yet everything. This was starting to make Alexa wonder: come September, would she be the only eighteen-year-old virgin on the North Shore? (Cam was such a gentleman. But was he *too much* of a gentleman?)

"Where are we going, anyway?" she asked Cam now.

"The reservation. I thought we could have a picnic. I picked up a couple of things after work today." She looked behind her at the center row of the minivan: sure enough, there was a Market Basket cooler bag there.

Even the drive toward the parking lot, with the marshes on the right, and the ocean air suspended around them, was sort of breathtaking, especially at this time of day, when twilight was turning the sky a purplish-mauve.

Most of the beachgoers were headed out as they were heading in, so it was easy enough to find parking—and the lot was vast. They walked together up the long boardwalk with the beach grasses waving at them from either side. They passed the pavilion with benches where a runner was stretching and tapping on the screen of a cell phone. They passed the sign that tells you what to do when caught in a rip current. When they got to the sand, they both kicked off their shoes and left them where they landed. Cam carried the Market Basket bag slung over one shoulder, and he handed her another bag with a blanket in it.

They stood for a moment, deciding which way to go. To the left you walked past the beach houses and toward the Blue Ocean Music Hall and the downtown strip, where people bought squares of beach pizza and ice cream and played in the arcades and listened to live music in the Bands on the Beach series. To the right was more solitude, a jetty, and, eventually, the part of the beach attached to the campground, where people let their dogs run around off the leash.

"Let's go to the right," said Alexa. "More privacy." It was low tide and the beach was flat and gigantic. There were hard, feet-massaging ripples in the sand closer to the water. They walked for a while in silence and then Cam said, "Alexa. I leave for school in nine days."

Alexa felt a drop in her stomach, and her voice sounded strange as she croaked out, "Nine days?" Had summer really gone by so quickly? It seemed like just yesterday she woke up in Cam's guest bedroom. Just yesterday, he was an affable stranger in St. Michael's spirit wear. "That's it? That can't be right."

"Yeah," said Cam. He stopped and looked out at the water, frowning, so Alexa stopped too, turning to face the waves. "I have to get back early for the team. We really ramp up practice before the semester starts. We have a few big tournaments right away in the fall. It gets pretty intense." There was a time Alexa might have smirked at the idea of intense golf training, but that time was in the past, and she understood and even admired how seriously Cam took his sport.

She scanned the beach. There were a few people left: the evening picnickers, the kids who'd begged their parents to stay just a little bit longer, the dog owners brash enough to flaunt the rules even away from the campground. Alexa looked out, and out, and out, all the way to the horizon. Full sunset was still an hour or so off, but the sky was changing by the second, going from pink-stripey to dark purple to navy blue. She felt a twist in her heart, a nostalgia for something that hadn't yet passed.

"And I guess I'll be leaving soon too," she said.

"Do you really want to leave so badly?" Cam took hold of her hand and they began to walk along the beach. It was stupidly romantic, with the waves beating against the sand, and the ocean—blue closer to shore, but along the horizon, black and infinite—laid out before them. Cam's hand was much bigger than hers, and warm, and comforting. "I mean, look where you live," he said. "It's so beautiful here." As if on cue, the setting sun turned the waves periwinkle. "Don't you ever feel lucky to live here, instead of wishing you could be somewhere else, all the way across the country?"

They had almost reached the jetty before the campground; they'd have to turn back soon.

"Not really," she said. "I just want to get started on what's next. I do."

"You know what Confucius said?"

"No," said Alexa, suddenly irritable. Must they philosophize now?

"He said, 'Wherever you go, there you are,'" said Cam.

"I don't get it," said Alexa, without really thinking. Far, far out, a sailboat glided along.

"Think about it," said Cam. Then—"Right? Make sense?" He was smiling eagerly.

Despite her best efforts not to understand, she thought she probably did. It wasn't that complicated. Alexa in California would just be the same as Alexa in Newburyport, although obviously tanner and probably with much cuter clothes, and, eventually, her own dog.

"I guess so," she said. She kicked reluctantly at the sand with her big toe.

"All I'm trying to get at, Alexa, is that I don't want you to miss where you are on your way to getting to somewhere else. It took me a while to learn that myself, but I think I finally have. And I think that might be what Confucius was saying."

Then Cam was putting down his Market Basket bag, and taking her bag from her to place beside his, and holding her face gently, a hand on either cheek, and he was bending down and giving her a glorious, glorious kiss. He stopped and pulled back for a second and said, "Okay?" She wasn't sure her voice would work—the kissing was really intense—so she just nodded and willed him to please start kissing her again. She put her hands on the back of his adorable, goofy, sexy golfer's neck and pulled him closer. He moved his hands down to her waist, and his grip was strong and sure.

Then he said, "No pressure. Whatsoever. But if you haven't moved yet, if you're still figuring things out, I'll be back for Thanksgiving. And maybe before that, if you have a free weekend in October, you can come up to St. Mike's. I'd love to show you around, and maybe you can come to a tourney."

Her head was saying, *Please don't say tourney*—some words are just not meant to be shortened. But her heart seemed to be saying something different, something—could it be?—nonjudgmental and hopeful. Her heart seemed to be saying, *October is not so far away.*

And then he took her hand and led her closer to the dunes and spread out the blanket. Her heart was beating so fast she felt like she had a bird in her rib cage.

There were no bad men. It was just her and Cam and the endless ocean, and everything was whole and good and safe.

"What's in the picnic bag?" she asked.

"Lots of good stuff," Cam answered. "Some of Market Basket's finest, if you want to know the truth." (Market Basket *did* have an excellent cheese selection.) "But I don't care so much about the picnic anymore," he added. His voice was husky. He was backlit by the setting sun.

She sat down on the blanket, and then she thought better of it and lay all the way down. Cam sat beside her and rested one of his hands on her stomach.

"Neither do I," she whispered. "In fact, I don't even know what Market Basket bag you're talking about."

And then he was kissing her, and kissing her, and kissing her.

63.

SHERRI

Rebecca mentioned Brooke's end-of-summer party casually. They had iced coffees from Soufflés and they were walking on the boardwalk after dropping the girls at nature camp. They would be sleeping overnight in Maudslay, and be collected at two the following day. Sherri had major reservations about letting Katie sleep outside in the woods—how easy it would be for someone to grab her from a tent!—but Katie had begged and begged and begged.

The day was sumptuous, the air plump and ripe, the river glistening as though it had just been hand-scrubbed. The marina was chock-full; there were boats from Key West and Camden, Maine; from Charleston, South Carolina; from South Padre Island. There was a long line outside the bathrooms at the harbormaster's hut, and happy, tail-wagging dogs coming off the rail trail.

Rebecca was talking about what she was going to wear. She'd worn her favorite off-the-shoulder dress two years ago to the same party and she couldn't wear that again. She wished she could borrow from Alexa but Alexa was so tiny. She stopped and leaned against the railing, resting her iced coffee cup on the flat surface of a post.

"This feels awkward," said Sherri finally. "But I don't know anything about this party." She fixed her gaze on the far side of the river, where she could see the big waterfront houses on Ring's Island.

"Wait, *what?*" Rebecca said, turning to her. "Are you kidding me? I just assumed—I'm so sorry. I thought she had invited you. She should have invited you! Are you sure she didn't? It was an actual paper invitation, not Paperless Post or Evite. Are you sure you didn't just toss it out with the junk mail?"

Sherri was sure. They didn't get much mail yet: she would have noticed an invitation. "Don't give it a second thought," she said. She was cringing from embarrassment for herself, but also for her friend. "I promise, Rebecca, I don't care at all. I don't even go to parties!" (In reality she cared a lot. She felt the sting strongly. If Sherri was out, was Katie out too? This now made at least three exclusions between the two of them. What about the lunch table? The lockers? They couldn't start over again, anywhere else. They *had* to make it work here.)

"How dare she!" Rebecca's face was tight with righteous indignation. "I mean. You've been to Brooke's house. You were at Esther's birthday dinner, back in the beginning of the summer! You were on the pontoon!"

"I was only on the pontoon as your plus one," Sherri reminded her.

"But you live here now, and Katie is friends with all their daughters. This is just so stupid. I swear, sometimes I just don't understand these people."

"Really, I promise, it doesn't matter. I don't care about that kind of stuff. I don't have anything to wear to a party anyway."

Rebecca was leaning on the railing of the boardwalk, thinking. Sherri watched as a little white terrier licked at a forgotten piece of ice cream cone. "You know what, though?" Rebecca said, suddenly and conspiratorially. "You should come anyway. That'll show them. They're far too polite to say anything if you just show up!"

"Oh, I could never do that," said Sherri. "I'd feel so awkward." She made a face to demonstrate the awkwardness she'd feel, showing up uninvited. Desperate.

"Well, in case you change your mind," said Rebecca, winking like an emoji. "You've been to Brooke's house, so you know where it is. And it starts at seven. Honestly, there'll be so many people there that I doubt anyone's checking the guest list. And they'll all be wasted by seven forty-five anyway. This party is insane. Legendary. You should come just to see the scene, if for no other reason."

"By seven o'clock I'll be in my pajamas, watching Netflix," said Sherri. "You can bank on that. I heard *Russian Doll* is good. Have you seen it?"

Rebecca hadn't.

But even as Sherri asked the question, something was licking up at her: a little flame of her former self. She wasn't going to stay home and watch *Russian Doll*. No way. Not this time. She'd had enough.

64.

THE SQUAD

Gina to Tammy: Who is Rebecca bringing?

Tammy to Gina: Sherri? She brought her on the boat.

Gina to Tammy: Isn't Sherri invited already?

Tammy to Gina: ☺

Gina to Brooke: Did you invite Sherri to Party?

Brooke to Gina: No. I used same invitation list I always use. Didn't occur to me to make changes.

As we all said later, it turned out that it didn't matter anyway.

65.

SHERRI

"Enough," said Sherri Griffin, formerly Sharon Giordano, standing in the dingy kitchen of their tiny half-house the next day. She'd survived a lesser branch of an organized crime unit. She'd sat in the FBI offices and told the agents everything she knew, and then she'd sat in a courtroom and she'd done the same thing. She'd gotten herself and her daughter out of a terrifying situation. She'd taken down men powerful enough that she would forever live with the fear that someone might still be looking for her. She'd changed her hair and her outfits and her address and her last name and her daughter's school records. She wasn't about to be done in by a bunch of yoga moms.

Excuse me, pardon me, *barre* moms.

Sherri had had enough of being meek, and plain, and of wearing unflattering, cheap clothes. She'd had enough of being 100 percent responsible. Careful. Sober. Boring.

"Enough," she said again. This house wasn't even theirs; they were renting it, and they shared it with a woman who banged on the wall when Sherri's child screamed in the night after waking from well-earned nightmares. "Enough," she said, when she bumped her elbow on the wall of the damp, unfinished, and very likely haunted basement, which absolutely contained mold or asbestos or maybe both. *Enough. Enough. Enough.* She was going to buy a new dress, and she was going to see if Alexa could stay with Katie, and she was going to go to the party. For one night, *just for one night,* she was going to be her old self.

While Katie was still at the nature camp sleepover, Sherri drove up to Portsmouth. She found a shop with pretty dresses in the window. The store was called Bobbles and Lace, and she realized after the fact that there was one in Newburyport too. Oh well. It was nice to get out of town, to drive north, to see a different city on a pretty late-August day. Portsmouth looked like Newburyport's older, slightly more sophisticated sister, with a wider main street and more shops and more tourists but a similar beautiful-city-on-the-water-in-summer self-confidence. The streets were thrumming with activity; she had to circle a bunch of times before finding parking.

She shopped quickly, choosing three dresses off the rack and asking the salesgirl where she could try them on. The salesgirl's name was Caitlin. She introduced herself when Sherri walked in and then went right back to scrolling through her Instagram feed, smiling to herself.

Into a pile on the dressing room floor went Sherri's cotton T-shirt, her sensible, ugly, ill-fitting bra, her awful, awful cargo pants. On went the first dress. She didn't need to try on the second and third dresses. She knew as soon as she put it on that the first one was an instant win.

It was gold. Back in the day she'd always chosen gold for a big night out. It matched her then-hair. "My golden goddess," Bobby used to call her and, yes, she could admit it, she'd loved it when he called her that. She often painted her nails gold too. Sometimes, gold eye shadow. She wasn't scared of standing out back then— she liked standing out. Bobby liked it too. He liked for them both to stand out. She even had a gold bikini.

It felt good to be wearing a pretty dress again. No, more than good—it felt amazing. Sherri Griffin took a deep breath and stepped out of the dressing room to access the three-way mirror. Caitlin, who was leaning on the counter that held the register, turned around, put her phone down, and started to look interested. "Wow," she said. "You look super hot in that dress." She didn't even add, *for an old person*. (At least not out loud.)

"Thanks," said Sherri modestly, but not too modestly. Because Caitlin was right. Sherri examined her reflection from every angle. The dress clung to her in all the right places. It fell to just above the knee, where it flared out a bit, but before it got there it lay flat against her stomach and hugged the curves of her hips. The dress had two thin straps across each shoulder and took a generous dip between her breasts. Sherri hadn't worn a dress like this in—well, it had been a long time. It had been so, so long.

She studied her reflection some more. In the beginning of the program, and before that, during the nightmare days of the trial, and before that, during the even bigger nightmare days following Madison Miller's disappearance, she'd lost too much weight, and her curves had departed without warning, like tired party guests. Her skin had started to sag. But over the course of the summer, ice cream cone by ice cream cone, lobster roll by lobster roll, she'd filled back out. She and Katie had put in enough hours at the beach that her color was good; the gold of the dress made her skin positively glow. And her cleavage! Her cleavage was back, like a dear friend who'd gone on a long voyage but now had returned.

"I'll take it," she told Caitlin.

"Uh, yeah!" said Caitlin. "Of course you will. Do you have shoes?"

"No!" cried Sherri, as horrified as if Caitlin had said, "Do you have syphilis?"

"I have the perfect pair," said Caitlin. "They're in the back, we haven't even finished unpacking them." She glanced knowledgeably at Sherri's feet. "Are you a seven?"

"And a half."

"Right back," said Caitlin. "And then we'll accessorize."

The shoes—heels! Sherri was back in heels!—were great, and so were the earrings Caitlin chose, which were long and fringy and felt like friendly little brooms sweeping at Sherri's shoulders. Sherri loved all of it, and as it turned out, the dress was part of the end-of-summer sale; the charges came only to one hundred and twenty-eight dollars, which, reflected Sherri, wasn't so bad for a total transformation.

Just past noon, Sherri texted Alexa to see if she was available. The gods of desperation and babysitting were on her side. Alexa was available.

Out on the street, catching her reflection in the shop window, she spotted her remaining problem. Her hair. She could wear it up. She could wear it down. But whatever she did it would still be the same drab color.

She pulled her phone out of her bag. First she called Rebecca to see if she wouldn't mind picking Katie up from nature camp when she collected Morgan. Of course Rebecca wouldn't mind—she was still chagrined about mentioning the party to Sherri; Sherri could tell she'd do anything to help. She could have asked Rebecca to change the oil in her Acura or aspirate a cyst and Rebecca would have answered in the same willing, cheerful way. Then she called the salon.

"You're in luck!" cried Brittany. "There's been a cancellation! Do you want it? How soon can you be here? How lucky are you?"

"Pretty lucky," said Sherri. "I want it." She believed that sometimes you made your own luck but that other times the luck was handed to you, a gift from an anonymous donor with no strings attached. This appointment would put her over her budget, but she'd cut back next week to make up for it. "I can be there in twenty-eight minutes," she said.

66.

ALEXA

Alexa's phone pinged with two texts as she was in the line at Commune to get a coffee and a crepe on Saturday, just past noon. Then her phone rang.

There were three people ahead of Alexa in line so she answered. It was Hannah, her coworker at the Cottage.

"Hey, Amazon!" said Hannah, and Alexa rolled her eyes. If this was about getting Alexa to work that day, no thank you, she wasn't interested.

"I can't switch shifts," she said preemptively, combatively.

"Calm down, Amazon. That's not why I'm calling." Hannah was chewing gum, loudly and right into the phone. If there was one thing Alexa couldn't abide, and there were many, it was gum chewers. If you needed to cleanse your breath and your toothbrush wasn't near, try a mint. "I just wanted to let you know that some guy was looking for you today."

"Some guy?" Alexa's hands tightened around the phone. Despite the generous air-conditioning in Commune, she began to feel warm. *The bad men are coming.*

"I told him you were off."

"What guy? Tyler?" She hadn't had any contact with Tyler since the night of the Yankee Homecoming fireworks.

"No!" said Hannah. "I'd recognize Tyler. Duh?"

"Cam, maybe?"

"Who's Cam?"

Alexa didn't feel like going into the whole story of her romantic entanglements just now so she ignored Hannah's question. "Was he wearing either golf clothes or St. Michael's College spirit wear? Was he smiling like a really big and enthusiastic smile?"

"Let me see." Hannah chewed her gum thoughtfully, right in Alexa's ear. Alexa held the phone a little bit away and rolled her eyes. "What specifically are golf clothes?"

"Khakis," said Alexa. "Golf shirt. Visor?"

"No, he wasn't wearing golf clothes. And he wasn't wearing spirit wear." There was an irritating pause while Hannah thought some more. "He definitely wasn't smiling. He was pretty serious." Alexa's mouth was dry now. *Bad men would be serious.* She headed for the tiny water cups that were lined up on a shelf running along the side of the shop. Murderers would be serious. Mob guys would be serious. She tucked the phone under her ear while she picked up the water pitcher to fill a cup. "How old is Cam?" asked Hannah.

"Nineteen," said Alexa. "No, wait, twenty." Her hands were shaking so that when she put the pitcher back down, some of the water sloshed out. She knocked back the water, threw away the tiny cup, and resumed her place in line, her heart hammering all the while.

"Oh, this guy was way older. Forty? Forty-five? I don't know, it's hard to tell, anyone between forty and sixty looks the same to me."

"Yeah, I know what you mean." Alexa was trying to downplay her concern, but she was getting really nervous. How old were gangsters, typically?

The person ahead of her had a credit card out, ready to slip into the machine.

"Anyway, he was older," continued Hannah. "I saw him get into a black SUV."

"A black SUV?" Panic began to drip into Alexa's bloodstream— a slow, ominous panic. "What kind of black SUV?"

"Oh, I don't know," said Hannah. "I'm not really a car person. Have you seen what I drive?"

"No," Alexa said irritably.

"It's really old. I bet you couldn't even guess what it is if you tried."

Alexa was absolutely definitely not going to try. "You didn't mention my last name, did you?"

"I didn't have to."

Alexa's heart was in her throat. No, higher: in her mouth. "Why not?" The drip of panic had become a flood.

"He already knew it."

"He knew my last name?"

"How would he be looking for you if he didn't know your name? I kinda have to go, Alexa, we're getting a line and I'm like totally hiding around the back and Lori is looking for me—"

Alexa pressed her knees together to keep her legs from trembling. "Just tell me one more thing. You said he was serious. But was he scary?"

"I don't know. He didn't seem scary. He was just a guy."

"You didn't tell him my address, did you?"

Hannah chortled. "I don't even *know* your address, Amazon. How would I tell him? I just told him to look for your Jeep if he wanted to find you."

"Next person in line!" said the girl behind the counter.

"You told him to look for my Jeep?"

"Yeah. Don't you live on High Street?" asked Hannah.

"Yeah," said Alexa. It was the only syllable she could muster.

"I don't know what number though."

"Near the high school. It doesn't matter. You told him to look for my Jeep?"

"Well, yeah. If he wants to find you. Anyway. Not to freak you out, but like I said, he knew your name, and you know, there is this thing called the Internet, and if you know someone's name and town it's not that hard to find out their address." Alexa sighed. Of course she knew *there was this thing called the Internet.* "Seriously," said Hannah. "I have to go now. Lori is freaking out."

"Yup," said Alexa. "You already said that. Thanks for calling, I guess." She wanted to throttle Hannah.

"No worries!"

"Next person!" said the counter girl again, staring directly at Alexa.

"Just a second," hissed Alexa hypocritically (she hated when people were on their phones when she was serving ice cream). She studied the menu, having completely forgotten what she was about to order.

But she couldn't concentrate on the crepes. Why had she read Katie's diary? After that, why had she told Cam what was in the diary? What if Cam wasn't the former Boy Scout he pretended to be? What if he told someone, and that someone told someone, and so on, and now an evil person from the Griffins' past was coming for her?

"Are you going to order or not?" said the girl.

"Yes," snarled Alexa. She thought she could trust Cam, but what if she couldn't trust anyone? Alexa placed her order and stood off to the side to wait.

She saw a black SUV rolling down Pleasant Street. The car stopped. Her breath caught. She looked more closely and recognized the blond head of Esther, Mom Squad member and mother of Morgan's friend Audrey. Alexa needed to relax. *Everybody drives a black SUV,* she told herself. *Everybody.* The SUV started moving again—now she could see that it had been letting the car in front of it pull into a parallel parking space. Merrily, the traffic rolled along, and Alexa felt her pulse quiet.

Once she had her crepe Alexa settled onto one of the couches and read her texts. The first was Cam, wondering if she wanted to hang out later. The second was Sherri, asking if Alexa could stay for a while that night with Katie while Sherri stopped by Brooke's party. That's right, tonight was Brooke's end-of-summer party, at her over-the-top house on the river. Brooke's party was legendary. Brooke's party meant a lot of drunk grown-ups dressed up and posting inappropriate and embarrassing photos on social media. And of course somebody would jump into the pool. Inwardly, in advance, Alexa rolled her eyes. Was there anything more depressing than middle-aged drunk people?

There was, in fact. Yes. Middle-aged drunk people who danced.

Alexa was surprised that Sherri Griffin was even going to that party. She probably had no idea what she was getting herself into. (What would she *wear?*)

She sent two texts back.

To Sherri: Sure. What time? She needed to keep Katie with her, to keep her safe. Katie couldn't stay alone during the party. *What if the bad men were coming for them both?* If they were, it was all Alexa's fault.

To Cam: Sry, babysitting. Talk to you after?

67.

REBECCA

Rebecca picked the girls up after their sleepover in Maudslay and dropped Katie at her house. She still didn't have anything to wear to the party. "Hey, Morgs, want me to leave you at home, or do you want to come to Marshalls with me?"

"Who's at home?"

"Just Bernice, I think." She checked her phone to see where Alexa was but her location wasn't visible. That app never worked.

"I'll go with you."

"You sure you don't want to shower?" Morgan smelled a little ripe.

"I'm sure. Can I get some of those sour gummy worms in the checkout line?"

"Absolutely not."

"Please?"

"No. The sugar epidemic is this country is for real, and I'm not going to contribute to it."

Morgan shrugged. "I'll come anyway."

Fine, okay. Maybe better if Morgan did come along. Rebecca had been putting something off and she knew it was time to face it head-on, before the party.

Marshalls on a Saturday! Oh, boy: the crowds. Rebecca wanted to make it quick. She headed to the dress section and started to flip through the dresses in her size, with Morgan joining her like a small but bossy personal shopper. "How about this?" suggested Morgan. "Or this?" She held out two dresses made for women twenty years younger.

"No strapless," said Rebecca. "No mid-thigh." She glanced at her watch. She did *not* want to spend all day at Marshalls. "I'll probably buy a few things and try them on at home," she said. "I hate going in the dressing rooms here. I'm sure one of these will work." She loaded up her cart with four not-terrible options in her size and considered heading to the shoe section. But then she spotted Melanie near the shoes, and she didn't want to talk to Melanie. If Melanie spotted Rebecca, she might say something in front of Morgan about who Rebecca was bringing to the party. And if Melanie was in Marshalls there was a good chance at least one other Mom Squad member was also in Marshalls, just based on odds.

She pulled Morgan down one of the housewares aisles. It was much more quiet in this part of the store. And wasn't the housewares section of Marshalls as good a place as any to do what had to be done?

"Listen, Morgan," she said. "There's something I have to tell you, before tonight."

"What?" Morgan was running her hands along the fluffy towels.

Rebecca breathed in, then let the breath out slowly. "I have a date," she said. "I'm going with a date to Brooke's party." Morgan looked up from the towels. "I've been seeing someone, Morgs. Dating someone. For a few months now. I've been sort of hiding it, keeping it a secret from everyone. But I decided recently I'm ready to stop doing that." She couldn't read Morgan's expression. "Does that make you sad?"

"Sort of," Morgan whispered. She stared hard at the bath

mats, blinking. Rebecca reached for Morgan's hand, but Morgan snatched it away. Tears appeared in Morgan's eyes, and then one fell out, mixing with the overnight camp dirt on her face.

"Here." Rebecca handed her one of the washcloths from the shelf, let Morgan wipe her face on it and then added it to the items in the cart. She waited and allowed an older woman with a cartful of beach towels make her way by. "I understand if it makes you sad, Morgs. I do. I promise, I'm taking it slow with this guy. I'm not trying to replace Daddy. You know that, right? Nobody will ever replace Daddy."

Morgan didn't answer that. Instead she said, "You mean like someone's going to pick you up and drive you there? Like a *date* date? A Disney Channel date?"

"Well, I'm going to pick him up, actually."

Morgan took this in and was silent for several seconds. She nodded sagely. "Because of equality?"

"Sure. Equality. And also logistics."

Morgan chewed her lip. "What's his name?"

"Daniel. His name is Daniel Bennett. And I know he'd like to meet you, just as soon as you're ready."

"I'm not ready," said Morgan, almost instantly.

"That's okay. That's totally fine. So when you are, you'll meet him."

"I might never be ready."

"That's okay too." (It wasn't actually. But she was pretty sure Morgan didn't mean it.) Once they checked out, she'd ask Morgan if she wanted to go out for a really late lunch/extremely early dinner and talk a little more.

"Do you know what I am ready for, though?" Morgan met Rebecca's gaze squarely. There was still a tear standing in each eye.

"What?" Anything for poor brokenhearted Morgan!

"Some of those sour gummy worms by the register."

Rebecca rolled her eyes. She'd been outsmarted once again. "Fine," she said. "You got it." She put one arm around Morgan and kept one hand on the shopping cart. This time, at least Morgan didn't pull away.

Rebecca could bet that they weren't the first people to have a heart-to-heart in the housewares section of Marshalls. And something told her they wouldn't be the last.

68.

ALEXA

In the early evening Alexa pondered her situation from the safety of her bedroom, with the door locked. The bad men couldn't possibly find her *here*, she reasoned. But perhaps they could. She moved to the back of her closet, and nestled among the expensive Silk Stockings clothes. *Or here,* she thought. She fell briefly asleep in the closet—a first, and hopefully a last; she crumpled one of her dresses. When she woke up she was confused and disoriented and slightly sweaty. She went to Morgan's room and looked out her window because it faced High Street. There were cars going by, but no black SUVs, and there was nothing unusual in the drive-way. Coast: clear.

She ate some carrots and pretzels with hummus—the Griffins' food options had not improved much over the summer, so she didn't want to arrive hungry—and was readying herself to leave when her mother and Morgan came in the front door. Clearly Morgan had not showered or bathed since her overnight in Maud-slay; she had dirt on her face and she was wearing a bandanna around her head. She looked like a *Survivor* contestant who had gotten knocked out in an early round. Alexa's mother was carry-ing a brown paper Marshalls bag, and Morgan was face-deep into a bag of the sour gummy worms from the checkout line. Morgan must have caught their mother in a weak moment.

"Oh, shoot," said Rebecca, looking at Alexa's car keys, her bag. "Are you on your way out somewhere? I was hoping you could stay with Morgan while I go to Brooke's party. I completely forgot to ask you. I'm not going to stay late. I don't really feel like doing the whole party thing tonight." She grimaced.

"I'm babysitting," said Alexa. "For Katie? So Sherri can go to the party?"

"Sherri's going to the party?" Rebecca's face registered surprise. "Why wouldn't she?"

"No reason," said Rebecca, glancing at Morgan. Her face softened and she said, "I'm really glad she's going. I realized at the last minute that I have nothing to wear. So I ran out quickly." She waved the bag in front of Alexa. Alexa was dismayed. Her mother was wearing Marshalls couture to Brooke's party? The only thing worse than a Marshalls trip for a special occasion was a *rushed* Marshalls trip for a special occasion. Alexa had seen her mother in a hurry at Marshalls before, when the time crunch compromised her better judgment. She wondered if any of her Silk Stockings dresses would fit her mom. Probably not. Her mom had those hips.

"Morgan can come with me," Alexa said. "I'm sure Sherri won't mind." It would mean less for her to do anyway; the girls would entertain each other, and then maybe Cam could come over. She thought again about the black SUV and her heart tripped its way back into her throat again. *Stop it, Alexa. Nobody is after you.*

Morgan brightened visibly and smiled, revealing a piece of a sour gummy worm plastered to her front tooth. "Yes!" she said. "I am in."

Her mother peered at Alexa. "Are you okay?"

Internally, Alexa was still jittery, but she didn't know it showed on the outside. "Sure," she said. "Yeah. Why?"

"I don't know. You seem—nervous."

"I'm not nervous," said Alexa nervously. She tapped her flip-flop against the floor. "You ready now, Morgs, or did you need to shower or change or anything?"

Morgan shrugged and said, "Meh. What's one more day?"

"That's the spirit!" said Rebecca. She kissed Morgan on the crown of her dirty head and patted Alexa on the arm, which was a shame because Alexa could sort of use a hug too. "I've got to figure out something with my hair," Rebecca said.

Alexa couldn't help but agree.

69.

THE SQUAD

Brooke's party was a tradition, practically an institution, and we all looked forward to it. She heated the pool up to the high heavens, knowing that at some point one adult was going to jump into it, and then another, until the whole thing felt like a Southern California scene you'd see in the movies. Nobody wore silk to Brooke's end-of-summer bash for exactly that reason. Nobody wore anything that needed to be dry cleaned, and people tried to remember to leave their good watches at home. But other than that: People. Dressed. Up.

Normally we would have a girls' trip in the works for September or October, and we'd be talking about that at Brooke's party. But the summer had been a funny one, and we hadn't planned anything yet. Rebecca hadn't said a word, and the rest of us were unsure if we could reasonably take the reins or not. We were in a holding pattern. Circling. There had been all of those changes with the group chat, and the splitting into factions. There had been the newcomer.

A brief rain shower had come on in the early afternoon, but the rain stopped in plenty of time, and the small staff of caterers was put to work placing super-absorbent towels all over the outside furniture. The sun came out in force around four. By the time we arrived at seven it was as if the rain had never happened.

The mosquitos had considered coming out to snack on the party guests, but Brooke's husband had invested in some sort of really expensive silent zapper, so the mosquitos changed their tune, and fast.

The party progressed quickly, the way Brooke's parties always did. Something about the end of summer made people feel both celebratory and frantic at the same time. We noticed it every year, and every year we got a little more frantic. A new school year always made us realize how quickly our kids were growing up, or, in a more general sense, that time was passing and we weren't getting any younger.

One of us had a mother suffering from dementia; another, a father with pancreatic cancer. One of us, although you'd never know it, it was all very hush-hush, had a stepchild in rehab. One of us had nothing saved for college, not a penny, and woke up at two thirty nearly every morning in a panic about it. We all felt the future, our futures, reaching out to grab us with terrible talons.

We assuaged that consternation at the bar. Brooke did some of the cooking for the party herself, but she always had caterers to help, and she always hired a bartender, which we believed was one of the reasons it was common for people to drink a lot, and quickly.

Some of the husbands were playing corn hole on the other side of the lawn. A couple of Brooke's children were wandering through the party, although the hope was that they would be safely ensconced in the media room before any of the behavior got really bad, especially the youngest, Taylor, who was in the group of girls with our daughters. We all feel it is important to set a good example for the younger generation.

We wondered where Rebecca and her Mystery Guest were— neither had arrived.

The sun began to move lower, bringing with it the sense not

just that the day was coming to a close but that summer was as well. We could feel just the very slightest hint of chill in the air, and we remembered that in July the sun set a full hour later than it did now.

Steam started to rise from the pool, the way it does when the water is warming up just as the air is cooling down. It gave the whole yard an otherworldly look.

And then Sherri Griffin walked in.

Okay, we almost didn't recognize Sherri. For one thing, she was blond! A bright, bright blond. Very well done, we decided, once she moved under the lights and we could get a good look at her. (Was it an Interlocks blond or a Shanti blond? We divided almost immediately into two camps.)

Then there was the way she walked into the party. Some of us were reminded of the scene in *The Devil Wears Prada* when Andy is walking down the street in New York City with this badass attitude and all of these gorgeous clothes, sprung from her mousy demeanor. It was kind of like that. Others of us thought about *Grease,* when Sandy puts on that black number and the red shoes and struts her stuff and sings "You're the One That I Want." It was a total transformation. Total.

Then there was her dress. We were shocked by that too. Looking back we weren't sure we'd ever gotten a good look at Sherri's body. Even at barre class (that one time) she wore something shapeless. Nobody wore shapeless clothes to barre class, so hers stood out—that's why we remembered. Not because we're judging. But anyway, we had no idea that she'd been hiding a rocking body under those bad clothes all summer. *No* idea.

(How was that possible? We live in a beach town. Had we never seen her in a bathing suit? Had she never been in the water? Hadn't we met her for the first time at surf camp, way back in June? We spent so much time quietly cataloguing each other's bodies for pounds lost or gained, lines emerging or erased, eyebrows that needed more or less shaping—how had we missed *this* body?)

Okay, and seriously? That dress was to die for. Somebody said later it had come from Bobbles and Lace. Maybe it was the Portsmouth location—we were in the Bobbles in town all the time and we had never seen it there. The shoes, the earrings, all of it. It was so very completely un-Sherri that we didn't know what to do. We just stared. Then one of us said, "Ohmygod, Sherri, you look amazing," and soon the rest of us followed suit, the way you do. OMG. OMG. OMG.

Except for Melanie. She had nothing to say; she was nowhere to be found. Later we learned that she and her husband had been at the far end of the lawn, just out of reach of the lights, arguing to beat the band.

There was no band, by the way. Brooke always hired a really good DJ from Boston.

Did we mention that the rest of us, excepting Melanie, and Rebecca, who hadn't yet arrived, were all standing near the bar when Sherri entered the party? The bartender Brooke hired was, dare we say it, easy on the eyes. She'd stocked the bar with some really good tequila. Like we told you in the beginning, it was the summer of tequila.

The bartender was making an Aperol tequila cocktail, which was a-mazing, even though some of us had never tried elderflower liqueur. We contemplated a round of shots before we got into the cocktails, and the bartender was kind enough to allow one of us to pick up a bottle from the bar while we thought about it. It was Roca Patron Silver, very good, though he was using a Blanco in the cocktail.

Yes, we decided. Yes. Summer was almost over; Brooke's party came around only once a year; the night was gorgeous; the very air felt full of longing and possibility. We all felt the need to make something happen. Or to let something happen. The DJ was playing something background-y and good vibe-y, something you didn't specifically notice, nothing you'd dance to yet, but something that echoed the mood exactly. The bartender readied the shot glasses.

And then, like we said, Sherri Griffin walked in, and our mouths fell open. She walked toward us, smiling an unfamiliar smile. Even her walk was different. Not like she was impersonating a hot person, no. Like she had *become* a hot person. Those of us who were blond may have attributed the change completely to her hair color, but the brunettes among us (there were a few) believed that there was more to it than that.

Sherri greeted us. She accepted our compliments. She watched some of us cast nervous glances at our husbands to see if *they* were looking at Sherri the way *we* were looking at Sherri.

Then Sherri said seven words that changed everything that night.

"Pass the bottle," said Sherri Griffin, without so much as a please or a thank-you. "And a shot glass."

We all looked at each other like, "Whaaaaat?"

And then we passed the bottle.

And a shot glass.

Honestly, it wasn't until a couple of days later, after the dust had settled, so to speak, that Brooke reminded us that Sherri hadn't even been invited to the party.

70.

SHERRI

"Pass the bottle," she told the nearest mom, Monica or Jessica or Nicole. "And a shot glass."

She didn't need the lime or the salt; she didn't need anything at all. She did one shot, then two, then a third, all the while looking Monica or Jessica or Nicole right in the eyes.

It felt good. She felt like herself again. She was reminded of what it felt like to have a roomful—in this case a yard full—of people's attention on her.

Then she gave a businesslike nod, a nod that said, *Time to get started here*. And she got ready to say all of the things she'd been holding back since that first day of surf camp, all those weeks ago.

71.

THE SQUAD

Okay, seriously? This new Sherri Griffin basically downed an entire bottle of tequila while we all watched. Maybe it wasn't an entire bottle. But it was definitely more than one shot. Two or three or maybe four. And we were like, what the hell? First of all, save some for the rest of us! And second, was she going to fall down drunk right in front of us, or, and we seriously hoped not, throw up in the pool? (That happened at Brooke's party in 2013, but we're not naming names. We will say that the involved party did pay for the pool company to come out the next day and hand-clean the filter, which was no small expense.)

With each shot of tequila Sherri became more composed, more steady. Her back, already very straight (and visible) in that (we had to admit, fantastic) gold dress, got even straighter. Her eyes, which were heavily made up, opened wider. She seemed to grow taller before us, like *The Nutcracker* Christmas tree. And it became a truth universally acknowledged: Sherri Griffin could hold her liquor.

The bartender, sensing new tension, made his first round of Aperol tequila cocktails, and we each took one. They went down easy. Also, they were sort of small, so a few of us went back for our second drink right away. Don't look at us that way. We knew the line would get long once the corn hole game ended, and we were just trying to be cognizant of the other partygoers. Okay?

Nicole was Sherri's first victim. Sherri turned to her and in no uncertain terms (there's some dispute about exactly what she said, which is why we are merely summarizing for you now) told her what a shitty thing it was to leave Katie and Morgan out of Riley's Boda Borg birthday party.

Nicole has that fair skin that hides neither shame nor alcohol, and almost immediately she reddened. She looked to some of us for backup, but nobody came to her defense. The next day some of us regretted that. But at the time, we were all too shocked. Seriously, Sherri Griffin had never been anything but unassuming and pleasant. Meek, you would have called her. *Milquetoast*, if you were being fancy, but we weren't typically that fancy.

After she had dispensed with Nicole, Sherri turned her attention to Dawn, and let loose on her for her telling everyone she'd been crawling around on the Laundromat floor at the beginning of the summer. How Sherri heard about that we do not know. That story had been told to just a few of us, in private.

After the evisceration of Dawn, Sherri set her teeth into Tammy. Not literally. But it felt like it. Her beef with Tammy had to do with an Instagram photo Tammy's daughter, Casey, had posted at a sleepover, when she'd tagged Katie even though she wasn't there—she hadn't been invited.

"Terrible," we all agreed later, hoping our daughters hadn't been guilty of the same shortcoming. "Real mean-girl stuff." We made mental notes to go home later and check Instagram accounts. And if we're being completely honest, Tammy doesn't always have the best judgment with that sort of thing herself. Sometimes, like mother like daughter.

When that was done, some of us slunk into the shadows, where the lights didn't reach, lest we were next. As it turned out, no single person was next. Sherri Griffin was addressing the whole group. She tossed her blond hair (definitely Shanti, we decided, probably that new stylist who had been brought in to do only color) and said, "Here's what we're going to do, ladies."

Even the bartender was listening.

"We're going to have a fresh start come fall. We're all going to be a little more accepting of newcomers." We nodded. "And I swear, if Katie comes home from school on the first day and tells me she didn't have anywhere to sit at lunch, or nobody shared a locker with her, or she didn't have a partner for the first group project, you're going to have to answer to me. And also?" She lowered her voice and we all leaned in. It was weird, how seductive she suddenly seemed. "I'd love to get in on that next trip to Nantucket. Whenever you guys are going. If one more isn't too much trouble." And she smiled, and she sauntered off.

Obviously Sherri Griffin did not bring a gun to Brooke's end-of-summer party. (Did she? No, of course not. Don't be stupid.) But there was something about the way she held herself that made us all feel like she had some sort of weapon—some power over us. It's hard to explain. It seems sort of embarrassing to talk about it now, especially considering what happened later. But at the time, well. We all took Sherri Griffin very seriously.

What did we do after that, you ask? Well, Gina saw Rebecca and her Mystery Man enter the party. She made a little noise of surprise and started off toward them.

But for a more long-term plan? What do you think we did? We told our daughters to make sure that Katie Griffin had the best first day of school in the history of first days of school. We had our girls fighting over who was going to sit next to her in the cafeteria. We had our daughters buying extra locker decorations so that whoever ended up with Katie Griffin as a locker partner would have the prettiest locker in the whole sixth grade. And when we planned the next trip to Nantucket, which, by the way, didn't take place for a while because of everything else that happened, you can bet your right index finger that Sherri Griffin was added to that text.

72

REBECCA

The party was clearly in full swing. Cars were lined all the way down the driveway. Music and laughter floated into the street beyond.

As soon as she saw all of this, second thoughts started marching through Rebecca's head.

"Maybe we should skip it," Rebecca said to Daniel. "Go to a movie?" Suddenly she wanted nothing more than to sink into one of the cushy seats at the new theater in Methuen and rest her face in a vat of popcorn. She'd see anything—even an action movie, or an animated movie, or *science fiction*. Anything.

"No way," said Daniel. "I have my party shirt on." Rebecca had been too agitated to notice his shirt; she looked more carefully now and saw that he was wearing a polo shirt in pale blue, rather than the navys and olives he typically wore.

"Fancy," she said. And then, because he really did look proud, she squeezed his hand and said, "You look very nice."

"I think it's funny that you're nervous," said Daniel.

"I'm not nervous," she lied. She was *so* nervous! This was the first time she was putting their relationship on display, and what a public forum in which to do so.

"Hey," said Daniel, before they walked into the backyard. "Come here, gorgeous." He pulled Rebecca toward him and kissed her lightly, so lightly that her lipstick stayed in place. "Thank you, Rebecca," he said formally. "For letting me into your life."

"Don't thank me yet," she said. She took his hand and led him through the gate. "First let's see if you make it out alive."

Naturally, the Mom Squad was clustered around the bar. As a unit, their heads swiveled when she and Daniel walked into the yard. Before they could get to the bar, Gina came toward them.

"I know *you*," she said. "Hey, Daniel."

"Gina." Daniel bobbed his head cordially.

"Are you guys dating?" Her head swiveled from Rebecca to Daniel and back to Rebecca again. Rebecca watched the understanding sinking in. She imagined she could see the whole history of Daniel's once-happy marriage, and Gina's friendship with Veronica the Cheater, the things Rebecca would never know or understand, and never *should* know or understand, because each friendship and relationship deserves its own private moments and secret backstory.

"We are," said Rebecca.

"Seriously dating?"

Rebecca glanced at Daniel again; he nodded. "It's pretty serious actually," Rebecca said.

"Is this where you've been all summer, Rebecca?" She couldn't tell if Gina was challenging Rebecca or if she was merely interested.

"All summer and for part of the winter too," said Rebecca. She found Daniel's hand and gripped it. A long moment passed.

"You should have told me," Gina said, half sad and half accusing.

"I wasn't ready to tell anyone yet," said Rebecca. "You know how this town is. You tell one person and it's the same as telling twenty."

"Oh, I know."

"I know you know," said Rebecca pointedly. Gina's eyes flicked from Rebecca to Daniel and back again. Gina didn't say *sleeping bag* and she didn't say *sorry* and Rebecca didn't say *distance* or *Morgan* or *holiday house committee*, but she thought that maybe in a few days, when they weren't at a party, when Daniel wasn't there, they'd sit down and talk it out.

"Well. I think that's great," said Gina finally. "You guys are two of my favorite people."

She opened her arms, offering a hug, and Rebecca hesitated only briefly before hugging her back. "We're all in high school for the rest of our lives," Rebecca had told Alexa earlier in the summer. Tragically true. But even high school sometimes offered redemption and second chances. Right? That was only fair.

"Okay, by the way," said Gina, "you are not going to *believe* what happened right before you got here." She pointed, and Gina turned. She saw a woman she didn't recognize walking away from the bar in a gold dress. And then she did recognize her. It was Sherri, with a new hair color, looking knock-your-socks-off gorgeous, disappearing into the shadows.

left on Merrimac, not too far from Brooke's house. She parked the Jeep.

"Change in plans," she announced. "Everybody out. We're switching cars with my mom."

"What's wrong with this car?" asked Morgan.

"It's running funny," said Alexa. "I don't want to take any chances with you two."

She didn't have keys to her mom's Acura on her key ring, but she banked on the possibility that whatever horrendous Marshalls outfit her mom bought wouldn't have big pockets (please, she prayed to the gods of fashion, *don't* let her be wearing something with big pockets) and that she would have left the keys in the center console, the way she sometimes did. Alexa would take the car, then she'd text her mom later and have her get a ride home with one of her friends. In the morning, if Alexa was still alive, she'd walk down here and pick up the Jeep. It would be a longish walk, but she'd try to appreciate the beauty of not being murdered.

Bingo! The keys were in the center console. It took some wrangling to get the Acura out of the driveway—this party was hopping, and there were cars parked every which way!—but Alexa had always been good at three-point turns. Peter, who could three-point turn out of a mason jar, had taught her well.

73.

ALEXA

Alexa forgot to be scared for a little while, she was so busy complimenting Sherri on her dress and her shoes and even her earrings and her hair. Her hair was blond! Like the Sherri from the newspaper photograph. But done in a really tasteful way. Shanti, Alexa could tell.

After Sherri left for the party, Katie and Morgan headed right for the TV and started watching *Pitch Perfect 3*. Alexa wondered if she should encourage them to choose a more age-appropriate movie, maybe *Paddington*, but she was still feeling jittery and she didn't have the energy for a battle. She paced back and forth in the tiny kitchen and kept checking her phone—for what? she wondered. Because the bad man was going to text or send a Snap before he came over?

"You girls want to go somewhere?" she said, when she could stand the feeling of being trapped not a second longer.

"Ice cream!" Katie and Morgan said together, and Alexa said, "Sure, why not? Why don't we go to Haley's?" Haley's wasn't in the center of town so she felt a little safer with that choice.

They all left the house and piled into the Jeep and then Alexa thought, *The Jeep!* She couldn't drive the Jeep around town while the bad men chased her down. "We just need to make a quick stop," she told the girls. She swung down Olive Street and turned

74

SHERRI

Sherri made her way toward the far end of the lawn. She was shaking, but she also felt really freaking amazing. The tequila had heightened her senses. The lights in the pool, which changed color like disco lights at a club, shone brighter. The music that the DJ was spinning sounded clearer. She felt the way Bobby looked like he felt when he did cocaine. Otherworldly. Invincible.

Don't worry, Katie-kins, she said in her head, sending her message up into the summer evening sky and back down into their little half-house, where Katie and Alexa and Morgan were all together, safe. *Mama's back, even if only for one night. And everything is going to be okay.*

A klatch of husbands stood around the corn hole game, and she headed toward them. She counted in her head while she waited for them to look at her.

One.

Two.

Three.

She'd met these husbands before. Some of them had been on the pontoon. One of them probably owned the pontoon, but she couldn't be sure. She could tell that to a man they thought they'd never seen her.

She watched them take in her gold dress and her blond hair and her breasts. She smiled.

"Gentlemen," she said.

"Hey there," said one of the husbands.

She pretended to wobble (well, she was sort of pretending, the heels were difficult in the grass) and put her hand on one of the husbands' arms to steady herself—this one was a different husband from the one who had spoken.

"Sorry," she said, smiling apologetically, demurely. "It's so hard to walk on this grass in these heels!"

The man's face took on a panicky look, and he said, "No worries, I've got you."

"Take them off," suggested another of the husbands. He was beefier than the other men (ex-football player?) but he was drinking one of the dainty cocktails, which made Sherri smile.

"You know what, I think I will," she said. She crouched down to undo the tiny buckles on the shoes, well aware that she was treating the husbands to a generous view of her cleavage.

She straightened, shoes in hand, and said, "Isn't anyone going swimming? Where I come from, we used to say that it's not a party until somebody jumps in the pool."

Some of the husbands looked nervous. The beefy one said, "Why not?" He put his dainty glass on one of the small tables scattered around the yard and tugged off his shirt, revealing a soft and surprisingly hairless midsection. "Big splash coming," he said. "Just to warn you." He nodded once, and ran with an unexpected amount of grace toward the deep end, cannonballing in. The splash was impressive, you could hear it even over the music, and Sherri stepped back to preserve her dress.

"Who's next?" asked Sherri. The men shifted. The beefy husband's head emerged from the deep end and he let out an exhilarative whoop. "This water rocks, man," he said. "It's like eighty degrees in here. You guys need to try it."

"*Who's next?*" Sherri cried, more sharply, and they all turned to look at her. *That's more like it*, she thought.

75

THE SQUAD

And just like that, Sherri was gone. We thought we saw her gold back disappearing into the crowd, toward the pool. The sun was beginning to set, and the sky had taken on that lavender late-summer hue that seems particular to New England. It was that in-between light where your eyes can play tricks on you. The deep end of the pool was difficult to make out.

Most of us thought Rebecca's mystery guest was *very* good-looking, sort of George Clooney-esque. He had kind eyes. It was always the kind ones who got cheated on, wasn't it? According to what Gina said later, Veronica the Cheater had always been difficult anyway. We thought Gina was close with Veronica. But that was Gina for you: one thing to your face, another behind your back.

It must have been a little while after we all met the mystery man that the argument between Melanie and her husband heated up at the far end of the lawn. There was shouting. Names were called. Somebody said a drink was thrown in a face, but that was never 100 percent verified.

We didn't know what had brought the argument on. Later there was talk that the argument had something to do with the summer nanny, who was from Argentina and had an accent that could make even the word *hemorrhoids* sound sexy, not that we'd ever heard her say that.

The cocktails were quite strong, and we'd seen Melanie's husband help himself to seconds and maybe even thirds within the first half hour. So anything could have happened. Aperol, we learned that night, is no joke on its own, but especially when mixed with tequila.

We were all standing around the bar, still somewhat in shock, partly in awe, over what had just transpired with Sherri, when Melanie crossed the lawn and joined our group. "I need to get out of here," said Melanie in a quavering voice. "But my car's blocked in." She had definitely been crying.

"Oh, sweetie," we said. "We're so sorry—tell us what happened." But we were phoning it in. We were still thinking about Sherri. (Melanie does this sort of thing a lot.)

"Take my car," said Rebecca. Rebecca always had more patience with Melanie's drama than the rest of us did. "You know which one it is, Melanie. White Acura. Keys are in the console. If you're okay to drive."

"I only had three sips of my drink!" cried Melanie. "I'm okay to drive, I promise." She swiped at her eyes and muttered, "I cannot believe this."

Melanie ran out to the driveway.

No, she didn't run. She was in strappy sandals with heels. She walked quickly.

The DJ ramped up the music. The bartender shook more cocktails. Then came the first cannonball. One of the husbands, obviously. We'd all worked too hard on our hair, or paid someone else to work hard, to ruin it at the beginning of the party. We couldn't see which husband from where we were standing. It was a fairly big splash, so most likely Dawn's or Jessica's. (They had played football together at UNH long ago; Dawn's husband had been a linebacker.)

You know what they say: the party doesn't start until somebody jumps into the pool.

76.

ALEXA

The frenzied end-of-summer feeling had invaded Haley's too, and the place was buzzing like a beehive. Alexa and the girls had to wait in line. Alexa left Katie and Morgan perusing the menu and turned to scan the crowd, looking for unfamiliar men, scary men. When she turned back, Morgan and Katie were digging in their pockets for quarters for the gumball machine. Alexa gave them all the quarters she could muster from her wallet and told them to stay in line for a minute while she took a stroll by the booths to keep an eye on the comings and goings in the parking lot. Haley's was decorated like a 1950s diner with a floor made of black-and-white checkerboard tiles and retro chairs and booths. The booths were all full of regular, non-scary combinations of parents and kids or clots of preteens and younger teens.

She paid for the girls' ice cream, forgetting to order something for herself, and wondered if they'd be safer in here, where the lights were bright and unforgiving, or outside at the picnic tables, where the light was fading but the mosquitos were unforgiving. Outside, she decided, and she stationed them at a table while she continued to patrol the parking lot. There was a lot of traffic going by on Route 1 and any minute a black SUV could pull in.

In fact, here was one now. Her pulse picked up.

Oh, never mind, it wasn't a scary man; it wasn't a member of a lesser-known crime family. It was someone her own age. It was Caitlin.

"Hey, Alexa," Caitlin said, hopping out of the SUV.

"Hey," said Alexa. Caitlin was coming toward her, blocking her view of the parking lot, so she moved to peer around her.

"I'm glad I ran into you, actually," said Caitlin.

"You are?" Alexa couldn't help it, her heart took a little optimistic, nostalgic skip. The light was seriously going now, and it occurred to Alexa that any old person could come off the rail trail and through the small section of parking lot, toward the picnic tables, before being discovered. You didn't have to arrive by car to Haley's; you could come by bike or on foot. You could even come by train and walk over from the station. Now that she'd realized that, she wasn't sure which way to face. Behind her, Morgan and Katie were giggling about something or other. A mosquito landed on Alexa's arm and she slapped at it.

"Alexa," Caitlin said. "I'm super sorry about what happened in March, that night at Destiny's. That's really what I wanted to get across to you at Popovers that day, but I didn't. I messed up. I told you that thing about Tyler instead . . ." She looked down at her feet. She was wearing her Jack Rogers Palm Beach leather thong sandals in white; Alexa mostly approved, although personally she preferred the bone white.

Here Alexa found herself facing two roads: the high and the low. It was a tough choice—each road looked attractive in its own way—but eventually high won out.

"You know what, Caitlin? I'm sorry if I've been prickly or hard to be with or whatever. I'm sorry if I overreacted." She took a deep breath and tried to put her complicated feelings into words. "But you and Destiny, your families are whole and complete, and they always have been. Mine's been broken not once but *twice*. I don't expect you to understand what that feels like. Honestly, I hope you never find out, or not for a long, long time. But you could have given me time to figure it out, you know? To figure out my own way to deal with it."

She thought she saw tears shining in Caitlin's eyes.

"Yeah, okay," said Caitlin finally. "I get that. I do. I'm sorry I didn't do a better job with that. I really am." She touched her artfully messy bun. Caitlin, Alexa had to admit, had always been really good at a messy bun, which, like most things, was harder than it looked.

"Thank you," said Alexa.

"I wanted to talk to you about something else too. About Tyler." She ducked her head. "We've sort of been—talking. Hanging out." She squinted at Alexa. "Does that bother you? Does that make you mad?" Her voice rose a little bit, pleading.

"Well, it doesn't surprise me," said Alexa. "Let's put it that way." Caitlin had had her eye on Tyler since freshman year.

"I mean," continued Caitlin, "if you have to know . . ."

"I don't," said Alexa. "I don't have to know."

"All he wants to do is talk about you," Caitlin continued anyway. "He's pretty broken up about how things ended with the two of you."

Alexa rolled her eyes so hard she thought one might roll right out of her head. *Bullshit,* she thought. "I'm sure he is," she said. Her voice sounded shaky. Another car rolled into the parking lot and she craned her neck to get a good view of it. She looked around for Morgan and Katie. They had finished their ice cream and were practicing cartwheels on the patch of grass.

Caitlin had always been so transparent about what she was thinking: she had no poker face, only tells. For a slice of an instant, Alexa missed their friendship with an intensity that gripped at her core. She felt herself softening further.

"Hey, listen. If you do start hanging out with Tyler, or whatever you want to call it—"

"Yes? What?" For a split second Caitlin looked like the old Caitlin, the anxious middle school Caitlin, who was the same Caitlin who'd once laughed so hard at Alexa's imitation of their algebra teacher during lunch in eighth grade that milk shot out of her nose.

Alexa paused. Her heart was still hammering and her insides were jumbled but this felt important enough to force all of those parts to be quiet for a moment.

"If you do hang out with Tyler, just be really careful, okay? He wasn't always that nice to me. Just—just watch yourself. Take care of yourself."

Caitlin nodded slowly. "Okay," she said. "Thanks, Alexa. I'll talk to you soon?"

"Yeah. Okay. Soon."

Caitlin went through the side door into Haley's, and as soon as she was gone the drumbeat started up in Alexa's brain again.

The bad men are coming. The bad men are looking for you. The bad men have found you. The bad men are coming. Are coming. Are coming. "Let's go!" she called to Katie and Morgan, trying to delete the panic from her voice. "Time to go, girls. Now. Right now. Morgan? Katie? Right now."

Back in the Acura Alexa said, "Change of plans. We're going back to our house, Morgs." They had to be safer at their house than at the Griffins'. Right? *Right?* Especially with the Jeep gone.

"But we had the movie paused at Katie's house!" protested Morgan.

The lie slid out. "Sorry. Katie's mom texted to see if I could take you both back to our house. I guess the party might go later than they thought."

"I'm not surprised by that," said Morgan philosophically. To

Katie she said, "Brooke's parties always go really late. Brooke's parties are crazy."

"Why do you know that?" asked Alexa.

Morgan shrugged. "People talk."

Understatement of the century, thought Alexa.

"Katie, you're spending the night," said Alexa. She pulled out onto Route 1 and then took the traffic circle back toward town, looking in the rearview mirror every two seconds.

"I am?" said Katie. "I didn't bring my stuff. Can we go back to my house to get my stuff?"

Before too long they were almost at Alexa and Morgan's house. The traffic on High Street was moving normally, no black SUVs were stopped in front of the house, but all of Alexa's organs felt like they were jumping. She said, "You can borrow some of Morgan's things to sleep in. It'll be more fun here, I promise. And maybe you guys can swim later." Two truths, one lie. No way was she letting them outside, and certainly not in the pool.

Katie looked dubious. Morgan was about three sizes smaller than Katie.

"Or mine," said Alexa, and in the rearview mirror she saw Katie brighten. Why the hell not? She pulled into the driveway, and said, "Everybody out."

Once the girls were inside Alexa locked the door, installed Morgan and Katie in front of the television and told them they could re-rent the movie and fast-forward until they got to the part where they'd left off. She said she'd make popcorn, and she was rummaging through the pantry for the jar when the doorbell rang.

Never until that moment had she truly understood the meaning of the phrase *"jumping out of your skin."*

Shouldn't she let someone know what was going on, in case something bad actually did happen? Shouldn't she let *Sherri* know? Alexa was responsible for two young girls, and they were in danger.

She typed out a text. She didn't hit send, but she got it ready. Just in case. I think you should come back. After a second she added, I'm scared. I'm really sorry but I found out who you are.

(Three truths, no lie.)

"Alexa!" called Morgan. "Door!"

The doorbell went another time. Whoever was ringing it was pressing down really hard, again and again, and the sounds were reverberating through Alexa's whole body.

"I know," whispered Alexa, too quietly for Morgan to hear her. *The bad man is coming,* she thought. *The bad man is coming.* The doorbell rang again, again.

The bad man is here.

She sent the text.

77.

SHERRI

Sherri had laid her evening bag (also gold, also purchased at Bobbles and Lace) on one of the many cocktail tables scattered across the lawn. There were at least five people in the pool, and others hovering around, looking like they wanted to join in. Once the pool extravaganza was under way she slid the phone out of her evening bag and looked at it, and her heart jumped directly into her throat and nearly straight out of her body. The text was from Alexa.

I think you should come back. I'm scared. I'm really sorry but I found out who you are.

Sherri's response to this text was visceral, immediate, physical. She left her shoes where they were, took her phone, and ran over to the side of the lawn, where she threw up into the bushes, just beyond where the outdoor lights reached. Her entire body was shaking. Her legs could scarcely hold her up.

I'm coming home, she texted back. I'll be right there.

Could she drive with the alcohol in her system? Should she? No, she shouldn't, but did she have a choice? Would she be faster running home?

No. She couldn't run in this outfit, and walking would take too long. She'd have to drive. The fear had sobered her up. She'd be fine.

But when Sherri got out to the driveway she saw that her car was blocked in by all the partygoers who had arrived after her. It would take some serious maneuvering to get it out. She saw Melanie wandering around the driveway too. "I've got to get the hell out of here," Melanie said. "I'm looking for Rebecca's Acura. But I can't find it."

"I've got to get out of here too," said Sherri.

78.

ALEXA

The person on the other side of the door had given up on the bell and was now pounding directly on the door. Hard, again and again and again. Then the person was shouting her name. "Alexa! Are you in there? Alexa. Alexa. Alexa!" Alexa realized, as she disentangled herself from the net of her fear, that she recognized the voice.

It was Tyler. It was just Tyler. She opened the door and leaned against the doorjamb for support.

"Tyler! What the hell? You scared me." Her knees were shaking but the rattling of her heart began to subside. "What are you doing here?"

Tyler was wearing a Newburyport Clippers Lacrosse T-shirt, jeans, and a Red Sox baseball hat. Under the glow of the porch lights—she had decided to keep them on, after much internal debate—his eyes were bloodshot and at half-mast. Pot eyes. "I just wanted to talk to you," he said. "Can I come in?"

Alexa thought about Caitlin. *He's pretty broken up about how things ended with the two of you.* She looked in the driveway, and out on the street. She didn't see his car. She stepped aside, and Tyler entered the house. She closed and locked the door behind him. "How'd you get here?"

"I walked. I was downtown."

"By yourself?"

"Yeah. I mean, I was with some of the guys. But they all stayed down there." He leaned in, too close. "So what's really going on with you and that golfer kid?"

She stiffened. There was something she didn't like in Tyler's voice. She didn't like the way he was looking at her—it was more of a sneer, actually.

"Nothing," she said. "We just hang out sometimes." The sneer deepened, and Tyler stepped toward her. She backed away.

"I know you're lying. I know where he lives too. Off Turkey Hill. I'm going to go talk to him."

"Talk to Cam? About what?"

"About you."

"How're you going to talk to him? You walked here. Are you going to walk all the way out to Turkey Hill? That's like three miles." She crossed her arms and she was briefly so irritated that she almost forgot to be scared.

"Can I take your car?"

"*No.* Of course not. No way. Anyway, mine has a flat. I'm driving my mom's."

"Can I take your mom's car?"

"Definitely not."

And here was where things got complicated. Tyler had known Alexa and her family for a long time. He'd been in this house, what, zillions of times. He knew where they kept the extra toilet paper and the backup pool towels and the Cap'n Crunch her mother bought for Tyler to have as a snack, dry, by the handful. He knew that you had to pull up on the handle of the door that led to the back patio to lock it and that the window screen in Alexa's bedroom fell out when a stiff wind blew. He knew that car keys went inside the small blue bowl on the hall table that came from

Fireside Pottery in Maine, and that was where he reached, before Alexa could stop him.

"Tyler. Give me the keys. You can't just take my mom's car."

But it was too late. He was already out the front door, and she saw that past the porch lights it was fully dark, with no moon to speak of. Blacker than the inside of a cow, as Peter used to say, until the motion-sensor driveway lights went on. With her eyes she swept the driveway and then the slice of High Street she could see. No black SUVs.

Then she remembered. She'd sent that text to Sherri. Except she hadn't told Sherri that she had moved the girls to her own house, so if Sherri was on her way anywhere it was to her own house.

"I'll bring it back safe, don't you worry," Tyler was saying from the driveway. "I just want to talk to the guy. Cam. See what I can do about getting my girl back."

"Ugh. Tyler, I'm not your girl. I was never your girl. I'm not anyone's girl."

"We'll see about that," said Tyler.

She heard him peel out of the driveway in the Acura. If anything happened to her mother's car, her mother was going to *freak* out. She'd just gotten that dent fixed.

Once again, she closed and locked the door. She peeked in on the girls—they were off the couch, and doing their own dance to *Freedom* along with Anna Kendrick and the rest of the Bellas. Katie had decent rhythm.

Okay. Deep breath. In, out. Everyone was safe.

She sent another text to Sherri. So sorry. False alarm.

79

CAM

Cam's parents were at the lake; he had the house to himself. Before it got dark he and the dog, Sammy, had walked all the way around the Artichoke reservoir—five solid miles, with hills—and they were both tired and content. He was waiting to hear from Alexa. She said she'd call him when she was finished babysitting. Cam had thought at first that he might be invited to go over while she was babysitting, but in the end he was glad, in a self-preserving way, that he hadn't been. He didn't want to compromise her babysitting reputation.

Cam was *so attracted* to Alexa. He couldn't even believe it. He understood in a way he never had before why people did crazy things for love: why they killed for it, died for it, ruined their lives or the lives of other people over it. Why they fought wars! He had never comprehended, when they were assigned *The Illiad* in high school, just how it was that Helen of Troy's beauty could have caused such havoc between the Trojans and the Achaeans. Now, though? If some guy named Paris of Newburyport tried to make Alexa fall in love with him and take her away from Cam forever . . . yeah, he'd put up a fight. He'd start a war.

Cam showered and settled on the couch with the Golf Channel on, Sammy's head resting on his bare feet. Some people liked to put on golf to sleep but to Cam there was nothing peaceful about it—golf, to Cam, represented edge-of-your-seat drama. In what other sport was utter concentration so necessary that even a small noise from the crowd, even a puff of wind moving in an unexpected direction, could change the entire course of the game?

The Golf Channel was showing a tape of Phil Mickelson's 2004 Masters win, one of the all-time bests. Even though Cam knew exactly how this would play out, even though he'd watched it dozens of times, maybe more, he watched, tense, as Mickelson and DiMarco strode toward the eighteenth hole. He listened to the tweeting of the birds and the whispered commentary of the announcers. The quiet of the spectators was so very quiet that it was almost a sound unto itself.

DiMarco putted, missed. With Mickelson gearing up for his final, tournament-winning, history-making putt, Cam's phone rang.

When he'd first started hanging out with Alexa, his friend Dex had said, "That girl? Bro! She is so far out of your league I don't even think your two leagues are in the same universe."

"I know," said Cam. "I know."

"Dude," Dex went on. "One day that girl is going to wake up, and she's going to look in the mirror, and then she's gonna look at you, and she's going to come to her senses. And that will be the last you see of her. You ugly bastard." Dex laughed and punched Cam on the arm—this was a habit he'd taken up after pledging Alpha Sigma Phi at Boston University.

"Okay, Dex," said Cam. "I get it."

Deep down, Cam wondered if Dex was right. Cam's parents raised him and his two older brothers to be respectful of girls and women, to be good Catholics, to undertake at least one service project a season, to work hard and play sports fairly, and to have some idea of the direction they wanted their lives to take so they were always marching along on a plane that was straight and sure. He could not believe that someone like Alexa Thornhill had ever given him the time of day, much less spent the better part of the summer with him.

Cam wasn't completely green when it came to the opposite sex, obvs. But he had heretofore dated girls like Shelby McIntyre: sincere, smart, pretty-but-not-so-pretty-you-couldn't-concentrate-on-anything-else girls, girls who took their sports and their grades as seriously as he took golf and his own grades. AP Bio girls, girls who made his mother sigh with happiness and say things like, "I *like* her, Cameron. You hang on to that one."

And then Alexa Thornhill came hurtling into his world, with her contemptuous smirk and her YouTube channel and her perfect, perfect body, and her skin that smelled like lavender, and her way of looking at him from underneath her lashes.

At Salisbury Beach the other night they had spread a blanket far back, close to the dunes. It was twilight. The sand belonged to the dog owners, the water to the whales or the sharks, if you believed the rumors. Nobody was paying them any heed. They took it easy at first, some kissing, some through-the-clothes stuff, more kissing, then it all started to heat up. Alexa was wearing one of her sundresses that fell to midthigh when she was standing, but inched up alluringly, up and up, when she was prone, offering, when the moon allowed, a glimpse of lace panties in virginal white. She pressed harder against him as they kissed, and, with his hand on the captivating protrusion of her hip bone, he thought he could die a happy man.

And then she had said, "It's my first time, Cam."

He couldn't be the first. Of course she had slept with Tyler. Right? Hadn't she?

"No," she said, shrugging her beautiful, beautiful shoulders in answer to his questions. And into his neck she whispered, "You're the first."

He said, "Are you sure? Are you absolutely one hundred percent sure you want this?" Because he'd been raised by two solid parents and he'd come of age in the #metoo movement and he understood his responsibilities to retain decency in a world that didn't always value it.

"Yes," she said. "I want this."

The awkward fumbling with the condom was the worst part of the whole business, especially considering the sand, but obviously necessary, and when that part was done he put one thumb on each of her perfect temples, and he asked one more time: "Okay?"

"Yes," she said, "okay."

And he didn't understand anyone who thought Alexa Thornhill wasn't nice. What people didn't see about Alexa was that beneath her tough exterior, beneath her beauty, she was actually smart and funny and even vulnerable, tender, like a lobster that had shed its old shell and hadn't yet grown a new one.

He paused the television to answer the phone. His heart jumped when he saw Alexa's name on the screen.

"Hey," he said. "What's up? Are you done babysitting? You can come over here, if you want, nobody's here, my parents are at—"

She cut him off. "I'm not done babysitting," she said. "I called to warn you. Tyler's coming. To talk to you. He's on his way now, from my house."

Cam stood up, disturbing Sammy, who roused and looked blearily up at Cam, offended. The remote fell to the floor.

"Tyler?" said Cam. "Tyler is coming here?"

"He's all worked up," Alexa said. "He came over here and he was, like, threatening you, and then he took my mom's keys, right from the bowl, and then he just took off in her car—"

"Wait," said Cam. "Where's your mom?"

"She's at Brooke's end-of-summer party. I had her car here. And Tyler is on the warpath. He's drunk or something. High. I don't know. It's like he's coming to challenge you for me. He called me his girl. Blech. How gross is that? And now I think he wants to fight you for me."

"He's coming to fight me?" A decade ago, Cam was briefly obsessed with martial arts; he went thrice weekly to Tokyo Joe's on the Bridge Road, where he'd made his way to the junior advanced level. But he was not, in general, a fighter. Tyler played lacrosse; he was a big guy, six one, at least, and strong. "And he's driving drunk?"

"Maybe high. Just don't engage with him, okay? And don't let him drive away, it's not safe."

Adrenaline surged through Cam. He stepped on the remote, and the Masters recording unpaused. Mickelson putted. Thirty-four years old, and he'd finally won his first major tournament. The crowd went wild. "Got it," he said.

"Do whatever you have to do, just take the keys and hang on to them. Promise? I really need you to promise."

"I promise," said Cam. "I'll take the keys; I won't let him drive home. What should I do with Tyler, though? Is there somebody I should call?"

"Throw him in the bushes, I don't care."

"I'll bring the car back to you. How about that?"

"No! No, Cam, don't do that."

"Why not? Are you okay, Alexa? You sound scared. Are you scared about something, besides Tyler?"

"Just stay where you are, okay, Cam? I'll call you later, and we'll deal with the car. Just take the keys, and stay where you are."

She disconnected the call, and now Cam's doorbell was ringing, and ringing, and in between rings someone was pounding on his door.

To call their exchange brief was a bit of an understatement, like calling a long iron shot into the wind moderately challenging.

Cam said, "Keys?"

"What the fuck?" said Tyler.

"Keys," said Cam firmly. He stepped out onto the front porch, held out his hand, and Tyler dropped the keys into it.

"What am I supposed to do now?" Tyler sounded petulant, like a little kid who had his electronics taken away by a parent.

"Call somebody for a ride, I guess." Cam made a great show of locking the door behind him. "I'm going to take this car back to Alexa's house."

She had told him not to. But he would go anyway.

80.

ALEXA

After she hung up with Cam, Alexa crouched down so she could look out the front window without being seen, and for the second time that night her heart stopped. There was a car in the driveway.

It was a black SUV.

This was it. This *had* to be the same car Hannah called from the Cottage to tell her about. It was sitting in the spot vacated by her mother's Acura.

That was when the doorbell rang again. And Alexa's breath caught and she started to feel a little dizzy.

The only answer was the one there had always been, as obvious, as inevitable as a sunset. *The bad men were coming.*

She shouldn't have told Sherri it was a false alarm.

The bad men were here.

"Alexa!" called Morgan. "The doorbell!"

"I know!" she called back. Her voice sounded amazingly normal considering how her insides were flipping around. The lights in the foyer were on. The outside lights were blazing.

Briiiing.

She couldn't answer.

She had to answer.

Briiiing.

She'd tell the bad man he must have the wrong house, the wrong person, the wrong idea. She'd tell him to go away.

She opened the door.

81.

CAM

Cam drove fast down Hale Street. He didn't like the way Alexa sounded. He wanted to get to her. He forced himself to rely on what made him a good golfer: patience, and focus, and calm in the midst of chaos. He thought about Mickelson and that final putt in 2004. He put his hands at ten and two on the wheel, the way he'd learned to drive. He focused on the road; he focused on Alexa.

"I'm coming," he said out loud. "I'm coming, Alexa." She had told him not to come, but of course he would. He'd get the car back to her; he'd make sure she was okay.

That's when the deer ran out in front of him and froze.

Cam's last coherent thought—his very last thought ever—was "That looks like a deer in the headlights!" which was something he'd have to remember to tell Alexa, because even though she'd roll her eyes he knew she'd laugh on the inside, and sometimes the inside laughs were the best kind.

He swerved to avoid the deer, and the pole was coming toward him, and there was the most terrific crunch of metal, and then everything went black. Except for a far-off light in the distance, no bigger than the head of a pin. And he wanted to say, "Alexa, hold on, I'm coming for you, I love you." But he couldn't say anything at all.

82.

THE SQUAD

Rebecca's car wasn't there after all, where Melanie thought it was, in Brooke's driveway. We didn't know what had happened until later, when the details of the night started to sort themselves out. Apparently, Alexa's Jeep was running funny. So she left her Jeep on Merrimac and took Rebecca's Acura.

At some point Melanie decided she didn't need to leave after all. Why should she be the one to leave, when she hadn't been (in her mind) in the wrong? Let *him* be the one to leave. She was going to stay and enjoy the party, and, yes, she would like to have one of those Aperol cocktails! And when that was done, she just might have another one. Since the line was getting long, why didn't she just grab two now?

Melanie found Rebecca, who was at one of the stand-up cocktail tables with the mystery man, whom by then we knew to be Daniel Bennett. Melanie told Rebecca she didn't see the car, but never mind, she'd changed her mind anyway. Rebecca didn't think much of Melanie not being able to find her car. By then the party was really very crowded, and the cars had more than filled Brooke's long driveway and were snaking onto Merrimac Street. She'd probably just overlooked it.

Did we hear the sirens from where we were? Some people said later that they had. But most of us viewed that as unlikely. Anyone coming from the police station would have cut up to High Street almost immediately to get more quickly to Hale Street. And it would have been nearly impossible to hear the ambulance from Brooke's backyard.

Somebody said later that before all of that happened, they saw Sherri Griffin throwing up in the bushes. That wasn't a surprise. Did you see how much alcohol she drank in a relatively short amount of time?

83.

ALEXA

There was a man outside. He was around her mother's age, with sandy hair and a wide freckled face. There was something about him—something in the set of his eyes, the shape of his nose, something that reminded her of someone she knew.

"Alexa Thornhill?" said the man.

"Maybe," said Alexa. Her fear was so strong and all-consuming that it felt like an out-of-body experience.

"I've been trying to get hold of you! You are one hard person to find. I went to your place of employment earlier, looking for you."

The man held out his hand to shake hers and Alexa thought, *Are these the manners of a murderer?* She found herself shaking back—really, it was the only way to keep her hand from quaking right off her wrist, and also, for good or for ill, she had been brought up to respond in kind when presented with an outstretched hand. She peered around the man to see where the other men were. The accomplices. But there was nobody else there. Maybe they were still in the SUV. Readying the weapon, preparing for a clear shot.

"And I was told that the specialty of the house is something called the Ring? Which involves a doughnut along with the ice cream?"

"The Ringer," whispered Alexa.

"Ah! Of course. The Ringer. Right." He chuckled and rubbed his belly. He was awfully friendly for someone who was about to kill her. But then again, so was the psychopath in *Killing Eve*. Right before she killed her victims, she was utterly charming—seductive, even. "I have something to show you, if you don't mind."

The man furrowed his brow. Again there was something familiar about him, a flash in his expression. He reached into his back pocket and Alexa's knees came close to giving out. She thought, *Here we go.* He was going for his gun, and she had nothing to protect herself with. She squeezed her eyes shut. Would Morgan know to call 911, once she heard the shot? Would Katie?

She waited for what seemed like hours but was probably an eighth of a second, and when no shot came she opened her eyes. The man was holding a small bronze coin.

"This is my five-year sobriety coin," he said. "I bought it on Amazon, and it cost less than six dollars, but it's incredibly meaningful to me. I told myself that when I earned this coin I would allow myself to come and find you."

"*What?*" Her veins were still flushed with adrenaline; she couldn't quiet her breathing into any normal pattern. "I don't understand."

"I'm sorry," said the man. "I should have led with an introduction. My name is Jacob." He paused. "Jacob Thornhill."

"Thornhill?" she said. "But that's *my*—"

"That's right," said the man. He waited, as though giving her a chance to figure something out. "Go ahead," he said finally, encouragingly.

"Wait. Are you my—?" No, this couldn't be right. This was insane. She couldn't bring herself to say the word out loud, and then she could. "You're my *father*?"

He nodded. "And I don't mean to intrude on your life, really and truly I don't. I only want to see that you're okay. I just want to know that you survived what I put you and your mother through. I can disappear as quickly as you want me to. We can have zero contact after this. I just needed to—" He took a deep breath and looked almost teary. "I just needed to see. With my own eyes. And look at you! You've survived *and* thrived. You're just as lovely as you are online, on your channel . . ."

"My channel?"

"And that's why I started leaving those comments."

"Comments?"

Alexa's brain couldn't catch up.

"Yes, as JT76—"

"JT76?"

"My initials. Plus my birth year. I tried to be kind. It's just, Alexa, I really needed to know I didn't destroy your life by giving things such a bad start. I don't expect to be involved in any way, but I needed to lay eyes on you and know I didn't ruin everything forever. That's why I got in touch with your mom, last year. Though I don't blame her for not answering, really I don't."

"Got in touch with my mom?" repeated Alexa. "Last year?"

"And I know I'm supposed to wait until your eighteenth birthday. But since you're leaving soon . . . I didn't wait. And I really do know a good Realtor in L.A. I really *can* help you get set up."

"Wait a minute," said Alexa. "I'm still catching up." Her phone, which she'd been gripping in her hand, started to ring. Her mom. She declined the call: she'd call her back.

Then it started ringing again.

"Seems like I caught you at a busy time," said Jacob Thornhill. "But I'm on the East Coast for a week or so. I'd love to talk more, if you're willing. I understand you may need some time to think about it." He pressed a business card into her hand. "There's no rush. Here's my number. When you're ready. If you're ready." He turned and walked back to his car.

Again Alexa's phone rang, stopped, started again. Her mother must have noticed that the Acura was gone from Brooke's driveway, and now, of course, there would be hell to pay.

84.

SHERRI

False alarm, said the next text from Alexa to Sherri.

She was starting to sober up now; getting sick in the bushes had sped that along.

In their situation, she didn't think there was any such thing as a false alarm. It took some serious maneuvering but Sherri was eventually able to work her car out from its spot and out of Brooke's long driveway.

She pulled up in front of the house on Olive Street. The front door was locked—that was good. She unlocked and entered. The kitchen light was on, and so was the light in the living room.

But nobody was there.

"Hello!" she called. Nobody answered. She screamed: "Katie! Morgan! Alexa! Where is everybody?"

Nobody was home.

Nobody was home.

She could hardly breathe. She pulled her phone out of her bag and texted Katie:

Where R U.

The reply came immediately. Morgan's house. Out in front w morgan there's a police man here.

Ohmygodohmygodohmygod. Katie, Alexa, Morgan, a policeman. *I found out who you are.*

Coming to get u.

She was leaving the house, locking the door behind her, when she saw Miss Josephine peering out of her own front door.

"All this yelling and banging around!" said Miss Josephine.

"I'm sorry," said Sherri hurriedly. "I thought Katie was here, but she's not. I'm so sorry to disturb you."

"And what on earth did you do to your hair?" barked Miss Josephine. "That color doesn't suit you at all."

Sherri was at Morgan's house in under thirty seconds. And yes: *There was a police car in the driveway.* Its lights were on. Morgan and Katie were sitting on the front steps in pajamas—Katie's were unfamiliar—the lights from the police car casting an eerie glow on their faces. When Sherri got out of the car, Katie ran up to her and threw herself into Sherri's arms. "Alexa's mom's car was in an accident," said Katie. "That's why the police are here. But Alexa's mom wasn't driving it."

"Who was driving it?"

"I don't know," said Morgan. "My mom's in there now, talking to the police."

"I want to go home," said Katie. "I don't like this. Can we take Morgan home with us?"

"Yes," said Sherri. "Yes, absolutely we can take Morgan home with us."

85

THE SQUAD

When Cam Hartwell's obituary ran in the *Daily News of Newbury-port,* we all looked at the picture for the longest time. In the picture he was smiling and holding a golf club.

The line for the wake at Twomey, LeBlanc & Conte, the funeral home, stretched a full block down High Street. The service, at Immaculate Conception, was standing room only. We didn't go; we didn't know Cam, or his parents. Cam and his brothers hadn't been through the public school system, and they were older. But Gina's ex-sister-in-law, Veronica, had once been in a book club with Cam's mom and she told Gina it was the saddest funeral she had ever been to. Ever. And that Alexa was inconsolable.

86.

REBECCA

Rebecca knocked on the door of Alexa's room the day after the funeral. It was ten thirty in the morning; the day was shaping up to be cruelly, unfairly perfect, with the sun resplendent and the air dry. Rebecca knew that Alexa would have preferred rain.

She expected Alexa to be asleep but she was sitting on her bed, fully dressed, in shorts and a tank. Rebecca was carrying a plate of Ritz crackers slathered with peanut butter. She didn't think Alexa had eaten since the funeral, and maybe not before. When Alexa was young, this was the snack that could draw her out of a bad temper or disappointment.

Rebecca had a very strict no-eating-in-the-bedrooms rule, and Alexa's eyes shot up in surprise when she noted the plate.

"I know," Rebecca said, interpreting the look. "I made an exception. Extenuating circumstances." She put the plate on the nightstand and sat down on the edge of the bed. Alexa moved over to make room for her.

What to say to her brokenhearted daughter?

By the time Rebecca had gotten back to the house on the night of Brooke's party (it had been no easy task to find a sober driver who could access a car), she felt like she'd had fourteen separate heart attacks. Esther's uncle, who worked for the Newburyport Police Department, had been the one to let Esther know a white

Acura had been involved in an accident. Until they had more details, naturally Rebecca thought it had been *Alexa* driving the Acura. Alexa hadn't answered the phone the first dozen times Rebecca had called, in her mind confirming her very worst fear.

"Listen—" said Rebecca. She found Alexa's calf under the blankets and laid her palm against it, flat and firm. "Listen," she said again. "Sweetie." Her voice was authoritative, but she had nothing to say and no confidence that she'd be able to come up with anything. They sat like that for a moment, mother and daughter, until Alexa spoke.

"It's my fault," she said.

Rebecca had anticipated this. She was ready. "It's not your fault, honey. It was an accident. You weren't driving. You didn't give Tyler the keys. It's *not your fault.*"

Alexa looked straight ahead, not at her mother. She hardly blinked. "But if Cam hadn't met me, he'd still be alive."

"Oh, honey." Rebecca's heart twisted for Alexa. "Honey," she repeated. "You can't think like that. You can't let your mind go down those rabbit holes. There is absolutely no point to it."

"But it's the only way I can think! I can't think any other way. I'm just lying up here, thinking and thinking and thinking." Alexa's face crumpled and she began to cry—first tentatively, then harder and harder.

Rebecca reached for a box of tissues on the nightstand. She said, "Can I tell you a story about Peter?"

Alexa nodded and gradually her sobs subsided. She sniffled and swiped at her nose.

"Two months before he died—" Even now, all this time later, Rebecca had to stop and catch her breath when she said that. "Two months before Peter died, he was offered a different job, with another company. It was more money, but he wouldn't have liked it as much. It wasn't hands-on, and the hands-on parts were the parts he loved. Nevertheless, he felt he should take it, for us. To provide more."

Alexa's face spasmed briefly. *That was Peter for you* was what her face said.

"But *I* didn't want him to be unhappy in the service of money. I convinced him to keep the job he had."

"And that's why he was in Dubai," whispered Alexa.

"And that's why he was in Dubai," affirmed Rebecca. "Do you know how many times I've lain awake at night trying to figure out if that aneurysm was just waiting for a reason to rupture? If it was going to rupture at that point in time no matter where he was, or if it was the long trip to Dubai that did it? Do you know how many times I've wondered if *Peter would still be alive* if he'd taken the job *I* convinced him not to take? The job he was leaning toward taking?"

"*Mom.* No."

"It's true. I have. I've thought about it so much. But the point is, I'll never know. So I understand what you're going through. But I also understand—I *one hundred percent know,* sweetie—that you can't blame yourself for what happened to Cam."

Alexa started to cry again. "I think I loved him, Mom. I really think I did. And I don't think I'm ever going to fall in love again. I think that was my one chance, and look what happened."

"Oh, Alexa." Rebecca thought of all the twists and turns her life had taken since she'd been Alexa's age. The early boyfriends, the missteps and misstarts. Alexa's father. Rebecca thought it had been all over for her after that; she thought she'd used up her chances. *Then* she'd met Peter and she'd thought that those blissful years were here forever. But she'd been wrong about that too. Now she knew Daniel, and there was nothing that said that he would be in her life permanently. You could take nothing for granted. *Nothing.* A lump in the breast, a slip of the ski, a turn of the wheel, a deer in the road—who was to say what was waiting around the corner for any of them. "That wasn't your only chance. I promise you. It wasn't."

"Mom?" Alexa motioned to the spot next to her at the head of the bed, and Rebecca, who hadn't cuddled with her daughter in who knew how long, leaned back against the headboard and put her arm around Alexa. Alexa pressed her head into her mother's neck—it wasn't the most comfortable thing in the world for Rebecca's neck, in truth, but she didn't want to spoil the moment. "How long until it stops hurting, Mom?"

Rebecca thought about that for a long time. Six months? Definitely not. A year? No. Longer. There was only one real answer in the end. "I don't know," she said. "I'll let you know when I get there."

Alexa didn't stop crying, and she didn't say *thank you* or *please help me through it*. But she did reach over Rebecca to take a peanut butter cracker, and that was something.

87.

ALEXA

Morgan wanted to go surfing one final time before sixth grade, so she asked Alexa and Rebecca to take her to Jenness Beach on the penultimate day of summer, the week after Cam's funeral. The day was almost cruel in its perfection, a big tease for all of the kids about to ready their backpacks and sharpen their pencils.

Rebecca said, "Parking will be a nightmare."

But Morgan persisted—she had checked the surf forecast, and the waves looked promising. So off they went, packing their stuff up in the rental car that insurance was paying for while the details of buying a replacement for the Acura got sorted out. It was the only time all summer that the three of them had spent the day together with nobody else around.

When they got their smoothies and coffees at Summer Sessions Alexa's mother refused Alexa's money and threw down her credit card. Alexa, feeling generous, stuffed a five in the tip jar that said "bikini fund" on it, even though she thought it was unnecessary for the surfer girls to have a bikini fund when clearly they got, like, the biggest discount ever from the Summer Sessions shop.

Alexa helped Morgan carry her board. Alexa's mom set up the chairs and the umbrella they'd had the foresight to drop off before parking in the backup lot. Then Morgan stepped into her wet suit and presented her back to Alexa for zipping. Despite all of the ice cream she'd eaten this summer, Morgan was still very, very skinny—she was the only person Alexa knew on whom a wet suit was actually baggy. When she was zipped she turned around and faced Alexa and gave her a giant smile. The zinc she had applied to her face was uneven, making her look like a clown who'd partied too hard after last night's circus.

"Don't go out too far," Alexa told her. "Be careful."

"I'll be careful," Morgan promised. She dragged the board down the beach, the leash trailing behind her, and Alexa watched to make sure she fastened the strap around her ankle once she got there.

Alexa and Rebecca had just settled themselves in their chairs when they saw Morgan flip off her surfboard. They stood as a unit and started toward the water, but before they got there Morgan's head popped out of a wave. Her board was bobbing beside her and she put one hand on it to steady it. She gave them the *shaka* sign, which Alexa took to be Surf-ish for *I'm okay*. They sat back down.

"Morgan is going to be all right," Alexa told her mother. "She's more resilient than we give her credit for."

"You think so?"

"I know it. I'm positive." The beach was starting to fill up; everybody wanted to get in one last day. "Mom?" said Alexa. "What do you think I should do about—" she couldn't call him *Dad*, but *Jacob* seemed strange too. "About my father," she said finally. She knew that Rebecca had been in touch with Jacob Thornhill to let him know about what happened the night of Cam's accident and that Alexa needed some time. Rebecca had all of Jacob's contact information for when (or if) Alexa was ready, and Alexa still had his card. "He didn't seem terrible, you know. He seemed—nice. Sweet, even."

"I believe it," said Rebecca. "He wasn't not *nice*. I loved him for good reasons, a long time ago. He meant well, even when he was sick. But he was really sick for a really long time."

"So what should I *do?*"

Her mother's eyes, behind her sunglasses, were inscrutable. "That's up to you, Alexa. You'll be eighteen soon. You're in charge of your own destiny. No pun intended."

"But should I call him, when I go out to L.A.? Should I see him?" (There had been talk of a Realtor, after all . . . and beyond that, maybe it would be nice to have a connection, starting out somewhere new. A *family* connection. Would it? Wouldn't it?) Alexa watched a black Lab race toward the water after a ball. Dogs weren't supposed to be on the beach at this time but the Lab looked so happy that Alexa hoped nobody said anything to the owner.

"I can't decide that for you, Alexa. And even if I could, I wouldn't know what to say. I mean, do I think you need to be careful, if you get in touch with him? Yes. Unequivocally, I do. I don't want him to hurt you. Again. I guess I don't want you to hope for too much."

Alexa flexed her foot in the sand and examined her toenails. "Because maybe he hasn't changed as much as he says he has."

"Right."

"But maybe he has."

"Well, sure. Maybe he has. And even if he hasn't completely changed—" Rebecca took a sip of her coffee. "Even if he hasn't. Part of growing up is acknowledging not only our own imperfections, but everybody else's imperfections too. And maybe even forgiving them." Did Alexa imagine it, or did her mother's voice catch? Alexa considered her mother's words. They made sense. And she didn't have to decide right this minute.

"Anyway," Rebecca continued, "I'm sure this is a moot point because there's no way you're going to move so far away from me.

Why would you leave all this?" She waved a hand to indicate the beach, the happy Lab, the surfers.

Alexa snorted. "A hundred reasons. This water is *freezing,* you can't even go in for more than three seconds without a wet suit. In California you can go to the beach year-round. And you won't be alone. You have the Mom Squad! You have Daniel! You have Morgan!"

Sixth grade for Morgan, with lockers and (ugh, poor Morgan) changing for PE for the first time and the springtime overnight trip to Camp Kieve in May. Kids around Morgan would start vaping or being interested in the opposite sex (or the same sex) and life would get confusing and sometimes intolerable for Morgan, the way it did for everybody who had to go through the onerous process of growing up.

Alexa looked down the beach and saw two familiar figures walking toward her: Caitlin and Destiny. She steeled herself. She had hoped that she and her mom and Morgan could pretend they were on vacation somewhere far away, just this once. Just today. Every time she'd seen anyone who knew about her and Cam since Cam's funeral she had had to endure their awkward condolences, or, worse, their bumbling attempts not to say Cam's name at all.

Caitlin was wearing a two-piece with a bandeau top which actually looked really good on her, Alexa had to admit, even though she would never in a million years have picked that style for Caitlin. Destiny was wearing a Summer Sessions sweatshirt with the neck cut out, *Flashdance* style. Alexa was going to leave the jury out on the sweatshirt for a bit longer.

After they said hello Caitlin and Destiny stood there uncomfortably for a minute, looking down on Alexa and her mom. Finally Caitlin crouched on the sand next to Alexa and spoke to her.

"Hey," she said softly. "I'm really glad we ran into you. I didn't get a chance to talk to you after everything happened." She was wearing sunglasses, so Alexa couldn't see her eyes but her voice sounded shaky, as if she was about to cry. "But I am so, so sorry for what you're going through. I thought a lot about what you said that night at Haley's, I really did, and I think I"—she glanced up at Destiny—"We owe you a big apology." Destiny nodded her agreement.

"Thank you," said Alexa. And then, truthfully, "That means a lot. It really does."

There was a pause then, and Rebecca stepped into it and did that mom thing where she made conversation with the girls, asking them if they were excited about college (yes!) and when they were leaving (day after tomorrow!). Alexa zoned out, watching Morgan. Morgan wasn't exactly setting the surfing world on fire, but every now and then she did catch a legitimate wave, and from this distance she looked almost graceful.

Maybe now that they were all moving on, she and Destiny and Caitlin didn't have to be former friends any longer, or frenemies. Maybe they could just be friends.

Then Destiny's eyes flicked over to Caitlin and she said, "I think we're gonna bounce now." Okay, Alexa *did* roll her eyes at that point, because nobody was saying "bounce" anymore, if anybody ever really was. But the eye roll was brief, and she kept it to herself, and she knew her own soul well enough to know that therein lay some redemption. "But we'll text you later, okay? We should do something, before we go. Like the old days."

"I'd like that," said Alexa. "I'd actually like that a lot." She didn't meet her mother's eyes because she knew they would be full of hope.

"Bye, girls!" said Rebecca, all hopped up on her Summer Sessions iced coffee. She stood up to hug both Destiny and Caitlin and Alexa thought, *Okay, let's not take it too far, Mom.*

After Destiny and Caitlin had gone she thought about what

Confucius told her, via Cam, *Wherever you go, there you are*. It wasn't the worst saying in the world, if you really thought about it.

"It was nice to see those girls again," said Rebecca, sighing happily. "I've really missed them."

Alexa let out a soft grunt in reply, because she'd missed them too.

The next night Rebecca and Morgan were going out to an early dinner with Mr. Bennett; Rebecca had told Morgan about him, and Morgan was uncertain but definitely curious. They'd go early, because school started the day after that, and Morgan had to do the important packing of the middle school backpack. Alexa was on the schedule at the Cottage, but she might try to meet up with them for dessert. Then again, she might not. She might give Morgan her own chance to get to know Mr. Bennett—*Daniel*, although thinking of him as Daniel seemed really weird—on her own terms, at her own speed.

Alexa heard her name and looked toward the sound. Morgan had beached her surfboard and was waving at Alexa, motioning her toward the water. Alexa rose from her chair. She knew she looked good in her bikini, and she could feel eyes on her, but that didn't matter now as much as it had in the beginning of the summer.

Although, please. Of course it *still mattered*.

88.

SHERRI

In the late afternoon the day before the day before the first day of school, Sherri got home from work early and called up the stairs to Katie, "We're going to dinner!" Katie didn't come down immediately and of course Sherri's heart started up the old ticking of alarm, so she called again, trying to keep her voice steady.

And here came Katie, holding a book, her finger tucked between two pages, acting as a bookmark. "Sorry," she said. "I fell asleep reading." She held up the cover of the book, which featured a pair of legs in blue jeans and the title *The Second Summer of the Sisterhood*.

"That looks like a nice book," said Sherri. "Where'd you get that?"

"Morgan," said Katie. "It's a series. This is the second one. But we're not allowed to read past book three yet because then there starts to be sex and stuff." She yawned as though the whole idea of that was terrifically boring. "That's what Morgan's mom said."

"Grab your shoes," said Sherri. "I'm taking you out to dinner to celebrate."

"To celebrate what?"

Sherri wasn't exactly sure. To celebrate the fact that they were still alive? That Katie would have someone to eat lunch with? That over the course of the summer Katie's nightmares had abated, so Miss Josephine stopped complaining about the noise?

"To celebrate the first successful summer of our new lives," Sherri said finally.

"Okay." Katie shrugged, maybe unimpressed, and got her flip-flops.

Brown's Lobster Pound in Seabrook was one of the many places Sherri had driven by this summer and said to herself, *We have to try that*! That happened to her all the time—the hazard and joy of a coastal town in the summer. *Try me*! called the taco truck that parked at the Plum Island Airport. *And me*! pleaded the gelato shop downtown. *Don't forget about me*! The food stands at Yankee Homecoming. The oysters at Brine. The sandwiches from Port City Sandwich Company. The whoopie pies at Chococoa Baking Company.

They took Route 1 toward the Salisbury Bridge, stopping at the hideous intersection where Merrimac Street and the bridge traffic came together and invited all the cars into a giant game of chicken.

Rebecca's Acura had been totaled in the accident, and, obviously, that poor boy's family had been totaled as well. Sherri hadn't gone to the funeral because that felt presumptuous—she hadn't known the boy. But she felt somehow responsible that anybody had died in this beautiful town this summer. Had she unwittingly brought darkness to a place that knew mostly light?

Brown's was a low tan building, unassuming except for the fact that the building extended into the water, so you sort of felt like you were on a moving boat. You ordered at the counter and brought your food to a table. Sherri stood for some time looking at the menu. Katie took her hand and looked very seriously into her eyes and said, "Mom. It's time."

"Time for what?" Sherri felt her heart jump with a familiar terror. Katie was going to say something that would shake Sherri to her core—something about Bobby or the other men, something she'd seen or heard that Sherri thought she had kept her safe from. Something unspeakable.

But Katie was grinning. "It's time to eat a whole lobster," she said.

The relief that flooded through Sherri felt almost like a warm liquid poured over her head. "It is? No lobster rolls?"

Katie nodded firmly. "It is. We've lived here almost a whole summer, and we haven't done it yet. No lobster rolls."

"Okay," Sherri said. She was weak with relief, and the relief made her feel silly, almost drunk. "Okay, Katie-kins! Anything you say!" They ordered two lobster dinners with the works, and they found a seat at one of the picnic tables on the outdoor deck.

The lobsters overran the edges of their paper containers. Around Katie and Sherri the other tables held a low, celebratory hum. Sherri would have ordered a stiff drink but she saw now that people were carrying in wine bottles and cans of beer in paper bags: it was BYOB, which somehow made it seem that much more festive. Truthfully, Sherri didn't need anything to drink.

"Did you know they used to feed these to prisoners?" Katie said. She was holding up her whole lobster and considering it.

"Who did?"

"I don't know." Katie shrugged. "People in the olden days."

"What olden days?"

"Not sure."

"Who told you?"

"Google. Or maybe Morgan. I can't remember which."

"I'm not sure what to do from here," said Sherri. She held up her lobster and looked at its creepy, incomprehensible eyes.

Katie said, "I got you," and took out her phone and loaded up a YouTube video on how to crack a lobster. Normally Sherri would not have allowed the phone at dinner, but she needed the help. Katie moved the phone to the center of the table and they both watched, trying to be surreptitious about it so that the other restaurantgoers wouldn't know what novices they were. Apparently you were supposed to twist the tail off before you did anything else, then the claws. You could use a small fork to reach up into the shell and pull the meat out of the claws; the meat in the tail normally came out in one big piece, and was firmer than the meat in the claws. They dunked the lobster meat in butter and stuffed it into their mouths like it was the first meal they'd had in weeks. They ate corn on the cob and coleslaw and onion rings. They ate all of it.

Katie hadn't even finished the last of her lobster when she said, "After dinner can we get ice cream? There's a place right across the street, Dunlap's? It's supposed to be good. Morgan told me it's good."

Sherri hesitated. Now that fall was here, she'd have to cut back on her spending, cook healthy food for her and Katie, maybe find some way to exercise regularly. (Definitely not barre class.) "I don't know—"

"Please? It's the second to last day of summer! It's the last *night* of summer, because tomorrow is technically a school night."

"Okay," said Sherri. "Of course we can, sure."

The day after tomorrow Katie would walk up Olive Street to High Street, where she would meet up with Morgan and a few other girls from the group to walk to the middle school, and Sherri would clean up from breakfast and take a shower and get in her car and drive to her job, where she would do all of her usual job things, which were boring but not mind-numbingly so, and she would try not to think about the fact that Katie was out of her sight and out of her control, and that, sure, the school had some sort of intercom system or whatever, but was it really safe, was it really secure?

Would anything ever be secure enough to satisfy Sherri?

Sherri hoped Katie never knew how close she'd come to real danger in those early days before they'd become safely ensconced in the program. She hoped that in time she'd forget all about the time in the motel and the bad food and the bad television and Louise the counselor with the velvety brown eyes, and also about the life they'd had before that. But not all of it, maybe, because that life was part of Katie's history, the only one she had.

The sky was becoming paler as the sun began to drop. It wasn't sunset yet, it was more like sunset's appetizer. Sunset's calamari. Sherri's favorite part of the day. She breathed in the briny smell of the water.

She would never not be scared for herself or for Katie. But maybe the fear would become a low thrum in the background of their lives instead of the crashing cymbals in the center of the stage, in the same way that Rebecca had explained to Sherri that her grief for Peter never left, would never leave, even as she fell in love with Daniel.

They cleared their plates and placed them in the appropriate bins; they walked across the street to Dunlap's. They were an ordinary mother and daughter on the penultimate night of summer. The line for ice cream was long, so they had a good amount of time to peruse the menu.

"What are you going to choose?" Katie asked.

I choose life, thought Sherri. *I choose happiness. I choose the light.*

She looked down at Katie, her forthright, strong, vulnerable, invincible, vincible child. She thought about a girl named Madison Miller who had probably gone out for ice cream with her parents dozens of times, never knowing that one day she wouldn't.

After Brooke's party one of the dads to whom Sherri had been talking had asked around for her number. (At the time she hadn't known he was divorced.) His divorce was new and shiny, just out of its packaging, and he wasn't quite sure what to do with it. He'd registered on Tinder, but it scared him, so he never used it. He had been impressed, he told Sherri, by her "bravado" at Brooke's party. Sherri thought what he really meant was that he'd been impressed by her breasts. Or maybe both. She was still deciding whether she was ready to date—whether she'd ever be ready to date. Right now her priority was getting Katie settled in school and doing a bang-up job at Derma-You so she could get more hours. Apparently, with the rapid expansion they'd be seeking a manager for some of their new locations. Jan said she'd told management that Sherri had a solid work ethic and a natural discreetness about her, which was a necessity in their business.

"Mom?" said Katie. The line was moving up; there was a family of four in front of them, and after that it would be their turn. "What are you getting?"

"I think I'll have my usual," Sherri told Katie. "Chocolate with chocolate sprinkles."

Katie rolled her eyes. "They have like four hundred flavors here and you're getting the same thing you always get? You're so predictable, Mom."

"I know," Sherri said. "I'm completely predictable." Sherri tried to look rueful but she couldn't do it genuinely, because predictable implied safe and safe implied boring and to Sherri Griffin on that evening, on the far edge of summer, on the outer reaches of Katie's childhood, *boring* seemed like the most beautiful word in the world.

She just had one final item on her to-do list.

89.

ALEXA

On the very last day of summer, Alexa served, among other things, one Ringer, three sugar cones of Moose Tracks, one cone of chocolate, and one dish of Green Monster. She was in the back, checking on the supplies of paper napkins and spoons, when the "ring for service" bell went off.

"Amazon!" called Hannah, and Alexa rolled her eyes, because wasn't it Hannah's turn to help the next customer? "Someone's looking for you!" Hannah called again, super chipper.

Alexa growled, "Coming," and tugged her apron back into place. She was arranging her face into her best customer service smile when she saw Sherri Griffin. Alexa hadn't seen Sherri since the night Cam died, since Sherri had taken Morgan and Katie away while Alexa and her mom talked to the police. She'd been waiting for this conversation, though: the text she'd sent that night, then the "false alarm" text after; obviously those wouldn't go without a follow-up.

"Hi, Sherri," said Alexa. She pretended cheer but she knew her uncertainty was showing through.

"Hello, Alexa," said Sherri, all business. Her hair, which was pulled into a ponytail, was back to brown; she looked much less arresting than she had the night of the party. No. Not arresting. Bad choice of words. Much less . . . eye-catching. But still, with the right styling, Alexa believed the brown could look pretty. Alexa could show Sherri a few tricks with a super-wide curling iron, if she ever wanted to see.

"Is Katie with you?" Alexa asked.

"Katie's at home," Sherri said. "Packing her backpack for tomorrow. I came to talk to you."

"Here?"

"Not here. No. Definitely not. Plum Island Grille. I'll be there at seven."

So much for catching the end of the meal with Mr. Bennett. This wasn't a question. This was an order. "Got it," said Alexa. "I'll see you there."

"Who was that, Amazon?" asked Hannah after Sherri had departed.

Alexa smiled as sweetly as she could manage and said, "Just a mom of one of my sister's friends. And please stop calling me Amazon. It's really getting tiresome."

Alexa got to the Grille at ten minutes to seven and secured a seat at the bar. The bartender was a girl who had graduated a few years ago, Natalie Gallagher. She was really tall and really thin and had freckles and that gingery hair that works on some people and not on others. On Natalie it worked. Alexa had heard Natalie Gallagher had been in a J. Crew modeling shoot the year before. She smiled at Alexa like she knew her, so Alexa didn't even try to order a drink. She got a seltzer with lime, and she saved the seat next to her—easier said than done; it was crowded. At exactly seven o'clock, Sherri walked in.

Sherri ordered a tequila shot, which she threw back without blinking.

Alexa couldn't help saying, "Wow."

"Listen," said Sherri. "You sent me a text, the night your friend died. And I haven't been able to talk to you about it, because, well . . . because obviously you were tied up with all of that awfulness, after the accident, and I wanted to respect you, respect your privacy. Respect your friend. And I'm so sorry about all of that. It's really terrible."

"Thank you," said Alexa, bowing her head, waiting for the "but."

"But. I need to know what you meant by the text that you sent me that night. I can't remember the exact words. I deleted it— I can't have texts like that on my phone."

"Of course you can't," murmured Alexa.

"I know you said *false alarm* after, but it's clear that you know something about me."

Alexa took a sip of her seltzer. Sherri was watching her, waiting for an explanation. "The thing I said about somebody being after me. That was a misunderstanding. A huge, embarrassing misunderstanding. I'm really sorry. I never should have worried you. I was panicked, and scared, and I was confused about what was going on, and there was somebody knocking on my door. I'm so sorry."

Sherri looked at Alexa for a long time, and then she said, "The part about knowing who I am. That part is what I'm concerned about here. I did a thorough search of Katie's room the day after the party, and I read her diary. I'm assuming that you read it too. That's the only way I can figure out that you'd know anything."

Alexa nodded. "I saw it in her room one day, and I opened it, I don't even know why I opened it, and once I started reading I couldn't stop. I just couldn't. And then I did some googling, and I put everything together. I'm so, so sorry."

Around them came the festive, slightly mournful sounds of an evening at the end of summer: the tinkling of ice in glasses, bursts of uproarious laughter, a hint of seize-the-day mania. The bar stools faced the salt marshes, and the windows were open so that the smells of Plum Island came wafting in. Far, far in the distance, if you squinted and tilted your head just right, you could almost see the Pink House, which would be turning luminous and mysterious under the last rays of the setting sun.

"That's what I figured," said Sherri. "This is a really big problem for me, Alexa. *Really big.*"

"I know." Alexa looked around the bar desperately, but nobody could save her from this conversation.

"You can't ever, ever say anything that you know about us out loud, do you understand me?" Sherri's voice was cold—Siberian.

"I know," said Alexa. "I won't. I never will. I swear. And I'm so sorry. I'm so, so, so sorry." She opened her hands and then closed them into fists. She didn't know what else she could say.

"The diary is gone," Sherri said. "I destroyed it, and then I talked to Katie about never writing anything like that down again. Ever. She simply can't."

"No," agreed Alexa. "She can't."

"I trusted you," said Sherri. "In my home, and with my child. I trusted you, when we were new here, and when we were most vulnerable. And we were *really* vulnerable, Alexa. We still are. We'll be vulnerable for the rest of our lives."

"I know," said Alexa.

"Now here's what I have to ask you," said Sherri. "And I need you to answer honestly. Does anyone else know? Did you tell anyone?"

Here Alexa found herself knee-deep in moral muck. She thought of Cam, the most trustworthy, most honest person she'd ever known, who'd wanted to un-know the truth about Katie and Sherri the second he learned it. He wouldn't have told anyone. She knew that with absolute certainty. If there was anyone who would take a secret like that to the grave, it was Cam.

Alexa shook her head.

"I need to hear you say it out loud. If you told anyone, Katie and I are in too much danger to stay here. We'll have to move away, we'll have to start all over again. New names, new hair color, new everything. I don't want to do that to Katie. She finally feels settled here." Sherri's voice tripped. "But I'll do it if I have to. I'll do anything to keep Katie safe. So I need to know right now, Alexa, if you told anyone else about what you read in that diary."

Alexa thought of Dave Matthews and her heart wrenched once again: *The wicked lies we tell to keep us safe from the pain.*

There were lies that we tell to save ourselves, and then there were lies that we tell to save other people. In the past Alexa had been a master of the former. Now, she supposed, as the New and Improved Alexa, it was probably about time to learn the latter.

"Nobody else knows," she said. "I swear to you, I haven't told, nor will I ever tell, a soul."

"Not your mother, or your sister, or anybody else," said Sherri. "Swear."

"I swear. I haven't told my mother or my sister." One truth. "I will never tell a living soul, Sherri, I promise." Two truths. "I would never share something like that. With anyone." One lie.

Sherri's face relaxed, and Alexa felt that for once she had done the right thing.

Some years hence, when the celebrity Alexa Thornhill has a child of her own, a little boy named Max who has a cowlick and a freckle on his ear and the biggest brown eyes you could imagine, a boy who is growing up in the dazzling Southern California sun, she will look back on this conversation. One day Max will get in an altercation with a bully at a playground. Alexa Thornhill will feel an innate, unquenchable urge to lift the bully up by the straps of his overalls and throw him into next week.

She will never do that, of course. It wouldn't read well on her social media feed, to her fans and followers, which number in the hundreds of thousands. But she will remember the intensity of Sherri Griffin's eyes as she said, "I'll do anything to keep Katie safe." And she gets it. She totally gets it.

But that is in the future. In the raw, unpasteurized present, the New and Improved Alexa, the nice Alexa, asked Sherri Griffin, "Is there anything I can do to make it up to you? Anything at all?"

Sherri thought for a minute. Alexa watched her eyes travel over the marshes of Plum Island, the piece of turnpike visible from the bar, the grasses dancing in the light wind.

"There is one thing," Sherri said finally. She looked around the bar, because it was a small town, and you never knew who you might run into.

"Anything," said Alexa eagerly. She polished off her seltzer and noticed that the bartenders had changed shifts.

She told Sherri, "Whatever you say, I'll do."

One truth, no lies.

90.

THE SQUAD

Monica and her husband, who were celebrating their thirteenth wedding anniversary the night before school started, had a seven o'clock reservation at Mission Oak. You'll never guess who was coming out as they were going in. Well, you might guess. It was Rebecca, Daniel Bennett, and . . . *Morgan Coleman!* Daniel was holding open the door for Rebecca and Morgan, and Morgan appeared to be giggling at something Daniel Bennett had said.

We had also heard, from Brooke, via Monica, who heard it from Dawn, who heard it directly from Gina, that Gina was in the process of breaking off her friendship with Daniel's ex-wife, Veronica the Cheater, out of loyalty to Rebecca.

On the first day of the new school year the girls had all planned to walk to school together, those who weren't on the bus route, which is how they've always done it. Always. Naturally Morgan was part of this plan. After the dressing-down at Brooke's party, Katie was too. We made sure of it.

Then! Early on the first day of school something surprising happened! Morgan texted the rest of the girls on their group chat and said that she and Katie wouldn't be walking with them after all. No explanation.

Esther had driven Audrey in from Plum Island. The buses are sometimes late on the first day, getting used to new routes, and

Audrey didn't want to take the chance of being tardy at the beginning of middle school, when there were so many new things to figure out: homerooms and lockers and the changing of classes and all of that. So it was Esther who told us that *Alexa drove* Morgan and Katie to school in her Jeep. And she didn't leave them at the drop-off on Low Street the way parents were supposed to. No. She parked in the parking lot and she walked them to the front door of the school, in full view of everyone.

We had heard that Alexa had deferred Colby because she was so heartbroken about Cam. We had also heard that she'd never gotten into Colby in the first place. We'd heard that she'd been signed by a talent agent and was moving to L.A., and also that she was moving to New York City, and also that she was reapplying to colleges in the Midwest to get away from it all. We'd also heard she might be buying the Cottage with her Silk Stockings money and would be staying local to run it.

It was reported by Gina, who works for the upper elementary in the same building and was helping to usher the students off the buses, that Alexa said, *really pretty loudly,* to the girls, "Take care, bitches. You go kill it in sixth grade, okay?" Then the three of them did some sort of complicated secret handshake which Gina, when pressed, could not re-create.

And off Alexa went into her future, glowing with youth and beauty and vitality and fame, and something more complicated but somehow also beautiful—something that had to do with grief. She left in her wake a bunch of scrawny, clumsy middle school boys, fresh off the school bus, whose bar for beautiful women had been radically and irrevocably set very, very, very high.

Acknowledgments

I am beyond grateful to the team at William Morrow, who have welcomed me so warmly and worked so hard for my books: Liate Stehlik, Molly Waxman, Julie Paulauski, Vedika Khanna, Jen Hart, and my fabulous and insightful editor, Kate Nintzel. Kate has twice taken *very* rough first drafts and worked her magic on them, not letting me rest until we have the best book we can have. (Even when I really, really want to rest.) Here's to the future!

My agent, Elisabeth Weed, has been my tireless champion and friend from the beginning of my publishing career, and I'm so thankful for her and all the people at the Book Group. Special shout-out to Hallie Schaeffer for keeping things moving smoothly and for smart editorial insight at just the right time.

While any mistakes in this book are mine alone, I owe a thank you to the FBI's Office of Public Affairs for answering my many questions carefully and thoughtfully over the course of several months. For additional detail I used the book *Witsec: Inside the Witness Protection Program* by Pete Earley and Gerald Shur.

This book wouldn't exist without the town of Newburyport, Massachusetts, which my family and I have called home for twelve of the past thirteen years. I moved around a lot as a kid and a young adult, and Newburyport is the place I've lived longest in my life—I consider it my hometown by proxy. Newburyport! Your restaurants, beaches, houses, history, rail trail, parks, ice cream, Yankee Homecoming festivities and general sensibility are all a big part of this book and I thank you for giving me so much to work with in life and in fiction. Thank you to Jabberwocky Bookshop and the other independent bookstores around the country that support authors and keep people reading avidly and shopping locally. The Book Rack, Newburyport's other independent bookstore, did not survive to see the end of 2019 but remains alive in this book because it did so much for so many (including me) for so long.

An author takes a certain risk setting a book in the town where she lives, and to anyone with concerns about this I have three words: fiction, fiction, fiction. My own Newburyport Mom Squad has only its (former) name in common with the Mom Squad of this book. My squaders are full of love and empathy and kindness, and that might not make for enticing fiction, but it sure does make for sustaining friendships and really fun dinners out.

In a busy household it can sometimes be hard to find a quiet corner to work, especially in deadline times. Thank you to Cindy and Marc Burkhardt for the generous use of their Salisbury beach house for the second book in a row. Thank you to Sandy Weisman at 26 Split Rock Cove in South Thomaston, Maine, whose beautiful artist's retreat apartment has saved me multiple times. Chococoa Baking Company, Plum Island Coffee Roasters, and Commune Café are all places where I have parked myself for long periods of writing time and really good beverages. The same goes for the Newburyport Public Library, except for the beverages, although I really like the new rule allowing covered drinks.

Jennifer Truelove and Margaret Dunn have been around now for six books (and a long time before that), serving as book-titlers, emergency readers, research assistants, laugh-generators, celebrity-introducers, and best friends. I am lucky to have them. I am also lucky to have the Destrampe and Moore families in my corner. My parents, John and Sara Mitchell, and my sister, Shannon Mitchell, have been longtime supporters of my work and my family as a whole, attending track meets and book readings and soccer games and plays year after year.

All of my books end up being about families in one way or another. To my daughters, Addie, Violet, and Josie Moore: while I do not write specifically about you (I promise!), I can safely say that without having all of you in my life I don't think I'd have anything to write. I am so proud of the people you have always been and the people you're turning into.

My husband, Brian Moore, always goes last in the acknowledgements in a last-but-not-least way because without him by my side I doubt I would have published one book, never mind six. Thank you for holding down the fort when necessary, reminding me that nicer is always the better choice, and teaching me that sometimes it's okay to cook without a recipe.

Insights,
Interviews
& More . . .

About the author

About the book

Read on

Meet Meg Mitchell Moore

Courtney Trembler

MEG MITCHELL MOORE worked for several years as a journalist for a variety of publications before turning to fiction. She lives in the beautiful town of Newburyport, Massachusetts, with her husband and their three daughters. *Two Truths and a Lie* is her sixth novel. ∾

Behind the Book

One of the questions readers ask me the most is which part of a book comes to me first. Plot? Characters? Theme? My answer can vary from book to book; sometimes I can't say for certain after the book is done which came first. With this book, the answer is easy: the setting.

As a "beach book"—a relatively new term in publishing, but one that has spawned dedicated tables in bookstores and bolstered the career of many a writer, me included—I wanted *Two Truths and a Lie* to entertain readers. I wanted summer cocktails, preferably involving tequila. I wanted people on beaches, in boats and parks, in restaurants and swimming pools. I live in a town that has all of these things in the summer. In fact, I live in *this* town, Newburyport, Massachusetts, where *Two Truths and a Lie* takes place, and the simplest answer to why I set this book here is because I love living here, and I wanted to write about it and bring the town to readers.

In New England, where winter can last through early April, when summer comes we throw off the last shroud of gloom, the one closest to the skin, with abandon, and we soak up every moment of light and heat the sun offers us. I wanted to capture that feeling in ▶

Behind the Book *(continued)*

this book. I wanted the town of Newburyport to be its own character, and I wanted to celebrate all of the places that draw locals out of their homes and tourists to our town in the summer.

But groups of people sitting on a beach or licking yet another ice cream cone don't make for compelling reading, unless there are currents—maybe darker and more complicated currents— moving under the surface of the water. I don't quite recall how or when I came up with the idea for the crime that propels Sherri and Katie Griffin into their new lives in Newburyport, where they struggle to fit into the Mom Squad, a large and welcoming/not welcoming group of mothers and their preteen daughters. What I do know is that the more I talked about the book after publication the more I realized that the theme of being an outsider is truly central, and that whatever it was that got the Griffins to the town it was their outsider status, and that of other characters, that I wanted to explore. Seventeen-year-old Alexa Thornhill has lost her connection with her former best friends during her final year of high school: she's an outsider hiding a secret online life. Alexa's mother, Rebecca Coleman, has suffered a big loss that sometimes makes her feel like a square peg in the round hole of her own friend group: she's an outsider too. Sherri and Katie Griffin are newcomers to an unfamiliar town, a different region of the country, a foreign and sometimes treacherous social dynamic. They are the ultimate outsiders.

Why is the outsider theme so interesting to me? As the daughter of a naval officer I moved with my family every few years throughout my childhood. As a result, I have no real hometown, although there are places I lived in longer than others, places where I put down tentative roots before the relocation orders came in and I had to pull them up. I'm not complaining about this. There are military families that move far more often than mine did, shuffling their children in and out of schools every few months. With the exception of our last move before I went to college, my senior year of high school (okay, that one I sometimes complain about), I had two or three years to settle into a place. Nevertheless, plenty of times in my life I have been the newcomer, standing uncertainly on the outskirts as I gauged the social situation, tested the waters, squinted until I could find my place. I'm a natural introvert, which makes it nearly impossible for me to walk into a roomful of strangers and say, "Hey everyone! I'm *here!*" I had to work at it, every time. I think this is one of the reasons I became a writer: not only were books a source of solace in every new place, but my observational muscles were strengthened early.

A little over thirteen years ago, when my husband and I had a four-year-old, a two-year-old, and a baby very much on the verge of being born, we moved to Newburyport, and with the exception of one year in California we've lived here ever since. Once again, I found myself starting over, the newcomer, studying the social dynamics to figure out where I fit. (Happily, my real-life mom friends are *much* nicer than the Mom Squad Sherri contends with!) And that's another reason I wanted to set this book here. I've paid my dues as an outsider; I've finally, well into adulthood, found my hometown. I wanted to honor it. Maybe in a sequel to this book we'll find out if Sherri and Katie Griffin are able to do the same. I'm rooting for them. ◠

Reading Group Guide

1. Why do you think the author chose to include the Greek chorus-style narration of the Squad? What does this add to the story?

2. How do Rebecca, Alexa, and Morgan deal with their grief over Peter differently? How does grief affect their family as compared to how it affects Sherri and Katie?

3. Why is Alexa so determined to move to Los Angeles in particular? What does the city represent to her, and why is it so appealing?

4. The Squad members stress that they try to keep their children away from their wilder parties in order to "set a good example for the younger generation." In general, what kind of example do you think they're setting for their children? Looking especially at how the younger girls treat Katie and Morgan, to what extent do you think their actions come from watching how their mothers interact with each other?

5. Do you think Rebecca was right not to tell Alexa about the letter from her father? What would you have done if you were in her situation?

6. The Squad blames Katie's arrival for the shifts that occur in their daughters' friendships. Do you think they're right, or are the moms using Katie's presence as an excuse for the fact that their girls are simply growing up and moving beyond their control?

7. Alexa reflects that "there were lies that we tell to save ourselves, and then there were lies that we tell to save

other people." Of the many lies that are told throughout the book, what are some examples of those told to protect the person lying, and of those told to protect other people?

8. What do you think of Cam's mantra of "wherever you go, there you are"? Do you agree with Alexa's interpretation that people stay the same even as their circumstances or location change? Or do you think the place you live does have an impact on who you are as a person?

9. Sherri tells Katie that "people who do bad things aren't one hundred percent bad. Hardly anybody is one hundred percent bad," but then admits to herself that it took everything she had to say that. Do you think Sherri really believes what she's saying about Bobby? Do you agree that most people have good in them?

10. Rebecca and Alexa both lose friendships due to their grief, but at the end of the book it seems they're both willing to give those friendships another try. Do you agree that both Caitlin and Gina deserve a second chance? Was there anything in the author's portrayal of female friendships that you particularly related to?

11. What role does social media play in the lives of the Mom Squad, the daughters, and Alexa? Do you think this is a story that could have been set in a pre–social media age? Why or why not? Did you draw parallels between the social media shenanigans of the characters and your own life?

12. What did you think of the book's ending? Were you satisfied with where all the characters ended up? ⌒

An Excerpt from
The Islanders

Chapter 1

ANTHONY

ON THE TOP deck of the ferry from Point Judith to Block Island Anthony Puckett watched a group of bachelorettes drinking from plastic tumblers. They wore identical skintight tank tops— white, of course, bachelorettes always wore white—that depicted a pair of cowboy boots with the words Ride 'Em Cowgirls above and Jennie's Last Rodeo below. Each tumbler was printed with its girl's name in large block letters: ASHLIE, LEXIE, SADIE, etc. (It seemed to be a rule that to attend this party your name had to end in *ie*.) He didn't know what was more depressing: The *ie* factor, or the cowgirl hats each girl wore, here in Rhode Island, so far from Texas or Nashville or anyplace where such a hat might be warranted. Or the orange juice he could see through the clear plastic of the tumblers, which meant they were drinking screwdrivers, the most unimaginative drink of all the drinks.

It was all depressing. Everything was depressing. Not to the bachelorettes, though. They were laughing, laughing, the way you do when you're young and carefree with a weekend ahead of you.

On the other side of the deck, at a safe distance from the bachelorettes, a little boy about Max's age sat pressed into his mother's side. His mother was on her phone, scrolling mindlessly through something, paying the boy no heed.

Don't think about Max, Anthony told himself fiercely. He wouldn't think about the way Max's face transformed when he was about to ask a cosmic, loaded question. For example: *If God made everything, who made God?* (Anthony's parents were staunch Catholics, and Anthony's mother, Dorothy, was indoctrinating Max on the sly, a fact that made Anthony's estranged wife Cassie's normally yoga-calm blood pressure rise.) Or, another example, when Anthony hadn't turned the channel from the nightly news fast enough, allowing Max an accidental glimpse of the aftermath of an ISIS bombing in Turkey: *Why is there evil?*

Anthony couldn't answer either of these questions properly. (Neither, it should be noted, could Dorothy.)

Anthony wouldn't think about Max, and he wouldn't think about Cassie, and he wouldn't think about Glen Manning, Cassie's smarmy art dealer with whom Anthony was positive she was sleeping. He wouldn't think about his future—financial and otherwise—which was as murky and inscrutable as a churning ocean. And he definitely, *definitely* wouldn't think about his father, Leonard Puckett.

He closed his eyes and dozed. When he felt the ferry slowing he opened his eyes. They were approaching land. He took a deep breath and surveyed his surroundings. Buildings were coming into relief, a jetty, a dozen or so moored sailboats. *To approach a place you'd never been before and to have the privilege of approaching it by boat—well, he supposed there was some sort of magic in that.* He head-wrote that sentence, and then deleted it. It wasn't very good. ▸

He'd told nobody where he was going, and he didn't expect to run into anyone he knew. Cassie certainly hadn't asked: she just wanted him gone. Nobody he knew vacationed on Block Island. They all went to Nantucket or the Vineyard or the Hamptons. It was a stroke of luck that an ancient uncle of a college friend had a Block Island cottage for which he needed a house sitter.

"Couldn't he rent it?" asked Anthony. "For actual money?"

"He could," said the friend. Ryan Fitzsimmons, his name was. In college they called him Fitzy. "But, dude, this place is *old*. It looks like something your great-great-great-grandmother would have lived in. And he can't be bothered to fix it up. But he doesn't want it left alone either. Comes with a car too. A Le Baron. Also old."

"Why don't you stay there?" asked Anthony.

"*Me?*" Fitzy laughed, long, deep, almost insolently. "No way. Charlotte's parents hooked us up with a sweet house on Nantucket for August. And I don't get that much time off from the bank anyway. Gotta keep making the coin."

Rub it in, why don't you? thought Anthony.

Anthony had wanted to go farther away, to a different type of island: Anguilla, Saint Martin, Barbados, someplace where a person could slip in among the beautiful and the glamorous. But his coin was gone. All of his coins were gone.

When the ferry docked he let the bachelorettes lurch ahead of him, pulling their weekender rollaway bags. He now observed that the bride-to-be had a white bow affixed to the side of her cowboy hat—he had missed this before. Her shirt, instead of saying Jennie's Last Rodeo, said My Last Rodeo. Clever.

Have a great bachelorette weekend, Jennie. Have a wonderful life and a happy, happy marriage.

Marriage is the worst kind of heartbreak, he wrote in his head. *That's what the disgraced, lonely man wanted to say to the young bride-to-be. Get out while you still can, Jennie. Run for the hills.*

Before he and Cassie got married she'd gone on a yoga retreat with her four bridesmaids. It was all very civilized and Zen.

He'd gone on a bender with his Dartmouth buddies, the details of which were hazy.

He plodded down the ferry ramp and stood for a moment. *The wave of summer humanity undulated around him*. No. Delete.

Just ahead of him was a large white Victorian-era hotel with a sign reading **HARBORSIDE INN**. Next to it, another one: **NEW SHOREHAM HOUSE**. Next to that, another inn, and another one. Any deck attached to any building was full of laughing, drinking people. There were dogs and children and ice-cream cones and sunlight, mopeds and bicycles and Jeeps. And here was Anthony Puckett, dragging behind him his own wheelie bag, holding in his hand a wrinkled piece of paper with an address on Corn Neck Road.

He supposed he'd have to find a taxi to take him to the borrowed cottage, the borrowed Le Baron. Did an island this small have taxis? Ubers? Anything? He could feel sweat dripping down his neck, and his jeans were sticking to his legs. He trudged up the hill that led away from the ferry, and he crossed the street. There his eyes snagged on a sign on a small building next to the post office. He felt a squeeze like cold fingers on his heart.

ISLAND BOUND BOOKS said the sign. And in the front window, of course, inevitable as death or taxes, Leonard Puckett's latest. The cover was fire-engine-red; no images, just the white letters of the title popping out, *The Thrill of the Chase*. Book number nine in the Gabriel Shelton series.

Even here his father followed him.

No, that wasn't right. The book had been here; Anthony had only just arrived. *Revise that, Anthony. Delete. Rewrite.* Once again, he had followed his father.

Twenty-seven Corn Neck Road was a weather-beaten little cottage with a long seashell driveway and, as promised by Fitzy, a large flat rock beside the front porch with a key hidden underneath. From the outside, it could have been any year. On the inside, time had stopped in the early 1900s. Lace, brocade, ▶

straight-backed chairs, heavy dark furniture matched only by the heavy dark rugs that lay under them. In the kitchen (small) it was closer to 1942, with ancient silver pulls on the drawers, a laminate countertop in pale green. The stove bore the word *Hotpoint* across it. He had never heard of such a brand. The door to the refrigerator closed completely only when Anthony pushed against it with all of his weight. No matter: there was no food to keep fresh in it, and only a half-empty ice tray in the freezer.

Or was it half full? This was a joke that at one time he might have made to himself, or even out loud. But he no longer felt like joking.

On the kitchen table, which was small and wooden, with four wooden chairs, as if the three bears had put out an extra for a guest, was a note from Fitzy's uncle.

HOUSE RULES, it said.

1. Garbage day is Thursday.
2. No pets.
3. No parties.

"That's it?" Anthony said out loud. He thought he could probably handle three rules.

On a sideboard in the living room sat a crystal decanter flanked by two glasses. Whether this was decoration or invitation he couldn't be certain, but it lent a certain sense of propriety to the place, like he'd just wandered into *Downton Abbey*. There was an amber liquid in the decanter. Brandy. Or sherry. *The lonely man had to stop himself from tipping the whole thing into his mouth, gulping it down like lemonade.*

What a boring story this would make.

He turned from the decanter and into one of the two bedrooms, which contained a four-poster bed whose posts looked sharp enough for him to impale himself on. (Not out of the question.) In his former life, he and Cassie reposed on an upholstered Avery bed from Room and Board on Newbury Street in Boston, chosen, of course, by Cassie. Paid for by Anthony.

Anthony tried not to think of how his wife might now be reposing on the Avery bed—or, more accurately, with whom. The thought that his despicable actions had brewed marital discontent was terrible to consider, but even more terrible was the possibility that the marital discontent had existed long before, like a chapter outline to a book that was yet to be written.

Oh, Anthony, stop it. What an obvious metaphor. You never used to be so obvious.

He wondered what Max was doing right then, right that very minute, and whether he'd been offered a reasonable explanation for his father's absence. But thinking about Max hurt too much, so he rolled up the thoughts like a sleeping bag, tucked them into their matching carrying pouch, and placed them tenderly in a corner of his mind, to be taken out later.

Anthony unpacked his single suitcase into the dark recesses of the dresser drawers. Next he started up the old Le Baron and followed the directions on his iPhone to the Block Island Grocery, a gray-shingled building that smelled of sea air and tourism. Once inside, he saw that the produce section looked like it could fit in the pocket of the produce section at his local Whole Foods. He spent three thousand dollars on four items. (Not really, but it felt like it.) Even to get those four items he had to fight through the throng of people waiting in line at the deli for their sandwiches to take to the beach. They all looked so happy, so hopeful. So sandy! He couldn't stand it.

As he was leaving the store he perused the notices on the bulletin board. Somebody was selling a mini-fridge; seven other people were selling surfboards; a housecleaning crew of six respectable, responsible women was looking for summer housing. But was anyone selling peace? Was anyone selling absolution? A place to live, a career?

He drove to the end of Corn Neck Road, passing three ▶

wobbly bicyclists—wobbly, maybe, because the big wicker baskets on the front of the bikes, stuffed with beach towels, set them off balance. The road ended in a small parking lot. Across a vast sea of rocks he could see a lighthouse, and a small pack of people trooping toward it on foot.

He turned the car around. Was this all there was to this island? Was this really *it*? What should he do now? He could go back downtown. (He put air quotes over the word in his mind; one street did not a downtown make.) He could get ice cream, but he wasn't hungry. He could buy a T-shirt, but he'd packed seven of his favorite gray shirts and didn't need one. And anyway those activities might require smiling. They would definitely require interaction with human beings. And for sure they'd require money. No, thank you, to all three.

He proceeded back down Corn Neck Road. In no time at all he came to the seashell driveway, the cottage.

Anthony had come here to hide from the world. But how on earth was he going to be able to hide in a place so *small*? ⌒